Grace
on the
Horizon

EMMA LOMBARD

THE WHITE SAILS SERIES
BOOK TWO

Paperback ISBN: 9780645105827
Large print ISBN: 9780645105834

This book uses British English spelling conventions.

Cover Design by Jennifer Quinlan, Historical Fiction Book Covers

Come join the crew! Subscribe to my newsletter at www. EmmaLombardAuthor.com for fun giveaways and to receive advance notice about future book releases.

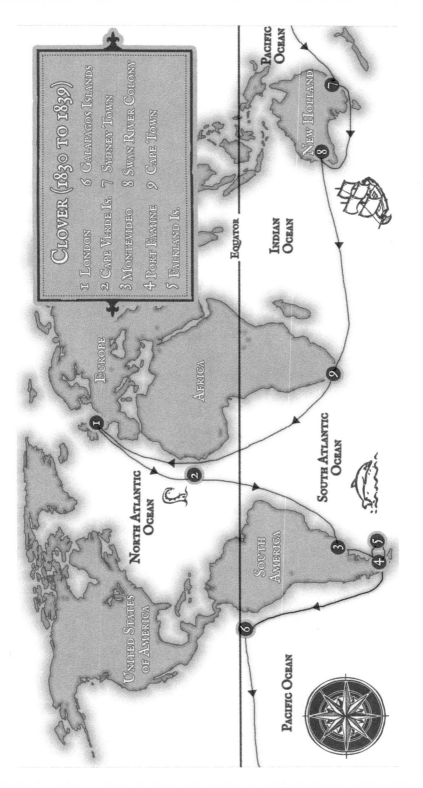

CLOVER (1830 TO 1839)

1 London
2 Cape Verde Is.
3 Montevideo
4 Port Famine
5 Falkland Is.
6 Galapagos Islands
7 Sydney Town
8 Swan River Colony
9 Cape Town

EUROPE

AFRICA

NORTH ATLANTIC OCEAN

SOUTH AMERICA

SOUTH ATLANTIC OCEAN

UNITED STATES OF AMERICA

PACIFIC OCEAN

EQUATOR

INDIAN OCEAN

NEW HOLLAND

PACIFIC OCEAN

Dedicated to my dear friend,
Rayelene 'with an e in the middle' Williams.
I will stew eternally in the juices of author remorse for
misspelling your name in my first book.
Here, you and your extra 'e' now have a whole book
to yourselves.

Chapter One

Grace's heart was filled with contentment, her belly with succulent roast duck. Across the dining table at Abertarff House, the dancing candlelight added a rosy hue to Uncle Farfar's already wine-flushed cheeks. The shadows darkened Seamus's fair hair.

After the revelations of Admiral Baxter's true parentage as Grace's father, and after her parents disowned her, Seamus had been inviting Uncle Farfar to weekly suppers so their new little family could discuss the shape of their future together. Grace had decided she would still refer to the admiral as her uncle rather than her father. It was far simpler and required no explanation to those nosy busybodies she bumped into on the high street.

Uncle Farfar tugged the front of his cravat as though the room had suddenly warmed. "Service in His Majesty's Royal Navy has always come with prestige and high public opinion."

Seamus half turned his head, his face crestfallen. "A lofty position from which I have clearly tumbled. Something I am glad my father is no longer here to witness."

"Come now, my boy," encouraged Uncle Farfar. "I've seen many commanders make difficult choices in the field. Your decision to retire from the navy does not come lightly."

Seamus jabbed a carrot slice on his plate. "I'm not the first disgraced commander left rotting in an Admiralty back office. My reputation would've been in utter tatters had it not been for your persuasion around town, sir."

Sucking a breath through his nostrils, Uncle Farfar smiled. "Least I could do, my boy. You're family, after all."

Grace ran her thumb over the gold band on her finger, her thoughts sliding to the wedding. It had been an intimate affair, but she did not mind. Of the few guests who actually deigned to show, some were only there to garner tidbits of gossip about her and Seamus. But none of that mattered when Seamus kissed her for the first time as her husband.

She swivelled her head at Seamus's chuckle. "My appetite for exploration as a young midshipman had me vowing never to be tied to shore by any marriage." He lay his long, warm fingers over hers. "Little did I imagine finding a wife whose craving for adventure would rival mine."

Grace raised her glass in a silent toast. His diminished career had gripped him in a painful state for far too long, and she was glad a decision had been made.

Uncle Farfar harrumphed. "The sea was a good enough mistress for me."

Grace bit back a giggle. These days, Uncle Farfar's position as port admiral kept him ashore and well within the terrifying reaches of eligible ladies. Though he was *not* having any of it. His one and only dalliance with Mother, resulting in Grace's arrival, had scared him off from falling prey to further female foibles.

Clinking the rim of his glass against hers, Seamus added, "I'm fortunate that my charts of South America have proven to be a popular commodity with naval captains and merchant masters alike. I've done my best over the past three years promoting them at dinner parties and clubhouses, and even the races, but it hasn't been enough to redeem myself."

Grace injected levity into her voice. "It's been a while since you stepped foot aboard a ship. What's on the horizon?"

Seamus's lips twisted. "Any merchant ship who'll have me. I'm nearly done with my book, too." The corner of his mouth tugged up. "Let's hope there'll be as much interest in my written exploits as in my charts."

Uncle Farfar cleared his throat. "No doubt there will be, my boy. Though you may just find yourself aboard another vessel sooner than you imagined."

"Sir?"

"I've recently joined the Geographical Society of London. A new institute to promote the advancement of geographical science. A topic dear to both our hearts, is it not?"

"Indeed, sir. But what has this to do with me securing another vessel?"

"A patron of the society, Colonel Hamilton, is suitably impressed by the quality of your charts. There have been discussions around the dinner table about tasking someone to head a round-the-world voyage to chart new shores."

"A private explorer?" Seamus hummed in contemplation, his spine lengthening.

Uncle Farfar nodded. "A fine opportunity, if you're itching to get back out to sea."

Grace sipped the wine, the fruity warmth of the vineyards adding to her good mood. "And what has Colonel Hamilton so interested in world charts?"

"Some men seek the glory of participating in exploratory endeavours," said Uncle Farfar, dabbing the corner of his mouth with his napkin. "Others, like Colonel Hamilton's investors, prefer to finance these daring ventures that deliver pride and prestige to the empire—leaving the muddying of boots to others."

Swinging her knife and fork together on her empty plate, she hesitated at the look passing between Seamus and Uncle Farfar. Her humour frosted like a winter snap. "What's the matter?"

Seamus rolled his wrist, and it clicked. *That* was never a good sign.

Uncle Farfar cleared his throat, his kind, grey eyes narrowing. "Some unfortunate news has come to light, poppet." He paled.

A barb of panic speared through her stomach.

"There's no gentle way to ease you into this." Uncle Farfar's voice was as thick as a ball of sealing wax. "Silverton isn't dead."

Grace's hand dropped to the table, her knuckle catching the silver knife, crashing metal on china. How could that be? She took a swill of her wine, and it soured in her mouth. Setting her glass down, she stared at her trembling hand—the same trembling hand that had been slicked with Silverton's blood. Her memories scratched the inside of her skull, their sharp claws raking an instant headache across her forehead: the gelatinous press of Silverton crushing the breath from her, the resistance of his flesh as she stabbed the bone knife into his back, and the stink of his putrid odour blending with the iron tang of his blood.

Grace startled as Seamus's long fingers entwined with hers again. They were steady and dry compared to hers.

"I'm sorry I didn't tell you earlier," he said. "The admiral and I toyed with not telling you at all. For your own peace of mind." He pinched his lips in Uncle Farfar's direction. "But it's out now."

Grace puffed out light breaths, trying to steady her thundering heart. She firmed the quiver in her chin. How could this be? "But you went to Highgate Pond. With Jim and Toby."

"I did, but Silverton's body wasn't there."

Her neck warmed, and she snatched her hand away. "Why didn't you tell me? I didn't presume to ask if it was sorted because I trusted you to have it done." His deceit stung like a nettle.

"Dulcinea." The gentle tone of Seamus's endearment—born from their first ever conversation about literature and Don Quixote—drew her gaze to his face. It was white and tight with worry. "He slunk away to Paris with his tail between his legs, purporting to have been set upon by highwaymen. As long as the coward remained there, he was no threat to you."

Grace dropped her face into her hands, pressing her eyelids to stem the prickle of tears. Good Lord! What would it take for her to be rid of that bastard? Releasing the tension in her forehead, she took a deep breath. "Where is he now?"

She shot her gaze across the table as Uncle Farfar spoke. "He's returned to London."

Grace gasped and Seamus's head snapped around, his neatly tied, blond hair flicking over his shoulder. He gripped her hand again. The hearty meal in her stomach liquified, and she swallowed deeply to keep it down.

"When?" she asked.

"I only discovered this myself today," said Uncle Farfar. "I was enjoying an afternoon at White's when that fermented bag of wind strolled in as though he hadn't a care in the world." Uncle Farfar shifted in his chair. "When he proceeded to speak ill of your fall from your parents, I demanded he cease discussing my brother's private affairs."

Seamus threw his napkin on the table. "I'll write to him. Insist he offer our family a formal apology for his slanderous insults!"

"What good will a letter do?" Grace's words were flat. The hope of the carefree life she had immersed herself in had been instantly snuffed. The memory of Silverton's attack—laid to rest under the reassurance of his death—swirled uneasily inside her inner fortress like a spectre haunting the halls of an ancient castle.

"Because if he doesn't," said Seamus firmly, "I'll challenge him to a duel and end this once and for all."

The cold unease trickling through her veins froze solid. "Please don't risk yourself so."

"It galls me to have never avenged you after Silverton nearly destroyed you. And now that he's stepped back into our lives, the fiend is liable to answer for his loose tongue." A log in the fire crackled, sending up a shower of sparks.

"But what if you're killed?" squeaked Grace. She could forgive her husband's mule-headed decision to keep this from her, but she could not forgive him if he got himself slain. Not by the hand of that slithering serpent.

"I've seen your husband handle a pistol well enough, poppet," said Uncle Farfar earnestly. "Besides, he's safe for now. No challenge has been issued."

Yet! The frozen dread in Grace's veins splintered, showering icy shards of panic across her palms.

A WEEK LATER, at the breakfast table, Seamus looked up from his boiled egg as Grace snorted and threw down the small, folded note. The corner dipped into the jam pot before flopping onto the tabletop, an unsightly crimson splotch staining the white cloth. Grace scrunched the letter into a tight ball and tossed it at the blazing fire behind her. The paper sphere bounced off the edge of the mantel and rolled tauntingly back across the carpet to stop near her chair.

"Stinking seaweed!"

He chortled and she turned on him with the speed of a striking snake.

"Are you laughing at me?"

He inclined his head at the offending ball on the floor, waggling his eyebrows in amusement. "I thought you a better shot than that. Heavens above, I've seen you fire a rifle and hit a target dead-on from two hundred yards."

Grace snorted again, sounding like the snuffling, long-necked guanaco he had hunted in Tierra del Fuego, which would spit in annoyance at anyone who got too near.

"It's the last wretched decline," she complained. "Not a soul is attending our dinner party."

He pushed his chair back and patted his lap. "Come here, Mrs Fitzwilliam."

Grace slid over with a rustle of skirts and sat, her bottom nestling perfectly in the valley of his thighs. Their height difference when standing made it a challenge for him to get this close to her face, but seated in his lap, he could study the dark emerald flecks in her eyes and breathe in the clean, freshly washed smell of soap and rosewater in her hair. She sighed and leaned her head against his shoulder, the skin of her forehead warm against his neck. Sliding one hand up her back, he rested his other comfortingly across her lap.

"There we have it—in plain writing—proof we are such pariahs that the whole of London Town is set to reject us," she said, pulling upright. Her mouth arched down comically, though the hurt in her eyes glistened.

"We've both given them plenty to talk about." Seamus patted her back. "There's nothing quite like a spicy bit of naval disgrace and a family shunning to set one adrift on the raft of shame in this sea we call society."

"You're right," she said, sniffing. "At the London Orphan

Asylum fundraising luncheon last month, Jane Twillbury almost burst with shame at having to share a table with me."

Seamus leaned in, silencing her misery with a kiss. He caught her bottom lip in his teeth, enjoying the familiar taste of her mingled with a sweet hint of strawberry jam. Curling his arm around her hip, he pulled her tightly against him.

"I'm so looking forward to sailing with you again, my love," she said. "I can't wait to leave this town full of self-righteous muckrakers behind."

"I want to meet with Colonel Hamilton soon. I'd like a solid discussion with the man to establish just what is expected of me."

A glimmer of sorrow drew Grace's brows together. "Regardless, no journey will be the same without Gilly."

The flash of memory lit Seamus's brain like a spear of lightning—McGilney's blood soaking in the foreign soil, his body a pincushion to a lethal arrow. "A waste of a damn fine clerk," said Seamus, pleased to hear Grace speak McGilney's name so easily. She bore such guilt about his death—he saw the terrors that plagued her sleep. Seamus knew it was not only Silverton who haunted her dreams. McGilney's murder was not easy for either of them to forget.

"The divine timing of having a friend like Gilly aboard can't be dismissed," said Grace. "I'm delighted to keep my promise and return the dress he lent me to his sister."

"See, some good did come of that fundraising luncheon. Had you not attended, you'd not have discovered that Miss McGilney remained in the orphan asylum's employ. Though it doesn't surprise me that Chaplain Agutter keeps on some of his waifs and strays."

"I wonder whether Miss McGilney will join me in a stroll around Hyde Park with Jim and Toby?"

Swallowing his misgivings at the social imbalance of Grace's occasional jaunts to Hyde Park with Buchanan and Hicks,

Seamus had grudgingly given her his blessing. It was not as though she had been overwhelmed with social invitations recently, and Seamus knew he was partly to blame for this. Several of his ex-naval colleagues had expressed their thorough disapproval of the reason for his resignation, this censure tainting their wives too.

"Hopefully, the letter of introduction you've sent Miss McGilney will win you a warmer reception than if you'd arrived in an unannounced blaze of glory," he said.

Grace quirked one eyebrow. "I've never arrived *anywhere* in a blaze of glory."

Seamus broke out in a toothy grin. "Oh, Mrs Fitzwilliam, I wholly beg to differ." He pressed his forehead against hers. "You most undoubtedly *have* arrived just so—numerous times." Her deep gaze of trust and adoration warmed him like a hot drink on an icy night.

"Speaking of which"—she smiled wistfully—"I wish we had a better outcome for our efforts."

Heaven only knew how much he had attempted to remedy *that* situation. He tightened his arms around her. "I'm sorry I've not given you a child after all this time."

Cuts of sorrow lined her forehead. "I see your disappointment whenever you realise my courses have arrived."

Seamus loosened his pressed lips as her fingers glided across the bronzed blond hairs of his forearm. He ran his thumb lightly down her soft cheek, his heart flipping at her worry and disappointment.

"My heart, as wonderful as it would be for you to bear my child, I need you to understand something." Seamus rested his forehead on hers, locking her into his imploring gaze. "*You* are all I need." He lowered his lashes, whispering, "Will I do for you?"

Grace threw her arms around his neck. "Oh, my love, of course!"

Tucking his face into the crook of her neck, he peppered kisses up her smooth throat. His mouth sought hers, tasting her vulnerability and masking his own by offering her a mooring line. No matter how the storm raged around him, he always found refuge in her kisses, when two became one. If only those two could make three.

Chapter Two

The following afternoon, Grace knocked at the chaplain's simple stone cottage. Dirty puddles of mud lined the flagstone entryway. While the clouds pressed dark and grey, it had at least stopped raining.

The door opened, and a warm waft of homely smells enveloped Grace—the aroma of freshly baked bread from the morning's breakfast, interspersed with the ammonic reek of a cat or two. Grace took a step back in surprise, her boot sinking ankle-deep in a muddy puddle. She was eye to eye with a feminine version of Gilly. The eyes were the same dark brown, but unlike Gilly's warmth, Sally's were filled with fear and suspicion. Also missing was Gilly's easy grin.

"Miss McGilney?" Grace injected warmth and welcome into her nervous smile.

The young woman nodded mutely.

"I'm Grace Fitzwilliam. A friend of your brother, Gil— um, Lambert." The woman's blank stare unnerved Grace, and she paused.

"No one's called him Lambert since the day me mam birthed him." Sally even had Gilly's speech intonation.

Grace smiled fondly at the memory of first meeting Gilly, his enthusiastic handshake and slap on the back. "Of course. Gilly told me as much when we first met. He was a remarkable man, your brother."

Sally's brown eyes dulled. "Got your note about you comin'. What you want?"

Grace ignored her barbed tone. "As I mentioned in my letter, would you care for a walk in Hyde Park? I've invited a couple of Gilly's friends from the *Discerning* to join us."

With a twitch of her slim, curved eyebrows, Sally nonchalantly acquiesced. "'Tis me afternoon off. Lemme fetch me coat."

The two women sat in Seamus's carriage as it jostled along the busy London streets towards the parklands. Sally sat stiffly, her red, chapped hands clasped in her lap.

Wanting to put the young woman at ease, Grace chatted about Gilly. "You may find this difficult to believe, but I first met Gilly when he recruited me to the *Discerning*. Of course, I was wearing trousers and not a dress."

Sally's gaze raked over Grace's hair, which she had earlier pinned up. "He must have been a dolt if he thought you a lowly lad."

Grace grinned, pleased to have elicited a response from Gilly's stalwart sister, whose own hair was tied back identically to her brother's. "I can assure you, he was no dolt. I had shorn hair, was sporting a bloody lip, and was dressed as a stable hand. Gilly can't be blamed for thinking I was anything but a lad." Grace swallowed her apprehension. She never liked discussing the reason for her start on the *Discerning*, but she was determined to win Sally over, and she risked sharing an abridged version of events with her.

Whether from disinterest or diplomacy, Sally did not press Grace further about who had put her in that state.

Heartened, Grace continued, "Back then, Gilly knew me as Billy. He made fun about what a great team we made. Gilly and Billy." The memory settled sadly in her chest. "Gilly also told me about you, Sally." She regarded Sally frankly.

Sally stiffened and stared dispassionately out of the window. Grace tentatively put her hand on Sally's clenched fists. The sullen woman did not respond, but neither did she pull away.

"Taking you to the orphan asylum was the most difficult thing he ever did," said Grace. "It tore his heart out to leave you behind, but the only decent paying job he could find was as a sailor. He never stopped thinking of you or talking about you. He loved you."

Sally pressed her forehead to the window, sniffing. Discreetly, Grace tucked her handkerchief into Sally's stiff fingers.

"He hoped his letters reached you. He was distraught when the asylum wouldn't furnish your whereabouts. He'd have been devastated to know you were in Chaplain Agutter's employ all along."

Sally scrubbed her face with the handkerchief and sniffed forcefully again.

Grace continued, "He bought you a dress, truly believing he'd see you again. It was his prized possession." Her throat tightened as Sally let out a small mewl. "Gilly selflessly lent me it after I was revealed to be a woman aboard the *Discerning*. It's beautiful."

Sally turned, red-eyed. "Hardly think 'twas a gown fit for a gentlewoman," she snuffled through her blocked nose.

"The dress wasn't only a sight for sore eyes, but it was also the most comfortable clothing I've ever worn." Endeavouring to lift the heavy atmosphere in the carriage, Grace scoffed lightly. "There's much to be said about fancy gowns at fancy balls. For one, you can't breathe with a wretched corset pulled so tight you see stars. And the lace deemed essential on a fine quality gown is *quite* the irritation, I assure you. And don't get me started about the buffoons who seize you with sweaty hands and crush your toes with their dismal dancing."

Her heart soared at Sally's wide-mouthed grin. "You have his smile."

The joy on Sally's face faltered but, wiping her nose once more with Grace's handkerchief, she said, "I can see why Gilly would have thought you were all right. You isn't like all the other posh ladies."

Grace laughed warmly and freely. "No, I'm not. Much to my husband's consternation, I fear."

Sally twisted around, interest animating her face. "Tell me about my dress, marm."

"I needn't tell you when I can show you." Grace slid a large, white box from under the carriage seat. Depositing it on Sally's lap, she lifted the lid. Sally fumbled with the layers of tissue paper, revealing the soft blue-and-white-striped dress, immaculately pressed. Her eyes glistened, and she ran her coarse hands over the fabric, her chapped fingers fiddling with the two forget-me-not-blue satin ribbons at the hem.

"Alas, it's a ribbon short," said Grace.

"Why?"

"Captain Fitzwilliam planned to use the ribbon as a binding for our handfasting. Alas, an event that didn't transpire." Grace brushed the soft cotton dress with her fingertips. "Gilly carefully unpicked the trimming himself."

"You still got your ribbon?" Sally's dark eyebrows rose.

"Yes," said Grace, smiling. "I hope you don't mind?"

Sally shrugged. "Well, if 'twas all right by Gilly, then I s'pose 'tis all right by me too."

Grace glanced out of the window as the carriage halted.

"Your dress will be perfectly safe in the carriage with Bartel to watch over it."

"Ahoy, Mrs F.!" The familiar voice pulled Grace around as she stepped down.

"Jim! Toby! Oh, how marvellous to see you both!" Grace reached out her arms, and each man took a hand.

Both had broadened at the shoulders, and Toby, once a skinny cook's boy, was now even taller than Jim. Toby's gentle grey gaze flicked politely at Sally.

"You'll never guess who this is." Grace waved at Sally. Seeing Gilly's sister shrink under the scrutiny of the two strangers, Grace quickly added, "Sally McGilney, may I introduce Jim Buchanan and Toby Hicks. They also served aboard the *Discerning*."

"Eh?" Jim's wild, black brows shot up, his protruding ears pinkening. "McGilney, ye say?"

"Indeed," said Grace, grinning. "Sally is Gilly's sister." She set off along the gravel path into the park, her heart swelling with happiness to be with her friends again.

Jim's round face split with his smile. "Crivens, lass! Pleasure to make yer acquaintance. We've heard all about ye."

Sally smiled at Jim's exuberance as he tipped his hat.

Toby dipped his neat, sandy-whiskered chin. "Miss McGilney. You've the look of your brother about you."

Grace beamed. "I said as much!"

"We can tell you a thing or two about old Gilly." Jim winked. "Had a habit of slapping yer back when he talked to ye."

Toby chuckled. "The first time his giant hand landed on me, I thought he'd knocked my lungs clear of my body. Could scarcely breathe."

"Me too!" Grace's grin broadened in mutual sympathy.

Sally's eyelids widened scandalously, but her upturned mouth betrayed her humour. "He must've got a right fright when he knew he'd slapped a lady."

"Ye got extra slaps if he found ye particularly funny," Jim chortled.

Sally let out a nostalgic huff. "I remember him bein' a funny bugger."

The biting wind that had encouraged the earlier rain had disappeared, and for a short while, the weak winter sun broke through the gloom of the low clouds. Grace delighted at the antics of cheeky squirrels cutting daringly across their path and chattering indignantly at them for interrupting their daily routine along the Serpentine.

Jim grabbed Toby's arm. "Remember the day Captain Fincham lined the *Discerning* along some godforsaken mudflats?" He turned to Sally, gesticulating wildly. "Captain was a stickler for us to regularly practise firing the guns. Though, he couldn't afford to waste cannonballs, so he'd hail volunteers to retrieve as many balls from the mud as possible. Gilly, Toby, and I volunteered."

"Meanwhile," interjected Grace, "the older sailors laid bets on who would gather the most balls. Winner of the bet would share his winnings with the successful collector."

The two men laughed at the recollection. Caught up in the enthusiastic reminiscing, Toby added, "There we were, skating around the mud with wooden boards strapped to our feet, scooping up cannonballs. Remember how Gilly tried carrying two at once?"

"Aye!" grinned Jim. "He was loath to release his precious cargo, but being front-heavy, he ploughed face-first into the mud."

"And the men on deck fell about laughing." Grace giggled.

"Did he win?" Sally's cheeks pinkened with laughter.

Jim and Toby nodded in unison as Grace answered, "He did! It was an utterly entertaining afternoon, despite everyone being thoroughly rolled in mud." Amusement curled on Grace's lips as she caught Sally's appreciative expression.

"Thank you for bringin' me brother back to me." The grief and sorrow eased on Sally's face.

"Oh, Sally. I'm so sorry for the hardship you've endured." Grace chanced placing her hand on Sally's arm. "Are you happy with the chaplain and his wife? All Gilly ever wanted was for you to be happy."

Sally glanced at some passing riders and then swivelled her gaze to meet Grace's. "Happy enough, marm," she nodded, patting Grace's hand. "Them's good people. They treat me nice."

Grace turned to Jim. "Speaking of happiness, how are your studies at Arrowsmith Cartographers progressing?"

"Grand!" Jim grinned. "Couldn't have managed it without the captain's patronage."

"Captain Fitzwilliam was suitably impressed with your quick mind on our last voyage." Grace dropped her hands. "You wouldn't have his backing if he didn't believe you up to the task."

"Aye." Jim's protruding ears flushed. "Well 'tis mighty fine of him, nonetheless." His boots ground the gravel path as he spun on the spot to face Grace, his long legs striding backwards with ease. She had never seen his face so alive. Excitement gleamed in his eyes, brown like a well-polished mahogany table. "Och, and ye'll never guess who I've unearthed after all these years?"

She twirled a wayward curl of hair and squinted at the tops of the trees in thought. "Hmm, someone from the *Discerning*?"

"Not even close." He spun on the spot, resuming his place beside her. "My brother—Rory."

Giving a breathy laugh, she exclaimed, "Good gracious! The one who left for New Holland?"

"Aye! The very one. I've sent several packets via passenger ships, hoping that someone about town would recognise my family name. Fortune shone her good luck upon me. I received a packet from him just yesterday."

Toby gripped Jim's shoulder with his slender fingers. "I'm that happy for you."

"What news of your family?" asked Grace, looping her arm in Jim's. Her head barely came above his shoulder, and his forearm was still firm and defined, honed by years of hauling sails.

"My brother said they were to be placed with other Scots folk when they arrived. But those government bastards lied!" Jim rubbed his thick black brows, spiking the hairs in all directions. "'Course, Da wasn't having any of that. He caused such a stramash about town that the governor made a deal with the largest sheep station in the colony to take him on. He's head of the shearing shed. Rory's there with him, too."

"Such excellent news! I'm so relieved." She knew how desperately Jim had missed his family. She squeezed his arm, flashing him a grin, before glancing at Toby and tipping her head. "How are you faring, Toby? Any grand news of your own?"

"Can't complain, Mrs F. Jim's been furthering my reading and writing of an evening. Of a daytime, Admiral Baxter keeps me on my toes running errands from the Admiralty." Toby's caring grey gaze wandered over to Sally. "Miss McGilney, is there much you remember about your brother?"

"Gilly was a scrapper, mostly on account of me," Sally said wistfully. "If any sod dared pull my pigtails or call me names, he'd advance with fists a-blazin'. I thought he loved me, but then he went and left me." Her voice thickened. She sniffled, glancing sideways at Grace. "I know you said he had no choice, but it don't make it any easier."

Grace considered taking Sally's arm in comfort, but seeing the woman's stiff countenance, she decided against it. They continued their saunter along the gravel paths. The sweet waft of roasting chestnuts floated over from the tin barrel on a handcart. The chestnut seller was an old man bowed as much by his years as by the cold. With soot-blackened fingers poking from ragged, fingerless gloves, he deftly flipped the large, brown nuts in the roasting pan.

Spotting Sally's longing gaze, the seller gave them a wide, toothless grin, his voice bellowing cheerfully, "Chestnuts all hot, a penny a score!"

Laughing, Grace pulled some pennies from the small purse in her skirt pocket. She made the exchange with the hawker and handed a hot cone of newspaper to everyone.

"By crumbs, Mrs F. You're a brick!" said Jim, beaming. Toby smiled in thanks.

"Thank you, marm," said Sally.

Grace deftly worked open the searing, crispy, fur-lined shell. The nut came out creamy, whole, and hot. She ripped it in two and blew on it. Grace adored roasted chestnuts. They reminded her of Uncle Farfar's visits to the nursery at Christmas—an innocent time when she'd believed that nothing wicked happened in the world. The chewy flesh crumbled between her teeth and a sweet, nutty flavour filled her mouth. She turned back along the path, leaving a Hansel-and-Gretel trail of chestnut shells behind her.

Nearing the entrance of the park, Sally scrunched her empty paper cone. "Has been a fine afternoon, marm, but I must be headin' back." A heavy note of regret tinged her voice.

"Of course. But fret not, we'll do this again. If you wish?" Grace offered.

"Indeed." Sally beamed, sliding a shy smile in Jim's direction. Grace's heart lurched again at how much she looked like Gilly.

Bartel was waiting with the carriage where they had left him. Grace swivelled her head between her two friends. "Where are you two off to now?"

"To sup at the alehouse," Toby replied, gesturing up the road with his long, slim hand.

Jim elbowed Toby's midriff. "Aye, and perhaps draw a song or two out of young Toby here. Has the voice of an angel with a few ales in him." Toby blushed at Jim's teasing. "Would the two of ye care to join us for a bite?" asked Jim. "'Tis grand chatting, but I'm that hungry I could eat a cow—"

"—without stopping to wipe its arse first." Grace and Toby finished Jim's usual catch cry in unison. They looked at one another and burst out laughing.

"Aye." Jim nodded, rubbing the back of his pinkening neck. "'Tis true though!" He glanced at Sally. "Will ye be joining us then?"

"Oh, no ta," quipped Sally. Grace sensed a heavy reluctance about Sally as she stared at Toby a beat longer. "Must be gettin' back. Mrs Agutter'll be expectin' me to put on supper."

Grace hesitated, torn between seeing Gilly's sister back home and an impromptu evening with her old shipmates. Sally must have seen her hesitation because she smiled warmly. "'Tis all right, marm. I can make me own way home from here."

"Nonsense," said Grace, looping her arm through Sally's. "Bartel will see you home safe, won't you, Bartel?" Grace arched her brows at Seamus's manservant.

"Yes, madam." Bartel stiffened. She was amused that he had the same uncanny knack as Seamus to keep his suit unrumpled all day, no matter what task was at hand.

"Wonderful! And please let Captain Fitzwilliam know I shan't be home for supper." Ignoring Bartel's censorious scowl, she deposited Sally safely into the carriage. "I know just the place," she said, hooking arms with Jim and Toby. "The Two Chairmen alehouse isn't far from here."

Jim eagerly widened his eyelids. "Aye, they serve the finest beefsteak and kidney pudding this side of the Thames."

Preparing to overlook her usual dislike of chewing on rubbery kidney for the sake of their company, Grace laughed. "Off we go, then."

Chapter Three

A short stroll later, Grace stepped into the noisy, cramped, and fuggy confines of the alehouse with her friends. They sat at a round table near the stairs leading to the upper floor. A red-faced, frizzy-haired serving woman dropped three pots of ale on the tabletop, slopping the earthy-smelling liquid. She took their orders.

Jim raised his pot. "To good friends and good times."

The three pewter pots clanged and Grace sipped the bitter ale, recalling her first ever taste of it at this very alehouse. An eternity ago.

Jim gripped Toby's shoulder. "How about ye sing us a song while we wait?"

Toby flushed and took a deep draught of ale. "I usually get a few more pots in me first."

Wanting to smooth Toby's unease, Grace grinned and leaned in. "Perhaps if the publican finds it entertaining enough, it might earn us a free ale or two?"

"Aye, lad," encouraged Jim. "Sing for our supper, won't you?"

Toby took another deep drink and wiped the back of his sleeve across his foamy whiskers. Fixing his gaze to the tankard, he began, his rich voice resonating above the din.

> 'Tis of a pretty female, as you may understand,
> Her mind be bent for ramblin' into some far-off
>   land;
> She dressed herself in men's attire, or so it did
>   appear,
> And she hired with a captain, to serve him for a
>   year.

The dumpy serving woman slid three steaming bowls onto the table, bringing an instant halt to Toby's efforts. Grace cupped her hands around her cool ale pot.

"Goodness! Is that about me?" It certainly sounded like her start on the *Discerning*.

Toby's neck flushed as he fumbled with his knife and fork. "P'haps."

Grace gripped his forearm. "Well, I think it's marvellous!"

"Yer not the first lass to stow away." Jim winked. "Sailors have been singing that tune for many a year."

Toby coughed and stabbed his suet pudding ball, splitting the round hole in the top of the crust. "I altered the words in the other verses a bit to suit."

Tendrils of steam carried the rich fragrance of gravy to Grace's nose. Digging into the surprisingly delicious dish, she poked around the kidney bits. She was famished—those chestnuts earlier had not even touched the sides—though the thought of chewing those rubbery morsels turned her stomach. She laughed at Jim and Toby's recollections of their time together aboard the *Discerning*.

Jim's fork hesitated halfway to his mouth, his gaze darting over her shoulder at a particularly raucous table.

A slurred voice chuckled deeply. "Ey lads, wouldn't mind sharing your toffer with us when you're done, would you?"

Four inebriated individuals grinned lewdly at Grace, the nearest one ramming his hands down his trousers to adjust himself. His stringy hair, the colour of sunburnt wheat, settled in greasy clumps across his wide forehead, and his grin revealed gums populated with more gaps than teeth.

"Och, don't mind them, lass." Jim tapped Grace's hand. "They're too far gone with drink. Pay no heed."

Grace rolled her eyes. "That's a first. I've been branded a maggot, and even a sphincter worm, but never a toffer. At least they've elevated me to the station of a high-class prostitute, and not some lowly dock whore." She chuckled, but then caught sight of Toby's pale face. "It's all right, Toby. Their words don't bother me."

"They bother *me*, Mrs F." A flush bloomed high on Toby's whiskered cheeks, and he pressed his lips. "No one should speak to a gentlewoman as such."

"They'll not likely be expecting a gentlewoman about such a place," reasoned Jim. "Let's finish up quick and be on our way."

Behind her, a chair screeched back heavily, and she tensed her spine as Jim and Toby both squared their shoulders. The sandy-haired man who only moments ago had thrust his hands into his pants wandered into Grace's periphery. She turned her head slowly, mustering a disdainful look.

"How 'bout I let ya climb aboard me, love? I'll even let ya ride rantipole," slurred the stranger, waggling his bushy eyebrows. Emboldened by their friend's first move, the three other men rose and staggered over to the table.

"Aye, I wouldn't mind payin' a visit to cock alley meself." The man in heavy work boots chuckled.

"Tell us, lads," said the red-shirted fellow, scrunching his nose. "She any better than a three-penny upright? You know the sort, cheap and up against the wall?"

The chunkiest one stroked Grace's curls. Jim snatched the man's pudgy finger and in one motion twisted it and rose, the movement wrenching his finger around with a satisfying crack. The man's deep chortle turned into a high-pitched squeal.

"Lay another finger on her and I'll tear off yer whore pipe and shove it down yer throat!" snarled Jim, thrusting the squealing man back. The man stumbled, crashing onto his backside.

Grace launched to her feet, whirling to face the advancing pale-haired man. Bleeding rats' tails, it had been *years* since she had raised her fists to anyone. *The throat. Aim for the throat.* She hoped they would stop staggering long enough for her aim to reach true. Where was a fire poker when she blazing well needed one?

Behind her, Toby exploded into action, his chair clattering over. "She's no whore!" he roared, sliding between her and the advancing man. Toby snatched his shirtfront. "Take that back this instant."

The lout took a drunken swipe at Toby, but he ducked. Toby drove his fist up from his waist and connected with the underside of the man's jaw. His teeth cracked together like an axe splitting wood, and the man toppled back, his eyes rolling.

The tubby man with the broken finger lunged. Jim intercepted him with a shoulder to his midriff. Driven off his feet, the man grunted. Ha! That would teach him to touch a woman's hair uninvited.

As Jim wrestled the pudgy man, a hobnailed boot swung into Grace's vision. "Jim! Watch ou—" *Blazing Hades!*

Jim groaned and slammed onto his back with a gasp of pain, his elbow clamped tight to his side. The booted man dropped across Jim as though he were a saddle, pinning Jim's arms with his muscular legs. Jim bucked like a wild stallion, railing against the hail of fists.

Although Ben Blight had taught Grace that the quickest way to drop a man was to kick him in his privates, she had never put it into practice. But now, Jim's straddled attacker was perfectly positioned. She lined up behind him. A solid shoulder crashed her aside.

Toby kicked the hobnail-booted man between the legs. Hard. The man moaned, deep and guttural, and dropped to his forehead like a sack of coal. A collective groan from the other patrons morphed into roars of approval and laughter as Jim thrust him away.

Grace snorted at Toby and grinned. "You beat me to it!"

Toby's head swung around wildly, vigilance vibrating from his entire body. "For the love of God, Mrs F! Get out of here."

The serving woman ran at Grace, brandishing a clay jug and shrieking, "Stop it! This instant! Take it outside!"

The pudgy man began to rise, and Grace snatched the gin jug from the woman. She cracked the clay over the man's head, showering them all in the pungent juniper-and-oak scent of a wrecked distillery.

The glowering landlord charged over. The strands of hair, usually pasted meticulously over his shiny scalp, straggled down his sweating face. "That's enough from you!" He snatched Grace's arm. "I'll not have you peddlin' your wares in here and upsettin' me customers like this. Out you go!"

Grace wrenched around, the fabric of her sleeve tearing at the shoulder. Blood pounded in her ears, and her cheeks flared. "I'm no social evil!"

"You're still trouble," snapped the landlord. "I want you out!" He lunged for her again, but she sprang back.

Jim leapt to his feet with the agility of a sailor used to a rolling deck. He snatched the red collar of the man pounding Toby with meaty fists and swung him around.

The tussling men collided with Grace, knocking her off balance. Her cheek smashed the table's solid edge with the wet crunch of a snapping rhubarb stalk. Her face burst in a bloom of pain. Grace collapsed, groaning and spitting globs of hot blood onto the sticky alehouse floor. Good grief, was that a piece of tooth? The room was a watery haze.

Jim gripped his opponent in a headlock and slammed his forehead against the table. The man's struggles ceased instantly, and Jim dropped him to the floor with a thud that shook the sticky floorboards beneath Grace's palms.

Panting, she sat up, swaying and spitting out another thick, slow taste of blood. Her tongue toyed with the sharp, jagged edge of her top molar. Gracious! This was going to hurt tomorrow! She wiped her arm across her mouth, smearing a red trail across the pale fabric. The publican's fingers pincered her arm again and he hauled her to her feet.

"Unhand my wife this instant!"

Grace winced at the lightning crackle of pain in her cheek as she turned towards the familiar voice. A swimming vision of Seamus filled the doorway, coatless and hatless, his chest heaving. A lethal blend of fury and horror blazed across his face.

THE FIRE in the hearth in Seamus's library roared, staving off the winter cold. Needling rain tapped at the window like a thousand impatient fingers drumming to come in. While the room was warm and cosy, Seamus made sure his glare at Buchanan and Hicks was not.

The two men stood before Seamus's desk like schoolboys before the headmaster, and Grace sat in the chair opposite him. Through his simmering anger, Seamus was smugly pleased to see both men looking suitably humbled, even though each one sported a ripe, shiny bruise on his face. Grace licked the bloodied corner of her mouth, and Seamus felt sick. He offered her his handkerchief.

"Mrs Fitzwilliam, pray tell, *what* possessed you to dine in a commoner's alehouse?" he asked.

Grace winced as she dabbed her mouth and steadily met his gaze. "It's where Gilly rounded me into service on the *Discerning*."

A theatre of emotions played out on her face. She was clearly prepared to defend her two accomplices. Heavens above! She certainly landed herself in some precarious situations. He turned a critical eye on the black-haired Scotsman.

"Buchanan, questionable nature of the establishment aside, would you care to elaborate how my wife, under the protection of not one but *two* men, ended up with a split lip?"

Buchanan's eyes, purple and puffed, were fixed with terror on Seamus. "Aye, sir. 'Twas an accident."

"And what of your own black eyes and Hicks's broken nose? Were those accidental mishaps too?" Seamus's voice was hard and unforgiving. These two were lucky they were not aboard a naval vessel right now, or they would both be strapped to the shrouds!

"No, sir. We were defending Mrs F.'s... um, Mrs Fitzwilliam's honour." Buchanan's wide ears turned a deep wine red.

Seamus shuffled forward a step. "Truly?"

"Yes." Grace dropped the bloodied handkerchief into her lap. Speaking with obvious care through her swollen lips, she launched into the details. She ended with a defiant sniff.

Seamus left a beat of silence before he sliced the air with his icy voice. "And which of those bastards laid his hand on you?" His gaze roved over her puffy cheek.

Grace shook her head. "None."

He erupted from his seat. "Mrs Fitzwilliam, I'll not have you defend those drunken louts on any account. Tell me which one of them hit you, and I'll have him arrested and dealt with *immediately*."

Her chin poked out. "Jim's right. It *was* an accident. I was shoved over in the struggle, and my face struck the table."

Seamus's heart thudded painfully in his ears, and he almost missed her softer words.

"I promise. No one hit me. Jim and Toby soon had the four of them sorted, as you well witnessed."

Seamus stretched his back, trying to crack the tension from his spine. He wanted to forget the hot flood of horror that had engulfed him upon seeing his wife bleeding and hanging limply in the publican's grip. Striding around the desk, Seamus bent over the fireplace, resting one hand wearily on the warm stone mantel, the other on his hip. Damn and blast! His name already bore the weight of enough disgrace. If he formally punished Buchanan and Hicks, then even more would know what had transpired this evening. Sighing, he beckoned his head towards the men.

"Over here, you two."

The two young men responded instantly, drawing stiffly before him. Seamus's deep breath thrust his chest out and, ensuring a dry, clipped enunciation, defined his displeasure.

"Since the Two Chairmen was my wife's suggestion, I can't apportion that blame to you." He hesitated, glancing at Grace's damaged face before locking on to the men before him. "I offer my thanks for coming to my wife's defence." Seamus swallowed deeply to force down a marble of bile. "However, let this be your only warning. You ever gamble to step out in public with my wife again without my full knowledge or permission, I'll personally see you locked in the stocks for a week." Seamus had known about their meeting at the park with McGilney's sister, but the alehouse was another matter. He glared at the two men. "*And* I'll nail your ears to the post for good measure," he added. "It'll also be the end of your naval careers. Understand?"

"Yes, sir!" Buchanan and Hicks blurted simultaneously.

Seamus regarded the two abashed men closely then flicked his head towards the door in dismissal. In perfect unison, they turned smartly towards the exit. The door fastened behind the departing men with a metallic click.

He leaned back against the mantel, shoulders slumped with unhappiness. In a gentle swirl of skirts, Grace stepped over to him and placed her hands over his knotted forearms.

"I'm sorry, Seamus," she whispered.

The misery in her eyes loosened the claws of anger in his heart. He had known she was not the mild and docile type when he married her, but by Neptune, her latest antics butted against his leniency like a foul-tempered billygoat.

She continued, "I'm sorry for upsetting you like this. Jim and Toby are good men—you shouldn't think too harshly of them."

"Good men or not, they aren't of our class. A stroll in the park is one matter, but to sup with them at an alehouse? Really, Grace!"

Her eyes hardened like emeralds. "What difference does it make who sees us together? No one will have anything to do with me anyway. Good Lord, I hate this place!"

Seamus was unsure whether she was about to burst into tears or shriek with anger. Straightening up, he pulled her into an embrace, and she sank her uninjured cheek against his chest, sniffing glumly.

"I know you do," he said, pressing a kiss into her dishevelled chocolate curls. Another couple of months had passed, and *still* no sign of a child. At least an infant would be a worthy distraction for her while he made plans for their departure.

IN THE PINK early hours of the following morning, Seamus awoke with a start. Grace thrashed restlessly, her head tossing on the pillow. Another bad dream? Pain from her injury? Her bruised jaw clenched and she let out a deep, guttural moan. For crying out loud, she looked a mess.

He gently shook her shoulder. "Grace, wake up."

She gulped as though she had been underwater and come up for a much-needed breath.

He slid his hand across her stomach and wriggled closer. "I'm here, my heart. You're all right." He nuzzled the soft, warm hair behind her ear.

Her stomach tensed as tight as a wooden board and she moaned again, croaking hoarsely, "Seamus. I'm going to be sick."

He snatched the empty chamber pot from beneath the bed. Grace sat up and heaved. The splattering contents of her stomach permeated the room with an acrid reek. He swallowed objectionably. Nursing was not his strong suit. He coughed and slid the pot beneath the bed again. This would serve her right for supping in questionable establishments.

She doubled over, grabbing her stomach. "Seamus, something's wrong."

Drawing open the curtains to let in the early light, he stepped back over to the bed and rubbed her bowed back. "Seems alehouse fare isn't to your liking after all." He laughed lightly.

She grunted again and tipped her head back. The rictus of pain across her face destroyed the humour in him. Heavens! This was no case of spoiled food or overindulgence of cheap ale. "I'll fetch the doctor."

She snatched his hand and squeezed as she bowed her head. "No, wait." She sucked and blew air through her teeth until the tide of pain passed, then pulled aside the bedcover. "I need to use the chamber pot." She slid her legs off the mattress and her shift rucked around her hips.

Seamus inhaled sharply. "Wait, Grace."

The bright stain of blood on the sheets sent a shudder of

panic rippling across his nape. Blind with fear and overwhelmed with helplessness, he inexpertly lay his hand on her hip. Another surge of tension rippled beneath his palm, and she clung to his arm as she slithered to the floor on her knees. Her primal moan was akin to that of a dying man, and Seamus dropped heavily beside her, his own knees shrieking in protest at the hard planks.

Grace lifted the edge of her bloodied shift and mewled. "Help. Oh, Seamus. Help me."

"Grace." He stared with equal horror and sorrow at the bloody mess between her knees. "It's a babe," he whispered, staring at her with agonising helplessness. It was faultlessly formed, with tiny toes at the end of its curled legs. The shadows of ribs through the transparent skin were as fine as fishbones. So tiny. So perfect.

Grace's chin jittered, and he recognised the signs of the aftermath of passing pain when the body suddenly realised it had survived a violent ordeal. Her voice was thinned by distress. "I'm sorry. I didn't know. I knew the absence of courses meant a child, but mine have always been sporadic. I would never have... oh, Lord." Her frame shook, and her breathing hitched.

Her vulnerability ploughed a furrow of grief through Seamus's chest. He gripped a firm arm around the small of her back and pressed her quivering knuckles to his lips, peppering them with kisses of forgiveness. "No, Dulcinea. Don't blame yourself."

She sagged back on her calves. Seamus tightened his grip. "Are you hurting?" Heaven help! What was he supposed to do? He felt so helpless.

She blew out a slow, controlled breath. "It's better now. The pain has stopped." Burying her face in her hands, she cried, "Oh, Seamus, I'm a wicked, wicked person."

"No, no. Don't say that." His voice was hoarse, and he swallowed painfully.

Rosy hues of sunlight peeked over the windowsill like the

light of heaven reaching down. It did not seem possible that such beauty could exist on a day of such sorrow.

Whimpering behind her hands, she opened her bloodshot eyes. "Forgive me."

He wanted to fall limp with grief onto the floor beside her. Instead, he scooped her up. "There's nothing to forgive. The sun has risen. The darkness is behind. Rest now, my heart."

Her purple, swollen lips quivered, and she buried her face in his neck, her tears damp against his skin. "How can I feel so much love for a child I never knew existed? This hurts more than I dreamt possible."

Seamus clamped his bottom lip to bite back the swell of emotion bubbling up in his throat. He cleared it with a dry cough, his tone softening. "Because it was the best of us put together."

She clung to his neck, her wracking sobs pulsing through him. How he loved this woman—each little wild, petite, frustrating part of her—with every living fibre of his being. He would do anything to protect her and keep her safe. He *had* to get her out of London before it ground her spirit to dust. Get her into the clean ocean air and away from these scrapes she seemed to get herself into with terrifying consistency.

While landlocked in London, the prospect of a child had great appeal, but raising a child at sea would be a dangerous occupation. It galled him to think it, but—perhaps—it was for the best she could not keep a child within. He would not forgive himself if anything happened to her.

It was time to press Baxter into arranging that meeting with Hamilton.

Chapter Four

Grace gripped Seamus's hand as he helped her into his carriage waiting on the street outside Abertarff House. She breathed deeply to expand the inexplicable tightening in her chest—the thought of leaving him always made her feel like this. Bartel had strapped Grace's leather travel trunk to the rear luggage rack, and the springs creaked in protest as he clambered to the driver's seat. Seamus stood by the open door, holding her hand.

"I'm sorry I can't accompany you to Oxford," he said.

She could not fault him for not joining her. His long-awaited invitation to dine with Colonel Hamilton had come at long last.

"Enjoy your supper. I know you stay home more often these days on my account. Now you will have all the free time in the world to surround yourself with the fug of pipe smoke, playing umpteen games of chess, and droning on about whatever secret men's business you lot get up to."

Seamus shrugged. "Your company is far preferable. While conversation with intellects can be enlightening, they can be a damned stubborn lot and quite set in their thoughts. Naturally, I'm curious to discover what Colonel Hamilton expects of me. However, once that lot start, one usually can't get a word in edgeways."

She wondered whether he was only saying this for her sake or whether he truly felt this way. "You should be quite used to not getting a word in edgeways, what with being married to *me*." She squeezed his fingers. "Worry not, my love. A month in Oxford with Billy and the Krantzes for company will do my spirits wonders."

She also hoped it would ease the tangle of guilt in her belly. Even though Seamus had assured her that she was not to blame for the babe, her remorse had twisted into a knot of confusion. Not wishing to impose her own childhood miseries upon another, she had always internally opposed the idea of having a child. But knowing it was a gift only she could give him, she had readied herself for it. Only, now she had lost his firstborn, and she was terrified of failing him a second time.

Dr Krantz was a physician at the Radcliffe Infirmary in Oxford who also taught at the university. Uncle Farfar had summoned his services after Billy was released from Newgate three years back, when Silverton's accusation about him attacking Grace had landed him there in the first place. Once well again, Billy had returned with Krantz to Oxford to continue his medicinal studies. Grace had never asked Uncle Farfar how he had delicately danced around the law to have the charges dropped against Billy without the case becoming headlines in the broadsheets again. He could have bribed the King for all she cared.

Grace would also not have cared if Dr Krantz had come from

the moon—his unconventional treatment of Billy's gaol fever had worked wonders. She recalled the first day he had swept into Billy's stifling, miasmic sick chamber at Seamus's London townhouse. Dr Krantz had promptly doused the fire and opened all the windows. He made Billy drink a mixture of ether and alcohol, and had swaddled his hands and feet in rags soaked in camphorated spirit of wine. All of which contradicted what Grace knew about caring for the ill. But it worked.

Now, Seamus chuckled, deep and low. "I'd have thought your unchaperoned jaunt into town the other week would've cured you of travelling alone. You risk such misadventure, madam!"

Grace took his teasing as another sign of forgiveness. She drove the poor man to despair, but it was not her fault—not most times, at least. And here he was, good-humouredly reminding her how she had been insulted by the clergyman who approached her as she stood alone on Regent Street after a morning of being outfitted. She had been waiting for Bartel to navigate the carriage through the throng of pedestrians, carts, horses, and carriages.

A whippet of a man with a white collar had pressed a Bible into her hands imploringly. "Take it home and read it attentively, my dear. I'm sure it'll benefit you." His lined forehead rumpled in concern.

Grace blinked at him in confusion until his disapproving pout and beseeching gaze made her realise who he thought she was. She thrust the black leather-bound book back at him, her hand raised in protest, her cheeks warming. "Pardon me, sir, you're clearly misguided. I'm *not* what you think. I simply await my carriage." Good gracious! What was it about men always presuming the worst of her? Was it that she did not take as much care with her hair and dress as others?

The thin clergyman bristled. "Well then, madam, no woman of class should be seen standing alone in public like this. You give one quite the wrong impression, which can only lead to misadventure on your part."

Grace repressed the urge to argue as she saw Bartel nearing, having not the time nor the patience to counter his objection. She smirked stiffly. "See, sir, my carriage arrives."

The clergyman then magnanimously announced, "In that case, madam, I'll wait with you and see you safely inside."

With her cheeks warming slightly at the memory, Grace patted her tapestried valise on the bench beside her and smiled. "Fear not, husband. I shan't parade myself on any more street corners. Besides, I'm safe enough with my pistol to hand."

She knew how repugnant he found the notion of her being armed, but after the fiasco in the alehouse, he had agreed she could carry her pistol for protection. A wild-haired woman brandishing a firearm would have stopped those drunken louts in their tracks. And then she would not have been knocked to the ground or lost—

Seamus's gentle kiss on her knuckles brought her back to the carriage. "Give Dr Krantz and Sykes my best, won't you? Mrs Krantz too," he said.

"Of course, my love." Countering the flicker of melancholy in her chest, she beamed. "I'll be back before you know it."

Seamus dropped his hand from the sill of the open carriage window. "Farewell, Dulcinea. Take care."

Grace blew him a kiss, and he banged on the side of the carriage to signal Bartel to drive on. Lurching back in her seat, she wrapped her arms about her chest. As hard as it was leaving Seamus, it was equally as thrilling to be seeing Billy again.

That night, seated at the Krantzes' dining table in their cosy cottage, Grace raised her glass. "To returned friends." She smiled as Dr and Mrs Krantz and Billy laid down their knives and forks and lifted their goblets in unison. Flickering candlelight from the brass candelabras and fire in the hearth cast a warm glow over their friendly faces.

"To returned friends," came the echo. Dr Krantz inclined his head.

Grace studied the physician. His brown hair was brushed with a severe side parting, but the greying clumps of his side-whiskers tufted out in rebellion, much like her own curls when she did not pin them down.

"Thank you, Mrs Krantz, for inviting me to stay," she said.

"The pleasure is mine, *liébling*." Mrs Krantz's words were clear and deliberate, unhindered by her Prussian accent.

After the stifling lifestyle in London, Grace's reunion with Billy and Dr Krantz was the breath of fresh air her soul needed, as was meeting the doctor's new bride, Anni Krantz. She was eight years Krantz's junior, the same height as Grace, though not as willowy—her stature fitting for her age and standing. Her brown hair was laced with the finest threads of silver.

Dr Krantz waved his glass at Billy. "Mr Sykes has earned the break. His apothecary knowledge, balanced with my surgical instruction, has tempered him into a fine physician indeed. He invests just as many hours into his vocation as I do."

Billy's face coloured, and he flicked his black fringe from his brow. "Thank you, doctor. 'Tis grand of you to say."

Grace beamed proudly at Billy. Here he sat at this table—a physician! She never could have imagined the possibility back on that dark May night when she had snuck into his room above the stables, battered and afraid.

Now, his warm brown eyes, so familiar from childhood, drew Grace to him. Billy lowered his glass and wiped his lips with his napkin. "Perhaps you might like to join me on the river next week?" he asked. "Weather permitting, of course."

"That sounds splendid!" gushed Grace, eager to spend some time alone with her friend.

"I pack a picnic?" offered Mrs Krantz. "Cold sliced tongue, veal pie, and perhaps Stilton cheese? You like ale and claret too?"

Mrs Krantz's Prussian accent elicited her yearning for a new adventure to foreign shores. "A feast fit for a king," said Grace. "Thank you."

Billy patted his stomach. "I hold Mrs Krantz responsible for this extra padding." His face had filled out, no longer haunted by black shadows of illness. His gaze settled on her, soft with fondness.

"I'm glad to see you looking so well, Billy," she said quietly.

He waggled his eyebrows. "The three of you didn't leave me much choice other than to get better." He winked and held his glass again. "To good health!"

Grace clinked the rim of her glass against his. "To good health."

THE FOLLOWING WEEK, Grace settled upon some comfortable cushions as Billy pushed the green punt along the River Cherwell. He handled the pole with ease, propelling them along at a leisurely pace.

"You've done this before?" she said.

"I have," he acknowledged with a grin. "Dr Krantz is an avid fowler. This punt's handy for retrieving the ducks he shoots from the reeds and shallows. I've done it enough times to have a handle of it now. But it wasn't always so."

Billy gave an extra forceful push, ducking as they glided under a low stone bridge. He raised his black eyebrows in amusement. "The first time Dr Krantz gave me the pole, I gave it an overly enthusiastic thrust, and the wretched thing caught in the weeds."

The fresh air and good company lightened Grace's spirits. "And what prevailed—you or the pole?"

Billy winced sheepishly. "The pole. I found myself hanging

over the water while the punt and Dr Krantz floated off without me."

"Did he return?" She giggled again.

"Not before I entertained the onlookers with a satisfying splash."

She threw her head back to laugh, and the punt wobbled dangerously, causing her to cling to the sides and shriek even more loudly.

After an enjoyable hour of gliding, Billy wedged them onto a shallow, muddy bank and opened the picnic basket. Grace accepted a bottle of ale, and he handed her a slice of pie on a plate.

She forked a piece of the meaty centre into her mouth, humming in appreciation. "Hmm, Mrs Krantz has turned the making of veal pie into an art."

"She has," said Billy. "Dr Krantz and I have no complaint on that account."

Grace grinned. "My uncle says Dr Krantz wrote to tell him you were his best student before you qualified."

"The good doctor's teaching expounded my apothecary learning. Working at the infirmary has been a marvellous opportunity to hone my medicinal skills." Billy shrugged one shoulder. "Dr Krantz travelled many a year with the Russian army, treating the camp fever that afflicted the troops." He flicked his black fringe aside. "Said some of his best learning came from working in the field. I only wish I had the chance of such hands-on experience. Though, I've been studying the procedures of obstetricius by James Barry, a military surgeon in the British Army. He's had success in ensuring the survival of both mother *and* child after performing a Caesarean section."

"What's a military surgeon doing concerning himself in such matters?" Grace cocked an eyebrow.

"As the Colonial Medical Inspector in Cape Town, he bore great responsibility, not only for the welfare of soldiers, but also for effecting great improvements to the whole litany of woeful souls in the colony. What I wouldn't give to work under him for a spell."

Would that she could remedy this for him. She owed him a year of his life. If it were not for her, he would never have ended up shackled in Newgate. The guilt squeezing her chest tightened with a tug reminiscent of Miss Hargrave's vicious pulls on her corset.

As a diversion, she asked lightly, "Are you terribly busy?"

"Indeed. Poor Mrs Krantz spends much of her time alone, with us spending such long hours with our patients."

"I'm sure she appreciates you not being underfoot." Grace took a sip and sat a moment in silence, watching Billy take a bite of sliced tongue. "Mrs Krantz has been marvellous company, but she also seems to know just when I need a moment of peace with my book. And she never stops feeding me!" She laughed.

Chewing and swallowing his mouthful, Billy nodded and grinned. "Clearly, Oxford is doing you wonders too. How's London Town treating you, flower?"

She blew out a long, slow breath. "You know how it is. The endless rounds of dreary tea and dinner parties, broken only by sporadic visits to museums and art galleries. An occasional theatrical show thrown in for good measure, all accompanied by bores and gossipmongers. I find the whole existence there rather burdensome."

"Haven't you grasped yet, burdens are for shoulders sturdy enough to bear them?"

Grace lowered her eyes, twisting her mouth. "I can bear my own well enough, but Seamus is working so hard to redeem himself. Unlike me, he cares how others perceive him."

"Captain Fitzwilliam's a fine gentleman. If anyone can work their way back into society's good graces, he can." Billy paused. "How are you faring? Within yourself, I mean?"

"Sleep is no longer the friend it once was."

"Is it bad dreams that plague you?"

"When I thought Silverton dead, he was no longer a physical adversary."

"But he's not dead," prompted Billy gently.

"Knowing he's alive has complicated matters. I was free of him when I believed him killed. Now, I worry he'll needle his way into my life again." She was afraid that even if she managed to escape her worry, her own personal guards in her inner fortress—fear and caution—would march her right back and drop her again at the feet of despair.

"Would you care to tell me of it?"

"I want to fight him for holding me in this dark place. Truly I do." She glanced at Billy's patient face and realised she had not confessed to anyone how she felt since discovering Silverton was still alive.

"Are you worried he will have you charged with attempted murder?"

"I was a little, but my uncle assured me Silverton is an abject coward who wouldn't want it known he was outwitted by a woman." Grace took a mouthful of warm, bitter ale, appreciating its lubricating effect on her dry throat. "It's more than that. I don't know what to do with this inferno within me. I fear if it continues to rage, there'll be nothing left of me but ash. I'll have no pieces left to rebuild." Grace pressed her fingers to her eyelids. "I feel that the slightest puff will scatter me in the wind. What good will I be to Seamus if I dissipate into nothingness?"

"You've too much fortitude about you to dissipate into nothingness." Billy reached over and patted her knee. "You need a distraction. Something to occupy you otherwise."

Grace blanched. "Actually, there is something that would be the perfect distraction." The heated creep of her blush reached the tip of her ears.

"Yes?" Billy fixed her with a look of professionalism.

With her gaze fixed on the half-empty contents of her ale

bottle, her throat tensed as she swallowed. "Seamus and I have been married a couple of years now." Seeing Billy sitting with an interested stillness, she continued, "But there has only been one instance... one potential chance of..." She sucked her bottom lip.

Billy's voice carried softly from the other side of the punt. "A child?"

Grace shot him a grateful look. "Only the beginnings of one —once. I'm afraid there's something wrong with me." Her voice caught, and she glanced at the tadpoles butting insistently at the edges of the long-stemmed reeds—looking anywhere but at Billy's empathetic smile. She pinched her lips together to steady the wobble of her chin. "I'm failing Seamus as a wife because I've not yet given him the child he desires. I don't know what to do."

Billy took a slow, deep breath. "I can perform an examination if you wish?" Grace's cheeks set alight at his suggestion, and he hastened on, "Or perhaps recommend another physician, if you prefer?"

"Um, n-no," she muttered, horrified. What was she thinking? That he could use divine intuition to determine the problem? She felt uncomfortably hot, and the warm prickle of the summer sun did not help.

Billy studied her intently. Brushing his fringe back, he took a deep breath as though reconciling himself to what he was about to say next. "I don't find myself attracted to the female form in any way." He shrugged one shoulder. "'Tis strictly business. I've no time for any emotional investment in the matter."

Grace smoothed her brow, and an odd sadness filled her bones. "Oh, Billy, who's to say what your future might bring? You shouldn't discount the matter so readily."

He shook his head. "I've no occasion for wives or mistresses. I'm married to my profession. Nuns and monks do it all the time —why not physicians too?" Billy straightened, his face searching hers earnestly. "Putting aside my impending bachelor-hood, will you pardon an impertinently personal question?"

She narrowed her eyelids warily and nodded minutely.

"Are your courses regular? Monthly?" he asked.

"No… yes… no…" Her tongue felt thick as it fumbled over her words. Had the ale bottle in her lap been a live creature, she would be strangling the life out of it. "No, not every month."

Billy ran his thumb around the opening of his ale bottle. He gave an understanding nod. "Have you heard of a condition called a wandering womb?"

"No."

"You have within you a female organ, a womb. 'Tis within this organ that a child grows, but it's a fickle piece of equipment, prone to wandering around inside you. 'Tis a pelvic disorder afflicting many women."

"Is that what caused me to lose my child?" Grace asked uneasily, not liking the sound of any organs wandering around inside her with a mind of their own. She needed Billy's redemption, because Lord knew she was incapable of forgiving herself. The fact that Seamus did not blame her only doubled her guilt.

"Alas, that happens more often than you think," he said gently.

She swallowed back the salty threat of tears. "So it wasn't my fault—you know—with the brawl…?"

Billy cocked his head, his voice lowering. "You'd be surprised what circumstances I've seen some mothers endure, only to have their babes arrive pink and squalling. There's no saying why that's so for some and not for others."

"Can this affliction be cured?"

"It can. And as a married woman, you're in the ideal situation for treatment." Billy leaned forward, elbows on his knees, his ale bottle swinging freely from his fingers. "A husband's strong and vigorous ministrations can alleviate the symptoms, especially if your own pleasure is obtained from the activity too.

Though if there's anything lacking in this department at home, I can always recommend a physician in London who can perform manual pelvic massage and douching."

Good Lord! If there was any truth behind the mythical existence of water horses, she longed for one to loom up now and swallow her whole. She swivelled her head, determining whether the other boatmen on the river were near enough to overhear their shocking conversation.

"N-no, Seamus... um, manages just fine... thank you." Goodness gracious, he did more than just manage! He sent her into earth-moving, toe-tingling, full-bodied paroxysms! Grace wondered whether she should mention this to her friend, but she found herself mute with mortification.

Billy's empty ale bottle clinked as he replaced it in the basket, his voice rich and warm. "Might I suggest a herbal decoction? Fair warning—tastes like a beggar's armpit, but it won't harm you."

"Very well!" Grace accepted, bringing a hasty end to the uncomfortable conversation.

THE TIME TO return to London came all too soon for Grace. Billy helped her into the carriage and slid her valise onto the floor beside her, clinking the glass bottles inside.

"There you are, flower. Those four bottles of decoction should see you through the next few months. Take care when lifting your bag, it carries quite a weight." He slammed the carriage door shut and, flicking his fringe aside with a toss of his head, grinned at her through the open window.

Grace reached out, and he took her hand, kissing it fondly. She swallowed the knot of emotion. "Goodbye, Billy. Thank you for a marvellous month."

"'Twas grand to see you too. Give Captain Fitzwilliam my

regards. I'll see you soon." He banged on the carriage door, and Grace heard Bartel's muffled order to the horses. Bridles jangled and the carriage jerked, pulling her hand out of Billy's. The leather seat squeaked as she sank back and squeezed her eyelids shut, unable to trap the lone tear sliding down her cheek. Goodness, it was hard leaving family, especially an eclectic one gathered through circumstance rather than birthright.

She was dozing lightly when the sudden halt of the carriage sent the heavy valise careening across the floor and crashing into the opposite bench. The glass bottles smashed riotously. She half slid off the seat, barely catching hold of the windowsill in time to avoid ending up on the floor with her case. Outside, a muffled voice yelled, "All passengers out, or we'll shoot your driver!"

Grace snatched at her valise, her fingers trembling with the clasp. Ripping open the lid, she cursed at her pistol and shot bag swimming in a puddle of brown glass shards and tangy herbal slush. "Bleeding rats' tails!"

"Out this instant! We'll not ask again!"

She snapped the lid of the valise shut. With a yank on the handle, she thrust the carriage door open and leaned out. "What's the meaning of this?"

Standing in the shadows of the thickly wooded track were two masked figures. Both had their feet braced on either side of the carriage tracks, their primed pistols pointing directly at Bartel.

"Out you get!" ordered the shorter man, squinting shiftily at Grace from beneath the low brim of his hat. Without Bartel to pull out the steps, Grace jumped from the carriage, landing with a light crunch in the dried leaves littering the track. The taller man's features were obscured by the heavy shade of the forest.

"Your money and your valuables!" the short man demanded, waving his pistol at Grace. The taller one trained his muzzle on Bartel still sitting on the driver's seat, leaving all the talking to his companion. "Don't you reach for no weapon. Keep your 'ands where we can see 'em!" Grace raised her hands, and the highwayman scowled. "Give me your valuables," he snapped again.

"You can have them with pleasure—but don't point your pistols at my driver or me." Grace raised her chin.

"Jesus bloody wept! Do as you're told, woman!"

"Certainly. I—" Grace reached into the open doorway.

"Hands up, I say!"

Grace glanced at the valise on the carriage floor.

"Uh, uh, uh!" cautioned the highwayman. "Keep your hands where I can see 'em. Want me to blow off your head?"

Grace inhaled sharply, her raised hands gesturing towards the man. "I'm *trying* my best to please you! You tell me to hand over my valuables, but when I reach for my valise, you tell me to put my hands up. Lower your pistol and allow me to reach for the belongings you so demand." The pistol swung in Grace's direction again, and her lungs almost leapt up her throat.

From the corner of her eye, a black blur launched from above. Bartel collided with the man in a fleshy thud. With deep-throated grunts, the two men rolled into the edge of the forest. Shielded by the open carriage door, Grace spun to her valise. Flipping the lid open, she snatched her pistol. They would not know it was unloaded. She aimed it at the taller man. "Drop your weapon!"

Bartel roared. The highwayman had the advantage, the muzzle of his pistol slowly lowering. Bartel strained to push the man's aim away. A thunderous explosion scattered the birds in the surrounding trees. Both men jolted. The taller man tore towards the scuffling duo, pistol raised like a bludgeon.

Grace squawked. "Stop! I'll shoot!" *Blasted useless lump of metal!* She lobbed it at the sprinting highwayman. It knocked off his hat, but his footsteps never faltered.

He smashed the stock of his pistol onto his accomplice's head. The sound of the bone-jarring crunch ricocheted through

Grace's teeth. The short highwayman crumpled with a startled grunt, slumping over Bartel. What on earth? He just hit his own man!

Puffing, she scoured the empty track, wondering whether she could make a run for it. She froze in confusion as the tall man tugged on the kerchief, revealing his face. He stared at her, unblinking.

A hot-and-cold wave of recognition washed over Grace. She stared at the familiar droopy features. It can't be? Surely? His thick, black hair was longer than the last time she had seen him —standing on O'Reilly's ship beside Holburton, before she had been whisked away in the hackney to Silverton's manor.

"Darcy?" spluttered Grace.

Darcy dropped his pistol with a thud on the compact dirt and raised his open palms. "Miss Baxter?" His serious mask broke. "Good day, madam. 'Tis good to see you." He swooped into a deep bow.

"Good Lord Almighty! What are you doing?"

"Don't mind me. I don't want your money."

"No, I mean, what are you doing *here*?"

Beside her, the tangled pile of arms and legs groaned. She nudged the unconscious highwayman with her boot. Beneath him, Bartel moaned. *Good Lord! He's alive!* With Darcy momentarily forgotten, Grace whirled and hauled at the short highwayman's thick collar. She grunted at the weight of him, then she yipped in surprise as Darcy's wide hand reached down and tossed the unconscious man aside.

"Won't you help your friend?" Grace knelt beside her manservant, not caring about soiling her skirts.

"Galloway's no friend. I'm but his lackey."

She sucked in a breath through her teeth. Bartel lay panting and gnashing, with half his face blackened by burnt powder. A red-raw trail snaked down his cheek. It ended in the tattered

47

shreds of ear tissue dangling precariously beneath his blood-matted hair. That *had* to hurt.

"Bartel! Bartel, are you all right?" Grace cupped the uninjured side of his face. The manservant blinked a few times before focussing on her lips. "Can you get up?" she urged.

"P-pardon me, m-madam? I can't hear." Bartel squinted at her. He raised his hand to his injured ear and studied his bloodied fingers in confusion. His eyes widened as Darcy stepped closer. Bartel grabbed Grace's shoulders and twisted, rolling protectively atop her.

Beside them, the short highwayman groaned, his moaning muffled by the kerchief still masking his mouth. Grace wriggled out from beneath Bartel. "It's all right, Bartel," she shouted. Her own ears still rang from the pistol discharge, and she could only imagine his deafness. "I know this man! He won't harm us!" At least, she did not think he would.

Bartel growled in pain, clasping his bloodied ear as he glowered at the man looming above.

"Let's get you out of here," bellowed Grace, snatching Bartel's black lapels. She ground her teeth as she strained to pull him to his feet. "Get up, Bartel! I can't lift you."

Darcy ducked around the other side of Bartel and thrust himself beneath his arm.

"Geroff me!" objected Bartel, struggling to retrieve his arm.

"I'm a friend. Let me help." Darcy hauled him to his feet, and the driver staggered. Grace slung his arm across her shoulder to steady him. Darcy gripped the back of Bartel's trousers as she guided him towards the open carriage door. The injured man slumped onto the floorboards, half in and half out. Wedging his shoulder against Bartel's rump, Darcy thrust him into the carriage.

Behind her, the short highwayman was rousing. He twisted onto his back, the whites of his eyes still showing. His grimy-nailed hand fumbled where Darcy had clobbered him. She snapped her head towards Darcy, who shuffled his boots in the leafy detritus, peering at her through lowered lashes.

"You've saved my neck again, Mr Darcy," said Grace. What was she to do with him now? Unable to pull him from his last precarious station aboard O'Reilly's ship, she quickly calculated his position. "Are you staying with him or coming with me?" she asked tersely. Rats' tails! Seamus was going to throttle her for this.

"Coming with you."

Well, that was that. She inhaled deeply. "Right then, in you go. Lay low, and don't let Bartel kill you on the way home."

Darcy's one eyebrow rose slowly. "And who'll drive?"

She lifted her chin. "I will." Admittedly, it had been many a year since William Sykes, Billy's father and stablemaster at Wallace House, had let her sit on his lap and take the reins out in the countryside. It would not be too difficult to recall, would it?

Darcy thrust his head in the injured manservant's direction and shook it. "It'll be safer for all if you ride with him and let me handle the horses." The two mares pranced skittishly. "Come on. They're keen to escape the pong of blood."

"Yes, all right," she agreed, slamming the door.

The carriage rocked as Darcy hauled himself into the driver's seat. The snap of reins and his goading yell dissipated in the empty forest.

Chapter Five

I n the cramped backroom of the Geographical Society, Seamus laid his elbows on the rickety table and stared at the dark panelled walls. Without windows to allow in any midday light, the miserly reeking, smoking tallow candles did little to alleviate the covert mood. Seamus slid his gaze between Baxter and Hamilton, peeved by the lack of audience. Where the devil were all these supposed intrepid adventurers?

"Who are the investors?" Seamus asked.

"Peers who don't wish to sully themselves by getting directly involved in the business side of things," drawled Hamilton, undoing the buttons of his waistcoat to accommodate his girth. He filled the chair like a monolith, erect and broad shouldered. "God forbid they be branded active industrialists. All dealings will be through me." He leaned back in his chair. "Plus, there's another delicate matter. I've been approached by Bishop Carmichael, who has requested passage for one of his priests."

Seamus's brow tightened. "Sounds like a reasonable request."

"Not when it comes attached to unsavoury circumstances." Hamilton withdrew a packet from his inside pocket and slid it across the table, the seal already cracked and flapping open.

Seamus unfolded the letter. It spared no detail of the death of Father Babcock's wife, including the news that his mistress had been accused of the murder.

"Babcock is an abomination to the church," elaborated Hamilton. "It's best for everyone that he be sent from England post-haste. The bishop wishes to protect the church by removing this canker."

Good heavens! Were it up to him, he would refuse Babcock passage. Hamilton watched him intently with sharp, grey eyes.

"It galls me to have a dangerous man of such ill repute aboard my ship. Especially with my wife aboard," said Seamus, scratching a prickle of sweat at his hairline.

"How many other offers of command have you received, Captain Fitzwilliam?" Hamilton pulled at the loose skin beneath his chin. "Should you wish to step aboard another exploration vessel, some concessions *must* be made."

Seamus stiffened. "I may not have the esteem of a serving navy man, but I unquestionably still have my pride, sir." He reached for his wineglass, needing to moisten his dry mouth. "And the welfare of my wife to consider too."

"Perhaps this might help?" Hamilton slid another packet across the table.

Seamus's wineglass stopped halfway to his lips, his narrowed gaze fixed on the bulging packet. The sputtering wicks spat out crazed shadows that darkened the neat, white package before him. "I can't be bought."

Hamilton waved a hand, his singsong voice grating in Seamus's ears. "Consider it a down payment on the excellent charts you'll be providing. You've quite the reputation in this department."

"It's true," added Baxter. "The sale of your charts has more than made up for the cost of your last voyage. Though it hasn't lessened the blight on your name."

Seamus laid his knife and fork together over his unfinished meal, his appetite gone. What choice did he have? He had means, but none so great as to finance an expedition of his own —especially not now, with that loan against Abertarff House.

At Baxter's recommendation, Seamus had invested in government bonds in Peru and Colombia. The Spanish Empire was crumbling, and their former colonies had big plans as burgeoning independent nations. The return on the bonds of these new countries was double that of British Government bonds, and it seemed like an excellent investment. Admiral Baxter's knowledge of affairs in that part of the world had assured Seamus it was indeed a prudent venture. That, and the fact that Baxter had made a sizeable investment himself.

Of course, he could always re-join the navy, but knowing his luck, he would likely end up commanding an anti-slaver. There would be no hope of Grace joining him aboard then—he would not risk exposing her to those atrocities. He was well aware of her yearning to leave London.

"So, you see, Captain"—Hamilton leaned forward, nudging the packet nearer to Seamus with one finger—"I've the utmost faith you'll deliver a solid return on my investment. Consider this favour regarding Father Babcock a personal one."

"Come now, my boy." Baxter's cheeks flushed red with wine and excitement. "Can you imagine what Mrs Fitzwilliam will say if she hears you've passed on such an opportunity?"

Laying his napkin beside his plate, Seamus reached slowly for the envelope, his fingers hesitating before curling around the generous wad.

SEAMUS PEERED EXPECTANTLY out of the street-front window of his library at Abertarff House. Grace was due home from Oxford today. He frowned. What the devil? His carriage clattered around the corner too fast. *Who* was that in the driver's seat? Seamus darted out to the mews to meet them, and his leather soles juddered to a halt on the cobbles. The horses were blown and frothing at the mouth. Grace's skirts billowed as she jumped from the carriage, and he glowered at the fabric stained with mud and—*is that blood?*

"By Christ! Where's Bartel?" He gripped her slim waist and held her at a distance to study her a moment more before crushing her in an embrace.

"Inside," she said, her words dulled by the press of her cheek into his shirt.

Reluctantly releasing her, he glared into the carriage. A dribble of liquid dripped onto the cobblestones, and he winced at the spicy herbal reek. Bartel sat with his back wedged against one bench and his feet against the other. Fresh red rivulets ran between the fingers of his hand pressed to his ruined ear.

His manservant's eyes were sharp and focussed. "Sir."

"What happened?" Seamus's gaze shot to the dark-haired stranger who had dismounted from the driver's seat. The man's hangdog expression and wary gaze matched the suspicious roil in his gut. "Who the devil are you?"

The black-haired man nodded politely. "Good day, sir."

Seamus cast equal measure at the three of them. "Will *someone* please tell me what is blasted well going on?"

"Highwaymen. Including that one." Bartel jerked his head at the stranger, hissing as his fingers clamped his head tighter.

"What happened to you?" demanded Seamus.

"That one's accomplice shot me," griped Bartel.

Seamus leaned his weight into his back foot, ready should the Irishman spring. "What's a highwayman doing driving my carriage?"

"Mrs Fitzwilliam permitted it," said Bartel.

Seamus frowned at his wife. Her wide-eyed concern weighed both men equally. Bartel grunted and shuffled stiffly across the carriage floor on the seat of his trousers, leaving behind a wet trail. Seamus gripped Bartel's arm to steady him. The stranger stepped closer to help.

Seamus pinched his lips, expertly assessing the stranger for any hidden weapons.

The man offered his open palms. "I'm unarmed, sir. You can check."

Towering over the Irishman, Seamus ran his hands around the man's back and trouser line and down the length of his slim legs. The fabric, splattered with the pungent juices of whatever had spilled in the carriage, was of superb quality, immaculately cut. He had clearly dabbled in a life of luxury. What was a highwayman doing in such a fine get-up?

His unconventionally bright pink coat, contrasting strikingly against his black tailored trousers, was marred by muddy scuffs and crushed leaf crumbs. The high starched collar of his dress shirt sat just below his ears and was finished with a black silk tie that had twisted askew. And Seamus knew he spoke the truth. He was unarmed.

Seamus shuffled beside Grace as Bartel bowed awkwardly, his hand still clamped to his ear. "Thank you, madam. You saved my life."

The Irishman fixed his dark eyes on Grace. "You have my gratitude too."

"Who are you?" Seamus asked tetchily. This was an unruly disruption to his otherwise peaceful day.

"Darcy, sir." He straightened his skewed tie with the ease of a man familiar with the motion.

Grace gripped Seamus's elbow. "Remember the indentured man I told you about, on O'Reilly's ship? The one who armed me with the knife I used on Sil—" She broke off, flushing. "You know who." She nodded at the man. "This is he. Darcy."

"Heavens, Grace!" Seamus widened his eyes at her, but she shrugged one shoulder. "You don't do things in half measures, do you?"

She patted his arm, her face softening with a silent apology.

Seamus glared at Bartel and Darcy. "Right. Come on, you two. Let's get you inside and cleaned up."

In the kitchen, Adair fussed around Bartel like a mother hen and frowned at the stranger. Seamus strode through the hallway, leading Grace and Darcy to his library where they might have a private conversation. He stomped over to his desk and, with a loud grating, pulled out a chair. "Sit."

Unperturbed by Seamus's sharpness, Darcy strutted over to the chair, and Seamus hoped that the vile liquid on the man's clothes would not taint the leather seat. Seamus offered Grace a seat behind his desk.

"Explain yourself, man." Seamus rubbed his scarred wrist, absently flexing his fingers in agitation. "The last my wife saw of you was aboard O'Reilly's ship. How the devil did you end up a highwayman?"

"While 'twas hearty to see Miss Baxter—"

"She's Mrs Fitzwilliam now," interjected Seamus.

Darcy dipped his head. "While I was glad to see her leave O'Reilly's ship, I was heartsore not to accompany her."

Grace uttered a small noise in her throat, and colour flooded her cheeks. "Oh, Darcy. I wanted to yell out to you, but I was afraid Holburton would realise our connection. I didn't want him to harm you."

Seamus stepped beside Grace, sliding a hand over her heated nape. Curious how the Irishman had evaded O'Reilly, he asked, "How *did* you sneak away?"

"One night, on shore leave, I saw a man beating a woman with a stick in an alley. 'Tweren't a fair fight. She had no stick of her own to fight him back. So, *I* took the stick and clonked *him* on the head. The woman was obliged. She took me home."

"She took you *home*?" Grace's voice pitched. "You—a perfect stranger?"

"Not a stranger for long. Madame Galloway put me up in her most esteemed establishment." Grinning, he patted the lapels of his pink coat. "As an important protector of ladies, from scoundrels who danced the blanket hornpipe but didn't pay."

"Blanket hornpipe?" Grace tipped her head.

Seamus coughed dryly. "He worked as a procurer in a brothel." Of course! What other occupation would be available to a man with his background? "How did you convince O'Reilly to release you from your bond?"

Darcy smirked. "Even O'Reilly had a price. And it was one Madame Galloway was willing to meet to keep me on as protector."

"Where are you from originally, Mr Darcy?" Seamus lay a hand between Grace's shoulders, savouring the feel of having her safely home. He rolled his other wrist, and his old knife injury clicked.

"O'Reilly took me off the streets of Dublin as a young boy to serve aboard the *Annabelle*. I had no home to recollect." Darcy tweaked his nose with a long finger. "Gave me my name too. Though the others didn't half give me a hard time about it, what with it being a lass's name and all."

"And just how did you turn highwayman?"

"'Twas *Mr* Galloway's mantra to take from the rich and give to the poor. A veritable Robin Hood, if you will. I were at his service by day and Mrs Galloway's by night."

"You're lucky you've avoided swinging on the end of a noose for your troubles," said Seamus stiffly. Fire and damnation! Had he known of this man's criminal behaviours, he would never have invited him into his house, no matter how indebted Grace was to him. "What now?" Seamus asked. What now, indeed. He still had half a mind to toss him back out on the street.

Darcy pinched his nose and sniffed loudly. "I've only ever been an indentured servant, at the beck and call of ruffians. Reckon 'tis about time I try my hand at being a free man. Put in an honest day's work." He settled his dark gaze on Seamus. "You still commanding a ship these days, sir?"

Seamus hesitated. "I hope to, soon."

"Might I ask for a position aboard? Best leave ol' London Town to the likes of the Galloways. The open ocean's a fine place to start a fresh life."

Seamus glanced down at Grace as she asked, "Can Mr Darcy stay at Abertarff House? Perhaps take a job in the stables in the meanwhile?"

"If he so wishes." He only entertained the notion because Darcy had saved Grace not once but twice now. But by Christ, it galled him to make the offer to a man with such questionable beginnings. He had his hands full ironing out his own past without adopting another man's woes.

Darcy's gaze roved between Seamus and Grace, his weathered forehead rumpled in thought. He nodded. "'Twould be grand. My first respectable post."

It might be a respectable post, but Seamus wondered how long the man would last on the lower wages of a stable hand when he had been used to a lavish life in London's most reputable brothel.

That evening, Seamus lay on his back in his nightshirt, hands clasped behind his head. It was too warm for covers, and he kicked them carelessly to the foot of the mattress. Grace clambered onto the double bed and flopped onto the pillow beside him.

"You'll turn me into an old man before my time, Dulcinea. Do you realise that?" He picked at an unruly curl spreading over her pillow, twirling it through his fingers before letting it spring back into place. The worry that had filled him upon seeing his carriage tearing into the mews with a stranger at the helm was still tight across his chest. He spoke in a low voice, "When I jested about you finding misadventure, I'd no notion *it* would find *you* on a dark, wooded road halfway between London and Oxford."

"Who could've imagined such an encounter?" she said.

He ceased fiddling with her hair, ignoring the menhir of guilt that he had been unable to protect her on so many occasions. It was an unreasonable burden to load on himself, since she always seemed to land on her feet like a cat, but it was still a difficult feeling to shake. Grace threw her arm over his bare chest, and he marvelled at her cool cheek as she settled her head against his shoulder.

"I'm home safe now," she said. "Bartel is no doubt relishing Adair's ministrations to his injury. And surely, you're pleased to repay Darcy for his kindness?"

Her fingers stroked the curls of his chest hair, and the restrictive bands of uneasiness lessened. He grunted. "The man should be a hardened criminal by now, given the life he's led. I'm unsure of his motives."

"He's also a proud champion of underdogs, or so he claims."

"His philanthropy towards you baffles me."

"Apparently, I remind him of his sister. He said as much back on the *Annabelle*." Grace twisted her face upwards. "Speaking of philanthropy, how was your meeting with Colonel Hamilton?"

Seamus hesitated, hoping she would not hear the increase in his heartbeat. "A little peculiar. I believed I'd be supping with the other members of the Geographical Society at their rooms on Regent Street, but it turned out to be a private affair with only Colonel Hamilton, Admiral Baxter, and me in attendance."

"Sounds rather clandestine," she said, and he caught the spark of excitement in her voice. He was tempted to shake his head, but a well of humour bubbled up at his wife's penchant for adventure. No wonder London life stifled her.

"Hamilton wants to lend me his support to complete the maps of the archipelago off Tierra del Fuego, as well as voyage onwards to the Antipodes." He avoided mentioning the financial precipice on which he stood. He had faith that his investments and new career would prove lucrative. And when it did, he would surprise her with a wardrobe full of silk gowns—without lace edges. She hated lace.

"Is that not a windfall?" Grace asked.

"Yes, of course." Seamus tightened his arm around her back. "I've also been tasked with ferrying a Father Babcock to Port Famine. He's to re-establish the mission there." She need not know the full measure of the priest's dark heart. Wanting to steer her curiosity from the topic of the priest, he moulded his hand around the curve of her bottom, smiling. "Did you at least have a good time in Oxford?"

"I did, and the weather couldn't have been more magnificent."

"And you found Sykes in good health?"

"I did. He's relishing his new life as a physician. He had quite a few tales to tell about his patients. Some quite macabre, some rather amusing."

"I'd relish a humorous tale."

"Well…" Grace dragged the word out as though carefully ordering her thoughts.

Intrigued, Seamus flipped onto his side, propping his head on his hand. His lips twitched, and he ran a finger along the open neck of her shift. "You look as though you've swallowed a secret that's difficult to keep down. Pray, do purge yourself of it."

"Well," she began again, nibbling her top lip. "Remember how Countess de Brienne counselled you in… the art of dalliance?"

His shoulders stiffened, tightening his nightshirt across his chest. He had not expected this, and she now most definitely had his attention. "I remember. She trained me well." His hand wandered over her thigh, his fingers fumbling with the edge of her shift. "And I remember giving *you* counsel on the matter too."

He thought back to their wedding night. Placing her head in the crook of his arm, Grace had listened enthralled as he elaborated on how he had learned of such pleasures as the one he had just delivered her. From the age of sixteen, every summer Seamus's parents had played host to their friend the Countess Isabelle de Brienne, a French aristocratic widow. She was nearly twenty years his senior, but this had not deterred her from actively pursuing him and propositioning him to bed her.

"I remember how helpless I felt that first time," Seamus had explained. "Ashamed to confess that I was unaccustomed to such propositions." Seamus had run a hand over his smirking lips. "Fear utterly withered my vitals."

After his clumsy and inexperienced first attempt to bed her, the countess had made it a personal goal to educate him in the art of lovemaking. She taught him that in the commerce of affection, his embrace of a woman afterwards was even more essential than the appendage between his legs, and that to feel truly loved, a woman needed his stroking fingers and murmured kisses to whisper their own language of love.

Now, just as she had on their wedding night, Grace wriggled closer to him with a laugh, easing the path for his venturing fingers. "Well apparently, Billy has taken a keen interest in female afflictions too."

Seamus's hand froze. "I beg your pardon?"

Grace stiffened. "Oh no, I don't mean to imply he's into dalliances! What I meant is that he has taken an interest in the welfare of women."

He dipped his brow even lower.

"From a strictly medicinal perspective," she added hastily.

He softened his scowl. "Go on."

"Well, I know you've not mentioned... what I mean to say is... I voiced my concern to Billy, about us..."

Seamus jolted from the pillow like the broken spring from an overwound clock. "You discussed our private affairs with *another man*?" He fixed her with a hard stare.

"Seamus!" Grace shot him a warning glower of her own. "Get off your blazing high horse and hear me out."

"Oh, Mrs Fitzwilliam, I assure you—*I'm listening*." He drew her nearer, the homely scent of her settling his thundering heart.

She lay her head on his chest again. "I wanted Dr Sykes's professional opinion on the matter," she said quietly. "Especially after... well, you know."

Yes, he did know. The muscles between his shoulder blades tightened. "Did Sykes make a diagnosis?"

"I spoke of my inability to bear a child." Grace shrugged. "He said I likely have a wandering womb."

Seamus offered an anxious smile. "Sparing me the intimate details of the affliction, did he have a remedy for it?"

"Yes, a tonic. Unfortunately, all four bottles were smashed during the holdup."

Ah, so that was the source of the stench. His carriage was going to reek for weeks!

Grace narrowed her eyes, and her slow, tickly finger teased the opening of his nightshirt. His heartbeat increased as she coaxed the fabric over the broad contour of his shoulder.

"There *is* one other remedy." She smiled as his skin peppered with goosebumps. "A jolly good drubbing from my husband."

"A drub—?" His words caught short as her warm mouth met his. Rolling atop him, she pressed him back onto his pillow, leaving him with no uncertainty whatsoever precisely *what* the physician had prescribed.

Chapter Six

Inside the newly decorated great cabin aboard the *Clover*, Seamus relished the shelter from the wintery bite of the air outside. The great cabin had been expanded by knocking through to the storeroom next door. A new double bed sat above a chest of two deep drawers, topped by a plump feather mattress. Upon it lay a thick quilt that had taken Grace the better part of a year to make. It featured a central, eight-pointed star of a compass—the heart of Seamus's exploration work. Seamus's favourite square was of the roofless, stone church at Port Famine, in which they had nearly been handfasted.

The new chart table, which also doubled as their dining table, was fixed in the middle of the floor. Seamus ran his fingers over the raised wooden lip, contemplating how many plates and inkwells it would save from sliding off in rough seas.

A portly black stove made a poor substitute for a grand fireplace, but Seamus caught Grace's reflection in the mirror of the washstand—she was rosy cheeked, and her pink lips curled. She smiled at him as though catching sight of an old friend.

"Are you pleased with your new home, Mrs Fitzwilliam?" He wrapped his arms around her from behind. Her neck made a beautiful line down to her shoulder, and he pressed his lips against her warm skin.

"It's perfect." She butted her head against him in pleasure like a cat. "Particularly those lanterns."

He had replaced the traditional brass lanterns with two lamps displaying an intertwined pattern of letters in the stained glass. S and G. Seamus and Grace.

"I'm touched by your thoughtfulness, husband," she purred.

"Did you doubt I could deliver?" He nibbled her earlobe, savouring the tantalizing taste of her clean skin. Her hair, knotted loosely behind, gave her a warm, affectionate look.

"No, but the space constraints will take some getting used to again."

She turned to face him. He curved his hands around her buttocks and cocked one eyebrow. "Is that doubt I hear in your voice?" He touched his lips to her soft mouth, marvelling at how much more enjoyable preparations for the journey were with her here.

"Perhaps I owe you a forfeit for not believing in your abilities?" she whispered.

"A forfeit?"

Twisting slowly from his grasp, Grace locked the cabin door. She turned to face him, her emboldened smile curling her lips. She arched her eyebrows, and he swore he saw amusement. "A forfeit," she confirmed.

With one finger on his chest, she pushed him towards the bed. He offered no resistance, his shoes scuffing back across the new patterned carpet. "Dulcinea. I must supervise the loading." His voice was laden with desire. He possessed the physical strength to easily resist her—just not the willpower.

"Isn't that what your first mate is for?"

Seamus's heart pounded at the delicious impropriety, and he laid back on the plumped pillows. His wife advanced like a leopardess slinking through the grass, crawling over him. Wintery sunshine poured through the new arched windows behind the berth and lit the auburn hues in her hair. Reaching up, she drew the heavy maroon curtains, sealing out the bustling dock and river. She kissed him deeply, and for this moment, she ruled him. Unquestioning and unchallenging, she invaded his soul and, by the heavens, did he enjoy her presence there.

She pulled back, clearly admiring the effect she had on him. He ran a finger softly along her jawline and melted under her gaze of adoration. "Stopping already?" he whispered urgently, his hands encircling her slim waist. He did not want her to stop. He wrestled with a fleeting glimmer of guilt at their salacious indulgence while the hands toiled above, but she pressed her weight onto him, and he stirred instantly. He groaned, his hands scrabbling desperately at the multiple layers of her skirts.

She reached down, her fingers curling around his wrist. "This is *my* forfeit. I'll pay it how I please. Hold still."

Grace shuffled down the length of him. Seamus gripped the pillow behind his head with both hands and licked the sweat from his top lip. She smiled at him with those pretty lips of hers, and his body responded. "By the saints and all that's holy!" The tendons in his arms strained as he gripped the pillow.

"You believe in saints now, do you?" She teased loose the laces of his trousers.

"Right now, I don't know what I believe in." The effort to speak was almost too much.

Shoes scraped outside the cabin door, and Seamus jerked his head at the two firm knocks. Shit! Served him right for shirking his duty. He grinned at Grace like a schoolboy caught secretly putting an apple on the teacher's desk. Sliding off the edge of the bed, he laced his trousers and tucked in his shirt. By Neptune, he was in for an uncomfortable afternoon. He waited for Grace to shuffle off and straighten her skirts before unlocking the cabin door.

Bosun Sorensen, a squat bulldog of a man, removed his cap. He was one of the men who had initially disapproved of Grace's presence when she was first discovered on the *Discerning*. But when news got about town that Seamus was recruiting for the new voyage, Sorensen had slunk into his library, cap screwed tightly in hand.

"Mr Sorensen, I must admit I'm rather surprised to see you here." Seamus had used a professional tone that made the man before his desk straighten up.

"Never miss a chance to serve under you, sir." Sorensen licked his lips.

"You're aware that Mrs Fitzwilliam will be sailing with us again?" Seamus remained still, latching his stare onto the man.

Sorensen slid his eyes away. "Yes, sir."

"Weren't you part of the mob who made it perfectly clear that you wished me to abandon Mrs Fitzwilliam ashore in a foreign country?"

"I'm most heartsore for that, sir. Cottoned on by the end that she was all right, like. 'Tis why I didn't scarper like the rest of 'em in Montevideo." The seaman shifted from one foot to the other. Seamus studied him in silence, seeing how long the man's nerve would hold. Sorensen coughed. "Besides, 'tis you I wish to sail under, sir. You're a fine man and a fair captain. A sailor can't ask for better."

"A fair captain who abandons his men in favour of his wife?" Seamus challenged him.

"As I remember it, sir, Captain Burns and his lot aboard the whaler wouldn't have survived another week out there." Sorensen stared at the carpet and lowered his voice. "Truth be told, I thought having Mrs Fitzwilliam aboard had made you soft in the head, but I was wrong."

"There's many a naval man who still thinks I'm soft in the head."

Sorensen stared stiffly at a spot above Seamus's head. "Aye, sir. But you still had the head of a captain when it truly mattered. You saved my brother's life."

"How so?"

"He was aboard the whaler you rescued, sir."

Seamus steepled his forefingers together and pressed them to his lips. "Very well, Sorensen. Though I warn you, you'll not have as much liberty with your knotted rope as before." The colour drained from Sorensen's cheeks. Grace had told Seamus how she had earned a clobber from Sorensen's knotted rope for fighting Holburton in the mess.

"No, sir."

"In that case, I welcome you as bosun."

"Yes, sir. Thank you, sir."

Seamus had studied the wide-shouldered man before him. "You know, Sorensen, not many are as willing to sign under the command of a disgraced man." He tapped his fingers lightly on the desk. "See if you can't round up some of the old hands from the *Discerning*, especially those who might be chasing a promotion. Peacetime usually leaves an abundance of quality sailors to pick from, but I understand their reticence. Tell them I'm paying better-than-average wages. That might lure them aboard."

"Yes, sir," Sorensen had replied.

Now, Sorensen's cough returned Seamus's wandering thoughts to the darkened entrance outside the great cabin. "Sir, if you please, Mrs Fitzwilliam's trunks have arrived."

"Very well, Bosun. I'll be up shortly."

"Oh, and there's a man on the dock asking after Mrs Fitzwilliam, sir."

"Did he state his business?"

"No, sir, but he gave his name as Sykes." Sorensen cocked a sceptical eyebrow.

Grace darted to the door. "Billy? Please, tell him to come aboard."

The bosun glanced at Seamus, who nodded. "Sykes has permission to board."

"Aye, sir."

On the upper deck, Billy Sykes towered easily near the gunwale. Seamus stiffened as Grace, unable to contain her excitement, ran the last couple of steps over to Sykes and linked arms with him. Her friend patted her hand with brotherly affection. Seamus threw a quick look into the masts, expecting an owlery of eyes to be watching his wife's familiarity with a strange man. Thank the stars Sykes's frock coat lent him a professional air.

Seamus instinctively scanned the swinging arm of the pulley hauling Grace's trunk from the dock. With his collar suddenly too tight, he studied Mahlon, whose hunched, skeletal shoulder was draped with a large coil of rope as he slunk past. Seamus was surprised Sorensen had picked him, considering his previous stance about having a woman aboard. Clearly his views had evolved. The pock-marked man's gaze slid away submissively, and his feet worked double-time.

"Billy!" Grace bounced on her toes. "Here you are—in the flesh."

"'Tis good to see you too, Mrs Fitzwilliam." Sykes's grin at Grace tempered into a respectful smile, and he tipped his hat. "Captain."

"Dr Sykes, a pleasure." Seamus inclined his head. "Welcome aboard the *Clover*."

A gust of wind ruffled Sykes's jet-black fringe over his eyebrows, and he flicked the wayward hair aside with a toss of his head. The boy had become a man, thought Seamus.

Grace beamed proudly at her friend. "Oh, Billy, I'm truly glad to see you!"

Cook Phillips tapped by on his wooden leg, weighed down

by a sack of grain. He wheezed through his moist lips as he passed. Although Seamus had found the cook's temperament disagreeable aboard the *Discerning*, he could not fault the man's cooking and, after accepting the man's formal apology for his previous misgivings against Grace, had welcomed him aboard the *Clover*. Grace was oblivious as Phillips nodded curtly at Seamus and made towards the mid-hatch. Seamus clasped his hands behind his back, listening to his wife's excited twittering.

He clapped Sykes on the upper arm. "Join us in the great cabin—to toast the journey. We'll be gone a good few years." He diplomatically ignored the anticipation bubbling from Grace.

A wooden water barrel rumbled past under the power of Buchanan and Hicks, their eyes masterfully averted. He doubted they would have signed under him had it not been for Grace's persuasion. Then again, Buchanan had discovered the where-abouts of his family in New Holland. It was unlikely the lad would miss this opportunity. Regardless, they both still trod lightly around him.

Sykes's smile subsided, and seriousness shadowed his eyes. "Very well, sir. Will your men see to my trunks?" His Adam's apple bobbed as he swung his gaze to Seamus.

Seamus frowned at the four sturdy, brown trunks stacked neatly on the dock. "That's a generous supply of medicine, Sykes. Though I'm sure Surgeon Beynon has packed what we need for the journey."

The doctor's brow furrowed. "You've another ship's surgeon?"

"Indeed. Beynon has proven his abilities time and again. It only made sense to secure his services." Sykes's crumpling face wrenched a twist of guilt in Seamus's gut. He knew Grace would have relished the companionship of her oldest friend, but he had long secured Beynon's services. Besides, was Krantz not preparing Sykes to take over the infirmary in Oxford when he retired?

"Surely two surgeons are better than one?" said Grace.

Seamus gripped his hands behind his back at her persuasive tone. *En garde, Dulcinea.* "Indeed, but two men means double the pay." What the devil was she playing at now?

She released Sykes's arm, her eyes sparking. "How can you put monetary value on the lives of your men?"

"Quite easily. It's called *commerce*," said Seamus.

"What if something happens to Surgeon Beynon? What if we have a smallpox outbreak or some such disaster?" she countered.

"Since it's a requirement that everyone aboard my ship is vaccinated against smallpox, that issue won't arise."

"What about me?" Grace's voice peaked. "Surgeon Beynon has previously professed to be unfamiliar and uncomfortable with women's business."

He took in the sight of his petite, wild-haired wife standing with her feet braced on his deck. The sun glinted off the gold heart brooch on her chest. He flinched as a thunderous crack resonated through the planks of the deck, splintering their discussion.

Bosun Sorensen roared, "Watch what you're doing, you bumbling halfwits!" Several seamen scrambled to right Grace's trunk, which had slipped from the ropes.

Grace's touch on his arm drew him back from the distraction, her tilted head clearly offering a peace settlement. Her fingers slid over the scar along his wrist. "Perhaps we might continue this conversation below?"

Sykes drew back his shoulders, and Seamus admired his composure.

"Good idea," said Seamus, casting his gaze across the deck. The trunk, while tipped awkwardly on one end, appeared to still be in one piece.

In the plush great cabin, Grace poured the three of them a Cognac. Seamus sat in the new armchair, squeak and creak free, at the head of the chart table. Sykes bravely squared his solid frame to face him. Grace's hand slid over Seamus's knee under the table, her warm touch appreciated.

"Captain," said Grace gently. "Dr Sykes isn't an enemy ship. You needn't look set to pull alongside him and blast him to smithereens."

Seamus pulled in a mouthful of Cognac, hissing through his teeth as the smoky, roast-peach-flavoured spirit bit the back of his throat. "As agreeable a companion as Dr Sykes is, I can't be taking on any superfluous supernumeraries."

Grace sipped her drink, wincing as though it were lime juice rather than his finest French offering.

"My studies under Dr Krantz also includes obstetricius," Sykes offered.

Seamus recalled his intimately personal conversation with Grace after she had visited Sykes in Oxford, and he frowned. "Midwifery is a woman's business. What are you doing meddling in it?"

Sykes drew his shoulders back like a man confidently armed by his knowledge. "With all due respect, sir. While it has always been the role of women to assist in childbirth, they lack the surgical skills to assist with more… *complicated* confinements. I'm an avid advocate that an unborn infant of a deceased mother can be saved by a surgical procedure known as a Caesarean section. Where the child is removed from the mother's body through an incision in the abdomen."

Seamus choked, his face heating like a lit fuse. "Your proposal is to avail yourself to carve my child from my dead wife's body?"

"No, sir!" Sykes shook his head, his long fringe whipping about. "I'm making a lousy effort of explaining myself. Forgive me, sir." Sykes's thumbnail tapped against the crystal rim of the glass. "With your permission, sir, may I please clarify?"

Nodding stiffly, Seamus drew his shoulder blades together.

"As long as it does not include talk of slicing open my wife's stomach."

"I'm quite sure it won't come to that, sir. Your wife is young and healthy. I don't anticipate her having any trouble."

The thought of having a child now squeezed acid up Seamus's throat. Heavens above! His first stint as captain aboard the *Discerning* had been a poor attempt. How on earth could he redeem himself in this capacity *and* be responsible for a child? He swallowed, the sting of guilt sliding into an unsettled pool in his gut.

"We needn't worry, Sykes. Despite your tonic, it appears my wife is unable to bear children."

Sykes's brow dipped towards Grace. "But I thought you... that you..."

Grace licked her lips and firmed her chin. Seamus narrowed his eyes. His heart kicked up a notch as he shuffled one foot forward, pressing it against hers beneath the table. She gave a watery smile, and his heart sped further as a blush flooded her face.

"Grace?"

"I'm with child again," she blurted.

Seamus wrenched back in his chair as though she had cleaved him in two with a broadsword. "But how?"

Grace's pink cheeks deepened into a merlot red. "Surely I needn't explain *how*? Besides, I'm not entirely certain. Which is why I invited Billy to sail with us."

Seamus huffed through his nostrils. "*Without* discussing it with me? Now who's broadsided who?"

Grace shuffled upright in her chair. "I've the utmost confidence in Billy. He and his father aided the birthing of many a foal—"

Her words yanked out the broadsword with which she had cleaved him. "You're *not* a horse, Grace!" Seamus took a breath and turned to the physician. "Sykes, please afford me a moment of privacy with my wife."

Sykes's chair scraped back hastily. "O-of course, sir."

Seamus pinched the bridge of his nose, fighting back the swell of panic at his next words. By Neptune's trident! He could not believe she had backed him into a corner like this. It left him no choice. At the thud of the cabin door closing, he opened his eyes again and stared at Grace's wary face. "You *must* remain in London. It's the safest option," he said firmly.

Grace inhaled sharply, her forehead scrunched at his betrayal. "You'd leave me behind—abandoned by my parents—shunned by society—at Silverton's mercy?" Her voice quivered as she uttered her nemesis's name through clenched teeth.

Seamus sunk his head into his hands, his fingers threading into his neatly tied hair and loosening it. The dark knot of wood on the table became a focal point. "Jesus, Grace. What choice have you left me?" He snapped his head up and ran his hand roughly across his chin. "Admiral Baxter won't sanction your coming to sea now. No father would risk his daughter's life like that. And no husband should either."

Grace rose, her back rigid with misery. She cleared the three glasses to the sideboard.

He rose too but did not approach her. "Why didn't you mention you'd invited Sykes to sail with us?"

Leaning back against the wooden dresser, she wrapped her arms around her chest. "Because I knew the unbending navy man in you would overrule any husbandly sentiments."

He pressed his fisted knuckles to the table. "With good reason! I needn't spell out the dangers you risk having a child at sea. Not to mention the cost of an additional man."

"I'd rather chance my child's life at sea than remain under Silverton's scrutiny."

For crying out loud—and she called *him* unbending!

She sniffed, rubbing her upper arms. "Besides, I owe Billy

for the trouble I put him through. When he expressed a desire to experience doctoring away from the infirmary, I knew I—*we*— could offer him that."

"I wish you'd confided in me." Though she was not wrong, he would not have conceded this easily had he not been ambushed so. Grace's chin rose—heavens, he was in for a hearty serving.

"If you won't take me with you, I'll follow on the next ship. I shan't have Billy to aid me, or you there to—"

Seamus burst away from the table, reaching her in a few quick strides. He silenced her mouth with his. The familiar taste of his favourite drink upon her mouth was intoxicating, and he drew her up for a deeper kiss. Heaven help me, he thought. Heaven help us both. Drawing back, he rested his forehead on hers, searching for any sign of concession, not truly expecting to find any.

Her chin quivered. "Aren't you pleased about having a child?"

"Of course I am. I'm thrilled!" He scooped an arm around her shoulders and drew her against him. "I'm also unashamedly terrified." A nervous laugh rumbled through his chest as he pressed his chin atop her curls.

"Me too." Grace leaned into him stiffly. "What if... if it happens... again?"

Clearly they were troubled by different concerns, but it would not do to add his apprehension to hers now. He lifted her hand between them, pressing his lips tightly to her cool, clenched knuckles. The lavender scent of her reminded him of springtime.

"I trust Sykes's vigilance will ensure you're well cared for." Pressing her palm against the battle drum beating behind his breastbone, he was aware of how slim and small her hand was beneath his. "Do you feel that?" he asked. She relaxed against him, and he trailed his free hand to the small of her back, squeezing her tighter as he whispered, "That's my heart, which has always beaten for you and you alone. But now it beats for two."

Grace's clear eyes glinted like the early morning sun off the water. "Does this mean we're coming with you?"

"I suppose it does." He kissed her warm brandied lips again, murmuring, "I'd best let Sykes know."

Her smile moved beneath his mouth. The little vixen had him in check. He tipped his king. Seamus wrenched open the cabin door, startling Sykes, who was standing a respectful distance away.

The physician's black brows rose, disappearing beneath his long fringe. "Sir?"

Seamus regarded him shrewdly. "You're confident you've the expertise and experience for the job?"

Sykes glanced over Seamus's shoulder at his wife. Sucking in a deep breath, the physician nodded. "Absolutely, sir. Without a doubt."

His face, so full of confidence, almost bordered on arrogance. It was only Seamus's knowledge of the man's character—of his previous protection of Grace—that dispelled this. Seamus held his contemplative stance. "I can't imagine Dr Krantz is pleased to lose you?"

Sykes shrugged one shoulder. "On the contrary, sir. He's happy enough to let me earn my own experiences before assuming command of his practice."

Brave man, Seamus thought, extending his hand and shaking Sykes's firmly. Having Sykes aboard would hopefully persuade Baxter to concede to this insanity. And as for the cost, he might as well put Hamilton's enticement to good use.

"Congratulations on becoming my wife's personal physician, Dr Sykes." Seamus dipped his chin. "You'll have to share a cabin with Father Babcock. It won't be for the entire voyage, though. I'm carrying the priest as far as Port Famine, where he's to re-establish the mission."

Seamus's earlier attempts to warmly welcome Father Babcock aboard had been met with a cold and pious glare down the man's crow-beak nose. He was not much taller than Grace, though his permanent scowl made it hard to pick his age. His hair, liberally sprinkled with grey, was fashionably coiffed and unnatural on a man of the cloth.

"Don't mind sharing a bit, sir," said Sykes amenably.

Chapter Seven

ST KATHARINE'S DOCKS, LONDON, 3 JANUARY 1832

On their last evening in London, Uncle Farfar had joined them for a farewell supper aboard the *Clover*. Now, Grace stood alone with him at the top of the gangplank, the ship's hull creaking as they tugged gently against the mooring lines attached to the dock. The evening was dark and cold, but Grace did not want to hasten his departure. She drew her shawl tighter, the wintery air not the only reason for her watery eyes.

"Oh, Uncle Farfar, I'll miss you terribly!" Grace burrowed her face into his broad chest, pressing her ear to his heart to memorise the beat of it.

"Come now, poppet, the years will fly by. You'll be having too much fun exploring the world to miss an old grump like me."

"Not true! I'll miss you every day." Tears choked off her words, and she squeezed him tighter.

"I must confess, I'm a little jealous of your impending expedition."

Grace lifted her head. "Why?"

"The thrill of the unknown, the clean salt air in your lungs, the blazing sun of the tropics, the uncharted lands. Knowing you share my spirit of adventure, I've no right to hold you back, though God knows I'd rather selfishly have you by my side than halfway across the world."

"You needn't worry. I've the utmost faith in Seamus."

"Couldn't agree more. To that man, sailing comes as naturally as breathing does to you and me. I too have the greatest confidence in his ability to see you around the world and deliver you and your little one safely back to me." Uncle Farfar's eyes shone warmly in the deck lantern's light. "Take care of your husband. He's an honourable and trustworthy man who is utterly devoted to you. Be a faithful and loyal wife, and you'll reap the benefits of his love and protection tenfold."

"I know." She fiddled with the heart-shaped Luckenbooth brooch on her shawl. Her smile faltered as he rubbed a hand across his chin, his eyebrows furrowing.

"I want to apologise to you, Grace."

She sniffed back an icy drip from the tip of her nose. "For what?"

"For the manner in which your true parentage was disclosed to you."

"Oh, come now, Uncle Farfar. That's in the past." She attempted a brave smile. She could not deny the pain Lord and Lady Flint's disowning her had caused, but it was a flame of anger now, rather than sorrow. "Besides, I've always preferred your company."

He enveloped her hands in his, his palms warm and comforting. "I beg your understanding, my darling girl. My excluding you from the truth was for your protection. If this has caused you any pain, then I humbly beg your forgiveness."

"Not at all, Uncle." Her steaming breath curled around her whisper.

"God's truth, my heart gladly sings that you know the facts of the matter."

"Mine too. You've never given me cause to regret anything." She balled her hands between his, smiling at the relief on his face.

"Here, I want you to take these." Uncle Farfar pressed a sizable leather pouch into her palm. Grace's fingertips, red and stinging, fumbled with the leather tie and she almost dropped it. "Good gracious, Uncle! I was expecting a packet of liquorice pomfret cakes, not a king's ransom of gemstones!"

Uncle Farfar chuckled, his gaze softening. "Don't want you finding yourself in need on the other side of the world, with me powerless to help. These will be able to buy you into or out of most situations. Though do this old man a favour, poppet, and don't land yourself in any pickles."

"I'll try," she said, sniffing. She pocketed the gems.

He swallowed deeply. "If I should happen across your thoughts from time to time, will you send word of your wellbeing? I'm not sure I've the right to ask this, but I ask nonetheless."

"Of course! I promise to write to you at every opportunity!"

Uncle Farfar's unsteady breath coiled white in the night air as he drew her into his chest again, patting her sturdily on the back. "I've never done well with goodbyes. Go well, poppet. God speed and good winds," he said thickly. He planted a final kiss on her head and abruptly broke away, pressing another wadded packet into her hand. Hurrying onto the dock, he disappeared into the shadows.

Fighting the sinking feeling of uncertainty, Grace peered inside the new packet filled with pomfret cakes bound in twists of wax paper. "Oh, Uncle Farfar! Still sneaking me sweets." She scrubbed her cooling tears from her cheeks and reached into the packet. Pulling the two ends of the twist with a satisfying crackle of paper, she freed the liquorice button and popped it into her mouth, anticipating the taste of her fondest childhood memories. A potent, cloying flavour coated her tongue. Grace gagged, indelicately spitting the sweet overboard and wiping her tongue with the back of her hand. Ugh! The joys of being with child!

OUT AT SEA, Grace lay with her head on Seamus's chest, listening to the ship waking up—the grinding of holystones scraping the deck clean, the clang of metal buckets used in mopping, and the muffled shouts between sailors. Sorensen's sharp whistle piped. Grace recognised the call. All hands, up hammocks!

Seamus sighed. "All hands—includes me." He leaned over to languidly kiss her, and she sensed his reluctance. She toyed with the long, pale strands of his hair, grinning as he patted her bottom. "You'd best get up too, lazy boots!" he said. "I'm taking breakfast with Johns and O'Malley this morning. Hicks will be here with your breakfast soon enough."

Toby delivered a hearty breakfast of creamy oatmeal boiled in milk and sweetened with dried raisins—a pleasant change from the runny, salty gruel of her previous voyage. Despite her harrowing time as a prisoner aboard the *Annabelle*, the one thing for which Grace had not been able to fault O'Reilly was the quality of the ship's food. It had been far superior to that of the *Discerning*.

Billy assured Seamus that the unconventional food he had introduced to the *Clover* would not only aid Grace's condition but prolong the health of the men too. She appreciated the qualities of limes for keeping scurvy at bay, but Billy had yet to convince her that Dr Krantz's Prussian delicacy of sauerkraut— cabbage boiled and preserved in saltwater that could keep for months—would do the same. Besides, the tangy, slippery leaves served no purpose if she could not keep them down long enough to digest. Though she was partial to the fenberries—the tart red orbs were a welcome palate cleanser after her regular morning disgorgement of bile.

That afternoon, with Seamus poring over his charts, Grace strolled along the gently undulating deck with her red tartan shawl pulled tight against the cool sea breeze. With it being a Sunday, she spotted a crowd of sailors on the forecastle deck. Some of the men smoked. Some lay on their backs with their heads pillowed by their hands. An amicable air of comradery, enhanced by the high blue skies, settled over them. Grace ascended the stairs and the jovial mood erupted into a scrambled frenzy as the sailors haphazardly dragged themselves from their state of relaxation.

Grace waved airily. "Gentlemen, please don't stand on my account." She studied the series of familiar faces staring back. Toby, Jim, O'Malley, Ben Blight. She recognised some of the new men from the foretop and maintop, but she was not yet versed in their names. Smiling at an unmistakably dark-haired father-and-son duo in matching coats, she said, "Mr Johns." Grace nodded at the first mate and his son. "I don't believe we have had the pleasure of being introduced. Grace Fitzwilliam."

The young man grinned and winked amiably. "Danny Johns is the name. Maintopman is the game." His young voice cracked as his father elbowed him in the ribs.

Barry Johns bowed formally. "Pardon my son's familiarity, madam. It appears he needs reminding of his manners. I'm your most obedient servant." Danny rolled his eyes. She waggled her eyebrows in amused commiseration.

"Mrs F., 'tis good to see you." Toby's Adam's apple bobbed, his gaze flicking towards the charthouse where Seamus was engrossed with his brass instruments.

She smiled reassuringly and placed her hand on Toby's arm.

"Don't look so worried. I have the captain's permission to sit with you a while on Sunday afternoons, even if it's done with a blind eye."

"In that case, will you have a seat?" Toby slid over the crate he had been sitting on, and she sat.

At a familiar chuckle, Grace turned towards Darcy. He looked right at home with the other sailors. Despite being modestly dressed in his sailor's garb compared to his highwayman's get-up, he still insisted on wearing a brightly coloured kerchief around his neck. Today's was yellow.

O'Malley inclined his ginger head at Darcy. "Tell us again, Darcy, how you met Mrs F." The Irish sailor stroked a sleek, black cat barely out of kittenhood that nestled in his lap. Nessa was his cat—rescued from being drowned in a bucket.

"Let's 'ear it then!" hollered another voice from the crowd. A chorus of cheers went up.

Seeing Darcy buoyed by the men's spirit of anticipation, Grace smiled as he drew his shoulders back. "Bloody Tibbot was a rascally pirate. He took me off the streets and stuck me on O'Reilly's ship. Much like he did with Mrs F." Anger rumbled through the men. Darcy's attention anchored on Grace, and she nodded at him to continue. "I was a penniless orphan, not fit to survive another winter. I thought when Tibbot took me aboard the *Annabelle* that I'd been saved. I had, I suppose."

"How many years were you aboard the *Annabelle*?" asked O'Malley.

Darcy shrugged, clutching his crotch. "Since before my merkin appeared."

Barry Johns snorted tea from his nostrils and doubled over in a fit of half coughing, half laughing. "A merkin is what's used to shield a woman's privy parts. 'Specially tarts."

Grace chuckled. "Darcy must be excused. He's likely acquired such vocabulary from Madame Galloway's."

"Ah, Madame Galloway." Danny sighed wistfully. "Famous

nunnery mistress of Covent Garden. Never did get to pay her a visit before we left."

Barry Johns tutted at his son.

"Yes," nodded Darcy, his sleek black hair bobbing as it dried in the sunlight. "Madame provided a bed and food."

"Bet that bed saw some action," chortled Danny. Laughter peppered the crowd and the men surged forward, eager to hear details.

Darcy's white teeth flashed in a grin, but he shook his head. "I protected the ladies. I didn't *dance* with them." The swell of voices groaned in disappointment.

"Is it true what they say, Mrs F., that O'Reilly delivered you to Lord Silverton for the prize money?" Danny's young voice pitched.

"Danny Johns! Enough!" Barry spluttered. "My apologies, Mrs Fitzwilliam. My son has had no experience conversing with women, let alone gentlewomen."

"It's quite all right. I'm sure everyone is thinking what he's brave enough to ask." Grace tucked a curl behind her ear, her lips pressed in a tight smile. "Lord Silverton had no right to offer that prize money for my return."

"Crivens, Mrs F.," hissed Jim, leaning in. "Ye've no need to explain yerself to this lot."

"Rather they learn the truth of it from me than from the scandalous gossip of some threepenny upright." Jim's nostrils flared at her use of the term that had been so liberally bandied about in the alehouse just before their brawl. She winked, and Jim snorted back a laugh. She knew seamen loved a good yarn.

"I gave Mrs F. a bone knife I'd crafted. For her protection." All eyes swivelled back to Darcy.

"Did you get to stick one of the pirates with it, Mrs F.? Like I showed you?" asked Ben Blight. The sturdy breeze that carried them along at a fair rate of knots stirred loose strands of his fiery hair.

"No. Only a pig," she said. Her hands tightened into fists at the memory of the knife jabbing into Silverton's flabby flesh. She jumped as O'Malley's kitten launched into her lap. "Ahoy, Miss Nessa." The kitten closed her eyes in ecstasy as Grace tickled behind her ears. She glanced around at the men. "Has anyone met Father Babcock yet? Dr Sykes says he's crippled by the plague of the sea."

Barry Johns shook his head. "Other than a brief greeting when he arrived, can't say I have." The others shook their heads too.

"Poor soul. There isn't a more miserable feeling in the world," empathised Grace, her mouth salivating as the contents of her stomach rolled again. At least her predicament was temporary—she could not fathom a permanent affliction. A loud rattling emanated from the feline as Toby tentatively reached out. Nessa sensed the approaching hand and glared up, her pupils in the pale hazel orbs of her eyes rapidly contracting into slits. Then she sniffed the offered fingers and affectionately butted her head against them.

Grace smiled at O'Malley. He quirked one auburn eyebrow and said, "D'you know a moggy's good luck aboard a ship?"

"Really?" asked Grace.

The young cat's back rippled in an arc of pleasure beneath her fingers. Grace caught Mad Mahlon's eye. His pock-marked skin rucked with his scowl as he glared at Nessa. Grace wondered whether his contempt was for the cat, or for belief in the superstitious twaddle. She had been surprised to see Mad Mahlon aboard the *Clover*. He did not appear to have a particular fondness for any of his old shipmates, but she supposed he was after the money, like everyone else.

The black kitten nestled in Grace's skirts, tail sliding smoothly through her caressing fingers. "Well, Nessa, you have the admiration of the men. Do share your secret with me." She sensed the mood of the men around her swell, encouraged by her good-natured self-mocking.

"You know what whips up the wind?" Danny Johns's young face lit comically, the shadow of the fluff on his top lip catching the sunlight.

"No, I don't," Grace said, laughing lightly.

Barry Johns, having just taken a deep sniff of snuff, spluttered and choked as he seized his son's arm. Sneezing repeatedly, he vehemently shook his head as his face coloured purple.

Unworried by his father's gagging protestations, Danny continued, "There's nothing better for a stiff breeze than a frisky cat."

After a moment of paused shock, as the hands took in the ribald slight thrown so carelessly at her, Grace burst into unladylike laughter. Nessa regarded her with cool disdain. The men gradually joined, and O'Malley wiped away tears of mirth. Barry Johns neatly clipped his son across the back of the head but, seeing Grace had not taken insult, did not put much force into the blow.

Grace lifted Nessa up. "We'll be needing all the wind we can take to make good time to the Cape Verde Islands." The docile kitten hung limply as Grace went nose to nose with her. "What say you, Miss Nessa? Who is the friskier one of us? What say we ask Captain Fitzwilliam?" She stood and tucked the cat under her arm, leaving open-mouthed sailors in her wake.

Chapter Eight

CAPE VERDE ISLANDS, 30 JANUARY 1832

"**B**osun Sorensen!" Seamus peered along the upper deck. "Lower the cutters."

"Aye aye, sir."

Grace slid beside him at the quarterdeck rail with that flea-bitten furball laid upon her arm like the Sphynx, eyes slitted with pleasure at the scratching behind her ears. Seamus had no sentimental fondness for the feline. It was welcome aboard his ship as a working animal—to curb the rodent population. His attempts to persuade Grace not to mollycoddle the creature into complacency had clearly fallen on deaf ears.

"Rather miserable-looking place," said Grace.

Seamus caught the disappointment in her voice as she stared at a dishevelled conglomeration of single-storey dwellings on the raised plateau. At least the green-tinged, conical hills in the hazy distance offered some hope of plant life on this godforsaken volcanic island.

"Miserable or not, it's home for the next month." Seamus peered over the rail into the clear waters where his men readied the rowboat. "Dr Sykes and I will survey the coastal perimeters."

"Billy?" Grace's voice peaked in surprise. "Surveying?"

"He's a physician, after all, and interested in the natural order of things."

Grace shrugged a shoulder. "I never took Billy for the surveying type."

Sykes's deep voice sprung from behind. "I'm not."

Seamus turned to see the physician ready to head to shore with his pack and sturdiest boots.

"Good Lord! You made me jump." Grace gasped.

The cat, startled by the interruption, wriggled free and sprang lightly to the deck. It was likely headed to the galley where Cook Phillips plied it with tidbits. Seamus would have to have a word with him about that—he did not want the cat shirking its rat-catching duties because its belly was too full of easily-come-by morsels.

Sykes's wide mouth twitched. "You always were easy to scare like that." He laughed as Grace punched him on the shoulder with teasing affection. "Careful now. Don't want my specimen jars broken before I've even left the ship."

"What are you stockpiling? Leeches to put in my bed?" Grace scrunched her nose.

Seamus coughed dryly. "I'll have no leeches in my marriage bed, thank you, Sykes."

Sykes's smile faded under Seamus's scowl of authority that he knew put the fear of God into most men. Grace placed a hand on both their arms. "Seamus, Billy jests. Besides, *I'm* the one who put leeches in *his* bed when we were younger."

Sykes raised a black eyebrow at Grace, and his mouth tweaked to the side. His wife's eyes crinkled with laughter. Seamus wanted to believe he was the master interpreter of the emotions that rolled across her face. But clearly, he was not the only one. Seamus shifted his weight to his other foot, chastising his foolish jealousy. The man was practically her brother!

"Tell me, Dr Sykes," said Grace. Seamus eased his shoulders, relieved she had spotted his discomfort and resorted to a more formal address. "What specimens are you after?"

"Herbs, roots, flowers. Anything that matches the greenery in my apothecary notebook. I'll warrant the locals have plants for doctoring their own. But first, I'll help Surgeon Beynon set up the surgical tent."

Ashore, Seamus ordered the camp be established outside the little town. He strolled through the dusty streets with Grace on his arm, gauging the political clime with an experienced eye. They passed the fortified military barrack, its turret standing to attention overlooking the approaching waters of the Atlantic. Men of various colours and creeds filled the ragged standardised soldiers' uniforms, but instead of guns or swords, many were armed only with wooden staffs. He eyed the toes of several soldiers peeping from their shoes. There was no threat here.

Despite the barrack's formidable military bearing, its pale-yellow walls and azure-blue-trimmed windows lent a distinctly tropical air to the garrison. The soldiers greeted him with casual grins and waves in an appalling lack of discipline. No, there was definitely no danger here.

Along the sandy, broad street, goats and pigs roamed freely. Shirtless children played in rowdy groups with streaks of pale dust smeared across their skin. They squealed and laughed, oblivious to yet another foreign crew alighting on their shores. The broad street ended in a small market square, in which a crowd of men, women, and children gathered.

Seamus peered through the noisy rabble. At the centre were two of the hugest prize-cocks he had ever seen, each angrily fluffed out at his opponent. With a roar of encouragement from the crowd, the two cocks crashed together with a violent flurry of flapping feathers and kicking spurs. With a vicious peck to the head, the red cock pecked out the eye of the white one, who collapsed with his wings splayed, panting. The red cockerel strutted about his fallen comrade, arrogantly kicking his legs back, scratching up plumes of dust.

The feathery massacre was over in seconds, but Seamus, spotting Grace pale, hastily steered her towards a mat laden with a pile of oranges whose enormous size warranted closer inspection. Cook Phillips hobbled around the fruit, his loud negotiating halting when he spotted Seamus.

"Phillips, these people may be limited in English, but I'm sure they're not limited in hearing. Could you please negotiate in more civil tones?"

Phillips grinned. "Beggin' your pardon, sir, but 'tis the first time I ever clapped eyes on oranges so richly coloured as to almost be jewels." He offered Grace a large orange. "I've just been sold one hundred oranges for a shilling. A shilling, I say!"

Seamus frowned. "A courteous tongue, if you please, Phillips. You can't be sure how much English they have. You wouldn't want us to end our stay here by having your loose-tongue understood, would you?"

"No, sir! Wouldn't want to miss *any* of the delicacies this island 'as to offer." Phillips's gaze swam to a pretty young woman carrying a basket on her head. He winked at her and she giggled, sashaying her hips. Phillips curtly dipped his balding head at Seamus and hobbled after the woman, his peg leg scratching urgently in the dirt.

That afternoon, Seamus indulged Grace's request to explore the volcanic shoreline. Large, brown-mottled skinks, unperturbed by their presence, absorbed the weak warmth of the sun. Seamus spotted Father Babcock alone near a rock pool with his easel set up. The beak-nosed priest peered into the water before leaning back and painting with theatrical strokes. His brown suit blended with the dark volcanic rock. Intrigued, Seamus sauntered over.

"Father Babcock, I've not had the pleasure of introducing you to my wife, Mrs Grace Fitzwilliam."

"By no fault of my own," Babcock greeted him gruffly. "My only companions have been that wretched bucket in my berth and that meddling sawbones who keeps forcing me to swallow his poisons!" Seamus noted his brusque manner had not eased since their departure from London, and he wondered whether it was shame that kept him abrasive. He must know that Seamus was aware of the details that had landed him on the *Clover*. Seamus dragged his gaze over the short priest. For a man of the cloth, he severely lacked humility.

"Fine day for some painting, is it not, Father?" Grace smiled, leaning in to admire the watercolour.

"Indeed, madam," replied the aloof priest, peering once again into the water, his lips pursed. Seamus glanced over the edge of the rock, curious what fascination held his attention.

"Oh, an octopus!" Grace's cheeks flushed with excitement.

"Genus, Octopus—family, Octopodidae—order, Octopoda." Seamus nodded.

Her aquamarine eyes widened, matching the clear colour of the rock pool. "I've only ever seen one in a book. It's almost invisible against the rock." The octopus, disturbed by the sudden attention, slid off the volcanic rocks and onto the sandy bottom, taking shelter beneath a clump of seaweed. "It's changing colours!" Waves of yellow and green rippled across the sea creature's skin as its beady eyes peered up indignantly.

"You've disturbed it," muttered Babcock sourly. "Can't paint it if I can't see it." Rolling back his shirt sleeve, the priest reached a long finger into the clear water, poking a multi-coloured tentacle.

"What does it feel like?" asked Grace.

Seamus smiled at her innocent curiosity.

"Soft, fleshy, smooth. Perhaps coated in a film of slime." Babcock curled his finger under the tip of the tentacle and flinched. "It has attached itself to me by some sort of suction pad."

"Take care, Father," cautioned Seamus.

Gently running his fingers under the creature's pliable arm, Babcock lifted the tentacle tip out the water. Sedately, almost like a caress, the tentacle curled around the priest's wrist. Man and sea creature eyed each other curiously. Babcock tugged at the tentacle, his skin stretching as he pulled at the creature's arm. Several of the suction cups popped free and he gave a triumphant holler. With an eel-like slickness, the octopus whirled in a swirl of tentacles and a cloud of sand. A womanish shriek erupted from the priest, and he yanked his hand back. The creature fitted snugly to his arm like a thick winter glove.

"God save me! 'Tis biting me!" squealed Babcock. "'Tis eating me alive!"

The paintbox tipped, gorging its contents onto the rocks like the flotsam of a shipwreck. In a moment of morbid fascination, Seamus leaned in closer to observe the octopus's interactions with its prey.

Grace snatched up Babcock's walking stick and hit the octopus solidly. The harder she hit it, the louder the priest screamed. "Stop! Stop! You're infuriating it. 'Tis biting me harder. Owww!"

Babcock collapsed onto his back and hooked his shoes into the octopus's spongy flesh, playing a macabre game of tug of war. "Stop biting my fingers, you goddamned devil!" Tears of panic and pain careened down his temples. Despite the tense situation, Seamus saw Grace's blink of surprise at the priest's foul language.

"Curl your fingers into a fist," urged Grace.

Seamus snapped back the hem of his coat and unsheathed his knife.

"Stab it! Kill it!" Babcock wailed.

Seamus hesitated. "If I stab it, I'll stab you too."

"Get the cussed sod off me!" Babcock exploded, still losing at tug of war. He grunted and rolled onto his knees, punching the sea creature's head onto the sharp volcanic rocks. After a minute of maniacal pummelling, he paused, sobbing with lung-wrenching gasps. His arm hung limply. The octopus was still firmly attached, but its head was a pulpy mess. With blue blood dripping thickly from the mangled flesh, black ink oozed out between the clamped tentacles.

Seamus frowned as Grace knelt beside Babcock, placing a comforting hand on the man's heaving back. "Father, are you all right?"

With gulping breaths, the fear-crazed man began to return to his senses. Absently using the sleeve of his free arm, he wiped away the hysteria-induced slobber. He peered morosely at the offending creature still attached to his arm. "Least it's no longer biting me."

Seamus tried to pull the tentacles off but, impossibly, they had a life of their own and gripped tighter than ever. He popped a few of the suckers off, unsympathetically noticing the blood-filled welts left on Babcock's skin.

"Give me the knife." Babcock held out his hand. Seamus would like to believe it was distress that dictated the priest's manners, but he was beginning to realise it was the man's inherent nature.

"Allow me, Father." With a few quick slices, Seamus separated the octopus's tentacles from its head. With a wet suck, the head pulled free from Babcock's hand, coated in the gore of the massacre. The priest roughly rubbed his hands together in the rock pool, the water instantly clouding in black swirls. He held up his inky fingers for inspection. Seamus identified several double puncture wounds, like snakebites, along his middle finger and on the back of his hand.

"Thank God they're still there!" Babcock wiggled his

fingers. "It stings like buggery—oh, apologies for the colourful language, Mrs Fitzwilliam."

Grace shook her head stiffly, but Seamus could see her taking measure of the man with each passing minute.

Clenching his hand into a fist, Babcock hissed, "Last time I felt something this painful was after a hornet stung me in the summerhouse at my grandfather's estate. My fingers are tingling. They're going numb."

Seamus placed a supportive arm under Babcock's bony elbow. "Let's get you to Surgeon Beynon."

On the short walk back to camp, Babcock complained of a fiery pain creeping up his mid-forearm. He also began to sneeze.

"Bless you," said Grace.

"Your wretched cat's to blame," snapped Babcock.

Grace frowned. "But she's not here."

"Pah! You put your paws on me earlier. Likely shed that devil's hairs all over me, what with you pandering it like it's some Egyptian goddess." Babcock stepped around the other side of Seamus.

"Aversion to cats aside, Father, it appears you've a case of envenomation," said Seamus dryly, pointing to the scarlet swelling on Babcock's hand. Would luck have it that he could be rid of this miserable little man sooner than planned? He shook his head briefly, rebuking himself for such uncharitable thoughts.

By the time Seamus got Babcock back to camp, most of the swelling had dissipated. In the surgical tent, both physicians attended the priest, who reclined with ease on the cot. Seamus, with Grace beside him, observed from the opening of the tent flap.

"Alcohol to clean off the ink." Beynon upended the bottle onto a clean muslin cloth and handed the soaked fabric to Sykes.

Babcock snarled, "Careful, you buffoon! Are you trying to melt the skin off my fingers with your potions?"

"Sorry, Father." Sykes wiped away most of the ink. "Can't

confess to know how to treat an octopus bite. Never imagined being witness to such an event." He tossed the inky rag aside. "Care for some willow bark? For the pain?"

"I'd rather a swig of whisky." Babcock's eyes fixed hungrily on the brown bottle.

"These spirits are for medicinal purposes." Beynon stiffened and tightened his grip on the bottleneck.

"What kind of physician denies an injured man comfort?" scoffed Babcock.

"Come now, Father." Grace stepped into the tent. "The surgeons are doing their utmost to help you."

Babcock drew his hawkish gaze over to Grace. "If it's your intention to deepen my discomfort, madam, your dithering about and offering empty platitudes is succeeding."

Grace stiffened at the priest's unkind words, and Seamus placed a hand of support in the middle of her back. "Father Babcock, adopt a gentler tone with my wife. Unless you wish me to withdraw the services of my physicians and leave you to tend your own injuries?"

Babcock's face puckered, and he rammed his uninjured arm behind his head like a pillow.

"We must remove the tentacles." Beynon conferred with Sykes. "Can't treat what we can't see." Beynon and Sykes manipulated the suction pads off one by one. Soon all eight tentacles filled a bucket beside the cot.

Sykes leaned in to inspect the pale man's arm. "Looks like you've been attacked by an army of leeches, though the haematomas will heal without trouble over time." Sykes's brow rumpled. "The bite wounds are the biggest concern."

"Indeed." Beynon nodded, shoving his spectacles higher on his nose with an inky finger. "Fortunate it's winter. The heat and tropical miasma of the summer months would only worsen this man's woes." He turned Babcock's hand over to inspect it. "There's still a good chance it'll become inflamed."

Babcock snorted. "How in damnation do they expect me to survive in some godforsaken backwater hole when I'm set to expire on the outbound journey?"

Grace pressed her shoulder against Seamus's arm, whispering from the corner of her mouth, "For a man of the cloth, Father Babcock has quite a liberal vocabulary."

"No wonder he had trouble attracting a flock back in England," said Seamus under his breath. She bowed her head, but he caught her chin quivering as she pressed back the laughter.

Cook Phillips's wooden leg tapped by on the dry earth, the patter halting abruptly as he caught sight of the bucket beside the cot. "Ah-ho! You done with those squid legs? I can make a right tasty dish out of 'em! Somethin' the little moggy'll enjoy too."

Chapter Nine

Grace discovered that Father Babcock made a pitiful patient. He was laid up in the surgical tent with weakness and headaches for three weeks. Billy had forgone any exploration with Seamus in order to treat the ungrateful man. The bite marks on Babcock's hand blackened and crusted over, trapping pus-filled pockets of skin that Billy kept lancing open to drain and clean. Despite this ghastly treatment, the wounds were healing and shrinking. Ignoring Babcock's protests, Grace assisted Billy with his patient so that Surgeon Beynon could attend to the usual ailments of the rest of the sailors. She whiled away evenings with Billy before an open campfire, sewing infant clothes.

Grace smiled at Billy's mask of contentment as he cradled his evening pot of tea. "A penny for your thoughts," she asked. He blinked and swung his gaze to hers. The dark shadow of his unshaven jaw aged him, but his grin was still the same. He flicked back his fringe.

"Contemplating life's simple pleasures." His brown eyes glowed warmly in the firelight. "A full stomach, a warm bed, and good company." He smiled again, but a ghost of sadness skimmed across his lips. "There's nothing quite like staring into the abyss of death to resurrect one's appreciation of life."

Grace tied off her thread and nipped it with her teeth before sticking the needle into the pincushion. She held up the tiny cotton garment for inspection. It was plain, without any embellishments. A nightgown perhaps? The bolt of cotton she had packed to sew into shirts and undergarments came in handy for infant clothes too. Folding the gown neatly, she laid it over the arm of her chair and reached into her sewing basket for the half-knitted infant night cap. Her hands worked by feel and familiarity of practice.

"Was it truly terrible in Newgate Prison?" she asked gently.

"'Twas *so* cold, so damp. You wouldn't believe how one poxy window could be such a curse. Too small to allow fresh air in and relieve us of the putrid odours, but plenty big enough to let in the bitter cold." His eyes dulled in remembrance. "At least I had Harley Suffolk to keep me company."

"Who?" Her needles clicked industriously.

"A bushranger from New Holland. Had the unfortunate pleasure of being jammed in with him in the cell."

"What on earth was a New Holland bushranger doing shackled in a London prison?"

According to Billy, his cellmate, Harley Suffolk, had the dubious honour of having been exiled *twice* in his life. Once on the grounds of forgery, where Suffolk was sent from Newgate to Port Jackson in New Holland; and once as a thieving bushranger, where he had actually been given his ticket of leave from the colonies back to London. "The scoundrel was even too much for the penal colony to handle." Billy shook his head. "I wouldn't have survived without his scrawny frame to wedge against. 'Twas that cold the centipedes and slugs burrowed beneath us for warmth." Her friend drained his pot and peered into the bottom of it. "What I wouldn't have done for a hot drink back then." He laid the empty pot beside his chair. "If it hadn't been for Harley Suffolk and his stories, I'd have gone barmy in that hell hole."

Grace tipped her head. "How did Mr Suffolk end up in Newgate again?"

Billy harrumphed. "Was sentenced for forgery a second time. Despite his shortcomings, Harley Suffolk was well connected and generous. He even paid the garnish for some of the debtors so they could go free. He never thought twice about buying luxuries for all the men in the cell—you know, extra food, candles, soap, tobacco, gin. To a scared and famished lad like me, Harley Suffolk was the best kind of friend to have," Billy finished thickly.

"Well then, may the Lord bless Harley Suffolk!"

A log settled in the fire, shooting sparks into the cold night air like fireflies.

"You know, not many folks get to hear a life sentence read out, let alone one with their name in it." Billy paused, his stare fixed unseeingly on his dusty boots. "There must've been noise in the court, but all I heard was silence. Felt an odd measure of calm knowing I wasn't alone. Poor sod before me had his fate read out, and I knew the man coming after me would have his read out too."

Billy stared into the flickering flames, and Grace gave him the silence to speak.

"The hardest part was that I had to relinquish the guilt of what my transportation would do to Da." Billy's lips pressed tightly. "I considered beating the bastards to the punch, but the thought of joining Ma in the afterlife seemed selfish, knowing I'd be leaving Da all by himself."

"Oh, Billy." His words wrenched through Grace's chest like a painful, jagged wound. "I can't even imagine having those thoughts." She rested a hand of comfort on his knee, and he enclosed it with his warm one. His palms were softer than Seamus's, and his fingers were stained green and yellow from meddling with his herbs and potions. "And then for your da to not hear of your pardon..." Grace's voice cracked, and a lone tear curved down the side of her nose.

Billy curled his fingers under hers and squeezed lightly. "Now, now, don't be spilling tears on the matter. I've made my peace with Da." He gently scooped up the tiny gown and smiled. "When a man gets a second chance at life, only a fool sits around and wastes it. There's nowhere I'd rather be, and no other company I'd rather keep, than to be here with you right now. My heart is full and my soul content."

CAPE VERDE ISLANDS, 7 MARCH 1832

Grace awoke before dawn, urged by the pressing need to empty her bladder. Again! Returning from the head in the adjoining cabin, Grace hugged herself as the chilly pre-dawn air slashed through her thin nightgown. She shuffled across the bed under the quilt to lean alongside Seamus.

He and the expeditionary team had returned to the *Clover* the previous day, bringing their month-long exploration of the volcanic island to an end. From his knapsack, he had emptied small animal skulls, fossilised teeth, and dozens of pressed leaves and flowers, all of which now vied for position on his bookshelves already crammed with books and jars of snakes and insects. It amused Grace how proud he was that their cabin resembled a miniature natural history museum.

They were due to leave the Cape Verde Islands today.

Beside her, Seamus lay on his back, his hands tucked behind his head, awake and gazing at the deckhead.

"Sorry," she whispered. "Didn't mean to wake you." She tucked her cold feet under his calves and he flinched, uttering a small noise of protest. She rested her head on his chest, marvelling at the contrasts between them: the smooth skin of her cheek against the wiry pillow of chest hair under his thick cotton nightshirt. He radiated so much heat that her cold cheek tingled as it warmed. She became aware of the unhurried rise and fall of his breast and the strong but steady beat of the pulse in his neck.

"I imagine this is how it might feel to lie on a hot rock baked all day in the desert sun." Grace sighed. She felt the rumble of laughter in him as he curled his arm around her back and pulled her tightly against him, cupping her breast with his other warm hand. He was even more fascinated with them these days since they had ripened with her condition.

"I take it you have extensive experience with rocks to be able to draw the comparison?" he mused.

Curling a leg over the top of him, she felt him harden against her thigh. "Mmm, it appears your chest isn't the only rock-hard part of you," she hummed. She bit his nipple through his nightshirt, and he reacted with a jolt and a cry of amusement. Finding the edge of his nightshirt, she deftly slipped her hand beneath it.

"Hell's bells, Dulcinea!" Seamus snatched her wrist, laughing, his voice smooth like warmed honey. "Put those frosty tentacles on me again, and I'll not remain at attention." He clamped her hand to his chest with his forearm. "Let's warm you up a bit first, shall we?" His hand fanned around the curve of her buttocks, squeezing and rubbing with a continuity that she found seductive—and inviting.

He released her hand from its fiery prison on his chest, and she ran her warmed fingers along his thigh, stubbled by his daily wearing of trousers. Finding him again, she hummed as he leaned down, fitting his mouth over hers with great tenderness. Gone was the tentativeness of his first kisses, stolen in secrecy aboard the *Discerning*. Now, his confidence promised himself wholly to her, cocooning her in a swathe of safety. After a languorous while, he lifted his head, his full lips curling with that smile he reserved for her. Grace's hand lay submissively against his thigh, its previous mission derailed by the delightful distraction of his kiss.

"Are you happy, my Dulcinea?" he asked, unhooking a curl caught in the corner of her mouth.

"Unreservedly so," she replied without hesitation.

"You don't yearn for England or the admiral?"

"There was no struggle in my decision to join you, Seamus. You've offered me a lifetime of love and protection. My heart is with you, always."

"Not only one lifetime. By the promise of heaven, I'll love you to eternity. Christ grant me the strength to keep up with you —and this little one." He enveloped the rounded mound of her middle with his whole hand.

The life inside her flickered and Grace sat up, the bedcover rumpling in her lap. She gripped her husband's hand harder to her stomach.

"Did you feel that?" Exhilaration warmed her cheeks.

"Feel what?" He drew up on his elbow.

"Inside me. Did you feel it?" She whispered as though speaking out loud would render the moment unreal.

"I—I'm not sure." His hand shielded her abdomen. "What precisely am I feeling for?" Seamus minutely adjusted his hand, his fingers defining the hard ball within. "I feel the new shape of you," he offered, his lips curling tenderly.

"No, it stirred. The babe, it moved."

Seamus's pupils dilated in the blue pre-dawn light. "Are you sure?"

"It felt like a—tic—like one you get under your eye."

"Perhaps it was the sauerkraut from last night's supper." Seamus grinned. "Probably nothing more than a rumble of wind."

Grace rolled her eyes in playful despair. "This was different." She shivered in the cold air and lay back, pulling the quilt under her chin. "It came from deep within."

"Well, in that case"—Seamus slipped into a broad Scottish accent—"I'll just nip below and have a wee word with the laddie."

She laughed. "So, the babe is Scottish now, is he?"

"Aye," he continued, keeping in character. "As ye well ken, the laddie has Scottish heritage, what with his wee granny hailing from the bonnie town of Inverness." She squealed as he dived under the quilt.

His voice was muffled, and he spoke in a hushed tone, "Heavenly Father, I pray you put angels to watch over my wife and my unborn child. If I'm not around for you to guide my sword of protection over them, then I entrust their safekeeping to you. Amen."

He placed both of his hands on either side of her small bump and kissed it, his stubble rasping on the fabric. Her chest tightened. Only a few moments ago she could not have professed to be able to love him more than she did, but now, hearing him whisper a prayer of protection over their child, it felt as though her heart was going to burst.

Despite the poignant moment, Seamus surfaced comically, his sandy blond hair crackling with static after rubbing against the underside of the quilt. "Right, he and I have had words."

"Have you now?" She stretched her smile. "And pray tell, what words did you have?"

"Secret men's business." He winked.

"And what if it's a girl?"

He blinked twice. "I hadn't thought of that. I..." His words trailed off as he absently tugged his left ear.

"You what?"

His left eye crinkled and he lay his head on the spread of her curls. "I'll love her—as much as I love her mother." As though struck by a sudden thought, he clasped his hand to his forehead. "Heaven help me if she's as headstrong and as spirited. What'll I do with *two* of you?"

TWO WEEKS LATER, they crossed the equator, and Grace and Nessa watched the initiation ceremony from the safety of the quarterdeck. Father Babcock was well enough to rise from his sickbed, and the other sailors showed him no mercy. She grimaced amusedly at the memory of the tar-swill brushing across her mouth and winced in sympathy as Babcock vomited as she had. Even Billy was not exempt from the tradition, and she laughed as he was tipped backwards into the canvas pool of water. Sloshing water spilled across the deck below, and Nessa's ears swivelled around, the slits of her pupils widening into perfect orbs.

"Go hide, Miss Nessa. Before the rum gives them any ideas about baptising *you* into Neptune's kingdom." She kissed the warm, furry head and tipped the cat onto the deck, impressed by the feline's ability to slink so close to the bulwark as to almost be invisible in the shadows.

Leaning her elbows on the quarterdeck rail, she shook her head at Seamus decked out as the preened and powdered all-powerful King Neptune. As before, the festivities went on well into the afternoon and transitioned into a night of rum and fiddler's jigs and singing.

It was late and Grace was heavy with weariness. Everything about her felt heavier these days, and she wondered whether it was the effect of the child within. Guided by the light of the deck lanterns, Grace weaved her way towards the rear hatch. A desperate, primal shriek cut through the evening's merriment, rooting her shoes to the wooden planks. Goodness, was it a man overboard? Though an icy chill crystallised across her nape, she rushed towards the bow where the scream had materialised. Could a man make such a shrill noise? Was it one of the new youngsters?

Surgeon Beynon's fiddle was silent, and men clustered around the gunwale, pointing and shouting at the inky water below. She caught sight of a familiar shape beside her.

"Toby!" Her friend was pale, the shadows of the lanterns painting dark streaks of worry beneath his eyes. "Is someone overboard?" She gripped his coat sleeve.

Toby glanced around furtively. "Wasn't a man, Mrs F." His voice was small and thin. "'Twas Miss Nessa, yowling in fright. Can't say I blame her. 'Tis a long drop with a cold ending."

A chunk of denial clumped in the pit of Grace's stomach as Toby's shoulders slumped. "Nonsense," she said. "She's likely in the galley. For all his grumbling about having a cat about, Cook Phillips adores her. That's why she's as fat as butter."

Toby raised his eyes sluggishly and a weight of dread squeezed her lungs. *Please, do not say it aloud,* she thought.

"She's as good as dead, Mrs F.," he said.

Grace wrapped her arms around herself, more to stave off the icy dread than the cool night air. "Did she fall?"

Toby stared unblinking, his lips pressing tight. She shuddered at the thought of the panicked kitten, who had escaped drowning once, floundering in the dark, cold waters. Poor creature! At her friend's silence, she grabbed his arm. "Was she *thrown*? Who would do that?"

"A cat overboard will fetch the worst luck on us," whispered Toby glumly.

"Surely you don't heed those superstitions?"

"Doesn't matter what I believe, Mrs F. It'll make the men

restless and careless." He ran the back of his hand across his chin.

A loud shout boomed across the jostling crowd, and Grace heard the anger in O'Malley's tone. "You bastard, Mahlon! You'll pay for this!"

She elbowed her way through the men, bursting into an opening where O'Malley had Mad Mahlon pinned to the foremast by the scruff of his shirt.

"I done nothin'," bellowed Mad Mahlon, wrenching unsuccessfully at O'Malley's wrists.

"Bollocks!" the Irishman snarled. "You've been upset with me all week for cleaning you out on the dice. Maybe you figured if you couldn't get your money back, you'd take something else of mine?"

"O'Malley, that's enough!" Seamus's voice wrenched her head around. "You're an officer, for heaven's sake." His powdered Neptune wig had slipped and his rouged cheeks were smeared after the long day, but the note of authority in his voice was unmistakable. And Grace saw that O'Malley had heard it too.

Barry Johns stepped up to O'Malley and laid a hand on his shoulder. "Come now, O'Malley. A moggy isn't worth a flogging, man."

Hissing, O'Malley released Mad Mahlon's shirt and stepped back, trembling with the effort.

"'Tweren't me, I tell you!" Mad Mahlon sneered, flashing his grey, gapped teeth. He swung a gnarled finger around the crowd. "What about Father Babcock over there? Complains endlessly how the cat makes him itch something fierce."

"Oi!" Babcock's objection burst from him in the unholiest of ways. "Hold your tongue, you blasphemous wretch. Lying lips are an abomination to the Lord!"

Barry Johns glared about. "Anyone witness the cat go over?"

Heads shook and voices murmured.

Grace chewed the inside of her cheek. Toby was right. The incident had indeed caused discord, and the rum so liberally dispensed by the purser earlier was not helping either. Who might inflict such wanton cruelty? Had the kitten actually been thrown overboard? Or more to the point, who wanted to rattle the peace?

Chapter Ten

Seamus stood on the quarterdeck, enjoying the sunny, cloudless day as he manoeuvred the *Clover* down the east coast of South America. Despite the mishap with O'Malley's cat, he was pleased with the expedition so far. The absence of the ship's cat had many aboard unsettled. It was a good thing the decent weather in this part of the world favoured his endeavours. He concentrated all his efforts in surveying the reefs, dredging seabed samples, and meticulously measuring and checking the lines of longitude against his previous calculations.

He watched in awe as Grace blossomed and swelled, keeping busy with recording the daily happenings on the *Clover*. In the evenings, he scanned over her meticulous logs, marvelling at the distances they had travelled, observing the rigid precision of the routine on his ship, and reminiscing about hands they had lost. A new foretopman had died after losing his arm. It had been caught in the tackle and, despite Beynon and Sykes's best efforts, they were unable to stop the bleeding. The sailor's body had been committed to the sea near the Abrolhos reefs. Two others had caught a tropical fever after fetching water from the Macacu River in Rio de Janeiro, both men succumbing to the teeth-chattering, skin-yellowing spread of an unnamed disease.

Hicks had proven a most pleasant surprise. Only yesterday, shortly before Seamus took the sun at noon, he heard Hicks make a wager with Buchanan.

"Bet you a week's rum I can predict the *Clover*'s coordinates." Hicks's soft-spoken voice carried no brag.

"Ye've a deal there." Buchanan beamed, shaking on it.

Not paying much heed to their game, Seamus took the measurements. Heavens above! Hicks was remarkably near to the mark!

Seamus chuckled, impressed. "What's your trick, Hicks?"

Hicks scratched his fine, pale whiskers with a dry rasp. "I keep a running account of the ship's way, sir."

"How?" Seamus expected him to pull a notebook from his pocket. Instead, Hicks flicked his eyes up briefly at Seamus before sliding them away again.

"In my head, sir."

Not possible! The detail of such an attempt required a staggering amount of mental arithmetic. "Indulge me, Hicks. How do you determine our coordinates without implements or paper to calculate your reckoning?"

"I keep track of the number of knots and our courses, sir. Provided the course doesn't vary much during the twenty-four hours, I can make up my reckoning easily enough."

"By heavens, Hicks, you're the first sailor I've met with that skill! It's remarkable!" And one that he fully intended to exploit. "Join Buchanan in his duties. Between the two of you, we'll hit our marks in good timing." If these two could make themselves this useful, he just might be able to forgive their past transgressions—especially that shameful alehouse brawl that had endangered Grace.

It was with great satisfaction that Seamus entered Hicks's phenomenon as the final entry on the last page of the leather-bound logbook. He carefully wrapped it in its waterproof bindings for safekeeping until he could present it to Colonel Hamilton. When he opened the new ledger, the leather spine cracked, and he admired the uncharted, blank pages before him.

Weeks passed where, some days, he would leave his wife in their berth with a morning kiss, and he would not see her or have the opportunity to speak to her due to his frenetic engagement with his brass instruments. He worked like a man with no tomorrow, eking out every second of daylight the tropics had to offer. He never tired of hauling his great brass theodolite ashore to peer through its double telescopic sights, recording the lie of the land with satisfying precision. Each evening when he was aboard, squalling weather excepted, he walked arm in arm with Grace. Pacing the decks, his footsteps confidently knew every knot and dip in every board.

The air this evening was calm and bruised purple with twilight. Grace sighed heavily, her protruding belly lifting then settling beneath her thick coat. Seamus knew she was not wearing a corset, refusing to bind herself, and he was pleased she was giving his child room to grow. He stopped walking. "Do you need to sit?"

"No, no. I'm but a bit breathless. Billy said the little one is likely using my lungs as a cushion for his head," she said, smiling grimly. "I look forward to the day of reclaiming my internal organs for their original use."

Seamus eyed the horizon. A menacing line of inky clouds broiled in the distance. He squeezed Grace's hand in the crook of his elbow. "We're in for a bit of a beating this evening. Why don't I take you down?"

Grace peered up at him trustingly. "Nothing you can't handle, I'm sure, my love."

The gale hit later that evening. Battering winds and unrelenting seas pummelled the *Clover*.

Days and nights blended. One afternoon, through a horizontal sting of rain that obscured the horizon, Seamus saw Beynon dissolve into the grey mist as he hastily lashed himself to the security of the wheel when he changed places with O'Malley. As ship's surgeon, Beynon would not ordinarily man the helm, but in weather like this, Seamus had asked each man to do his bit. Seamus winced in sympathy as O'Malley staggered to the mid-hatch, beating his chest and stamping his feet on the wooden deck to return the blood flow.

Seamus turned his attention to the vast, green-grey waves driving ceaselessly across the decks and crashing into him. The waves were warm compared to the wind, though he knew the momentary relief would not last. As the shin-high water poured unhindered through the gunports and drain holes, the frigid air hit him again. Razor-edged hailstones scratched at Seamus's raw cheeks.

Buchanan, now alternating his duty with Hicks, followed Seamus to inspect the chronometers in the chart house for the umpteenth time. Discarding his oilskin, Seamus scoured his hair with a dry rag and then used it to dry the glass top of each machine. Buchanan scattered a sprinkling of flour across the glass to absorb any residual traces of moisture. Seamus peered through the glass and, despite seeing his chronometers and gimbals miraculously still fully functional, his heart sank. It had been days! Would this storm ever release her grip on them? He made short work of his observations and turned to Buchanan.

"Buchanan, the weather is worsening. Have Carpenter James secure the gunports. We must ease the amount of water coming on deck."

With his black fringe dripping down his forehead,

Buchanan's thick brows furrowed, and Seamus sensed a moment of hesitation before the man responded. "Aye, aye, sir. Have Carpenter James secure the gunports." Buchanan shrugged into his oilskin.

Seamus set about cloaking his precious instruments with their own oilskins as a lashing squall snaked through the open doorway, engulfing Buchanan in a grey wall. Too late, Seamus realised he should have also ordered Buchanan to take food to Grace. He decided to fetch her some, fancying a pot of hot tea himself.

He approached the galley off the men's mess. It was gloomy, with only a couple of lanterns lit, and he eased through the sodden hammocks that reeked of wet tobacco and old bacon. The off-duty men were comatose with exhaustion. Buchanan and the broad-shouldered carpenter huddled in the tiny galley with the one-legged cook. All three men strained towards the blistering iron of the sealed stove, steam rising from their backs. Cook Phillips's tone told of a man unimpressed. "The lot was taken from the stove by the roll of the ship! Fish, potatoes, and coppers all rollin' about the floor together. Saucepan landed in the pantry! 'Twas a right mess, I tell you. 'Tis why Mrs F. had hardtack and salt beef like the rest of us today."

Seamus, still tucked out of view, noticed Buchanan's dripping coat forming a wide puddle at his feet.

Buchanan spoke up. "Carpenter James." He rubbed his hands briskly over the stove. "Captain's ordered all gunports to be fastened." The pots and pans swung wildly, and Seamus winced as they clanged like an out-of-tune, out-of-time band. He strained to listen to the conversation.

With a groan, James patted his clothes he had clearly been trying to dry out since his last watch. Seamus was aware he would not be completely dry yet—there was never enough time between watches.

"Right you are, Buchanan." James stood stiffly, giving his

hands one last valiant rub over the stovetop. Seamus was about to step into the galley when Buchanan spoke again, his tone of caution halting Seamus's feet.

"Carpenter James?"

"What is it, Buchanan?" asked James.

"I was wondering if perhaps ye might like to keep yer hand-spike about ye? Should ye have haste to open the gunports again, ye understand?"

Seamus's cheeks warmed in annoyance at Buchanan's implication. Cheeky beggar! Was he questioning his order to close the gunports?

"That another order?" asked James.

No, it blasted well was not! Seamus shivered as tendrils of warmth crept up the cuff of his coat. It was only Buchanan's violent blush and hasty blustering that stopped Seamus barging into the galley.

"Ehm, well, not exactly. I… um… 'tis only that…"

Seamus caught the carpenter's profile as he nodded silently at Buchanan. He knew Buchanan had trained on the gun deck under Gunner Ash, a man whose experience and logic he could not fault. He was also aware of the young man's intelligence, or else he would not have sponsored his apprenticeship with the cartographer. Doubt washed over him in a cold wave. Was he right to batten the gunports? He straightened his shoulders. *Pull yourself together, man. You're the captain, for Christ's sake.* He was confident the *Clover*'s last modifications would see her through anything.

James placed his meaty hand lightly on Buchanan's shoulder. "I take your meaning, Buchanan. I'll keep my handspike nearby."

Seamus's blood pounded in his ears. With all thoughts of food and tea forgotten, he spun around and headed to the great cabin. His bones ached with cold and, even though he had no dry clothes to change into, the thought of warming his tingling skin against Grace hastened his footsteps. He needed to be near her, to have his reassurances mean something, and not to have his judgement questioned. Nor to question his own judgement.

He nudged the great cabin door ajar, hoping to quickly slip through without letting the swirling warmth of his home hearth escape. He jarred to a halt at the sight of Father Babcock on his knees, hanging onto the chart table leg. He was so deep in fevered prayer that he did not even open his eyes when Seamus entered. The priest's unfamiliar odour of boiled cabbage and old broadsheets was an unwelcome assault in this sanctuary.

Panic seared the cold from his bones at the sight of Grace slumped over, arms spreadeagle, forehead lolling on the tabletop. "Are you well, Dulcinea?"

She lifted her head, and his knees nearly buckled with relief as the ship rolled over another wave. Her bundled hair, scooped into a wiry nest, wobbled lopsidedly. "Yes," she groaned. "At least I've no dinner threatening to toss itself into my lap. Earlier, my tea sloshed over my hardtack and beef." She grimaced. "Nothing kills an appetite faster than food swimming in a sea of cold tea in the bottom of your plate." Her smirk dissolved into concern. "Oh, Seamus, your face is bleeding!"

"But a few hail cuts. I'm fine."

The priest wailed like the pitifully low moan of a violin as the ship rolled precariously, scattering a cascade of books from the shelves across the room like heavy confetti.

Seamus scowled at Babcock. "What the devil are you up to, man?"

The priest remained mute.

"He came to offer me a word of comfort," Grace replied instead. "But he's been that way for the past hour." Babcock quivered and his knuckles whitened around the table leg, his only reply a juddering groan.

Cowardly fool! Seamus seethed, his patience worn thin by

the almost insurmountable pressures of seeing the *Clover* through the worsening foul weather.

Grace's darkened eyelids were sunken in her pale face. "It's been days! How much longer is this storm going to last?"

"Can't say. She's in fine form, though."

The priest mewled again in terror, crushing his hooked nose against the wooden leg, his eyes squeezed shut.

"Worry not, my heart," said Seamus, holding firmly onto the back of her chair as the floor undulated. "The *Clover*'s built to weather anything. Only the shore can sink her, and we're miles from that." He hoped his voice sounded as confident as his words.

For crying out loud, where was Wadham when he needed him? Seamus suddenly missed his former fellow officer with a ferocity that scared him. He would have done just about anything right now for the lieutenant's council. Seamus rolled his scarred wrist, the tension in it clicking before releasing.

"I can't walk around with the same steadiness as you." Grace gave a strained laugh. "In my current state, I can barely manage that on a smooth day." She rubbed her bulging belly. "How am I to sleep properly in this?"

Seamus growled at Babcock. "I'll help by hauling this yabbering pillow thumper back to his berth." He leaned in to kiss her. She stank of wet wool, but her lips were gloriously warm. The prickling heat creeping over his body had nothing to do with the warmer cabin air. "When you're tired enough, you'll lay your head anywhere it pleases."

After unceremoniously marching Babcock back to his berth, Seamus went above again to see that his orders were being carried out. Impossibly, it was colder than before. He gripped the gunwales as the swathes of water churning across the planking threatened to upend him. He squinted grimly into the rigging as his crew risked life and limb to keep order about the masts, spars, and web of ropes. By Neptune's forked trident! Her canvas was saturated, and with marrow-freezing dread he comprehended she was too top-heavy. Squeezing the stabbing pain of cold in his injured wrist, he calculated that the already fraught situation was deteriorating rapidly.

At the helm, Ben Blight had joined Beynon to wrestle the wheel, and the two men warily eyed the straining, crackling masts above. Blight's flaming whiskers fluttered red like a muti-neer flag. Amassing, mountainous waves rose under the *Clover*'s hull, angrily sacrificing themselves against the bow. Seamus staggered over to the helm to help.

He had kept a main topsail and reefs for better steerage, but he knew they could not possibly carry them any longer. Not in a blow this big. As though to confirm this, the gale's claws screeched through the rigging, trying to ravage the canvas and wood. Seamus roared his orders at Sorensen.

The bosun held the speaking trumpet to his mouth, the wind slapping his words into near oblivion. The saturated rigging sprang to life again with small figures responding immediately to the order with rehearsed meticulousness.

Exhausted, Seamus strove valiantly to maintain control of his brigantine, but the incessant gale mocked his efforts. He was losing her! Several cries in the rigging alerted him to the merci-less wall of green water heading directly towards them.

"Come on, you bastard!" Seamus cursed into the wind, quailing as he strained his neck back. That devil was almost as high as his ship was long! *Give us a chance to ride over it,* he prayed silently.

With heart-stopping dread, Seamus stared at Mahlon hugging the protruding bowsprit. The wave fully absorbed the sailor as the *Clover* bravely scrambled up its taunting face. The torrent gorged the bow of the ship, and Seamus's knees turned to jelly as Barry Johns, clinging to the bowsprit netting with arms locked around his son, also vanished. Seamus clung to the helm beside Blight as the *Clover* pushed upwards, her deck shuddering as she pitched almost vertical. Time slowed as the *Clover* hovered over the bottomless chasm that opened up.

With a gut-swooping drop, the ship skidded uncontrollably down the back of the wave into the abyss. Unbelievably, Mahlon was still clasped to the bowsprit, vomiting seawater. A thin cry of terror cut through the howling wind, and Seamus's anal sphincter spasmed as Barry Johns's saturated head pivoted wildly, searching the empty netting beneath him. Heavens, no! His boy!

The *Clover* bobbed deliriously in the frothing ocean, spluttering to catch her breath like the near-drowned seamen in the rigging. Seamus was not ready for the next impact and knew his ship was not either. He held his breath and tightened his grip on the helm, tempted to join the inexperienced men who were wailing prayers in despair.

The plucky brigantine rose up the face of the second wave, but she swung wildly to the side before toppling over the summit of the living mountain, slewing broadside down the back slope. The *Clover* twirled aimlessly in the swirling melee at the bottom of the wave.

"Turn her to face the next wave, Blight!" Seamus roared over the tempest, his clawed fingers gripping the wooden wheel.

"Helm's not responding, sir!" yelled Blight, wincing as another squall lashed him.

Avoiding the crazed terror in Beynon's eyes, Seamus blinked away the stinging pricks, struggling to distinguish between the sweeping, blackened rainclouds and another grey breaker. *Great heavens above, please do not let another come.* Lightning flashed and turned his green-grey world black and white. Temporarily blinded, Seamus thought he heard a cry, but it was whipped away in the wind before he could be sure. By Christ. There it was. The dreaded third wave, tall enough to loom over the roof of Abertarff House in London, gathered momentum and arched over the *Clover*. Of all the deaths—drowning!

"Oh, Dulcinea—I'm sorry!" he cried.

The wave tore into the ship with the ferocity of a full broadside of cannon, fired from a frigate twice their size. Seamus hooked both arms around the helm, the wood biting into his flesh as all light disappeared. This was it. His candle was snuffed.

The sounds of the flailing and thrashing of his men told Seamus his candle was still well lit. He was in an unprecedented fight for his life—as were his men. When the light returned, he clung limply to the helm, disoriented by the world that had tipped over. Blight and Beynon hung by their rope bindings beside him, struggling against their bonds.

He shook his head to clear his bewilderment. The *Clover* lay on her side, floundering unsuccessfully to right herself. With spine-tingling horror, he grasped that the larboard bulwark was well below the surface, pinned by an inescapable amount of water because of the gunports he had ordered fastened. Damn and blast!

In the swirling chaos, he spotted the cutter's new-fangled davits, holding the rowboat securely to the *Clover,* stubbornly defying all efforts to unwind. The swamped cutter clung to the ship with the tenacity of a drowning sailor clinging to his rescuer, equally threatening to pull them all under. The ship's bell clanged unchecked like jangling knells issued by the *Clover* herself, warning of the approaching disaster.

Squinting against the stinging needles, Seamus caught Sorensen, Buchanan, and three others maniacally swinging their hatchets at the manila ropes tangled around the arms of the davits, trying to free the rowboat. Seamus searched frantically for a tool to help his men, but the crashing waves had wiped the deck clean.

Carpenter James stood alone at the bulwark, in waist-deep water. He was trying to reach below the foaming surface, and Seamus instantly recognised his attempts to release the gunport with his handspike. James gasped with the panic of a non-swimmer trying not to submerge his head. With a snarl of defiance, Seamus released his grip on the helm and, fighting the rush of water against his hips, pushed towards James.

At a victorious cry from behind, Seamus spun in time to see the cutter slither free. Buchanan powered past Seamus towards James. Reaching James first, Buchanan snatched away the carpenter's handspike and, taking a lungful of air, disappeared beneath the frothing water. With his own breath drawn, Seamus waited for Buchanan to appear. James searched the water with equal intensity.

"Buchanan!" James yelled, his face twisted in anguish.

Buchanan exploded from the beaten surface of the water with an agonised roar before plunging below again to unseal the next gunport. He burst up again further away, staggering. He repeated the motion several more times. Seamus ploughed towards him and snatched at the precariously wobbling handspike.

"Is it done, Buchanan?" shouted Seamus over the chaos.

Buchanan whimpered and scrubbed hands over his scalp as though to encourage warmth into his skull. Seamus shook his assistant's shoulder violently.

"Buchanan! Is it done? Are they open?"

The Scotsman's bloodshot eyes blinked slowly. "A-aye, sir. 'Tis done."

Seamus clenched his violently chattering teeth to see if the *Clover* would right herself, or if it was too late. A fiery surge of hope shot through him, temporarily warming his stiffened muscles, as the ship shifted beneath his feet. The lad had just jolly well earned himself a keg of rum! Seamus's tentative hope wavered as he scanned the surrounding ocean through the maelstrom. Please, no more. They would be done for.

The *Clover* sluggishly swung upright. His courageous little brigantine staggered painfully to an even keel. She was low in the water, but she had not given up yet. He peered blearily through the blinding squall for the fatal wave. He was aware that the storm was toying with him like a cat toys with a lizard. And just like a lizard loses its tail, his ship had lost bits in the struggle.

"Come on, you bastard! You can't beat us!" His maniacal laugh turned into a howl of relief when he recognised that no more rogue waves approached.

An hour later, the ferocity of the wind died, and he took control of the *Clover* once again. Watching the storm shrug petulantly back out to sea, he bit back an exhausted sob as he scoured the damaged decks. The aft hatch had been torn clear. Grace! He threw himself down the ladder.

"Grace!" he roared, slamming open the cabin door that hung limply from its remaining leather hinge. Water dripped off the deckhead. He crashed through books, candlesticks, saucers, inkpots, shoes, and a myriad of their personal belongings. "No. Please, no!" His wife lay in a soggy puddle against the bulkhead, the sodden carpet rumpled against her.

He plunged to his knees and roughly shook her shoulder, his voice pitching in panic. "Grace! Grace, do you hear me?"

Her dress clung to her skin like a frosty veil and she was icy to touch. She flopped as he twisted her onto her back. Her face was as pale as any corpse he had seen. Whimpering, he pressed his cheek to her icy bodice. His own thumping heart and ragged breath drowned out any sounds of life from her.

"Sweet Jesus, no, no, no," he whimpered, his hot tears scalding his icy cheeks. He slapped her ashen face. "Open your eyes, for pity's sake!" He thrust his head onto her chest again and held his breath. Nothing! Pulling her bodice lower, he laid his ear against her pale, clammy skin. He sucked in his breath. A soft lub-dub patted his cheek. The sweetest sound in the world.

"Oh, thank heavens!" With a violent sob, Seamus collapsed onto the floor, his back crashing against the bulkhead. Scooping Grace into his lap, he cradled her head against his shoulder and willed all his body heat into her.

His breath hitched as she blinked dozily at him, the veins in her eyes red and crazed like an ancient Roman mosaic. He inhaled her warm breath, his soul thawing. "I couldn't wake you. I thought I'd lost you!" His voice cracked. He peppered her face with kisses and tucked a stray hair behind her ear, tracing his fingers down the jugular in her neck that pulsed reassuringly. Grace curled into his chest, and he tightened his arms around her in an unspeakable intimacy.

"You were right." Her words were muffled by his sodden coat. "When tired enough, you truly can fall asleep anywhere."

"I love you, Grace," he whispered.

"I feel your love," she whispered back. He heard her breath catch in her throat. "Just as I feel the life you placed within me."

Oh, thank Christ! The babe.

"The three of us are one," she murmured.

"No matter what," he agreed.

Chapter Eleven

race's stomach rolled as she stared at the eight names she had written on the page. Eight good men lost during the storm. With the great cabin destroyed, Grace sat in the sunshine on the quarterdeck at a small desk while attending her administrative duties. She keenly felt the loss of her shipmates. Especially Danny Johns. She ached at his loss, having observed him mature from a cheeky man-child into an exemplary sailor under his father's tutelage.

While every panel of wood and piece of rope on the ship was still sodden, her spirit lifted marginally as the sun warmed her back, thawing the cold, hard knot of loss inside her. It felt marvellous not to have the heavy weight of damp clothes hanging off her enormous belly.

Her stomach rolled again. Willing herself not to be sick, she wondered whether Billy might have something in his medicine box to help. The men were all engaged, cleaning up after the storm, and she was loath to ask one of them to summon Billy for her. She was quietly pleased that in a gesture of goodwill, Seamus had allowed the men in the saturated forecastle to lug the contents of their cabin onto the usually immaculate upper deck to dry. Chests, bedding, and two miserable goats bleating in distress were lugged up, and brooms, buckets of water, swabs, scrubbing-brushes, and scrapers were ferried down.

O'Malley and Ben filled a large tub with freshwater. The hands set about washing the clothing, piled like a stinking hillock on the wooden deck—much of it mouldy from lying wet for such a long time in dank corners. Clothes hung across all available ropes and rigging. Wet boots and shoes were spread out in the sun. Grace winced, knowing how difficult it would be for her proud husband to see his ship dressed like a domestic back-yard on washing day.

Jim clambered up the quarterdeck stairs, and Grace smiled at her wide-eared friend. "It's a good day for washing."

"Aye, 'tis indeed." He rubbed a hand across the back of his neck, an uncharacteristically sheepish grin creeping across his face. "The lads want to strip off their kegs for a wee wash, but they're not likely to do so with ye watching on."

"Do they now?" She cast a glance across the activity below. The men were already filling more buckets with freshwater and soaping and scrubbing one another's backs with towels and bits of canvas. Laughter passed between them as easily as the shared buckets of soapy water. A newly scrubbed Ben threw a bucket of water at O'Malley's sudsy back. The Irishman gasped then roared triumphantly.

"That must be wretchedly cold." Grace giggled, the men's high spirits infecting her own mood.

"Aye, but 'tis worth the dousing to feel clean again."

Barry Johns was hunched before a small looking glass atop a water barrel, shaving. His pale, half-shaven cheeks and red-rimmed eyes exposed his misery.

Grace wanted to cry at the agony of his loss, equally as much as she wanted to cry at Danny's absence. "How is Mr Johns faring? Since losing Danny?"

"Those two were joined at the hip." Jim shook his head sadly. "Despite his free spirit and liberal tongue, that lad was a fine sailor."

Goodness, his poor wife back home would only find out about this in several months. Sighing regretfully, Grace rose awkwardly. "I'd best head below now anyway. Sort out my own sodden mess and see if Dr Sykes has salvaged any of his ginger tea."

Closing the heavy leather cover, she rose and made her way down the main hatchway into the bare gunroom. Outside Billy and Father Babcock's cabin, she halted at Toby's low tone coming from inside. Someone gave a trembling squeak. Wrinkling her nose at the dank, briny odour of the saturated hull, she tucked herself back against the bulkhead to eavesdrop.

"You'll do as we say, you reprobate," said Toby, his words snipped short.

The snivelling sounds came from Father Babcock. "Y-you can't force me to."

Billy's normally mild-mannered voice sounded harder and more insistent than Grace was used to. "If you know what's good for you, you'll oblige us in this matter, or else—"

Babcock growled. "Or else what? You don't scare me."

"We mightn't," said Toby, "but last week, I caught you snooping about the galley. One word from us that you're a food thief and you'll be in irons in the hold before you've finished stumbling through the Lord's Prayer."

"I was only fetching some water!" the priest squeaked indignantly. "It'll be my word against yours, you pagan papist."

Toby scoffed. "Oh, I don't think we'll have too hard a time convincing the captain, do you, Dr Sykes? 'Specially since he already caught you visiting his cabin uninvited during the storm."

"Not at all," said Billy resolutely.

"We all heard what a blubbering coward you are," said Toby.

"I'm no cow—"

"Shut your mouth, you jabbering turkey," said Toby. Billy's laughter resounded deeply. "Save it for those who might actually care. Now back to the topic at hand—"

"I'm too ill to perform a funeral service for the lost men," Babcock's voice warbled.

"Oh, but you *will*, Father." Grace heeded the new note of authority in Toby's voice. "Don't underestimate how far we're prepared to go for our own. You'll perform the service if you don't want the whole ship to find out your little secret."

"I've no secrets," objected Babcock snippily.

Toby snorted. "Beg to differ. You know the men love a good yarn. Imagine their interest to hear about your wife's murder."

Murder? Grace pressed her palms against the cold, damp planks behind her. A hot trill shuddered up the back of her neck.

"You insolent oaf!" Babcock's voice rose a notch.

"Now, now, Father. We know the church shipped you off to be rid of the scandal," said Toby wheedlingly.

"A scandal you say, Mr Hicks?" Billy's voice toyed curiously. "What sort of scandal?"

"The good Father here had himself a mistress. And this mistress didn't care much for Mrs Babcock stealing her lover's attention, so the tart and Babcock dispatched poor Mrs Babcock in a grievous manner," explained Toby.

Billy gasped animatedly. "You don't say?"

A strand of doubt plaited around Grace's intestines. Surely Seamus would never knowingly allow a murderer aboard his ship? And certainly not without cautioning her about it?

"Lies!" screeched Babcock. "Lies from a worthless little tow-rag. You have no proof!"

"Oh, but I *do*, Father," Toby uttered confidently. "Came across a letter in the great cabin from your bishop, asking

Captain Fitzwilliam to squirrel you away from England, for a fair fee of course, in order to save the church's reputation. You let your mistress take all the blame for your wife's murder while *you* got away."

Babcock made gargling, huffing sounds as though he had swallowed a chilli pepper.

Billy's voice dripped with humorous condescension. "I wouldn't say that, Mr Hicks. Being sent to the godless ends of the earth is a fitting penance."

Babcock's voice was high and tight. "I'll inform Captain Fitzwilliam you've been snooping in his private papers—"

At a solid thud against the bulkhead, Grace jumped and Babcock yelped in pain. Toby's voice lost all its pleasantness. "Listen up, you spineless pudding-heart. There's a ship full of men, heartbroken at the loss of their friends. So, tomorrow, you'll say a few words of comfort about their untimely departure. You'll do it in such a way that offers condolence to each and every one of them. Do that and we'll let your dirty past stay a secret a little longer."

Grace was astounded that Toby knew so much, but she also knew how a ship like this had ears. He must have snooped through Seamus's papers, but then again, it was hardly snooping when Seamus granted him privileged access as Jim's assistant. She knew she could not broach the subject with Seamus without landing either Jim or Toby in hot water, but she bristled with disappointment that Seamus had kept this from her. He was likely protecting her—that was usually his excuse for his bull-headed decisions—but the betrayal still stank like the musty planks she was pressed against.

"That's blackmail!" Babcock squeaked.

"Ha, that's the pot calling the kettle black," said Toby. Billy joined in his laughter. "Just do as you're told!"

Grace silently backed up a few steps and, with a precursory cough, she knocked on the cabin door.

"Oh, I'm glad to find you here, Dr Sykes." She hoped her blush was neatly disguised as a flush of surprise. "Good day, Father Babcock." Grace barely held back her smile at the priest's goggling.

"Mrs F.," Toby greeted her enthusiastically. "You're just in time."

"For what?" Grace arched her eyebrows innocently.

Toby loomed over the short priest cowering against the bulkhead. He gripped Babcock's nape in a deceptively friendly gesture and pulled him round to face Grace. "Father Babcock was just telling us of the funeral service he's planning for the men tomorrow. Isn't that so, Father?" Toby's fingers tightened, and the pasty-faced man winced.

"Y-yes. Th-that's right. T-tomorrow."

Placing a light hand on Babcock's hairy one, Grace simpered, "Oh, Father, will you really? That's *ever* so thoughtful of you, especially since you're not feeling your finest. I'm sure the men will gain much comfort from your ministrations."

"Never fear, Mrs F." Billy grinned, nudging a stinking bucket beside Babcock's berth with his shoe. "The Father will be accompanied by his trusty companion."

"I... ehm... yes, well... best get to planning it," said Babcock, dipping his head. "Good day, Mrs Fitzwilliam."

Babcock's combative gaze slid sideways to Toby, who still held his neck in a fierce grip. With an extra squeeze and a jovial wink, Toby released him. The priest scuttled across to the desk like a ship's rat.

Grace pressed a finger to her lips to silence her laughter and nodded in thanks to her two friends.

Chapter Twelve

T wo days later, with the aired clothes, chests, and bedding returned neatly to the forecastle and gunroom, Grace stood on the quarterdeck beside Seamus as the *Clover* limped into the port of Montevideo. The grey-walled fortress with its whitewashed ramparts stood sentry over the city. Once they had docked, the drenched contents of the hold were disgorged onto the shore. She helped Jim and Toby remove Seamus's sodden charts and journals from the chart-house. Not many of his specimen jars had survived either.

With her heart sinking at how few salvageable items were carried to the large, dry storerooms near the dock, she headed back towards the gangplank. From the corner of her eye, some-thing moved in the shadows of some crates draped in mildew infested rope. Grace stopped, one foot on the gangplank and one hand holding the railing as she inspected the precarious pile. Either one of the large ship rats had made its escape or else— could it possibly be—surely not, after all this time? Nessa? She stepped towards the crates, holding her breath against the musty stink of the blackened netting. Had the plucky ship's cat been aboard all this time? Had someone been hiding her? Keeping her safe?

"Nessa," she crooned, reaching into the gap between two crates. The creature hissed and Grace yanked her hand back. Two pale green eyes stared at her from the recesses of the shadows.

"Come on, silly. It's me." Grace held out her hand again. A cold wet nose touched her knuckle, and the cat rubbed its whiskered cheek against her skin. Grace let out a gasp of a laugh, the warm rush of relief flooding up her back and over her shoulders.

She curled her hand beneath the soft furry belly but the cat stiffened and sprang back, hissing again. Grace tutted softly—the sound had always succeeded in calling the cat out of hiding before. She did not blame the poor feline. What with almost being thrown overboard, and then the storm, the kitten's reluctance was understandable.

"It's alright, puss-puss. I understand you not wanting to come aboard again. Your secret's safe with me." She glanced around the bustling docks. In a patch of sunlight in the alley between two warehouses, a tabby cat and two ginger kittens lay stretched out, ignoring the human activity.

Grace peered into the recess again. "I suppose there are worse places in the world to live than here. At least it's warm." She reached for a farewell pat, but finding only empty air, curled her fingers in disappointment.

She turned towards the ship, her gaze fixed on Seamus's grim face as he peered over the taffrail. Despite her advanced state, she was determined to be useful, and she waddled back up the gangplank.

"Not all is lost," she said perkily, hoping to alleviate some of his gloom. "The ship's books bound in oilskins have survived. As have the flowers you have pressed between the pages." She leaned it to whisper, "And I do believe our ship's cat survived her earlier ordeal, as well as the storm. She must have kept to the hold, or someone had her hidden. Though now she's ashore, I'm unable to persuade her aboard again."

The corner of her husband's mouth tugged up, but his eyes lacked humour. "I've bigger issues to worry about—like the impending expense and lengthy repairs. If I wait to send word to Colonel Hamilton, we'll be delayed for months." He slid his arm around her back, and she tucked herself against his hip. "As his agent, I've my work cut out to convince the suppliers to accept promissory notes."

"I have the gems Uncle Farfar gave me. You could use those."

Seamus squeezed her tighter. "Our current shortage of coin isn't enough of a predicament to warrant using your gems. Besides, I'm confident Hamilton and his backers will honour the accounts."

"Where shall we sleep tonight? At Lord Ponsonby's?" asked Grace.

"Lord Ponsonby has taken his diplomatic prowess over to Belgium. I'm hoping that Thomas Hood, the British consul-general here in Montevideo, might accommodate us."

Thomas Hood was waiting in his library to greet them. "Welcome back to Montevideo, Captain Fitzwilliam." He took Grace's hand. "Mrs Fitzwilliam, the pleasure is all mine. I don't believe we met on your last visit?" Hood kissed Grace's hand, his smooth-shaven cheeks the golden tan of many an Englishman in this part of the world. His brown hair was combed back, exposing a startlingly broad forehead.

"Thank you for your hospitality, Mr Hood. I'm sorry we only seem to drop in on your fair city whenever disaster has struck," said Grace.

"Nonsense! The pleasure of hosting such pleasant and respectable company is all mine." Hood's discoloured teeth showed through his wide smile. "I trust there are no prize hunters after you this time, Mrs Fitzwilliam?"

"None that I know of." She scrunched her nose and caught the white press of Seamus's lips from the corner of her eye. Hood's attempt at humour failed in the face of Seamus's exhaustion. She squeezed her husband's forearm, and his muscle flexed beneath her fingers. "Might I please beg a bed, Mr Hood?" she asked.

Hood's curious gaze flicked to her midriff. "Of course, my dear, you must be utterly spent after your ordeal." He looked at Seamus. "Perhaps once you're rested, Captain Fitzwilliam, you might like to join me for a brandy? I do love catching up with the latest from London, and yours is fresher news than mine."

"Of course." Seamus dipped his head.

DESPITE HER FATIGUE, Grace woke for the umpteenth time in the night with the dull ache in her back throbbing and with the unending pressure of needing to relieve herself. She stumbled out of bed to use the chamber pot, emptying herself of a dissatisfying amount of liquid.

Still squatting, Grace rested her elbows on her knees, sinking her face into the warm palms of her hands. They smelled faintly of Seamus's lemony fragrance, which did little to disguise the exotic fruity tones of banana—the only food she had stomached for supper the night before. She yearned to return to the soft bed, invitingly filled with the solid and warm body of her husband. Rising and adjusting her shift into place, Grace stepped aside as a warm trickle dribbled down her inner thighs. *Now* her bladder emptied itself? She let out a yelp of frustration and squatted over the chamber pot again, studying Seamus snoring softly into his pillow.

"Wretched rats' tails!"

Using one of the clean rags piled neatly on the washstand, she cleaned herself up. Her soaked shift clung uncomfortably to her legs in the chilly night air. She shuffled over to her trunk and scrounged for a dry shift.

Seamus stirred in the bed, his voice instantly alert. "Dulcinea? Are you well?"

"I'm fine," she whispered. "Go back to sleep. Just a little… accident. Nothing a dry shift can't fix."

Despite her instruction, Seamus rolled off the mattress, his unrumpling nightshirt stopping above his knees. He agilely stepped around the edge of the trunk and took the dry shift from her.

"Let me, my heart." His long fingers pulled at the bow at her neck, and he lifted the saturated slip over her head like he was undressing a child.

She blushed in the dark. "I can do it." She was ashamed enough that he knew she had soiled herself, let alone having him clean her up. She wanted to push him away, but standing cold and naked in the dark, what she wanted more was to be warm. Seamus slid the clean nightdress over her and guided her back to bed. The sheets were still warm. She squirmed backwards as he curled in behind her. He slid his hand over her swollen abdomen, caressing the babe within with tender circles.

"That feels good." She sighed. Behind her, Seamus stiffened as a wave of tension rippled across her tight belly, cresting into an uncomfortable cramping.

"You're as tight as a drum. It can't be doing the little one much good for you to be so tense. You'll crush the poor creature."

"Keep rubbing. It helps." She felt him relax as the tension in her abdomen subsided. Minutes later, another wave descended, causing her breath to catch in her throat. "My back aches terribly." She moaned into her pillow as Seamus's long fingers pressed into the ache.

Gasping with another wave of pain, she sat up and swung her legs over the side of the bed. "It's as though a giant has his hands around my middle and is trying to squeeze me in two." She slid off the bed, hanging onto the bedpost until the incessant squeezing relaxed. Her husband rose again and lit the lantern. He slid to her side, supporting her elbow. She turned to face him.

His lagoon-blue eyes were wide with anticipation. "This is it." His voice filled with wonder. "Our little one is on his way."

"Or *her* way," groaned Grace through gritted teeth as another band of steel rolled across her midsection. "You needn't look so pleased with yourself. One of us has a huge amount of work ahead." Squeezing his biceps and resting her forehead on his chest, she felt his laughter vibrate through him. Closing her eyes, she drew on his energy and excitement.

"Should I send for Sykes?" he asked as she sunk back on the bed.

"No, he explained it'll be a while before anything happens once the pains begin." Outside the large window, palm tree silhouettes stood to attention like marines against the pale pink sky. "It's nearly dawn. I think we can let him have his breakfast first."

Seamus sat beside her. "Are you hungry?"

"Not just this minute." She curled her fingers in his. "Since we have a moment—" A new pain started, and she dipped her chin to her chest, waiting for it to pass. She blew out a long breath. "I know about Father Babcock."

Seamus's jaw muscle twitched. "Know what precisely?"

"That you hid his past from me." Her own undisclosed knowledge of his secret sat like an undigested lump alongside the babe in her belly. Seamus's fingers tightened around hers as she continued. "But what I'd really like to know is—why?"

Seamus rose and wrenched off his nightshirt. He tossed it untidily over the clotheshorse. The muscles in his back flexed as he reached for a freshly laundered shirt from the wardrobe. He turned slowly, his long fingers fastening the buttons with efficient precision. "I had my reasons."

"I assumed as much, which is why I didn't press the matter before. But we promised to not keep secrets from one another." Grace rose and swayed from one foot to the other to ease the ache in her back. "I'd hoped you'd tell me yourself—in time." She paced over to the dresser, gripping the edge for support as another crushing wave came.

Seamus stepped behind her, his hands sliding beneath her elbows. She leaned her head back on his chest. She had imagined she would be angrier having this conversation with him. But now, swirling in the melee of her current situation, her need to know the truth was a beacon of distraction to latch onto.

Seamus's voice rumbled through his chest and into her back, the deep reverberation of it comforting. "I was ashamed."

She tipped her head around. "Of what?"

Snuffing through his nostrils, he said, "I all but took a bribe to take him as a passenger."

"A bribe? From Hamilton?"

"Yes."

"Was it not simply the church's payment for his passage?"

"It was sold to me that way. But Hamilton showed me a letter from the church—"

"The one sending him off to re-establish the mission?"

Seamus's forehead rumpled. "Ah, so you've seen it?"

"Yes," she lied neatly, turning to pace across the room again. "What concerns me is that you hid it from me. Why?"

"As I said. Shame. I was coming to terms with the circumstances of my career and our position in London." His wrist clicked. "It was a difficult time for me."

"All the more reason to share the burden," she reasoned, taking hold of the bedpost. Oh Lord, another one. She gritted her teeth.

Seamus waited for her breathing to return to normal.

"There's little honour in a financial predicament forcing a man's hand."

She was aware of his reduced social standing—they had been in the same boat—but financial difficulties? How much more had he kept from her? She licked her lips, already dry from her labouring. The pains were coming much quicker now. He would need to set off soon to fetch Billy from Beech's, the lodging house in town run by a British widow.

Grace pressed her forehead to the cool wooden post. "Just how much of a predicament are we talking about?" Jiggling one leg on the spot helped distract her from the impending onslaught.

"None to worry about. I've investments that will deliver long before we return to London." The calm in his voice was reassuring. He scooped the mass of curls from her neck.

The cool air was bliss on her overheated nape. "Please tie my hair back." She doubled over, her fists sinking into the soft mattress. She groaned loud and long. The time for worrying about money had passed. "It's time to get Billy."

The sun was high in the sky by the time Seamus returned with Billy. He set up the birthing cot in the bedroom. Back in London when they had been loading the ship, she had seen Billy carry the lightweight bed aboard. He had explained how a portable cot negated the need to awkwardly manhandle patients around the ship.

"Is that really necessary now?" She dubiously eyed the narrow cot that looked wholly uncomfortable compared to the plush double bed beside it.

"You'll thank me when you've your clean, warm bed to crawl into afterwards." Billy flicked his fringe back, smiling warmly.

She was almost past the point of caring which bed her child was going to be born in. She leaned over the high edge of the portable bed and gripped the sheets, her knuckles white and the muscles in her forearms straining. It felt as though she had swallowed a giant dose of pain. Worry squeezed the air from her lungs, and she groaned deeply.

"Easy there, lass. How long have you been bearing down?"

"Long enough!"

"Climb up for me," coaxed Billy. "I'd say you're nearly there."

"Just get it out!" She let out a deep, guttural groan.

Seamus rubbed her back in long, soothing strokes. The luminescent pressure in her belly spread to an all-consuming energy drain that radiated from her lower back to around her midriff. Earlier, she had changed into a clean shift with a short petticoat underneath. Billy had suggested the petticoat to maintain her modesty during the birth. Modesty be damned! She wanted to curl up and die!

Billy's warm voice sliced through her haze of pain. "Come now, flower. 'Tis time. Sir, you'll not want to stay about for the next part."

A fist of fear gripped Grace. "Don't leave!" She reached wildly behind her until she found Seamus's hand, knotting her fingers around his.

Her husband's voice, calm and low, eased some of her panic. "Come now, my heart." With little effort, he lifted her onto the cot. Grace grabbed his hand again in a double grip, a piece of life-saving driftwood in the storm currently raging around her.

"Don't go."

"'Tisn't the norm for the man to be present during the birth," said Billy, pulling a stool to the foot of the cot.

She glared at Billy over her swollen stomach. "You're a man, and you're here!"

"Aye, but I'm the physician. Ah, here's the crown. Try again."

A crackling grip, like slow-moving lightning, crawled up her spine to her lungs. Grace squeezed her eyelids shut, pressing the back of Seamus's hand against her mouth to prevent her from crying out. The pit of snakes in her belly writhed more angrily than before. When the agony passed, her eyes were moist with tears as she implored both men for help. "I'm going to be sick."

"'Tis all right. 'Tis part of the process for some." Billy patted her knee. He glanced at Seamus. "Bring her that bowl over there."

Seamus obeyed Billy's instruction unhesitatingly, the authority in the room transferring seamlessly.

"Knees up, lass."

Grace did as she was bid, focussing on Seamus's face. She sucked in a lungful of air through clenched teeth as the crushing began again. "I can't do this!" she wailed.

"Look at me, Dulcinea." Seamus had his face nearly touching hers. "Remember what Admiral Baxter said about you? You're a warrior with a fighting spirit. You can do this." He wiped her forehead and kissed it tenderly. "I'd gladly take your pain as mine. Since I can't, I'll be with you every step. You're not alone, my heart, I'm here. Now and for always."

Grace breathed in puffs and pants, but she never broke eye contact with him.

Billy's dark head popped up from the end of the cot. "This is it. Bear down now. Push for all you're worth."

Seamus's lips pressed with the resolve of his promise, and Grace took a deep breath. She trembled under the strain and opened her mouth, releasing a primal roar. Gasping sharply, she sagged. Oh, good Lord! The relief! Was it over?

"'Tis a wee lassie!" Billy raised the babe up by the ankles, his grinning face materialising from behind her petticoat.

She glimpsed the pink squirming body of her daughter. Purple twists of the umbilical cord disappeared back under her skirts, but she cared not about the mess. Her delirious smile faded at Seamus's face contorted in horror. The babe's tiny face was squashed and malformed.

"Billy! What's wrong with her?" she rasped. Seamus's hand tightened around hers.

Her friend chuckled. "A babe of the highest luck. She's born with a caul!" With a sleight of hand, the transparent veil disappeared, and the round, unblemished face emerged, mewling and squawking. Billy fumbled behind her skirts, and with a firm snip of the scissors the babe was free. He swaddled the infant and offered her to Seamus. "Would you care to take your daughter, sir?"

A smile played on Grace's lips as Seamus took the squalling child. A warm flood of contentment filled her at how enthralled he was by the tiny, indignant face. Appreciating that now she would have to share his adoration, she did not mind one bit. The babe's frantic cries calmed to a couple of hiccoughed gulps.

The little one opened her silver-blue eyes and Seamus gasped. "She has my blue eyes!"

"All babes are born with eyes that colour." Billy chuckled before disappearing below her petticoats again. "You won't know the true colour for a few months yet."

"May I see our daughter?" Grace's voice was hoarse, and she wanted a drink. But more than anything, she wanted to hold her child.

"Oh, Grace." Seamus's voice hitched. He leaned in and pressed his lips firmly to hers, kissing her mouth and cheeks and nose and forehead. "She's absolutely the most beautiful creature I've ever laid eyes on." He kissed her lips again. "Thank you."

He gently handed the squirming bundle to Grace, and she pulled the edges of the wrap away. The babe's fists were bunched tightly against her cheeks, her hair dark like wet feathers on a newly hatched chick. Her tiny mouth pouted, her little tongue licking the cold air experimentally. Grace enclosed the dome of her daughter's skull, then stroked her tiny earlobe.

"It's thinner and softer than even the finest silk," she

marvelled. "And her hair, it's so dark." Her smile grew. "She's perfect."

Seamus rested his forehead against Grace's. "She's indeed perfect. And she's all ours." Tears magnified the intensity of his liquid blue gaze.

"Look what we did," she whispered.

"Our daughter is undoubtedly my most crowning achievement. I can't imagine anything surpassing this experience."

Grace outlined the babe's face with her fingertips. "I can't adequately describe the feeling, but I'd gladly give my life for this child, right now. I'd not hesitate." She looked at her husband. "There'd be no choice in the matter—it would be her over me, every time."

He slid a warm hand over her shoulder. "I know that feeling well. It's precisely how I feel about *you*." He pressed his lips to her temple, and Grace breathed in the sweet essences of her husband and new daughter.

"I want to name her Emily."

"Emily." Seamus tested the name on his tongue.

Billy's voice came from the folds of her shift. "That's a fine name. Strong. 'Tis Latin, you know? From the Roman family Aemilius." Billy peered briefly over her knees, his wide grin almost stretching to his ears. He dipped his head again. "My name, William, means resolute protector. Rather fitting, wouldn't you say? Is a physician not the resolute protector of people's good health?"

Grace studied her daughter's small, round face. The babe squinted fiercely at the world. "And what of my daughter's fortune? What'll her new name bring her?"

Billy gave a snort, glancing at Seamus with a humorous twinkle in his eye. "I'm not sure you'll appreciate this, sir, but little Emily there'll have a profound yearning to voyage and seek adventure. She'll be wanting to set her own stride through life without being ruled by convention."

Seamus raised one eyebrow at Grace. "Hmph, somewhat like her mother."

Despite the troubling prediction, she could see Seamus's euphoria was too great for it to be a worry, and he grinned boyishly at her. "I'd like her second name to be that of my grandmother on my father's side. Elizabeth." Seamus shot Billy a sharp look, though his voice was warm with humour. "I'll thank you to keep your fortune-telling to yourself on that one, Sykes. I'm happy enough it's a family name." Seamus kissed Grace on the head. "Let's leave it at that, shall we?"

Billy chuckled. "'Tis all right, sir. Elizabeth means God of plenty."

"Does it now." Seamus nodded sagely. "Sounds like God and I will have our hands plenty full with this little one." His fiery blue eyes were bruised with exhaustion, his normally groomed hair a spiky haystack. He looked as spent as Grace felt. But he also had never looked more magnificent than he did at that moment.

Billy's head popped up again. "I'll have Cook Phillips prepare your caudal."

"What's that?" asked Grace warily. Her tastes had been utterly dull for so long, and she was not sure she could stomach anything too rich or exotic.

"'Tis but a syrupy gruel with spices and wine," explained Billy. "Ideal for restoring your health after all these months of hardtack and ginger tea."

Grace winced.

"Rest up," said Seamus. "There's no hurry. The *Clover*'s repairs will keep us here for a couple of months yet."

She closed her eyes. Good! A couple of months of sleep sounded heavenly right now.

Chapter Thirteen

A few months later, seated at Hood's dining table, Seamus studied the city's head of police, Garan Dias. The candlelight reflected off his shiny, domed forehead. At Hood's question, Seamus turned his gaze. "How are the repairs coming along, Captain?"

"They're complete, sir. There's only the loading left," said Seamus.

Hood inclined his head. "I imagine the cost was prohibitive?"

Seamus coughed dryly to clear the ball of discomfort in his throat. "The *Clover* sustained more structural damage than met the eye. Colonel Hamilton is good for the repairs, as well as the replacement of goods lost."

Hood ran a hand along his brunette, sleeked-back hair. "It's understandable you're keen to get going again."

Dias rubbed his nose briskly. "Is he a man of honour, this Colonel Hamilton? He will honour those promissory notes?"

"I believe so." Seamus nodded. He had better honour them. The repair bill was eye-watering. The last thing Seamus wanted was any lucrative outcome of his South American bonds sunk to settle another man's debt. Besides, his acquaintance with Hamilton was at Admiral Baxter's recommendation, and Seamus's faith in Baxter was sound.

Dias stiffened formally. "Speaking of men of honour, Captain, I need *your* assistance."

Seamus's ears pricked to the man's flattering tone, and his instincts flared like a match struck on a moonless night. "If it's within my power to help, of course." He pasted a stiff smile to his face.

"There's a serious insurrection brewing with some of the troops at the garrison."

Seamus wiped his mouth with his crisp, white napkin. "This rebellion is most unfortunate, Senhor Dias, but I don't see how it concerns me. I'm but a private explorer."

Dias's fork stopped halfway to his mouth, a piece of roast beef skewered on the prongs. "Captain, these insurgents broke open the prison and armed the prisoners. They've planted artillery about the town and presently command some of the key streets."

Grace glanced over the rim of her wineglass. "What is their grievance, Senhor?"

"Put simply, madam, they're displeased with the re-shuffling of the former constitutional government." Dias offered her a quick explanation before glancing back at Seamus. "I'm in a unique position having continued power through both govern-ments, therefore remaining entirely neutral in a political sense." Dias lay down his fork. "My duty is to maintain law and order in Montevideo and protect its people and property."

The edge of Grace's wineglass clinked on the edge of the china plate as she set it down. "Pray tell how this concerns us,

Mr Dias?" she said, and Seamus spotted the flush on Dias's wide forehead.

It was clear that plain-spoken women were not plentiful in Dias's world. Seamus enjoyed watching the man wrestle with the challenge. However, he had a sinking feeling in his gut that Dias was about to ask him to intervene between the warring parties.

"I understand your dilemma, sir, but I'm duty-bound to my survey expedition. Not to quelling minor insurrections in far-off lands."

Hood interjected with a discrete cough. "Captain Fitzwilliam?" Seamus swung his head to the sophisticated dignitary at the head of the table. "It's my personal request, sir, that you afford the British residents in Montevideo any protection in your power."

Hell's bells! Was this Hood's instigation? The roast potato in Seamus's stomach solidified as he studied Hood's pleading face. "Sir, I no longer carry the authority of a Royal Navy captain."

Hood leaned forward, his fingers steepled over his lips. "Captain Fitzwilliam, it's the duty of every British citizen to protect their own."

Seamus rolled his shoulders back. "Are the lives and property of British residents in danger from these rebels?"

Hood nodded grimly, his pursed lips denting the dimple in his cheek. "They are."

Grace swung her head animatedly, giving each man equal measure. "Is a week long enough to quell an insurrection?"

Dias's tanned brow rucked in confusion. "Why a week?"

Grace tipped her chin at Seamus. "Is the *Clover* not due to sail next week?" He sensed the reluctance in her voice, pleased that it matched his.

"She is indeed, madam." Seamus sucked in a slow breath, examining Dias, whose top lip glistened with sweat. "Very well, Senhor Dias. Please enlighten me."

Dias's spine lengthened, and his hands became animated.

"The rebel troops are in possession of the fortified garrison where all our ammunition is kept. The few soldiers we have left, and some armed citizens, have the insurgents contained inside the citadel, but I fear bloodshed is imminent."

Seamus's tone firmed with authority. "Precisely what do you require of me?"

"Armed men. We must hold the fort above the city—it's the seat of government. At least until the reinforcements I've sent for arrive."

"And how long will that take?" asked Grace, her firm tone drawing a censorious scowl across Dias's brow.

"A few days. A week at most."

Seamus squeezed the bridge of his nose to ease his throbbing headache. It was exactly as he had feared. Meddling in foreign affairs was a chancy vocation. Lowering his hand, he swung his steely gaze between Hood and Dias as he digested the information. Hood's generous hospitality had seen his daughter safely delivered. How could he refuse the man?

"Very well. Thirty men armed with muskets, cutlasses, and pistols. We'll meet you on the pier at dawn. You'll lead the way." Seamus reasoned if he was going to do this, then Dias must do it *his* way. Seamus looked pointedly at Hood. "I'll station another ten armed-men around your residence, sir. I ask that you make the welfare of my wife and daughter your absolute priority."

Hood nodded solemnly. "You have my word, sir."

Seamus turned to Grace. Emily was with Hood's housekeeper this evening, affording Grace a reprieve to enjoy an uninterrupted meal, but there was no one he trusted more with Emily's protection than her feisty mother. "You'll keep Emily close?"

She nodded. "At all times."

WITH ALL HANDS back on the repaired *Clover*, it was not hard to muster them. The men milled restlessly. Some were keen to know what news had dragged them from their hammocks, others displeased at having their prized sleep interrupted.

The damp of the night bit the back of Seamus's throat and he coughed to clear it. "We've been asked to lend arms to quell the current discord about town. Since we're not here in any official capacity, I can't order you to do this. We're to hold the fort to prevent the rebel troops from accessing it while we await the arrival of the reinforcements."

"How far off are they, sir?" piped Buchanan.

"They should be here any day," replied Seamus. "Our role will be to shore up the fort with the best defence possible."

O'Malley stepped forward, head cocked, the red and orange of his hair catching in the lantern light. "Heard the rebels have taken the garrison with all the ammunition. How can we stand against such firepower?"

Seamus pulled his cuff over his scar to protect it from the bite of the night air. "They're presently imprisoned inside the garrison by armed citizens and a handful of soldiers. Hopefully, they'll remain that way. But should they break through, we'll hold our position at the fort."

"What if they start ransacking the town and killing inno-cents?" Father Babcock snapped, his beaked nose scrunching. "Your actions to take up arms will only infuriate them more. Is it really your business to go poking around in foreign affairs like this?"

If it had been Babcock's intent to stir disharmony, Seamus was thrilled to see several men throw impatient scowls at the bumbling priest and shuffle nearer to Seamus. Ignoring Babcock, Seamus clasped his hands behind his back and squeezed his fingers to focus on keeping his voice calm. "When an ally asks for help in the interests of keeping the peace, I can hardly see how we can refuse. It's also why it's every man's decision whether to be involved."

Babcock bristled. "I'll head into the cathedral to pray for peace. I'm sure the padre there won't object to the added blanket of protection over his flock."

Blasted coward was going to hide behind the cloth!

"Come on, lads!" O'Malley rallied. "We can lie idle in our berths, or we can lend this fair city a hand. Who's up for a bit of sport?"

"Sir, have we permission to fire the fort's cannons?" Sorensen asked eagerly.

"If needs be," nodded Seamus. "The *Clover*'s gunners will be instrumental." He scanned the crowd again. Several more men stiffened with resolve. "For those interested in protecting the fort, see O'Malley for a rifle and shot bag. I also need ten volunteers to guard Mr Hood's residence." He hesitated. "And my wife and child."

"I'll guard Mrs F., sir," said Ben Blight.

Seamus fixed his gaze on the towering, red-whiskered sailor, some of his worry dissolving—Blight was a solid fighter, his square physique a pleasing deterrent. Buchanan and Hicks stepped forward too. Ah, his wife and daughter were in good hands. Those two would risk their lives for Grace and Emily without hesitation. If only Sykes were here. He and Beynon were at Hospital de Caridad, offering their services and replenishing the ship's medical supplies. Blast! There was no time to summon either man now. Though should any of his men need attention, they would be well served to have both ship's doctors already stationed at the hospital.

"Thank you, Blight. You'll take the lead on that." Seamus scanned the rest of the crowd. "For those remaining aboard, you'll see the *Clover* safe under Mr Johns's command. I'll not have a band of pitch-fork-wielding dissidents sabotage our ship or delay our journey. We'll meet Senhor Dias at the pier at dawn."

As the early morning clouds pinkened with the start of the new day, Seamus and thirty armed men followed Dias up the steep road to the fort. He scoured the thickets of bush along both sides of the wide, dusty road, ready for an ambush at every step. Behind him, the city was still blanketed in pre-dawn grey. Would they approach from behind? He scanned every crevice of the substantial stone fort for movement from a hidden enemy. The citadel stood stony and silent.

"Senhor Dias." Seamus puffed lightly from his uphill trek. "I expected some opposition. This is too easy. I don't have a good feeling."

"Fear not, sir. The rebel troops are still holed up. Once I've seen you into the fort, I'll return to town to negotiate with them to lay down their arms."

Behind Seamus, the men's tension hummed through them, a mix of nerves and excitement. Each man looked comforted by the weight of the loaded rifle in his hands. As they poured into the echoingly empty square in the centre of the fort, Seamus drew his pistol in readiness and squinted to sharpen his vision.

"Where the bleedin' 'ell are they?" A disquieted voice from the crowd of sailors echoed around the empty stronghold.

Seamus turned to face his men. "They've been successfully detained for now. Don't let our easy march here allow for complacency. Keep your weapons loaded and ready. Gunners, prepare the big guns. Since you already own the skills to defend a ship, this fort should not prove any more complex. Get to the high ground, gentlemen, and be on the lookout."

"Thank you, Captain. I must head back now. I leave the safety of this fortress in your hands," said Dias.

Seamus shook the dry, dusty hand on offer. "Luck to you, Senhor Dias. I'll bar the doors behind you and not open them again until next we meet."

O'Malley dropped the heavy bar into place, and Seamus surveyed the shadows on the ramparts, sharpening into distinguishable men as the sun rose. He had every direction covered, including out to sea.

Seamus made several rounds of the ramparts himself during the morning. The city, harbour, and ocean remained uncannily calm. He had expected at least a little resistance. The men would soon be lulled into lowering their guard. After four hours, he ordered his men to switch lookout positions.

With the noon sun blaring down on the quiet, dusty square, Seamus sent Sorensen to the kitchens to find food. He returned, grinning with the success of his search as he scurried across the courtyard with a tray of reasonably fresh meat.

Soon, the roasted aroma of sizzling beefsteaks over the open campfire filled the air, and the knot of worry in Seamus's gut that had stolen his appetite at breakfast had eased. His mouth salivated.

He was on the last bite of his meal when the distant, lone pop of a pistol launched him to his feet. This was it!

"To your stations!" He roared. Wiping his greasy fingers on his trousers, he took the stairs to the rampart two at a time. The beefsteak he had so enjoyed sat like an anchor in his stomach. He circled the top wall, scouring the horizon in every direction. He halted beside O'Malley.

"Looks like 'twas but a lone shot, sir." O'Malley leaned his rifle across his shoulder and peered over the rampart.

"I think you're right. But best be alert," said Seamus.

"Aye, aye, sir."

By late afternoon, and after several watch changes, Seamus was studying the steep road to the town when a hot-and-cold trill swept over him. Men! Armed men! Several sailors' cries bellowed with practised, booming voices.

"Men approaching!"

"Soldiers!"

The lazy haze that had settled over Seamus since he had filled his belly evaporated. A bevy of rifle muzzles swung down, and the gun crew at the nearest cannon scrambled to action. Seamus spotted a familiar dark head bobbing in the lead of the approaching troops. Dias!

"Hold your fire!" Seamus ordered, waving his hand. "Hold your fire!" As quickly as the tension had arrived, it left. "Open the doors."

In the square, Seamus faced a beaming Dias. "Your reinforcements, Senhor?"

"Yes, yes! They surrounded the garrison in great numbers! The rebel troops surrendered quickly."

"I heard only one shot fired," said Seamus in a congratulatory tone.

"That was not us," shrugged Dias.

"Glad to hear no blood was spilled."

"Thank you, once again, sir, to you and your men. You are indeed a man of honour. I hope to have the opportunity to repay you someday." Dias gripped Seamus's hand in a two-handed shake. Seamus nodded, a flood of weariness replacing the nervous stiffness that had pulsed through him all day. It had been a long time since he had stood on watch for so long.

Seamus turned to O'Malley. "See the men back to the ship, O'Malley. And no detours past El Hacha either."

"Aye, aye, sir."

IN THE COOL corner of her room in Hood's residence, Grace ran her finger across Emily's soft, smooth brow. The babe snuffled awake, resuming her long-jawed draws from Grace's breast. Through the open window, fragrant smoke of Ben Blight's pipe curled in on the warm breeze as he passed by for the dozenth time on patrol.

Her three-barrelled pepperbox lay loaded on the table beneath the window. It had been a while since Grace had loaded a weapon, but her fingers had worked with a memory of their own. Not that she believed for one second she would need it.

Voices—familiar ones—filtered in. Babcock! What does that snivelling weasel want now?

"I've come to pray with Mrs Fitzwilliam. Offer her some comfort at this dark hour," droned Babcock.

Poppycock! Bastard only ever did anything if it served his own purpose. Probably coming to hide under Hood's wing. Grace tutted in irritation and gently eased Emily from her comfort. Her milky lips pouted, quivering in objection before the milk stupor carried her back to sleep. Grace laid the babe in the bottom drawer of the dresser and adjusted her bodice. Stinking seaweed. She had been looking forward to a nap—the babe had kept her up most of the night—but now that firebrand was going to sap her remaining energy with his hot-aired drivel.

There was a knock at the door. Grace resolved to send the priest away. Plead a headache. Although she did not have one, he would give her one soon enough. She gripped the brass knob and inhaled a slow, deep breath.

Hood's liveried manservant towered in the doorway, and Grace blinked in surprise. She tilted her head, expecting to find the stumpy priest behind him. The clock in the empty hallway chimed two.

"May I help you?" asked Grace.

The man's feverish eyes cast a furtive look around the room before fixing on Grace. "You meddling foreigners!" His words hissed as though his mouth was dry.

He lunged, and Grace caught the blur of a blade in her periphery. Her dormant fighter's instincts flared like a well-struck match and ignited her muscles. He was too tall and powerful to attack head on. Evasion was her only chance. Using her stature to her advantage, she ducked and twirled away, her skirts flaring like the cape of a matador. The bull of a man grunted as he overbalanced and stumbled.

Capitalising on the man's clumsiness, Grace's hopes flared. He was no experienced fighter, or he would not have missed. She lunged for the pepperbox on the table and swung it around, both hands gripping the stock.

"Stop!" she roared. In the drawer, Emily startled awake, her wail building to a healthy crescendo. The quivering knife in the servant's hand was not that of a man confident with weapons. "Come any closer, and I'll fire," she warned.

The servant's neck stiffened and quivered, as though straining against an invisible hand holding him back. Fear and uncertainty slicked the man's face, and he let out a gasp of desperation. "You must die!"

Outside, urgent cries of alarm rallied.

"What, by Jesus, is going on in there?" Ben's deep voice bellowed.

"Sweet mother of saints! Mrs F.! I'm coming!" Jim's frantic words bounced down the passage ahead of his thumping footsteps.

Father Babcock squeaked as Toby yelled, "Out of my way, waster!"

The servant's eyes widened to show the whites, and Grace's breath swelled in her chest. No! Their approach was going to force him to attack. A desperate man was easily pushed to do desperate things. She might have persuaded him to drop his knife, but not now. The babe's high-pitched screams were accompanied by indignant hiccoughs, but Grace narrowed her focus on the man before her. She locked her elbows and tightened her finger on the trigger. Blasted thing was wretchedly heavy. If she did not fire soon, her receding strength would compromise her aim.

"Stop!" Her warning was as much for the servant as it was for the army of men thundering down the hallway.

None obeyed.

The tall stranger lunged again, and Grace squeezed the trigger. The explosion drowned out the approaching chaos, and she flinched against the mule-kick of the butt. She shook her head to clear the painful ringing in her ears and squinted through the musty, sulphuric smoke. Had she got him? She must have, or he would have got her by now.

The three sailors burst through the open door, their broad shoulders colliding as though jostling on a drunken night out.

"Crivens, lass! Are ye harmed?" Jim powered over to her. "For the love of—you're bleeding." He cradled her right arm.

The red stain blooming on her arm did not hurt. "Just a flesh wound." Her voice was steady, but she readily released the pistol as Jim slid it from her trembling hands. It was not fear that shook her hands but the thrill of firing a weapon—it happened to her every time.

Ben Blight kicked the servant's thigh, and the man's wigless head wobbled. "Straight through the heart."

Toby eased in beside Jim, his gentle fingers tearing the cut of her sleeve so he could take a closer look.

"See?" Grace laughed shakily. "Won't even require stitches."

Toby's lips pressed thin behind his sandy beard, and his nostrils flared. He withdrew a clean handkerchief from his pocket and bound her arm. Grace flinched as he tightened the knot. The belated searing pain had finally shown up, and she swallowed dryly.

Hood and Father Babcock dithered by the door. Hood took one step into the room. "Good God! You've killed him."

"He attacked me," said Grace, bending to scoop Emily from the drawer. Her babe was hot, damp, and as red as a ripened tomato. "Oh, come here, my darling." She bundled the weepy infant over her uninjured side and patted her tiny back. She rocked instinctively as she glared at Hood.

"What the devil possessed you to shoot my man?" he demanded.

Jim took a step towards Hood. "Ye might want to ask just what the devil *he* was doing attacking Mrs F. with a blade?"

"She only defended herself, sir," added Ben.

"And her babe," said Toby softly.

Jim was clearly after answers. "He was *your* man, sir. What was his qualm?"

"I'm afraid I don't know." The regret in Hood's voice sounded sincere. "I'm equally as horrified that my manservant deigned to try kill a gentlewoman."

"I warned the captain that interfering in this town's political squabbling was poor form," piped Babcock, smoothing his robes.

Averting her gaze from the obnoxious little man, Grace pressed her lips to Emily's sweet, hot neck, peppering it with soothing kisses. Emily's ribs jerked with intermittent hiccoughs, but she was settling.

"How was I to know the damned fool was a dissident?" Hood puffed up. "It's not as though he wore a band upon his arm announcing him so."

Babcock's scowl deepened. "Indeed. Had Mrs Fitzwilliam not shot him dead, we might've been able to question him."

"Come now, sirs," objected Ben. "Spare Mrs F. this inquisition. She's had quite enough for one day, wouldn't you say? P'haps we might leave her to comfort her child?"

Hood addressed the men in the room. "I trust you can clean this mess up? God knows what will happen to the British citizens hereabouts if word of this spills." The three sailors nodded stiffly and he harrumphed, stepping over his servant.

Babcock's shifty gaze slid from Grace to the body on the floor. A prayer for the man's soul, perhaps? Babcock sniffed and turned. She sucked in a breath. Wishful thinking.

Toby ran a hand over Emily's head. "I'll be right outside your door."

"Thank you, Toby. That's most comforting."

Ben and Jim hauled up the limp corpse and shuffled from the room.

SEAMUS HEADED down the guest wing, his shoes tapping quickly on the black and white marble tiles. Grace was pulling back the bedcovers, and she jumped when he swung the bedroom door open. He strode forward, hastily undoing his weapon's belt. It clattered carelessly to the floor.

"Seamus?"

"Grace!" He scooped her up, burying his face in her cascading curls. His words were muffled by her hair. "What in Neptune's name happened here?" He lowered her to the floor and tucked her dark mane behind her ears.

"I can't explain." She blinked rapidly and her chin firmed. "I heard Father Babcock arrive, half-heartedly offering to pray with me. I opened the door to a knock, and Hood's manservant lunged at me with a blade."

The right sleeve of her nightshift bulged with a bandage, and he squeezed her shoulder gently, fighting the urge to pull her into another crushing hug. "Heavens, Grace! I shouldn't have left you."

"It's all right," she placated, placing her hands on his chest. At her touch of reassurance, his heartbeat steadied. "It didn't even need stitches."

"How did you fend him off? He's no small man. And you're a—sprite."

"But a quick sprite," she grinned.

"You almost seem to have taken pleasure from the event."

His wife's relaxed demeanour settled the worm of angst trying to gnaw its way out of his gut.

She cocked one brow. "I was taught by the best."

Of course he was aware of her formal training by Sergeant Baisley, but he had always tried to suppress the knowledge that she had also been drilled by Ben Blight during her time disguised as a lad on the *Discerning*.

"I had your pepperbox ready," Grace said confidently. "Got him squarely in the chest. Didn't even need to turn the barrel to prepare a second shot." She tipped her head at a jaunty angle. "Bet I'd still be able to rival Sergeant Baisley's aim."

He rubbed a fatigued hand over his face. "Thank heavens for Baisley's rigorous drills."

She pressed her body against his, and his desire dampened all traces of his previous dread.

"What of the fuss at the fort?" she asked, stepping onto her toes to kiss him.

Burnt gunpowder, mingling with her sweet milkiness, filled his nostrils. He wanted—no, *needed*—a distraction. "All that fuss amounted to naught," he murmured into her hair. His hands moulded the curve of her backside, his fingers trailing the line where her thigh met her buttocks—his favourite part of her body. A perfect distraction. "Hmm, you smell good."

"You don't." She laughed, swatting him, but there was an edge to her laughter. "What do you mean it amounted to naught?"

"We marched right up to the fort. Waltzed in without resistance." Seamus backed her into the bedroom wall. He kissed her roughly, desperately. By Christ, he could devour her on the spot! "The whole affair was rather mild. We even had time to cook beefsteaks." His words were muffled by her hair as he kissed and nipped her neck with urgency, his need for her growing. "Early this evening, the reinforcements arrived."

"And what of our men?"

Seamus drew her arms around his neck and slid his hands down her body, pulling her tighter to him. He groaned at the pleasure. "All tucked in their beds. Without a shot fired." Filled with a desperation never experienced before, he fumbled with his breeches.

Grace pushed against his shoulders. "No, Seamus. It's too soon. Since the babe."

"Christ Almighty!" His shame almost strangled him. He was set to use her body like a common doxy! "I'm sorry, Grace. Have I hurt you?"

She framed his face in her hands, her fingers gently scratching the two-day stubble along his jaw. "No, you haven't."

"I was about to take you in a foul and indecent manner." Fiery remorse flooded through him. What had just happened? He had been set to use her—and use her *hard*.

"But you didn't." Her voice was as soft and gentle as her touch. She waggled her eyebrows. "I daresay I'd have thoroughly enjoyed the experience…"

He rested his forehead against hers again, breathing hard and inhaling the same air as her. "My plucky Dulcinea. I didn't understand the meaning of courage until I met you." His voice was hoarse, his face warmed with self-consciousness. "You have me accepting the courage in my heart, even when I feel like a failure for being afraid for you. And now, you forgive my base impulses threatening to overpower me. What did I do to deserve you?"

Grace slid her hands into his hair at the nape of his neck, and he shivered in delight. Peering intently into his face, she held his stare silently and powerfully until he relaxed his shoulders. "Your fear for me is real. As is your need of me. Don't *ever* feel ashamed of showing me the depth of your love." She pulled him down and kissed him with a passion that dissolved all residue of his embarrassment.

With difficulty, he lifted his head, the sombre realisation of her situation dampening his earlier enthusiasm. They could not remain here now. He had to get her away from Montevideo—and fast. Blight, Buchanan and Hicks would not breathe a word of the manservant's death, of this he was certain. Babcock was another matter.

Chapter Fourteen

PORT FAMINE, TIERRA DE FUEGO, 7 JANUARY 1833

G race appreciated how the newly repaired *Clover* sailed more smoothly than before, her hull having been scraped of barnacles as well as her masts rigged with new canvas. It made their stop-start journey down the east coast of South America easier to bear. As expected, the weather turned colder the further south they sailed, but Sailmaker Lester had fashioned a miniature guanaco-fur coat for Emily from a tanned skin he had acquired in Montevideo.

They had made good time to Port Famine in the icy archipelago off the tip of South America. Now, the rebuilding of the stone church was nearly complete. They would soon leave Father Babcock to his mission. Good riddance!

Grace had forgotten about the ever-present wind in the rocky hillside cemetery, and she gripped her shawl tighter around Emily. At six months old, her daughter was furiously curious about the world. She had Seamus's ice-blue eyes as well as his mop of sandy hair, though she had Grace's curls. Despite it being summer, the day was no warmer than a mild winter's day back in London. At least it was not raining.

Wild grass blanketed the mound of Gilly's grave. The white wooden cross that had marked his final resting place was long gone, replaced by a clump of tiny white star-shaped flowers that waved in greeting to all who approached. Grace plucked a stem and held the balled head of blooms to her nose. She remembered the perfume. Cocoa. Emily reached for the floret, and Grace neatly rescued it from her daughter's chubby hand.

"It might smell delicious, little one, but it won't taste half as appealing."

Grace glanced around the rugged graveyard, her attention drawn to the snaking trail of men heading up the trampled path from the beach below. They were bowed by sacks and barrels of food hauled from the *Clover*'s cutters.

Behind her, in the grounds of the newly roofed church, the men had pitched tents in a homely camp. This sacred place, where she and Seamus had almost been handfasted to one another six years before, was just as she remembered. She recalled Seamus pinning the Luckenbooth brooch to her shawl the first time, and now traced the warm golden hearts of the brooch that came with her everywhere. The wind whispered echoes of her wedding vows, eventually made in a near-empty church in England—*I vow you the first cut of my meat, the first sip of my wine.*

From beneath the grove of trees beside the church, Seamus stepped from their steepled tent. He was dressed to toil alongside his men, though the alluring opening of his collarless shirt stole her attention. Her fingers tingled at the thought of trailing down his golden chest hair and slowly unfastening—

"'Tis a grand view from up here, is it not, Mrs F.?" Jim's chirrup rescued Grace from her deliciously improper thoughts.

Heat flared in her cheeks, and she hoped Jim would mistake her blush for windburn.

"Indeed." She lay her hand on the cold, compact earth. "Just paying my respects to Gilly. Sally wanted me to pass along that she's forgiven him. And to thank him for her dress."

"Aye, I'm sure he'd appreciate that." Jim stood, head bowed, gazing at the flowered mound. He slapped his cap against his thigh and slid it back on. "We finished the storeroom and animal keep today," he said. "Would ye care for a look?"

"I would," she said. Emily flapped her hands as Jim scooped her up. Grace stood, dusting the dirt and grass from her palms before reaching for her daughter. "I should lend a hand with the vegetable garden. The quicker we're finished here, the quicker we can leave Father Babcock to his own devices."

"Aye, wee bit of an enigma that one." Jim screwed his lips wryly. "For a man of the cloth, his sharp tongue doesn't exactly endear the men to flock to hear him preach."

Grace stared at the short priest, who was hacking at the hard earth with a hoe. "I can't help but feel that there's more to him than we know."

The tips of Jim's wide ears turned beetroot red. "Ye recall me warning ye of some of the men's ill intentions towards ye on the *Discerning* all those years ago?"

"I do," said Grace, linking her free arm with his. "And you were right to caution me so."

"Aye, well I'm plagued by the same omens as I had back then. Only this time, 'tis the men who've been pitted against one another."

Grace knew he was right. Mad Mahlon was even more surly these days, barking at the younger men, his increasingly bedraggled appearance and fishy odour doing little to humour his berth mates. It was almost as though he had stopped caring. Grace had witnessed O'Malley nimbly avoid Mad Mahlon since the altercation over his cat. It was only O'Malley's position as second mate that forced him to behave, or else she was sure he would have exacted revenge on Mad Mahlon by now. The privilege of being an officer had its downsides.

"Well, he won't be our problem for much longer." Grace hoisted Emily into a more comfortable position on her hip. She had never warmed to the odd priest either. Despite him appearing in her presence at puzzling intervals to offer empty prayers—during the storm, then again at Hood's residence in Montevideo—she was not going to miss him. No length of devotions could ever make up for the man's despicable attitude. Rude gnome of a man!

Beside the vegetable patch, Carpenter James was hammering together the last of the newly hewn pews for the refurbished church. Grace sat Emily on her checked shawl.

Darcy approached, coughing dryly. "Beggin' your pardon, Mrs F." The muscle in his jaw tensed as he snatched off his hat. Grace was in awe that such a man, dragged through his last years of childhood as an impressed sailor aboard O'Reilly's ship, could be so gentle and gracious. Not even his years as a brothel henchman, or a highwayman, had jaded his kind spirit.

"Good day, Darcy."

The man's face twisted peculiarly. "I was wonderin'… um… if I might give our Em a little somethin' I made?"

"Of course. How lovely. Thank you." Grace was thrilled that Emily's arrival had lifted the men's mood. Her presence kept the men better behaved and civilised. It tickled Grace to know her daughter had a ship full of adoring uncles. She knew from experience about the power of a loving uncle. The sailors who were fathers back home were the most attentive, chucking Emily's chin and spoiling her with trinkets. Except Mad Mahlon and Father Babcock—they both looked through Emily as though she did not exist.

Darcy bent down, and Emily beamed a gummy, one-toothed welcome at him. "Here you go then, our Em." He handed her a whittled wooden cat. Emily snatched the toy with her pudgy fingers, gnashing on it. He patted her head like a puppy. Straightening, his eyes lingered cautiously on Grace. "Might I have a word, Mrs F.?"

Relieved to lay down the hoe and straighten her back, Grace stepped from the half-tilled vegetable patch. "What is it?"

Darcy's soulful eyes fixed to his fisted hands. Grace could see the press of his knucklebones through his skin and wondered what tale of woe she was about to be presented with.

"'Tis like this," he began quietly. "I haven't exactly lived the life of a saint, even though circumstances pressed me into... certain situations."

"None of us can cast the first stone, Darcy," she said gently. "You've more than redeemed your past transgressions with acts of kindness." She had intended her words to offer the man solace, but his eyes darkened.

"That's mighty kind of you to say. But 'tisn't how I feel in my heart. I feel I've a penance still owing."

Sensing that he had more to say, she remained mute, her brows raised.

"I've been speaking with Father Babcock—" He broke off as she winced.

She could not wait to see the back of the inept priest. It bothered her that he had been in Darcy's ear. Plastering a gracious smile to her lips, she nodded. "Go on. I'm listening."

"I'd like to stay behind with the blessed Father at the mission."

"Pardon me?" Unable to keep the yip from her voice, Grace frowned.

"What better way to redeem my sins than to gather all the lost souls here and share the Good News with them." Darcy waved a hand at the wilderness in a wide arc.

"I didn't take you for a prayerful man," she countered uneasily. She was sure Seamus would not want to lose a man at this stage in the voyage. "You're needed aboard the *Clover*. You've quite the head for heights, and you man the sheets splendidly," she added, hoping that flattery might alter his thinking.

"'Tis kind of you to say, but I feel 'tis the only way back into the Heavenly Father's grace."

That sounded like the hot air she had come to expect from Babcock's mouth. "What'll you have me do about this?" she asked.

"Have the captain's ear. 'Twould mean the world to me to have his blessing."

She snuffed a light laugh through her nose. "You sound like a man with his mind already made up. You don't need his approval. You're a free man."

Darcy's gaze roved over the unfinished vegetable patch. "It'll be a while before we can produce our own food. Could you find it in your heart to persuade the captain to leave my rations? So I don't starve."

Grace folded her arms. The sweat she had built hoeing cooled uncomfortably down the middle of her back. "If you're absolutely sure that's what you want—to live here, with Father Babcock?" If it had been Mad Mahlon standing before her with this request, she would not have batted an eyelid. The two unsavoury characters were a good match, and they had gravitated towards one another in light of their alienation from the officers and crew. But Darcy? It didn't make sense.

Darcy's eyes sparked, and he nodded vigorously. "'Tis what I want. More than anything."

"Very well. As you wish," said Grace, bending to retrieve her hoe. Biting back a protest of pain, she wrapped her blistered palms around the rough wooden handle. "I'll have a word with the captain this evening."

A MONTH after the completion of the building, Father Babcock declared the new church of St. Martin's Mission open for business. Grace thought he had quite the gall naming the mission after himself! His power and superiority had him strutting about like a blazing peacock—it was well past the time to bid the popinjay farewell.

Down the hill, the cutter sat idly on the beach half out of the water, the four oarsmen leaning patiently on their oars. The *Clover*'s hands clustered about Darcy on the stony shore, the earthy, muted tones of their sailors' garb contrasting starkly with his gaudy cerise suit—the only remnants of his days as a highwayman.

Grace dragged her feigned interest back to Father Babcock. He gloatingly drawled, "I'm more than ready to plant the Gospel in this virgin soil, sir."

Beside her, she caught the forced enthusiasm in Seamus's words. "I'm sure you are, Father. I'll keep you in my prayers and ask for a fruitful gathering of a new flock. Take care."

The priest's eyes burned with zeal. "I shall pray for *your* safe onward journey."

Grace shuffled a step back at the priest's seemingly innocuous words. How could a blessing sound like a threat? She tightened her arms a little more around Emily's chubby body and followed Seamus's gaze over the calm bay where the masts of the *Clover* swayed peacefully. She was imagining things. What harm could one bumbling priest bring? She turned back stiffly to face Babcock.

Seamus cleared his throat. "We'll return briefly in a month, after we visit the Falkland Islands. See how you and Darcy are faring. Until then, Father." As he nodded curtly at the priest, Seamus's hand filled the small of Grace's back.

She accompanied him to the beach, her shoes crunching on the pebbles. Darcy chatted amiably with the crew. At their approach, he beamed at Seamus. "Thank you, sir, for allowing me to stay."

"You're welcome," said Seamus, stiffening formally.

She pressed back a stab of sadness at farewelling the man who had saved her life—twice. Loyalty like that could not be bought. She had tried several times to persuade him that he need not subject himself to a life of hardship in this remote mission, but the man had made up his mind.

Seamus's voice was rich with gratitude. "It's the least I can do."

"Goodbye for now." She clasped Darcy's hand. "See you when we return in a month." Leaning in to kiss him on his cheek, Grace whispered in his ear, "It won't be too late to change your mind about staying."

Chapter Fifteen

Grace lifted her head from the logbook and cast a glance out of the stern windows at the rowdy sea, churning objectionably in their wake. The *Clover*'s journey eastwards, from the coast of South America to the Falkland Islands, had been smooth sailing—so far. With Father Babcock gone, her mood was immeasurably lighter. The lantern above her writing bureau swung drunkenly from its hook, causing waves of light to oscillate across the open double pages.

After a light tap at the door, Toby ducked as he entered, smirking shyly, the tips of his ears reddening. The crockery on the tray tinkled lightly as he slid it onto the table.

"Your meal, Mrs F." Toby's voice was a deep, rich timbre that did not match his tall, skinny countenance. Wafts of aromatic pork soup reached the writing desk, and her stomach growled.

"Thank you, Toby." She seated the inky nib in its stand.

"'Tis but the broth. No lumps. Just as you like it. And some of Dr Sykes's pickled cinnamon apples." Toby's solemn eyes watched for her response, and his knotted brow lifted when she smiled.

"How kind."

"Cook Phillips has been experimenting with those dried herbs again." Toby dubiously eyed the bowl.

She nodded at the abundance of wilted greens swimming in the steaming broth. "I'll be sure to let him know if he's used too many. Pity Dr Sykes's suggestions for modifications to our dietary intake didn't come with recipes." She grinned at Toby. "Any sight of the Falklands yet?"

"Not yet." His grey eyes softened. "Is that all, Mrs F.?"

"No, actually." She cut a slice of soft apple and popped it into her mouth, savouring the spiced, fruity bite. "Would you please retrieve the new bolt of cotton from the hold?" It had been awfully kind of Mrs Beech, the widow of the boarding house in Montevideo, to sell her the fabric. Though Grace was sure it was Billy's charm that had persuaded her more than the money. Grace licked her fingers. "It should be in the wooden trunk with the brass bindings. Emily is growing so rapidly I can scarcely keep up with sewing her clothes."

"Right away." He scampered off.

Grace finished her meal, the warm broth, baked biscuits, and spiced apples satisfying her stomach. She finished recording the previous day's log, and the leather spine of the logbook creaked as she shut it. She frowned. What was taking Toby so long? Glancing at Emily asleep in the bottom drawer of the dresser, she took her woollen tartan shawl from its hook and went above. The wind buffeted the men and sails equally, the full set of canvas straining joyously.

"We're making good headway." Seamus's voice startled her from behind. He hugged his hat safely under his elbow while his wheaten hair whipped across his grinning face. The smile line to the side of his mouth had deepened a little more with weathering. "It's a trifle windy for a saunter."

"I'm not sauntering. I'm after Toby. I asked him to fetch me a bolt of cotton from the hold, but he hasn't returned. Have you seen him?"

"I haven't." Seamus's gaze roved masterfully up the sails before shifting over the horizon. She waited patiently as he checked his compass and signalled to O'Malley at the helm. "Steady as you are, O'Malley." The wind whipped away O'Malley's reply.

With her hands clasping her shawl, she scanned the busy deck for Toby's gangly, blond-haired form. She studied the activity below. Jim's footsteps were heavy and sure under the weight of the wooden box balanced on his shoulder. Sorensen patrolled among the men, his knotted rope spinning lazy circles on its strap.

"As soon as Sorensen completes his rounds, I'll have him scout for Hicks," said Seamus.

The bow of the *Clover* juddered sluggishly through a rogue wave, the fragmented splatters of sea-mist shrouding Grace. She gripped Seamus's elbow to steady herself. He was anchored to the deck like an embedded fence post. He gave her a look that as much as asked, *Heading back down to the safety and comfort of the cabin?*

She tutted playfully. "I'm on my way, Captain. I know when I'm being soundly berated by those blue eyes of yours." Giving his elbow a final squeeze, she headed towards the inviting opening of the rear hatch.

At the bottom of the hatchway stairs, Grace shivered as she flicked the droplets of water from her shawl. She waited a moment in the relative warmth for her sight to adjust to the dimness. Good grief! Her afternoon of sewing would disappear before she had the chance to turn one stitch if Toby did not hurry up. Making up her mind, she unhooked the lantern from beside her and slid down the nearest hatchway into the hold. The air was thick with the reek of human excrement mixed with the ammonic tang of livestock urine. The stench of mouldy dry rot mingling with the fermented airs of ale and rum threw her straight back into a memory of the forecastle cabin on the *Discerning*.

Grace scoured the narrow central passage between the barrels, trunks, and pieces of furniture piled to the deckhead and securely lashed in place with thick ropes. She eyed the tightly packed cargo, and her heart sank. Gracious! Even if she found the right trunk, she would never free it from this pile. The increased light from her lantern revealed some undefined lumps to be sacks of dried goods, piled high on a wooden pallet to keep them off the damp floor. At the advance of her light, three grey rats squealed and bolted for sanctuary between the sacks.

Old Bailey's Bells! Grace clamped back her squeak with her hand across her mouth, momentarily repriving her nostrils of the oily ammonia stench of the rat infestation. If only Nessa were still here, she would sort out the vile creatures in no time! Grace danced back on her toes as the scurrying creatures slunk behind the hessian bag to carry on their indignant conversation. The bulging bellies of casks sloshed, and the *Clover*'s bowels groaned and creaked in time with the motion of the sea.

A hiss and a muffled moan interrupted the ship's orchestra. Grace's padded footsteps faltered, and her stomach clenched as she strained to listen to the muted snorting coming from behind the stockpile of sacks.

In the dark shadows, Mad Mahlon's naked, hairy behind clenched and relaxed as he grunted. His long, stringy hair moved rhythmically across his shoulders. Between Mahlon's legs, braced and shackled by his dropped breeches, was another pair of pale, gangly legs scrabbling to gain a footing on the wooden planks.

Toby's fuzzy face lay at an awkward angle, his muffled cry

caught by the leather strap gagging him. Mahlon pressed a knife to Toby's neck, his other hand scrunching the back of Toby's shirt like a handful of reins. Mahlon's thrusting hips and bowed legs gave the notion of riding a horse. Except it was not a horse he was riding. Bleeding rats' tails!

"Keep still, ye squirmy bastard!" Mahlon snarled. "At least 'til I've got me cock seated—"

With her vision growing dark-edged, Grace roared, swinging her lantern at Mahlon. The metal base of the lantern smashed against his skull with a wet thud, and the glass exploded. The thick candle inside snuffed on impact, throwing the hold into a dizzying darkness. Mahlon collided with Grace, and she crashed to the floor with a bruising thump. Shrieking, she scrambled to her knees, blindly groping towards Toby's sobbing. Her hand slicked across Mahlon's hot, sweaty face, lumpy with scar tissue and prickly with sparse patches of whiskers.

Recoiling in revulsion, Grace winced at the putrefied odour wafting from him as he groaned. She clambered around him. Her palms ground against the shattered glass. Ignoring her stinging hands, she scampered over to Toby's muted struggles. Sightless, Grace touched her friend's quivering back, tracing her hand up his slim torso to his head. She wrestled the gag from his mouth.

"Toby! It's me!" Her feathered touch outlined his wet cheeks and soft, bristled whiskers. "Stand up. We must get out of here. Hurry!"

"Mrs F.?" Toby's strangled croak delivered a punch to her heart.

"Come on, Toby. We must go. Before he rouses." Mahlon's groan of agony echoed in the black air, accompanied by the heels of boots scraping wood. Her heart caught in her throat as she peered around blindly. The bastard was so near, yet utterly invisible—where was he? The darkness pressed on her with an unwelcome swirl of violence.

Gripping her friend's bony elbow, Grace dragged him along,

using the wall of sacks as her guide. Toby heaved. Hot, semi-digested porridge splattered across her sleeve, the earthy oats turned rancid by stomach juices.

"S-sorry, Mrs F."

The shame in his voice rallied her. "Never mind. Keep walking. I've got you."

An iron grip bit her ankle. *Get off!* Grace kicked out, her shoe crunching against flesh and bone. Mahlon groaned but held his grip. With a violent yank, he pulled her foot from under her. Grace collapsed, losing her grip on Toby and cracking her elbow on the gritty planks. A dry crunch of pain shot up her arm, and she shrieked.

"I'll teach you to clonk me over the head, my son," growled Mahlon, his voice ten times more ominous in the dark. "Gonna have to try harder than that to keep *me* down." Roughened, spindly fingers tore at Grace's blouse as Mahlon shifted his weight and pinned her with his bare thighs.

An avalanche of dread coated her in icy terror at the memory of Silverton's bulk pressing her helplessly to the patterned carpet. She had been unable to twist her way out of that situation because of his weight. It was only providence that had delivered her a reprieve—Silverton's sensibilities disgusted by her womanhood. Except, this bastard was not half as heavy. And she was not in as vulnerable a position.

"Eh? What do we have here then?" Mahlon's voice rose with surprise. His hands raked over her chest, twisting brutally. Her milk-engorged breasts flared, and she yelped. Mahlon slurped a wet suck before giggling dementedly. "You aren't exactly to my liking. Though p'haps you might like a taste of me. Eh? What d'you say?"

"Get off me, you foul, fishy bastard!" screeched Grace. She did not know what would be worse, having light to witness the pock-scarred leer of her attacker, or trying to gauge his unpredictability in the dark. Having a naked man astride her was disconcerting, but not distracting enough to keep her from knowing what she needed to do next.

His toughened hand fitted round her throat. "On second thoughts"—Mahlon's hot, rancid breath puffed against her cheek —"don't really fancy poking around in a soggy cockle cave that's already been harvested."

The blood pounded in Grace's ears, and she gargled. She fought the urge to lash out with her legs, instead jerking them up and planting her feet squarely on the floor. Mad Mahlon squeezed tighter, and sparkles of light flashed before her eyes like the smattering of stars in the southern sky. She could do this! Ben had drilled her against this defenceless position countless times. She crossed her arms over his, smashing her forearms into his. Mahlon's elbows buckled, and Grace bucked her hips like an unbroken stallion.

He grunted as he tipped headfirst over her shoulder, his head thudding into the wooden planks like a mallet driving home a stake. Rolling onto his back, he gasped and swore, "Goddamned harlot! I'll teach you to—"

Grace twisted with him. She pummelled her fists into his soft gut, propelling herself back onto her knees. Ha! His hairy legs were in the perfect position, arched and splayed around her—his soft sack of vitals would contain nothing more than raisins by the time she was done. Thrusting her hands against his knees, she sprang to her feet and swung her booted foot with her full weight behind it. It kicked the black air before her. Blasted hell—he must have moved. Off balance, Grace staggered.

Mahlon snatched her skirts and yanked hard. Tripping back over the fabric barrier, Grace's back slammed onto the spongy planks, chewed through by damp and rot. She opened and closed her mouth, desperate for a sip of the dank air. She knew she was only winded, but it gave Mahlon the advantage. *Get up. Get up!* Grace dug her boot heels into the floor, her nails clawing the wood. She did not think it possible to lose any more air from her lungs, but Mahlon's knee in her gut drove out the last precious taste. With a soul-deep groan, she winced in anticipation of his next blow. If only she could see him. He was going to kill her! Oh, Emily! How would her babe survive without a mother?

Mahlon's calloused hands circled her throat again. "If I must swing, might as well make it worth my—"

A fleshy crack abruptly halted his noxious rambling, and he slumped heavily, crushing her.

Grace retched, painfully swallowing the air. Oh, dear Lord! Even Mahlon's vile odour of rotting fish and rancid pork fat was easy enough to ignore with each sweet breath. His crushing weight disappeared, and backlit shadows sparkled before her.

Seamus's voice tore through the drumming of her heart in her ears. "Grace! Grace, do you hear me?" He wrenched her ungently by the shoulders.

She squeezed a rasp from her bruised throat. "T-Toby?" Placing her hand on Seamus's chest, she squinted curiously as her touch left bloody handprints on his white shirt. Had Mahlon cut Toby? She searched the crowd of faces. "Where's Toby?"

"He's above. With Beynon." Seamus gripped her hand. "Bring the light here, damn you!" His voice was tight and sharp. The surrounds lit up like an instant sunrise as Sorensen's and Jim's anxious faces peered over Seamus's shoulder. Her husband grunted as he inspected the wounds on her palms. "Oh, Grace."

Oh my, all this blood was hers.

Sitting her upright, Seamus reached into his pocket for his handkerchief and wrapped it crudely around her more severely lacerated right hand. In one smooth motion, he picked her up, heading along the narrow alley of the hold.

Gripping his solid neck, Grace glanced back at the cacophony of thuds, grunts, and whacks behind the sacks.

Seamus spun. "Don't kill him," he growled. "That right belongs to me and, by Christ, I will have the highest satisfaction seeing that devil swing madly from the yardarm."

Billy arrived in the great cabin. He cleansed Grace's palms with neat brandy, and she bit a mouthful of quilt. Blazing Hades! It was like ten wretched wasp stings. The cleaning hurt far more than suturing her right hand did. After three generous helpings of brandy, Grace was distinctly comfortable by the time Billy got to examining her elbow. With professional scrutiny, he inspected her minutely, his capable fingers palpating her arm and gently investigating her range of movement. "Not broken, only bruised. Though it'll need time to mend."

"How's Toby?" Grace slurred.

Billy's face hardened. "A man can't endure such treatment and not carry a deep shame within." He knotted the sling and, giving her a satisfied nod, he turned to set right his medical cabinet. "I've nothing in my doctoring box to fix that hurt." He wound up the suturing thread and returned it to its little drawer.

"He'll need minding with tenderness." Grace blinked at the deckhead, trying to order her foggy thoughts. "And to be shown kindness."

Billy made a small derisive noise through his nostrils. "On a ship like this? Gentleness and kindness don't exactly sprout in great abundance, flower. The life of a sailor is a hard one, and the men know it."

She jutted out her chin. "We must try. I'll have the captain issue a warning that any man who lays a hand on Toby Hicks will feel the end of the cat."

"Take heed. You'll do Toby no service by earning him favours from the captain. The men won't stand for that."

Grace pulled the bedcover higher, resting her bandaged hand on her abdomen, finally firm again after Emily's birth. Her chest slumped. "What can we do then, Billy?"

Billy sat on the edge of the bed. "You, of all people, know of the men's loyalty below decks. One bad apple hasn't spoiled the whole bunch. The lads will take care of Toby in their own way." His dark eyebrows tipped upwards, his face softening.

"Remember how you told me they took you under their wing when you arrived aboard the *Discerning*? Buchanan. Blight. Gilly too. They'll do right by Toby. You'll see."

Grace closed her heavy eyelids, allowing herself into the warm sleep that had been beckoning for the last half hour. Billy was right, of course.

Chapter Sixteen

FALKLAND ISLANDS, 28 FEBRUARY 1833

A rriving in the East Falkland settlement of Port Louis, Seamus had expected to find a thriving harbour with abundant fresh beef and freshwater, including excellent anchorage, but this place was uninhabited. And what the devil was the Union Jack doing hoisted up that pole? Where was the prosperous Argentinian settlement he had heard about?

Beside him, Barry Johns, dressed smartly in anticipation of company, lowered his spyglass. "The place is a deserted ruination, sir."

Seamus panned his spyglass around. Semi-demolished rock cottages and sprawling turf huts dotted the barren landscape. "Those boats are damaged. Whoever departed left in a hurry and with no intention of anyone following," added Seamus.

He lowered his glass, casting a side look at his first mate. Johns held his shoulders stiffly, his sorrowful stare meeting

Seamus's. "I see vegetable gardens, at least the remains of some, and a smattering of livestock. They couldn't have left that long ago."

"But leave they did. There's no one there now." Seamus squeezed the brass tube and rolled his stiff wrist until it clicked. Squinting at the dotted wild cattle in the distance, he turned to Johns. "Lay anchor. There's still a promise of fresh beef and water here."

"Yes, sir."

The anchor splashed into the azure shallows, and Seamus studied the ruined shore again from the forecastle deck. A high-pitched whizzing and yells of surprise spun Seamus on the spot. His heart thudded in dismay as the last of the heavy anchor cable whipped loose of the capstan and slithered overboard like a snake dipped in hot oil. Several men bawled out the alarm.

"Blasted cable must've snapped!"

"God 'elp us. We're too shallow."

Seamus roared, "Let go the stern anchor!" A flurry of activity livened the stern, but then a cry went up that sent a chill to Seamus's fingertips.

"Crivens! We've lost the second anchor!" Buchanan paced, his protruding ears reddening in alarm. "Cable's cut!"

One snapped cable was wretched luck. Two was impossible —not without foul play. With a realisation that twisted his neck and shoulder muscles into a knot, he glared at the shadows lurking beneath the transparent water. The rocks! They were drifting too fast on the current. He bounded from the forecastle, pounding swiftly along the upper deck towards the helm. "All sail! Hard to starboard, Blight!" In the rigging, all available men swarmed upwards with the urgency of ants disturbed from their nest. Blast! He only hoped the current did not work against them. Glaring at the approaching shore as though his scowl might frighten it back, he quickly turned his attention to Blight at the helm. The broad-shouldered man had wrenched the wheel to hard lock, the sinews of his neck straining as he held it in check.

"Hold her tight, Blight," Seamus encouraged. The whooshing, buffeting canvas dropped, catching hold of the breeze. *Come on, you beauty. You can do it.*

The shudder of the deck vibrated through the marrow of his legbones as though a giant holystone were being dragged across the scrubbed planks. Seamus held his breath as the *Clover*'s bow began to slowly swing away from the shore. For pity's sake, it was not enough—she was still kissing the rocks! Several men hesitated at the rough scraping. Now was not the time for idle hands.

"Carpenter James!" Seamus ensured his words carried loud and clear. "Bring up the spare anchor. Affix a new cable. Quick as you can." He clasped his hands behind him, ignoring the trickle of sweat tickling the middle of his back. "And while you're down there, assess the damage." Concentrating on steadying his breathing, his relief grew as the *Clover* eased her way back into deeper water.

Johns stepped beside him. "That was quick thinking on your part, sir. Saved us running aground."

"We'll find out whether I have or not shortly, Mr Johns." He pressed his lips together.

Johns turned his head stiffly. "Someone severed both cables."

"I'm aware." Holding his face neutral, he lowered his chin, angling it towards Johns as he spoke in muted tones. "Find the saboteur. By any means necessary."

The first mate cleared his throat and licked his lips.

"What is it, Johns?"

"Well, sir. Since his shackling, Mahlon's started spouting on about the surprises we're going to find aboard the *Clover*." Johns wrung his hands. "I thought they were but the ramblings of a mad man. His words barely make sense anymore."

Seamus turned his attention to the gang of six hauling the spare anchor from the mid-hatch. Carpenter James followed, a heavy anchor cable coiled across his thick shoulders like a sleeping boa constrictor. At least the weather suited repairs. It was as though King Neptune sensed the wrath rippling through Seamus's veins and offered him a favour.

"The hull, Carpenter James?" said Seamus.

James hoicked the coil higher on his shoulder. "All clear, sir."

Releasing the fists clenched behind his back, Seamus nodded. "Very well. Carry on."

He turned his head swiftly to Johns. "Were Mahlon not already beaten to a pulp, that would be my next course of action." He rolled his neck to ease the tension. "Once the anchor is repaired, lug Mahlon up here. Let's see if we can't extract some more answers."

"Yes, sir." Johns's voice wavered.

Seamus narrowed his eyes. "Is there something else, Johns?"

"Permission to question that whaler over there first, sir?" Johns's stub-nailed finger pointed at the squat neighbouring vessel. "Perhaps they might know more about the affairs ashore?"

While he was aware of how stoically Johns bore his son's loss, his enthusiasm to question the whaler's crew told Seamus he would be glad of the distraction of extra responsibility. The whaler across the water, newly painted and tarred, glittered prettily in the morning sun. Her crew had lined the gunwale, hooting and cheering at the *Clover*'s close call, and Seamus's innards had shrunk at being the source of their entertainment and amusement. The last thing he wanted was to face her captain.

Seamus nodded. "Good idea, Johns. I look forward to your report. I'll have O'Malley bring Mahlon up for questioning."

"Yes, sir."

The late afternoon land breeze carried odours of the abandoned settlement, livestock dung, tilled soil, and remnants of cold campfires to Seamus's nostrils as he stood with his feet planted on the quarterdeck. Sykes and Beynon flanked him. Mahlon stood slouched and shackled before them. Sorensen had a firm grip on his arm. A deep cut on Mahlon's jaw dripped blood onto his stained shirt, his left ear a mangled cauliflower of cartilage. Seamus stared at him stonily.

"Mahlon, you're already being detained for the detestable and abominable vice of buggery committed against Toby Hicks and the attempted murder of my wife. What—"

"Ha!" interrupted Mahlon. "Squirmy little shit didn't keep still long enough for me to succeed. Not before I had me brains bashed in by that witch."

"You don't deny this offence? Even though it's punishable with death?" asked Seamus.

Mahlon coughed and rubbed the back of his neck, gazing out at the distant shoreline. His lack of eye contact did little to persuade Seamus of his innocence.

His thoughts wandered back to the sight of Hicks bursting from the hatchway on the day of Grace's attack. The man was in a grievous state, half undressed and gibbering incomprehensively, his clay-grey eyes packed with terror. A leather collar hung loose about his scrawny neck. It was only when Seamus spotted Hicks's bound wrists that the uneasiness slicking through his gut had turned into a hot, gushing torrent of boiling oil. Grace! Seamus strode over to Hicks and snatched his arm.

"Where is Mrs Fitzwilliam?" Seamus had barked, his throat dry with fear.

"D-down the hold, sir. Oh, sweet mercy! Mahon's got her. He's going to kill her."

Seamus wanted to forget the vision of a trouser-less Mahlon straddling his wife, one hand pinning her wrists and the other choking the life out of her, her eyes already rolled back, her tongue protruding grotesquely. He had kicked the back of Mahlon's head with his heel, the thudding connection that reverberated up his shinbone both satisfying and horrifying. He had feared he was too late.

O'Malley's snarl brought Seamus back to the sunny deck. "What about the anchors, you turncoat? That you too?"

"Aye, 'twas all me. Well—not only me—but a little of me."

Seamus frowned at the convoluted confession. "You admit to meddling with the anchors?" He had not expected the confirmation to come so readily. "Pray tell, who is your co-conspirator?"

Mahlon cackled, gripping his ribs in support. "Why, the devil 'imself."

Ah, not so readily after all. "I've no doubt about *his* involvement here, Mahlon. But even the devil has his minions. Who aided you?"

"You'd never pick him in a million ye—"

Sorensen backhanded Mahlon with an open hand. Mahlon's head snapped back with a ferocity that might have left a weaker man with a broken neck. With his head lolling, Mahlon snorted. A bubble of mucous and blood inflated from one of his nostrils. It popped, and the red glob dribbled over his lips and down his chin.

"Indulge us." Seamus spoke with a forced degree of patience. "Who is this man who has so smartly evaded detection?"

"Babbling bloody Babcock, o' course!" Mahlon tipped his head, hooting. The motion opened the split on his jaw, and a fresh trickle of blood coated the black, dried crust on his neck.

Seamus's stunned silence was interrupted by the guttural growling and squalling of a curious giant petrel soaring overhead. "Father Babcock? He's no longer aboard." Seamus's voice pitched. "Have you lost your mind?"

"Not to play the devil's advocate here," interjected Beynon, unhooking his thumb from his fob pocket and waving his hand airily. "But I feel it prudent to mention that Mahlon *isn't* in his right mind."

Seamus jerked his head around, his gaze whipping from Beynon to Mahlon and back to Beynon. What the devil was he playing at? "Explain yourself, Beynon."

"We've already lost two men to tropical fever. 'Tis my diagnosis that this man is suffering from a parasitic invasion. He's been to me four times in the past month to let his blood due to excruciating headaches that have affected his sight."

"And what does that have to do with *this* interrogation?" asked Seamus.

Beynon smoothed his thick-whiskered lip with his finger and thumb. "Mahlon may not be the friendliest soul aboard, sir, but no one can accuse him of shirking his duties. He has become increasingly erratic since his health began declining."

"Are you justifying his abominable behaviour?" Seamus clipped his words.

"Certainly not. What he's accused of is inexcusable. However, I believe it only fair all the facts be known. I believe Mahlon is suffering an incurable condition."

"Incurable? So, he won't heal?"

Beynon shook his head, his bristled top lip twitching.

Beside the ship's surgeon, Sykes shuffled his feet and ran his palms down his frockcoat. "Had he more time, we might be able to treat him."

"And why is he so pressed for time?" Seamus glanced at Sykes's black, bushy brows drawn that were together before turning back to Mahlon. Through the slits of his blackened, pulpy eyelids, Mahlon glared at his judges with a liberal dose of belligerence.

Taking a deep breath, Sykes elaborated. "The man's coughing up blood. The beating he's received has irreparably damaged his insides."

As though to confirm Sykes's diagnosis, Mahlon gave a

guttural hawk, and phlegm splattered like bloody seagull excrement onto the clean wooden boards beside his dirty feet. Vibrating with anger, Seamus fixed his gaze on the distant shoreline, the flat green line hazing at the edges. What he would not give to strangle the sod this instant! If the man's health was already in slow decline, strangulation would probably be the quickest and kindest end for him. Seamus caught a flicker of movement, but it was just a lone cow grazing. Beynon was an excellent surgeon and Sykes a knowledgeable physician—he had no cause to disbelieve them. Though, disease and mortal injury aside, Mahlon had still committed a crime.

Sorensen's gnarled face twisted as though he had sucked a lime. "Snivelling bastard is rotten to the core. Should be hanged before he snuffs it." He drew his lips up and bared his teeth. Mahlon blinked sluggishly, his shoulders slouched.

Beside Seamus, O'Malley stiffened. "Mahlon, do you have anything to say in your defence?"

Mahlon ran his swollen tongue over the gaps where his teeth had been. He sucked noisily. "There's one thing you milksops hasn't had the bollocks to say out loud." He flinched, and Seamus was not sure whether his grimace was a spasm of pain or a deranged grin.

O'Malley spoke like a father indulging a young child's inane request. "And what would that be, Mahlon?"

"That until that sorceress came aboard, we was doing just fine. But then Fitzwilliam went and got himself bewitched, allowing that scrawny bitch to stay on our ship. The lot of ya know a woman aboard is ill luck." Mad Mahlon absently crossed himself. "But no one did nothing about it. The two of them cavorting around like 'twas no man's business. An' look at all what's happened to us since she arrived. Cap'n Fincham snuffed out his own wick. Gilly speared to death. Neptune's wrath—a tempest so fierce as to rattle even the hardiest of men."

Seamus's brow dipped. "You realise not all those events happened aboard *this* vessel?"

Mahlon jerked his head back, frowning. "Eh? What you talking about? I been aboard the *Discerning* four years now!"

Seamus sucked in a deep breath and stared at Mahlon for a beat before shaking his head. "Mahlon, we are aboard the *Clover*, not the *Discerning*."

The crazy-eyed man gave a short bark and doubled over, growling deep and low as he convulsed in a coughing spasm. A strand of thick, blood-stained mucous swung unchecked from his bottom lip. He stooped listlessly, his face a purple twist of pain, his bloodshot slits leering. "Was doing you all a favour by snuffing out that curse. Tell you one other thing—and I won't even charge you for the pleasure—feeling that she-devil choking beneath me hands gave me the hardest cockstand of me life!" He attempted a mirthless laugh, but instead gasped small puffs of agony as though he had just run the length of the Thames.

O'Malley hissed in objection and Sorensen muttered uncomfortably. Even Seamus had to admit he had not seen this turn of events coming. Curses, he would have the devil's own job pulling his ship to order again.

O'Malley stepped closer to Mahlon, the muscles of his forearms knotted with restraint. "Will you now admit you murdered my Nessa, in retaliation for me taking all your winnings on the dice?"

"Told ya I never done it," murmured Mahlon sullenly.

Seamus scowled. "Then why attack Hicks?"

Mahlon gingerly shrugged one shoulder. "Heard the bastard saying 'twas me what did the cat in."

Sorensen shook Mahlon's arm, shouting, "And he was right, you bastard! 'Twas all *your* bloody fault we was hammered by the biggest storm God saw fit to throw upon the ocean!"

The volume of his protest reverberated around the deck, and several seamen stopped and glanced around. Seamus hoped their knowing the truth would return order to his ship. He fixed his steely gaze on Mahlon. The blood from the crazed prisoner's wounds had darkened against the purple-mottled hue of his skin. Bowed to the right, Mahlon eased upright, his pock-marked face tightening in discomfort. He let out a short grunt as he stood fully erect.

"Pah!" Mahlon swallowed painfully, feigning disinterest. "The lot o' you can go to hell!"

"Take him below," ordered Seamus. He doubted there was any more information coming from this prisoner, at least not any he could trust.

WITHIN THE HOUR, Johns returned from the whaler. Seamus shielded his brow with his hand, squinting against the orange hues of the sinking sun. Johns's heavy footfalls halted beside him on the quarterdeck. "What news, Mr Johns?"

The first mate cleared his throat. "The Falklands was indeed a thriving settlement, sir, before an American whaler ransacked the place a while back. Scared the settlers off into the country."

Seamus frowned. "Then how did the *British* flag come to be hoisted?"

"After the ransacking, seems Captain Onslow of the *Clio* exploited this wee lapse and reasserted British sovereignty." Johns waved towards the hillocks in the distance. "But he left only a few days after claiming it so. No one's sure who it belongs to right now."

Seamus chuckled mirthlessly and pressed his thumb and forefinger against his eyelids. His eyeballs felt hard and hot. Lack of sleep did that to a man. Blinking, he shook his head at Johns. "With its lack of regular authority, I daren't chance stepping foot ashore. Heaven knows what happened last time I ended up drawn into foreign affairs. I'll not be lured onto this inherently lawless island—no matter how tempting that fresh beef is."

He glanced at the furled sails, their neatly wrinkled folds hiding in dark shadow. Grinding his back molars at the colossal waste of time and resources, Seamus lowered his gaze steadily to his first mate. "We'll return to Port Famine on the turn of the tide. I plan to shake Father Babcock until he spills all his black-hearted secrets, or until every last tooth of his has rattled loose."

TWO DAYS LATER, with the *Clover* headed back to Port Famine, Mahlon drowned in his own blood, just as Sykes had predicted. Standing beside the gunwale, Seamus watched the hands commit Mahlon's shrouded body to the sea.

Beynon stood beside him, rigid to attention. "I hope, sir, you'll put on record that Mahlon committed those atrocities without sound mind?"

Sweet heavens! This voyage was producing more twists and turns than the hedge maze at Hampton Court Palace! Seamus desired a return of normalcy. He nodded at Beynon. "Yes, of course."

As the *Clover* drew nearer to the rugged shore off Port Famine, sunlight sparked golden off the brass tube of Seamus's spyglass. He swung it level with the approaching land. In the right light, the scene might have been quite romantic, with the glassy water of the cove, the cutter perched lopsidedly on the sand, and on the hill, a wisp of smoke curling from the tree canopy. Despite the tranquillity, Seamus could not shake the feeling that something was amiss, though his mood was still soured by the incident with Mahlon. He scanned the narrow strip of pebbled beach and sucked in a breath through his teeth. Ah, just the man he wanted—Babcock!

Up on the yardarm, Blight yelled out, "Father Babcock's on

the beach. He's bald." He capped his hand to his forehead, squinting. "And without clothes!"

"What the devil is he doing sitting on the beach in his smalls?" Seamus murmured, snapping the scope shut and rasping his calloused hand across the back of his wind-burnt neck. It appeared as though someone had already thoroughly interrogated the priest. Seamus only hoped Babcock was of sound enough mind to face the volley of questions he had primed and ready to fire.

Chapter Seventeen

Seamus sat stiffly in the bow of the cutter as it cut effortlessly across the choppy water. The instant the bow crunched into the beach, he sprang out. While his men seized the sides of the boat and ran her high and dry on the pebbles, he hurried over to the stricken priest.

"Father Babcock?" Seamus extended his hand to the crumpled man. Shit! The state of him!

Babcock squinted, the wrinkles around his eyes creased black with dirt. "Sir! Oh, thank the Lord! You've returned!" The man gripped his hand, and Seamus winced as his knucklebones ground together. Wiry stubble sprouted from the crusted, bloody clumps on the priest's scalp and cheeks. He began panting hard before breaking into a wet sob.

"Calm yourself, Father." Seamus put a steadying hand on the blubbering man's bony shoulder.

"Get me out of here. Away from these heathens!"

Seamus glanced at the church on the hill. What the devil—it was a burnt-out shell! "Where's Darcy? What happened?"

Babcock laughed maniacally. "From the moment you left, those bastards plundered me daily. Isn't a sodding thing left."

Seamus guided the staggering man across the beach. He waved at the hands to ready the cutter. "What prompted that?" He knew Babcock was disagreeable but, as relieved as he had been to be rid of the man from his ship, he could not fathom what the priest must have done to upset the locals so.

Babcock wiped his running nose with his hairless arm. "They surrounded my cabin, day and night, making incessant inhuman noises. So unrelenting! Rendered me sleepless with dread."

That explained the bloodshot eyes, but not the missing eyelashes.

Snatching at Seamus's sleeve, Babcock's hairless brow arched. "Oh, dear God! He's coming back! He's one of them. He let them attack me."

Seamus spun, alarmed at Darcy's lone figure heading his way. His square-set shoulders and the determined crunch of his boots told of a man displeased. As a precaution, Seamus signalled his men to ready their weapons. Darcy charged at Seamus, stopping dead at an uncomfortably close distance, his dark-shadowed eyes unreadable.

Seamus took a slow breath. "Darcy? What on earth is going on?"

Darcy jabbed a stiff finger at Babcock. "*He* is a contemptible man."

Seamus studied Babcock's bowed, naked back, the knobs of his vertebrate pressed tight beneath his skin. He glanced back at Darcy's pale face. "Explain yourself, man. How have you allowed a clergyman to sink into such a state?"

"He's no clergyman," Darcy snapped. "He's a fashion plate who names sacred places after himself."

Babcock spluttered. "I did no such thing! My mission was named for Saint Martin of Tours—that venerated Christian soldier who split his military cloak in two to share with a beggar. A man of the highest morals who—"

"You're the devil's spawn!" Darcy yelled.

"I'll have no Irish heathen give account against me." Babcock cowered back a step. "You let those men attack me with wooden staves and rocks. I believed I was done for, sir! I tried to placate them with gifts"—the priest's voice quavered—"but they tore and dashed everything to pieces!"

"Silence, Babcock!" Seamus retorted. "I'll hear *all* accounts, thank you." Babcock slunk behind him, muttering under his breath. Seamus studied Darcy a beat longer. "What happened, Darcy?"

"I caught him drinking the holy wine. What man of the cloth commits such an atrocity?" Darcy drew back his slim shoulders.

"As sacrilegious as that is, it's no excuse to allow the man to be tortured." Seamus wrenched his arm away from Babcock's deathly grip and frowned at Darcy.

"'Tis a flaming blasphemous way to treat a man of the cloth!" said Babcock. "Those ungrateful heathens aren't save-able. I daren't fall asleep for fear *he'd* slit my throat in the night." He jabbed a begrimed, jittering finger at Darcy.

Ignoring Babcock's ranting, Seamus glowered at Darcy and hiked his thumb over his shoulder. "Did you do this to him?"

"No." Darcy shook his head emphatically.

"But you didn't stop it either?"

"No, I didn't. The wine loosened his tongue. He told me how you'd all die without anchors. Be dashed upon the rocks. He spilled all about his plans to kill Mrs F. in Montevideo. He's an evil man!"

Seamus reached back and, gripping Babcock's bony elbow, yanked him to the fore. Babcock whimpered as Seamus squeezed him tighter. "Explain yourself, man. Mahlon already revealed your plan to sabotage the *Clover*'s anchors. What's this about you killing my wife?"

"Look at me!" Babcock squeaked, fresh tears spilling easily without lashes to hold them back. He swayed with fatigue, the wizened, sagging skin beneath his chin quivering as he bawled. "They plucked out *all* my hair. One by one. It took *hours*!"

Darcy clicked his tongue with disdain.

Seamus switched on all authority in his voice. "I'll do more than pluck your hair if you don't avail me of the truth this instant, Babcock." He dropped the priest's clammy arm in disgust and wiped his hand down his coat. "On second thought, I think I'll just leave you here."

"Dear God above, please no! I'll tell you everything. Just get me away from here." Snot dribbled over Babcock's shrivelled, peeling lips. "I realised that Mahlon was succumbing to a malady that was slowly sending him mad. Didn't take much to tip him over. I persuaded him to slash the anchor cables. Dashing the *Clover* upon the rocks was supposed to take care of all witnesses."

Seamus scoffed. "And naturally, you waited until you were safely deposited at Port Famine before unrolling that devious plan."

Babcock whimpered and shrugged his shoulders.

Through a clenched jaw, Seamus uttered, "You're a fool and a coward, Babcock!"

"I know this well enough." Babcock sniffed with a wet suck. "I need no one's forgiveness. God will forgive me."

"He's not welcome to stay!" scowled Darcy. "Take him back to England. Tip him overboard, for all I care."

Seamus blew out a slow breath through puffed cheeks. What was he to blasted well do with a rogue priest for the remainder of the journey? "Will you come with us, Darcy?"

Seamus followed Darcy's gaze along the beach to a small, fierce-faced woman cloaked in a fur wrap, standing in the shadow of the tree line.

"I've a wife awaiting." Darcy blushed.

Blinking in surprise, Seamus asked, "A wife? Already?"

Darcy nodded. "The locals are good people. They've already learned a few words of English and I of theirs."

"What of the mission?" Seamus peered at the hill again. The spiralling curl of smoke he had seen earlier had stopped.

Darcy's lashes lowered. "'Tis gone. Razed to the ground. When I learned of Babcock's atrocities, I wasn't about to stand by and let him sink his devil's talons into these innocents."

Seamus bit back a retort about the waste of supplies, not to mention the cost. "Are you sure I can't persuade you to return to England with us rather?"

Darcy secured his gaze firmly on Seamus and shook his head with the surety of a man with his mind made up. "My wife doesn't wish to go to England. She's scared of the big ships. And frankly, sir, England hasn't been kind to me." His gaze softened as he panned the rugged coastline. "Thought I'd start anew. Where my past transgressions aren't burned like a brand upon my cheek."

Seamus placed a hand on Darcy's solid shoulder. "Fret not, Mr Darcy. I shan't leave this scoundrel to spoil your shores."

Bidding Darcy farewell a second time, Seamus tipped the near-naked priest into the cutter, where he curled into a ball in the grey puddle of seawater swilling about in the bottom. Right, it was time to get this canary to sing.

Back aboard the *Clover*, the men parted for Babcock as though he carried the plague. Seamus released Babcock's arm, and he dropped to the deck with a heavy thump. "Bosun Sorensen, prepare a noose," Seamus ordered.

"Wha—you can't hang me. I've had no trial." Babcock scrabbled to his knees and hung onto the hem of Seamus's coat.

O'Malley shunted Babcock aside with his foot. "Hands off the captain."

"Fret not, Father. As you said, God will forgive you. I'm simply expediting your journey to face Him."

O'Malley glanced sideways at Seamus. "What's the charge, sir?"

Raising his voice, Seamus curtly announced, "Father Babcock, you are hereby charged with the attempted murder of the crew of the *Clover*. I have borne witness to your testament by which you have admitted your guilt."

"I did not!" Babcock squealed, lunging for Seamus's coat again. "This is murder!"

"Sir." O'Malley's voice was low and respectful. "As disinclined as I am to defend this weasel, I must ask whether this is wise?" The afternoon sun set O'Malley's orange hair ablaze. "The priest's right. He's not stood trial."

Seamus elongated his neck. "It's my responsibility as commander to decide what offence Babcock has committed, and its within my authority to choose his punishment." Of course, O'Malley was right, but Seamus needed Babcock to think he was above the law—or at least that he was mad enough to disregard it.

"You've no proof. No witnesses!" Babcock wailed.

"Out on the open ocean, the captain's law *is* the law," said Seamus coldly. His mind raced over the Articles of War. If he could repeat some resemblance of them now, they would lend a legal air to this carnival. "Any persons being guilty of profane oaths or cursing, and corruption of good manners, shall be punished as a commander sees fit."

"God will damn you for this, Fitzwilliam!" Babcock bellowed.

Unwavering, Seamus droned on with all the naval authority he could muster. "No man shall presume to quarrel with the commander of the ship or disobey any lawful command. Any person guilty of such an offence shall suffer death."

Ignoring the curious scowls and questioning looks of his crew, Seamus peered up at Carpenter James and his mates on the cathead, protruding from the bow. They were making quick work of erecting a scaffold. He continued dryly, "Any persons making any mutinous assembly, upon any pretence whatsoever, shall be punished with death."

Seamus pinned high hopes on the priest's cowardice. The notion of Babcock martyring himself was almost laughable. Except Seamus was in no laughing mood.

"Any man entertaining intelligence to or with any enemy or rebel without leave from the commander shall be punished with death," Seamus droned on. The pounding hammers ticking rhythmically in the afternoon sun drilled into his brain with each strike.

Grace sidled up to him with Emily pouched in her shawl, the babe's pink, pouted lips sucking contentedly on her chubby thumb. His wife's green eyes widened in horror as she took in the priest's hairless, scabbed body. "Seamus, what's happening?"

He drew her over to the gunwale by her arm. "This isn't a sight for the babe, Grace."

She rocked in time with the undulating deck, patting the solid curve of the shawl. "She'll be asleep soon enough."

Seamus usually adored watching his daughter struggle to fight off the last vestiges of sleep, her droopy eyelids darting open so as not to miss the moment. All it took was his finger stroking her brow to persuade those long-lashed lids to close, his gentle caress his unspoken promise to always be there for her. To keep her safe. But just this minute, he had a spineless priest to hang.

"I'm stringing Babcock up for his crimes."

"Is it your place to prosecute the man for murdering his wife?" Grace whispered urgently.

"Trust me, Dulcinea. I know what I'm doing."

"Trust you?" She rammed one hand on her hip. "You knew of Babcock's unsavoury past but kept it to yourself."

Oh, heavens. His feisty wife's temper was up, but by Christ, so was his. He was in no mood to negotiate her down right now either. Why did she always choose these inopportune—and wretchedly public—moments? He gritted his teeth, attempting to control his voice. "I did what I needed to protect you."

"Poppycock! That's the sword you fall on every time. But it doesn't cut it this time, Seamus."

Seamus squeezed the wooden railing, his thumbnail aggravating a splinter of wood. "I never envisaged matters escalating to this. For crying out loud, Grace, I would never deliberately deny you the truth if I thought you at risk."

"I don't give a *rats* about me—I can take care of myself. But Emily? She needs the protection of *both* parents. How do I protect her when I'm unaware of the dangers lurking beneath my nose?"

"Be fair. How were we to know those dangers came laced with treachery and deceit?"

"I might have, had you enlightened me from the start."

Seamus pulled at his cravat, which was growing increasingly warm. "How did you find out about Babcock?"

Grace waggled her finger and pursed her lips as she shook her head. "Uh, uh. You'll not steer this conversation away like that. *How* I discovered it is not as important as the fact that it was *there* for me to discover in the first place."

She leaned in, and Seamus straightened his neck, glad of his height. If he were dry kindling, the sparks in her eyes would have set him ablaze already. Her closing the door on her source confirmed it was either Hicks or Buchanan—or both—who had spilled his secret. Blast those two. He knew he should appreciate their unwavering protection over Grace, but he was peeved enough right now to want to string them both up beside Babcock.

She spoke under her breath, her lower register more unsettling than when she yelled. "I thought we promised never to keep secrets?"

He took a step back. No, she was not going to make him feel guilty for assuming command of his family—for believing his decision was in their best interest. Below, the water was a shallow, pale blue, and he suddenly envied the fish in their emotionless, calm world where a wife's hot accusations could not scald.

"Now is not the time, Grace. Christ knows which other ears Babcock has whispered his black lies into. I must sort him out."

Grace's bottom jaw stuck out. "Hang the man without trial, and you'll find yourself dangling from a noose of your own."

Seamus leaned low, his words hissing angrily between his teeth. "Do you think I don't know that?" He needed her to head below—this instant. "I have a plan—one that you are about to sink if you carry on like this."

The splash of pain across her face doused the flames of his own anger, but the coals still smouldered inside. Oh, he would pay for those words later, but right now he needed to capitalise on his gamble that they would send her below in a rage. He felt like a prize shit for manipulating her so, but it was for the best.

She cocked her head to one side. "No need to explain yourself, *Captain*. My wifely foibles couldn't *possibly* cope."

Seamus was glad of his daughter's presence, or Grace's wrath might have over-ridden her sensibility and had her flee ashore like it had in the past. But she would never leave Emily. Grace wrapped her arms around the curiously blinking babe. His wife's courageous effort to control her trembling chin equalled his effort to not reach out and scoop them both in his arms. She turned stiffly, and he instinctively reached for the small of her back but curled his fingers at the last second.

With the sun lowering in the sky, Seamus stepped over to where Babcock cowered on the deck. On his order, Sorensen and Buchanan manhandled the quivering priest up to the scaffolding. He kicked out weakly at his captors, his movements limited by his short legs. The noose hung from a long rope over the yardarm. Sorensen roughly shoved the rough-fibred rope over Babcock's ears and yanked it tight around his throat. Babcock struggled in the grip of the two sailors on either side of him, his fluent string of curses spraying out into the sea breeze.

The peak of Seamus's cocked hat tipped, and he squinted against the setting sun. "Any last words, Babcock?"

The man stilled, wild eyes darting around the waiting crowd, deep breaths heaving in his chest. Gulls shrieked. Someone in the crowd sneezed.

"I was only following Hamilton's orders. God curse you!" Tears coursed down Babcock's puce face. He swallowed, and the rope undulated around his throat.

"What orders?" asked Seamus.

"To sabotage your efforts. Ensure you didn't return to London."

"So you meant to kill us?"

Babcock lifted his chin, his drooping eyelids so pitiful that Seamus's earlier flare of danger spluttered. "Not directly by my own hand. I was to make it look like you'd fallen foul of circumstance."

"Why?" Seamus thrust his hands behind him. "Why would Hamilton front an expedition like this just to foul it?"

Babcock shrugged one shoulder. "Wasn't his money. He has backers."

An expedition of this duration always required philanthropic support, though Seamus had not cared about the investors—until now. "Who?"

"L-let me down and I'll tell you."

Seamus nodded to Sorensen. "Make ready, Bosun."

A yellow stain bloomed across the front of Babcock's grubby smalls. "No, wait! Stop! I'll speak!"

"Then speak," Seamus said calmly. His throat was dryer than a strip of salt beef left in the sun for a week.

"Oh, good God! What an unholy mess!" Babcock's voice quivered. "Um... there's, uh... Milner—an Old Etonian friend of his father's. And… um… the industrialist, Lemmons. Oh, and Lord Silverton—"

That cursed bastard? His was the last name Seamus had expected to hear. More was amiss here than he had originally believed. And this was not a conversation he wanted bandied above deck. Ripping off his hat, Seamus scratched at an itch on his damp hairline. He waved the brim at Sorensen. "Cut him down and bring him to my cabin."

Chapter Eighteen

T hat bloody, bloody man! Seamus's betrayal left Grace feeling like she needed to soak in a tub of hot water with a jolly good scrub of lye soap. Her niggling doubt about Babcock's secret had been a concern for a while now, but *nothing* had prepared her for what had just transpired. Uncurling Emily from her shawl, Grace sat her in a basket padded with a grey ship's blanket and handed her the wooden toy cat to chew.

The gash of her husband's disloyalty nearly sliced her heart in two. She had taken his professed love for granted—and he had neatly strung her along. What a fool for naively believing their marriage would endure any hardship. Now she was left holding a soggy handful of his dishonesty. She wanted to hurl it across the room and watch it splat against the bulkhead, but instead she curled her fingers into a fist.

And that condescension! He had not tried that on her in years. Good grief, his brain must be as addled as Mad Mahlon's. It was the only thing that made sense—that he was failing from some tropical ague. But if that were true, then where were the sweats and the chills? Grace paced the great cabin, her hands on her hips, as she sucked in gulping breaths to stem her tears. Had she missed other tell-tale signs? She had once jested with him, asking, *Is love not blind?* But it appeared it was she who was blind.

Grace snatched one of Seamus's dried shirts from the line strung in the corner. Her trembling hands fumbled with the folding. Shrieking, she tumbled the cotton into a white ball and flung it with great satisfaction. It landed beside the potbellied stove, and she smirked to see it streaked with ash. Ha! He could wash his own wretched shirts from now on.

The cabin door opened, and she whirled with the speed of a bobbin on a well-treadled spinning wheel. Seamus closed the door behind him and remained motionless. Grace stared back, her chest heaving as though she had just swum beneath the *Clover* and burst up on the other side. This reminded her of a postcard she had seen once of a Spanish matador standing before a black bull. Only, who was the matador, and who was the bull?

Seamus moved first. "Grace."

"Did you kill him?"

He blinked hard, his feet shuffling to a halt. "No."

"Then why the performance?"

He licked his lips, and his cravat moved as he swallowed. "It was a ploy—to get him to speak."

Grace folded her arms. Father Babcock was the *last* subject she wished to discuss right now. She wanted to hurl all her pain and humiliation at her husband and watch him fumble with it. Instead, she asked, "And? Did he?"

He swept his hat from his head, disrupting his neat hair. His grip crushed the woollen fabric as he pressed the back of his knuckles to his mouth. He peered at her over the black brim, and her fervent wish for him to go and swim naked in a barrel of crabs wavered. He looked as though he were about to tell her that the hull had been torn open and the ship was about to be lost. Just what had he discovered?

Seamus's breath exploded from him. "Christ, Grace. He tried to murder us—and somehow, Silverton's hand is in this."

She staggered back a step. *No! Not possible.* He drew before her, his long, warm fingers catching her elbow and anchoring the moving world beneath her feet.

This news should have negated her anger at Seamus, but, instead, her hatred of Silverton squeezed alongside the rage in her chest, crushing the breath from her lungs.

Her words came out in stuttering gasps. "I gave you my trust. Yet you invited a murdering priest aboard without informing me. And now you tell me Silverton's behind it all?"

"Grace, I—"

She snatched back her elbow. "When your decisions involve our daughter, I expect—no, *demand*—to be kept appraised." Her voice warbled on the edge of tears.

"Emily wasn't even born—"

"You *can't* control every eventuality, Seamus. How do I trust you now?"

"For crying out loud, Grace. It's my duty to provide for and protect my family." He threw his hat upon the table that she had laid for tea earlier. The black hat upended one of her best china teacups, bell shaped and creamy-yellow. His long fingers curled over a chairback. "I made a poor effort of this back in London after retiring from the navy—I meant for this voyage to redeem myself in your eyes." His face paled, except for two pink spots high on his cheeks, a sure sign he was more upset than angry.

But she was upset, too—she was damned if he should suffer it alone. "I've *never* questioned your honour, no matter how bloody-minded it made you."

Bony knuckles rapping hard on the cabin door interrupted them.

"Enter," called Seamus, straightening up.

Sorensen thrust Father Babcock through the door. The priest's bulging eyes gave him the look of a panicked, hairless rat. Grace's irritation prickled at the beak-nosed priest polluting her home once again. Catching sight of her, Babcock squeaked and crossed his hands across his sagging, sodden underwear.

"Thank you, Sorensen. Please wait outside," dismissed Seamus. "Right, Babcock. Start talking." Grace recognised the tone of Seamus's voice—Babcock was headed towards an inter-rogation that would rival the Spanish Inquisition.

Emily dropped her toy cat and lunged over the side of the basket to reach it. Tipping, the basket emptied her onto the floor with a wooden slap. Her slow wail built to a healthy crescendo. Grace scooped her into a hug, nibbling at her soft, warm neck to distract her from her tears.

"Not with *her* unashamedly ogling my nakedness." Babcock attempted an air of nonchalance.

Shifting a sniffling Emily over her shoulder, Grace turned her head from the nefarious urine-soaked napkin that competed with Babcock's fetid stink of fear. She snatched the grey ship's blanket from Emily's basket and threw it at him. "I know your sordid truth, Father. That the mission was but a ruse." She glared at the priest, desperate for answers.

"Speak or I'll chain you to the bilge pump for the remainder of the journey." Seamus's voice was hard and unforgiving. "You barely survived in a comfortable berth with a doctor to hand—you won't survive down there for long."

Cloaking his bony back with the blanket, Babcock's gaze fixed hungrily on the fruitcake in the middle of the table. "I haven't eaten in days. They took all my food. I've eaten nothing but foul-tasting insects and grass." He roughly rubbed his eyelids, dragging grimy streaks down his cheeks. "Give us a slice, and I'll tell all."

Good grief! She had better tend to the coward—rally his spir-its. He looked likely to expire before they had the full tale. One-handedly hacking a quarter of the thick, moist cake, Grace dumped it on a bone-china side plate and thrust it to the edge of the table.

The skinny, drooping man stuffed giant bites of cake into his mouth with his hands, the wet snaps of his chewing plucking at her taut nerves. She slid across a cup of black tea. Babcock threw it back without first swallowing the cake. Less frenetic with food and drink in him, he shoved the cake into the pouch of his cheek, his words coming out muffled. "As I said, I was only following orders to do away with your wife."

Seamus snapped his hands behind his back. "I thought your devious plan was to do away with us all? When did you target her?"

The priest wiped his mouth with the back of his arm. "Tried several times. During the storm, I went to her cabin under the guise of prayer. Planned to make it look like an accident. An awry chest. A loose bookshelf. But God knows my own terror of dying that day overtook my senses." Babcock smacked his scabbed lips. "Then there was Hood's manservant in Montevideo. I caught him in a compromising position with a stable hand. It was easy enough to threaten to expose him. I ordered he kill you during the siege—as though a rebel had retaliated against your intervention at the fort."

"You bastard!" snarled Seamus, pressing his knuckles into the tablecloth weighed by frilly lace corners. He laughed dryly. "You clearly underestimated my wife's capabilities."

"Clearly." Babcock sucked wetly, his emaciated finger digging for cake remnants along his gumline. "Later, aboard the *Clover*, Mahlon had already developed a decent case of melancholia before I started whispering in his ear."

"He nearly killed me!" Grace scowled, fingering the bruised echoes of Mahlon's fingers around her neck.

Babcock's head whipped around to her. "Only you?"

"He assaulted Toby Hicks first." She held her glare steady

like a cobra poised to strike. "Did you order Mahlon to strangle me?"

Babcock held up a stubby-fingered hand. "Not I."

Seamus stepped over to her and pressed his arm against hers. Babcock was clearly not holding back on the truth, and the anger thrumming through her core vibrated in harmony with Seamus's. He leaned into her, his blond brows flickering when she leaned away and handed Emily a silver teaspoon to chew on.

Grace wanted to roar at the priest, but she did not wish to frighten Emily. "You've lost all your hair but none of your gall!"

Seamus glowered. "Why should we help you? After everything you've done?"

Babcock's eyes lingered on the slices of cake in the middle of the table before sliding to Seamus's face. "If you take me back to England, I'll hang."

"That's not our problem," said Seamus.

"I beg to differ, Captain. You promised Hamilton you'd see me spirited far from England. Would you risk Hamilton revoking his financial backing for my measly neck?"

Grace frowned. What knowledge did this whimpering flea have of Seamus's finances? He was likely bluffing his way out of the threat of punishment with this show of bravado.

"Very well," said Seamus. "Until I can hand you over to a passing ship, you'll be confined to quarters, Babcock." His wrist clicked. "I don't care what excuse earns you passage with them, you'll not stay aboard my ship a minute longer than is necessary."

Seamus's glare frosted like a winter snap, and a shiver of confusion feathered the hairs on Grace's arms. That was it? He was giving in to the priest's demands?

Babcock rubbed his grubby hand across his scabbed scalp. "We have a deal, Captain."

"Wait. What of Silverton's involvement?" asked Grace.

Babcock shifted his militant gaze over to Seamus. "One

afternoon, as I awaited a meeting with Colonel Hamilton, I over-heard him speaking with Lord Silverton, who seemed interested in your movements and your commitment to this voyage. Hamilton became agitated with the line of questioning, but when his lordship threatened to withhold his investment, Hamilton conceded."

"Conceded to what?" asked Seamus.

Babcock shrugged his bony shoulders. "I only caught the tail end of their conversation. Didn't care for details, as long as Colonel Hamilton delivered on his promise to see me safely away from England."

"What else?" Grace demanded.

"I heard my own name mentioned but presumed I was a lowly pawn in a bigger game."

Seamus inhaled deeply. "So, Silverton knew about you?"

"Only by name, as far as I could tell."

Grace was smugly satisfied as Babcock withered under Seamus's stoicism.

"I doubt that," said Seamus dryly. "What else?"

"Th-that's all I know."

Grace drew her shoulders back. Had Seamus's meeting with Hamilton really been all business? It had clearly pushed her husband into a decision about himself—but it also set the stage for events that affected her. Yet, he had not granted her a chance to arbitrate in her own fate. Again!

"Did you not meet Silverton?" asked Seamus.

Babcock shook his head. "Colonel Hamilton has one door into his rooms on Regent Street and another out. None of his acquaintances ever meet. I didn't care to be introduced to his lordship. He had an impudent drawl. Enough to make one's ears bleed."

Much like your sermons then, mused Grace humourlessly. Her mind raced over all the possibilities of what Silverton could be up to. Was his depravity so deep he would see himself profoundly out of pocket just to ruin the life she was trying to build with Seamus? And what hold did he have on Hamilton? A slow-sinking dread deadened her legs.

Seamus yanked open the door and summoned Sorensen to take Babcock away. The door closed, and he leaned back against it, warily watching Grace from afar.

"I'm not sure what just happened," she said stiffly.

He took several steps towards her, his long legs lithe and sure-footed on the rolling deck. "I'm but a man—with many failings. But I'm sure of one thing, Grace—I love you."

No. His biggest failing was never letting her words through that naval façade of his—it was as wretchedly impenetrable as the *Clover*'s elm hull. "Then *show* me by entrusting me with what's going on beneath that granite skull of yours." Grace jabbed a finger to her forehead.

"It's not that I don't trust you."

"Afford me *some* consideration—share what's in your heart. Some days I swear I'm nothing more than a warm body in your bed."

"That's untrue!"

Oh, that struck a nerve. Good! Grace lowered Emily into her basket again. "As I assured Captain Fincham all those years ago, I'll not be wilting or expiring on your watch. So, *trust me.*"

Seamus scraped back a chair and dropped into it. He laid his palms on the table. "Back in London, I had several setbacks that needed remedy. I believed this expedition to be the cure-all."

"Then why are you letting Babcock go? Isn't he the key to unlocking all this madness?"

Seamus's jaw stiffened and he tilted his face down, his fingers curling. "I can't dishonour my agreement with Hamilton." Raising his chin slowly, he fixed his gaze on Grace. "I can't afford to."

Her heart thumped guiltily in her chest. He looked... broken. Swaying closer to him, she resisted curling her hand over his broad shoulder. "I knew you were hurting, but Uncle Farfar told me it wasn't my place to heal your injured character. He said you needed to find your own way in the world again."

He blew out a slow breath. "As a navy man, my path was paved before me. I knew my place and where I fitted. But outside of this, I was... I am..." He bounced a clenched fist lightly on his chin.

"Lost?" she finished.

His shoulders sagged. "Yes. I was."

"And now?"

"Now, I'm learning to live with regret." He scratched one eyebrow with his thumb. "For not refusing Father Babcock passage when every instinct I owned cautioned me against it. For backing myself into a financial pickle. For not sharing my burden with you." He lifted his head as though it were filled with wet sand. His hand reached towards her. "Because heaven knows I could have done with the easing of it."

His declaration melted her icy resolve like a sugar cube in hot tea. Grace shuffled into the curl of his embrace. He drew her in tighter, lowering her to his lap, his ear pressed against her breast. She wrapped her arms around his head, her fingers playing with the silky strands of his hair. This always soothed him.

His words were muffled. "I didn't want to burden you after... losing the babe. And I truly believed all was in hand. Plus, I had Admiral Baxter's confidence."

Grace played with the smile on her lips, offering him another line from that long-ago conversation in the *Discerning*'s great cabin. "Well, I suspect we've already survived the worst this ship has to offer."

He tilted his face up, the growth of his chin rasping on her cotton bodice. "I hope you're right. Forgive me, Dulcinea."

Decision swelled in Grace's chest like the bulging ribs of a fermenting whisky keg. If she held on to the sooty residue of hurt and betrayal, she risked bursting with frustration—who knew what might be said then. The close confines of the ship would afford no escape for either of them. Her hatred of Silverton had taught her that the only person it hurt to hold onto resentment was herself. If she could show *that* bastard mercy, then surely she could forgive the man who safeguarded her soul?

Cupping his face, she kissed him. His mouth was warm and reassuring, full of new promises and absolution.

A COUPLE OF MONTHS LATER, Seamus once again navigated through the Straits of Magellan, documenting new islands and sections of seabed that he had not charted on his last voyage in these waters.

An American private merchant, the *Gannet*, dropped anchor alongside to exchange news and trade wine, tea, sugar, and tobacco with the *Clover*. The American captain, Gregory Chittenden, told Seamus he was heading to California to collect a shipment of furs bound for Boston, but not before he ferried the Reverend Walter Laurel to the established mission on the tropical shores of Tahiti.

Would ridding the *Clover* of the priest guarantee the safety of his ship and his crew? Although it did not prick his conscience one iota to keep Babcock detained in a cabin for the remaining years of the voyage, off-loading the irksome fool now at least meant one less mouth to feed. Would Grace also not be safer once they arrived back in London if Silverton believed his plan foiled and his minion dead? He arranged a passenger transfer for that afternoon.

Below in the gunroom, Seamus ordered Babcock to gather his meagre belongings, shooting down the priest's objection to being offloaded on a strange ship this far south.

"If you don't come above for a proper introduction to

Reverend Laurel, I'll dump you ashore to fend for yourself," Seamus growled.

"Y-you promised you'd see me safely delivered," said Babcock in a snivelling voice. "You can't give my real name, or Hamilton will find me."

Seamus inhaled deeply. "Then how shall I introduce you?"

"Um… as H-Harrington. Father Harrington."

Seamus sighed. "Very well, *Father Harrington*. I'm sure that without any papers to prove otherwise, you'll be able to spin your web of lies."

Babcock's belligerent silence was a blessing. Seamus emerged from the main hatch, turning as he heard the priest gasp behind him.

"Dear God in heaven. It reeks of rotting meat!" Babcock's patchy-lashed eyelids expanded. Not all his lashes had grown back. Seamus swivelled to study the schooner. The white sails were neatly furled. She might stink like carrion begging for a decent burial, but she was a tidy vessel.

Babcock stumbled forward a few steps, his baggy eyelids wrinkling in the sharp light. "Oh, my blessed hat, that smell will send me to an early death."

Seamus drew alongside Captain Chittenden, who matched his height but not his breadth.

"How long before you make your way back to Boston, Captain Chittenden?" asked Seamus. The man had the snowiest shock of hair that had nothing to do with age. It shone like the glistening back of the white whale Seamus had seen breach a few weeks before. A most peculiar colour indeed.

"'Tis a three-year round trip," drawled Chittenden, his Bostonian accent dropping the r from the end of year. "But this'll be my last. I'm selling this old tub for a packet. Going to try my hand at the opium run."

Seamus nodded. "A lucrative endeavour if you have the

contacts." He clasped his hands behind his back. "I appreciate you taking another passenger."

"What's another clergyman when I'm already transporting one?" Chittenden chuckled.

Seamus bit down hard on his back teeth as the Reverend Walter Laurel glided towards Babcock with barely a ripple in his black robes. It was almost as though he were floating—a sharp contrast to Babcock's clomping feet.

"Ah, Captain Fitzwilliam, and who might this be?" Laurel smiled serenely. From the corner of his eye, Seamus caught Babcock's lips part.

"Reverend Laurel, may I introduce Father Martin Harrington," said Seamus.

"The pleasure is all mine." Laurel beamed. "A crying shame, Father Harrington, about your unfortunate circumstances." He peered down his long, straight nose.

"Eh?" Babcock scowled, shooting Seamus a barbarous glare.

"With the natives. At Port Famine?" Laurel elaborated, waving a long-fingered hand.

"Oh, that," mumbled Babcock, his brow unrumpling.

Laurel smiled. "You'll find the natives in Tahiti agreeable and quite amenable to spiritual teachings. The village is well established. Our barn is set up for threshing and winnowing our grain and corn."

"And didn't you tell me there's even a blacksmith's forge?" Chittenden inclined his snowy head.

"There is indeed," enthused Laurel.

"Praise be!" Babcock shuffled his feet, his eagerness growing with every promising feature Laurel described about the village.

"And of course, no village would be complete without a cricket pitch, now, would it?" The reverend's warm gaze panned over Babcock's glistening face.

"A cricket pitch!" Babcock's usually grey, dour face flushed.

"Indeed. The London Missionary Society likes to keep things as civilised as possible."

Babcock beamed at Laurel, the zeal in his eye matching that of the taller priest. "'Tis our duty to wage a spiritual war against all who have not discovered the state of grace."

"I couldn't agree more." Laurel nodded sagely.

"You know, when I... when Father Babcock—God rest his soul—and I were attacked at St Martin's by spears and stones, I felt myself to be God's warrior, at war with the sins of ignorance and greed."

Babcock's words were like hot coals upon the fire of Laurel's enthusiasm. "I'm sure you both fought bravely, Father Harrington. If you'd had a real army of Christian soldiers at your back, you no doubt could've achieved great things that day."

"Yes!" Spittle sprayed from between Babcock's teeth. "I'm so glad you understand."

Kindred spirits, the both of them, thought Seamus mulishly, focussing on the schooner. A much better view than the evangelical efforts of these two pillow thumpers.

"Sounds like a remarkable setup, hey Fitzwilliam?" Chittenden asked.

Seamus swung his gaze back and nodded stiffly. "Indeed. Sounds as though an enchanter has planted a little piece of home there with the wave of his wand."

Babcock's scoff made Seamus glance down. "Such blasphemy, sir! 'Tis the *Creator* who has provided, not some wand-waving heretic."

Seamus held Babcock's gaze with aloofness. The bald priest blinked and looked away. "I trust you're happy to become a passenger aboard the *Gannet*, Father? Now that you've laid Father Babcock to rest?"

The priest rolled his shoulders and glued his eyes back on Seamus.

Ha! Bastard did not trust Seamus not to spoil his chance of escape. Coughing, Seamus cleared the laughter in his throat.

Babcock intertwined his stubbled knuckles before him and adopted a reverent tone. "If the good reverend can find it in his heart to offer me a place at his mission, then yes, I'd very much like to leave the *Clover*. Have you written to Colonel Hamilton advising him of poor Father Babcock's demise?"

Seamus nodded stiffly and held out the sealed packet. "I have."

Babcock snatched the sealed letter with the same fervour used when ramming fruitcake into his mouth after his rescue. "I'll be sure to pass on this tragic news to London."

"I'm sure you will, Father Harrington. I'm sure you will," said Seamus.

The fawning little man did not deserve this decent hand, but Seamus was not sorry to see him go. Good riddance!

Chapter Nineteen

G race stared at the slow, fat raindrops pattering against the round brass scuttles like thrown pellets. The warmer clime of the South Pacific made a delightful change to the wintery bite of the South American archipelago. Not even a few days of rain could spoil her mood. She knew Seamus was well pleased with this part of the journey. The ease of hopping from island to island in the Pacific and noting which of them delivered precious supplies, such as fresh water and edible wildlife, had him in his element.

Like a topman on watch combing the horizon for the umpteenth time, Grace gazed at Emily asleep in her little berth. Carpenter James had torn out one of the large wardrobes in their cabin and enclosed a small, raised bunk. Above was Emily's bed, and below was a safe place for her to play without being underfoot.

The French polish of the writing bureau gleamed with the

gloss of well-buffed silver. Grace jiggled open the narrow wooden drawer and scooped out a pile of Uncle Farfar's letters, delivered by passing ships since the start of the *Clover*'s voyage four years back. Chips of red wax crumbled from the long-broken seals, speckling the desktop. She drew the lamp nearer, the thick honey-yellow whale oil swilling inside. Shuffling the letters into the order in which they were written, she began to re-read them for the dozenth time.

H.M. Dockyard, Chatham
1 September 1833

My most darling Grace,

What adventures! What excitement! I have read your letters so many times I know them by heart. They are so familiar to me now, I often confuse them with my own memories. I apologise for not writing sooner, but it is challenging sending letters after a ship that never rests! No doubt this letter will have been traded back and forth between many a passing ship before arriving in your lovely hands.

Your letters bring me such joy to hear news of your little one. The portrait Dr Sykes sketched of you and Emily is one of my prized possessions. The man is a magnificent artist. He captured your likeness so vividly. Emily's angelic face certainly takes after yours. And those curls! A true delight! It warms my heart immeasurably to know you and your family are well. And these qualities are doubled by her good fortune at being born with a caul—the girl simply cannot go wrong!

However, your recount of the storm in which your ship and your life were nearly lost does leave me wondering whether having a babe at the mercy of the ocean is sensible? I shudder to think what might have become of little Emily if she had already been born when you were caught in that tempest. There comes a time in life, poppet, where one has to consider others before one's self, and this proves truest when one becomes a parent. I know I am in no position to lecture you on the virtues of being a good parent; my own actions negate that privilege. However, should you decide to return home to England with little Emily while Seamus continues his expedition, I will happily care for you.

"I know you will, Uncle Farfar," murmured Grace. "But we're staying put." She peeled back the page with a papery crackle to expose the second letter.

H.M. Dockyard, Chatham
9 October 1834

What a turn of events with Darcy. He is a prime example that fealty is a human trait that can transcend any social barrier. It appears the man has his work cut out for him after the murder of poor Father Babcock at Port Famine! I hope Darcy will be able to redirect his new kin from their grievous ways.

Grace's gut tightened as she scoured Uncle Farfar's words in response to the stretched truth she had sent him. She had not dared tell him that Babcock was alive, for fear of her packet being intercepted in London like last time. Goodness knew what Silverton was up to—undoubtedly something unwholesome. Seamus had scribed that letter to Hamilton, advising him of Babcock's demise, and she thought it best that her correspondence reflect the same tale. She loosened her grip on the letter and continued to read.

I am pleased to hear that you carry a pistol for protection. If your husband has faith that you are capable of protecting your-self in this manner, then who am I to argue?
 In the case of Mahlon, it goes to show you cannot be too

careful or trusting. This bears repeating, and I shall not raise it again, but I am now unsure whether a ship is an appropriate environment in which to raise a daughter. By your accounts, Emily appears quite a wayward little thing—wearing trousers like a boy and scampering up rigging like a monkey, even if she is secured to a maintopman by a rope. Although I do not doubt the vastness of the education she is receiving while discovering the world, I cannot help but worry that she will lack the etiquette and decorum required of a young lady when you return to London. As her mother, I trust you will educate her in the finer nuances of life too?

"Yes, Uncle Farfar." Grace tittered. "I'll teach our Em how to sip tea like a lady. And how to cross her ankles but never her legs." She turned to a new letter, skimming to the paragraph that flipped her stomach each time she read it.

Wallace House, Mayfair, London
12 June 1835

I wish to advise you of some events that, while they happened some time ago, I have refrained from telling you for fear of upsetting you too much. Please forgive my silence on this matter, but I have been torn as to whether it should wait until your return.

I am so sorry, poppet—Lord and Lady Flint have both died. Lord Flint took his own life with his pistol. Lady Flint found him in his library. While those two undeniably had an unconventional marriage, it cannot be said that your mother did not love my brother, because she collapsed upon finding him and never recovered. She slipped away in her sleep.

As it turns out, although you were removed from their will after they disowned you, I was left as sole beneficiary to their estate. I was quite surprised that my brother had not followed

*through with his threat to remove me too. So, I am now living
in Wallace House. I hope this news is not too upsetting for you,
truly I do. I must confess, writing this, a weight of responsibility has lifted from my shoulders.*

Time and distance had helped alleviate the pain of parting
from her mother and the man who raised her as a father, but
news of their demise left her feeling uncomfortably guilty that
she had not been there. Her shame did not make sense. Why
should she feel remorse at their passing when they had treated
her so cruelly her whole life? Swallowing the thickening in her
throat, Grace continued reading.

*In another surprising turn of events, your young acquaintance,
Miss McGilney, appeared on my doorstep looking for work.
Chaplain Agutter from the orphans' asylum encouraged
McGilney to seek employment elsewhere so that he could make
way in his house for another of his urchins. McGilney is a
lively enough lass, and she has proven to be a hard worker. I
needed a housekeeper, and she has easily mastered all that
goes into running a large household such as Wallace House.
We still have old Mrs MacDougall in the kitchen. She is a
cantankerous she-devil—but, by God, can she cook!*

Grace smiled at the familiar names of the servants. She
closed her eyes, picturing Sally McGilney walking the halls of
Wallace House. It had stopped being home long ago, but the
thought of the place filled with people she so dearly loved left
her with a satisfying warmth. Opening her eyes, Grace turned to
the final page.

*If I had not travelled the world myself and borne witness to the
wonders out there, your tales of erupting volcanoes and
ground-shattering earthquakes would have sounded like fiction*

to me. The west coast of South America is undoubtedly untamed and fraught with many dangers. I know many months will have passed since you were caught in the earthquake in Chile, but the notion of you being trapped in the city by the devastation chilled my blood. Thank God you all escaped unharmed.

I sensed your pride in setting up a tent hospital and caring for the sick and injured alongside Dr Sykes and ship's surgeon Beynon. Your recount of the massive destruction around you was vivid and raw. I am suitably impressed you were able to save the man who lost his leg. I too have experience in trying to save a man who lost his leg to a cannonball. There was so much blood, and the poor wretch screamed himself to death. He certainly did not go peacefully. It is an image that, even after all these years, still haunts my memories. I am glad the outcome of your patient was so favourable.

Promise me you will always use that head of yours to keep you and your family out of harm's way. I read these words and laugh! This is a warning I should bestow upon your husband— to keep you safe—but I thought it better you hear the plea directly from an old man who has seen how easily life can go awry when the proper precautions are not taken. On that note, I shall keep you in my prayers and wish you fair winds and calm seas as you continue your voyage. And poppet, please do keep your letters coming.

Affectionately always your Uncle Farfar,
Admiral Arthur J. Baxter

Chapter Twenty

GALAPAGOS ISLANDS, PACIFIC OCEAN, 15
SEPTEMBER 1836

Seamus squinted at the albatrosses, petrels, and gulls screeching and swarming around the sails of the *Clover*, their fluttering bodies blocking the sun.

"Up please, Cappy!" Beside Seamus, Emily stretched up on her four-year-old toes, straining to peer over the taffrail at the approaching island. Her pet hen, Petal, was tucked securely under one arm.

"At your service, milady." Picking her up, Seamus shook his head good-humouredly at the inventive name his young daughter had given him. It was not until he had heard her mimicking the sailors that he understood she was trying to say *Captain*. Seamus had encouraged her to call him Papa, but his daughter seemed determined to address him the same as the others.

Emily's grubby bare feet curled around his waist like a lemur clinging to a tree. He tickled Petal under her chin, and the hen craned her feathered neck to give him better access. It took Seamus all his powers of persuasion to convince Emily that at night, Petal was safest tucked in the henhouse with her feathered companions instead of in her berth. Carpenter James had created comfortable living quarters for the hens, since eggs were precious to all aboard. Though he knew the *Clover* could be guaranteed no eggs for at least a week after any decent squall.

"Pooh! What's that smell, Cappy?" Emily wrinkled her button nose. Seamus swallowed deeply against the thick, powerful reek. "It's like dead crab but worser."

He laughed as he readjusted Emily on his hip. "That, our Em, is the stink of whalers. See those ships over there?" He pointed at several nondescript two- and three-masted ships anchored in the bay. He swore the chicken's beady eyes darted across the water with interest, as though hopeful that the white sails were in fact fat, white grubs.

Whalers were always easily identified by their cranes and boats and by their stumped topgallant masts. For the most part, he thought they had a slovenly look about them, with their slack rigging, worn-off paint, and untidy rope binding. He frowned at the sailors wandering about the deck without much order to them. They looked more like blasted farmers who had just stepped from the countryside, he thought. Despite the eyesore, he knew there to be no better seamen than the masters of whalers when it came to handling a ship and skilful navigation.

Aware of Emily's unworldliness, he elaborated, "They catch whales!"

"Why?" Emily pinched her nose.

"We need their oil for our lanterns and candles and soap. Their bones are used as stays in corsets and as handles for whips and umbrellas." He tapped the chicken's soft red comb. "Just as we use feathers for our pillows."

Emily kissed the chicken on the head. "Mamam doesn't like corsets."

Seamus smiled at Emily's maternal term of endearment, and he winked at Grace beside him as Emily prattled on, "They're squishy!"

"They are indeed!" Grace agreed.

He tweaked Emily's nose. "Pop Petal back in her pen, and run along with Mamam. We'll be in company soon. I'd like you looking like a respectable young lady and not like a mucky little monkey." He nuzzled his nose into his daughter's soft, damp neck, and she squealed.

"I's climb like a monkey!"

"I know you do, my darling, but now is the time for washing and dressing, not climbing."

Emily tipped her cheek towards the hen. "Kisses, Petal."

As though on command, the hen pecked at her earlobe. She hunched her shoulder and giggled. Seamus did not have the heart to point out that the chicken was merely taking an opportunistic peck at a freckle. What was the harm that she believed the creature kissed her on demand? He lowered her to the deck.

Emily set Petal down. "Come, Petal." His daughter set off towards the forecastle and, like a feathered dog, the hen gave a delighted squawk and faithfully darted after her, its long talons tapping the wooden deck. Seamus was amused by his daughter's obsession with the hen but more so by the hen's reciprocation. Trust Emily to discover the most loyal chicken in the world. Just as well she did not have the whole hen house under her spell. One feathered fiend soiling his clean decks with its green-and-white calling cards was enough.

At the helm, Barry Johns gripped the wheel with white-lipped concentration as he guided the *Clover* into the harbour. The anchor splashed, and Seamus ordered the cutter to be lowered, turning a blind eye as several of the men scurried back to their berths to fill their pockets with tobacco to barter with the locals. He tasked the first crew of five with filling the empty water casks. Once the first lot of passengers had been deposited, he watched the returning rowboat a moment longer before heading below.

In the great cabin, Emily hummed softly while Grace stripped her down before the tall washstand. Seamus breathed in the homely aromas of the liquorice pomfret cake, citrus bergamot soap, and lavender powder. Emily's face twisted with curiosity. "Cappy, are there turtesses on this island?"

He bit back a laugh. "I think you mean tortoises?"

"Yes, turtesses. Can I ride them?" Emily's skin glowed pink from its scrubbing as Grace slipped her shift over her unruly mop of curls.

"Yes, they're big enough to ride."

Emily's excited grin disappeared behind her starched petticoat as Grace slid it over her shoulders. She tied it off at the waist. Next came Emily's favourite red dress, scattered with a pattern of golden feathers.

"I'm going to ride the turtesses." Emily stuck her jaw out determinedly. Grace turned Emily around again to tie the high-waisted sash at the back.

"We'll see about that," said Grace, sliding him a side look. She brushed out the tight twists of Emily's hair, splitting a parting down the middle. Seamus sat on a stool, appreciating the nimbleness of Grace's fingers as she expertly plaited two braids. She looped the braids together and fastened them with a white ribbon. She had always been good with the ropes.

Turning Emily by her shoulders, Grace dipped her chin. "Don't pull your ribbon out."

Seamus smiled as Emily's shining blue eyes assessed him. "You won't mess your pretty hair, will you?" He held his arms out, and she toddled over.

"No, Cappy."

He knew no matter how her fingers itched to pull out her ribbon, her wayward locks would remain fastened. She might be a little tear-around, but she *was* obedient.

A square brick of a man met them at the end of the long pier. The golden beach alongside was tinged by an olive-green mineral. Grace stood behind Seamus, holding Emily's hand. He scanned the rocky domes of the volcanic island, several of which had their tops hidden in the low cloud. Emily stooped to pick up a grey lump of rock with a mesmerising sapphire sheen, and he smiled at the thought of the rock joining her growing collection.

Seamus inclined his head at the man. "Captain Seamus Fitzwilliam, commander of the explorer, *Clover*."

The man's clean-shaven face accentuated his hard eyes. He had a squat, short neck with a roll of skin protruding over the back of his tight collar. "Colin Lawrence, acting governor and penal colony prison warden of the Galapagos." Lawrence smiled mildly. His gawkish gaze flicked over to Emily, and he broke into an enthusiastic grin.

Seamus spotted Grace's fingers firm around Emily's.

"And who do we have here then?" A grey front tooth marred Lawrence's oily smile.

"Emily Elizabeth Fitzwilliam," offered Emily formally. "I'm four."

"Well, Miss Emily, the pleasure is all mine." The warden bowed, but Grace's eyes shifted uncomfortably to Seamus and she scooped Emily up.

"Mr Lawrence, we've been told there are giant tortoises on your island. Is this correct?" Grace asked. He placed his hand in the small of her stiff back as she pressed her hip into his.

Colin Lawrence hesitated a beat, some of the warmth sliding from his eyes before he broke out his sardonic grin again. "Indeed, there are! I'll show you them myself."

Seamus's stomach flipped coldly at Grace's tone. "We wouldn't want to keep you from your business, Mr Lawrence. We'll find our way around."

Seamus did not like the way Lawrence tipped his head,

shrewdly eyeing Grace. "Won't want to do that, Mrs Fitzwilliam. This island is a penal colony. Dangerous men live here."

Seamus studied the half-dozen men who were unloading his survey equipment. Heavens above! The only discernment between prison guard and prisoner was that the guards had boots on their feet. All appeared equally miserable. He turned his attention to a lone guard who gripped a coarse rope attached to a square-headed dog. The dog's tan hide quivered and it flattened its ears against its head, intently inspecting the new arrivals.

"Surely you keep your prisoners locked up, Mr Lawrence?" Seamus pressed his elbow against his hip to check that his knife was there.

Lawrence tipped his head back, guffawing. "We do indeed have locked buildings, sir. But 'tis the warders who lock themselves in at night—for their own safety, of course."

What the devil? A knot of concern pulled Seamus's brows together. "Are your prisoners not detained at all?"

"No. Therefore, as a matter of safety, your men are forbidden to sell or barter any knives or weapons with the prisoners."

"Where do they sleep? How do you maintain law and order?" The same discomfort he had seen on Grace's face a moment ago now slithered down his own nape.

"In groves and rocky outcrops. Some opt to camp with the whalers, though God knows the stink of those men is enough to make any man prefer sleeping with the flamingos." Lawrence gave a disinterested wave towards a flock of vibrant pink birds wading in the shallows further along the shore. Most stood with one pink leg tucked up tightly, while others dipped their long, curved necks below the water surface, foraging upside down. Their honks were not unlike geese. Seamus swung his attention back to Lawrence.

"Any prisoner who steps out of line feels the end of this." With a flick of his wrist, Lawrence's riding crop snapped into his thick fist. "Any further insolence earns them an intimate inspection of *this*." He seized the ivory handle of his pistol and pressed it to the head of a passing prisoner. The weather-beaten prisoner froze, his eyelids twitching closed.

Seamus's blood pounded in his ears as he slid Grace behind him. Beneath his damp palm, he felt Emily's stocky leg tighten its grip around Grace.

"Holster your weapon this instant! My wife and daughter are present, man! Are you expecting unrest?"

Lawrence's glare sliced across the quaking prisoner. Unhurriedly, he slipped his pistol back into his belt. At the stinging flick of the crop, the prisoner scurried off. "My prisoners are but a handful of dissidents—foolish soldiers captured after yet *another* unsuccessful coup on the mainland." Laurence sized Seamus up, the air thick with tension.

Blustering buffoon—flaunting an air of authority he did not possess!

Laurence ran a finger beneath his nose, sniffing. "There's nothing to say these men don't have murder in them. A few months back, a handful of them stole a boat at night and boarded a brig in the harbour. Fortunately, some might say, they sent the captain and hands ashore in their boat before making out to sea." He flicked his head at the *Clover* bobbing peacefully at anchor. "Might want to keep a bright watch aboard your vessel at all times."

Seamus could not blame the poor fellows with the likes of *him* in charge. "I have the safety of my vessel well in hand, thank you, Mr Lawrence," he said dryly.

With a nonchalant shrug, Lawrence's demeanour switched back to hospitable host. "Where are my manners? Would you like to visit my tortoises, Miss Emily?"

"Yes, please!" Emily squirmed to be put down, and Lawrence offered her his hand.

Seamus's fist curled as the thick-set man lead his daughter away. He beckoned for Blight and O'Malley to accompany them, and he hooked his arm around Grace's back, hoping to ease her worry.

The warden led them into a clearing and past a couple of encampments. From the odorous stench, it was clear these were whalers' tents. Emily pinched her nose again.

A man with a worn leather hat jammed on his head sat stoking a nearby campfire. He grinned, waving good-naturedly at Emily. "Howdy, little lady." He pulled his beaten hat off, exposing spiky brown hair. Emily released her nose to wave back at the friendly-faced man, whose eyes crinkled with humour. Seamus noted the man wore shoes, and he rolled his neck in relief. Not a prisoner then.

On the outskirts of the clearing, Emily squealed as a giant tortoise loped towards a tuft of grass. Releasing Lawrence's hand, Emily ran towards the gargantuan tortoise, the back of its shell level with her chest. Grace gasped as Emily bolted, and she took a hurried step. Seamus tightened his arm around her waist, gently holding her back. She frowned as he lowered his mouth to her ear.

"Let her be. She won't come to any harm." His wife's brow quivered indecisively. Seamus whispered, "I promise."

Grace leaned into his embrace and together they walked to where Emily had both her hands on the tortoise's shell, her fingers curiously outlining the square plates on its carapace. His daughter's azure eyes sparkled. "Oh Cappy! Mamam! Can I ride him? Please!" Despite her impassioned plea, Seamus hesitated as the tortoise's long, leathery neck extended an extraordinary way from its shell. It snapped at a mouthful of grass, slimy remnants staining its mouth green. The docile creature eyed him with its beady, watering eye. He had not heard of anyone succumbing to a tortoise bite.

Before he could reply, Lawrence said, "Of course you may! Tortoises are perfectly harmless." He scanned the thicket nearby.

"Satan's boar, on the other hand, is another story." He gripped Emily's torso.

Grace stiffened, and Seamus stepped forward, his hand pressing Lawrence's forearm. "Allow me, sir. She's my daughter after all." Lawrence hesitated. Seamus curled his fingers tighter, and the warden's hands slid away from Emily. Seamus swallowed dryly and scooped up his daughter. She perched happily atop the tortoise, giggling as it waddled a few steps towards a fresh clump of grass.

Scouring the nearby brush, he kept his ears pricked for any snorts or snuffles.

Chapter Twenty-One

Grace spent the night back on the *Clover* with Seamus and Emily. Emily was disappointed not to be camping with her beloved tortoises nearby, but Seamus had put his foot down, and Grace concurred—the notion of camping alongside unrestrained prisoners was too ludicrous to entertain. She had seen several large tortoises roaming the wilds of the island, and she had promised her daughter that in the month Seamus was due to survey the islands around Galapagos, she could revisit them.

She lay awake, listening to Emily's soft snores. The curtains of the stern windows were drawn. She curled into her husband's firm body as he moulded around her back. His arm draped heavy and comforting across her shoulder, his fingertips twirling her wedding ring. His light touch trailed the length of her arm, and he softly swept aside her hair to expose her neck, his stubbled lips kissing her as he inhaled. A shimmer of pleasure rippled across her décolletage.

"You smell like a field in spring," he murmured against her skin.

She hummed, wriggling her bottom into him. Her pleasure sobered as a dark thought invaded her mind. She rolled over. "Seamus?"

"Mmm?" His warm lips were distracting as they moved down her neck.

"Do you think it's too dangerous for Emily to be aboard the *Clover* with us?"

He lifted his head. "Where's this coming from?"

"Today, on the island, whenever Colin Lawrence touched Emily, I was overwhelmed by a sense of foreboding, like something bad was going to happen." She swallowed audibly. "I couldn't shake the feeling. I still can't."

Seamus hugged her tighter, his voice vibrating through his chest and into hers. "When you first told me that Emily was on her way, I was trapped between feeling as mighty as a lion and as helpless as a tortoise on its back. Despite my strong sword arm and straight shot, I knew I would be unable to shadow her my whole life. Neither of us can." His moon-blue gaze lured her in. "You're a wonderful mother." He cupped her face, his long thumb gently stroking the arc of her eyebrow. "Don't doubt that for a moment."

Grace gripped his hand to her cheek. "Sometimes I feel so afraid for her I can hardly breathe."

"Me too, Dulcinea." She savoured the comfort in his voice. "Me too."

"Why must there be such evil people in the world? I want our daughter to grow up fearless, and discover this wondrous world in which we live. But when I think of Babcock, and Mahlon, and Silver—" Seamus pressed a finger to her lips. It smelled familiarly of brass polish from his surveying equipment.

"Knowing fear is important. It's what sharpens our wits. Alerts us to danger. Fear can be the greatest teacher in life."

"I know, but she's still so young, so vulnerable. I want her to have more time before she learns the true measure of the world."

"Emily doesn't only have a mother and a father to guard and guide her, but a ship full of fierce protectors too."

"Well, when you put it that way." She traced a finger down his pulsing neck.

Seamus's eyes burned intelligently in the lantern light. "When we speak, it's as though I'm conversing with my own soul." His words flowed over her, calming her fears and filling her heart. "I want to be a better man because of you. A better father. Man wasn't intended to be alone, and I thank Christ every day for giving me you." His unconcealed longing guided her towards him like the far-off beam of a lighthouse on a cloudy night. "The intimacy of my eyes is for you and you alone."

He leaned in, kissing her with a passion that sent tingles to her toes. She had a good one here. Loyal husband. Devoted father. Dependable captain. She squirmed beneath him, the glow of his desire illuminating the way to him.

IT RAINED FOR SEVERAL DAYS, so it was not until the first sunny day that Grace made for shore with Emily and a small army in tow. Toby Hicks, Jim Buchanan, and Ben Blight had muskets slung over their shoulders as between them they juggled the picnic basket, a small wooden fold-out table, and a couple of tri-legged stools. Grace adjusted the leather musket strap on her shoulder. Seamus had left that morning in a cutter to survey the island's rugged coastline, which meant he was not there to stop her bringing the weapon along. But she was fast regretting the decision to carry the blazing heavy thing this far. The ache in her shoulder was almost not worth the effort, especially with her personal guard to hand. She should have opted for a pistol instead.

With Seamus's uncanny knack of direction, Emily confidently marched past the whalers' camps to the far side of the clearing. Three giant tortoises milled around the edge of the brush, and she raced up to them. Two of the tortoises withdrew into their shells, and she stumbled to a halt. She whipped her head around, the whites of her eyes flaring.

"Their heads fell off!" Her face scrunched, tears trailing down her rosy cheeks.

Ben reached her first, his red-bearded face grinning sympathetically. He dropped to his haunches, lowering the two stools he was carrying. "No, no, our Em. Look, they're only hiding. You gave 'em a bit of a fright, is all."

Gulping back sobs, Emily scrubbed at her tears with her fingertips, painting grimy lines on her skin. Over their initial surprise, the tortoises experimentally poked their heads out to peer around. Emily clapped her hands and darted towards the nearest tortoise, slapping her palms against the uneven shell. "Hello, Mr Mountain."

Grace gauged their proximity to the whalers' camp then scanned the evenness of the ground. A few hand-sized rocks littered the ankle-length grassland. Perfect. She unslung her musket and laid it in the grass, rolling her neck to ease the twinge.

She drew some comfort in being near the whalers, even though they were strangers. Especially on an island where prisoners and wild pigs roamed free. The sound of men's voices, wood chopping, and water sloshing carried across the clearing. Grace's cheeks ignited as a near-naked man walked around the edge of the tent. It was the whaler who had waved to Emily on their first day on Floreana Island. His stride was stable and unhurried. Grace averted her head, but her eyes traitorously strayed towards him. He wore tight, white long johns that hugged his narrow hips so tightly he may as well have been wearing nothing.

She had seen many of the men shirtless in the summertime and, of course, she had seen her husband completely naked plenty of times, but something about this man held her gaze. *Have you no shame, Grace Fitzwilliam? Look away!* she scolded herself. But something about his lithe frame kept her gaze glued to him. She swallowed deeply. She was no artist, but she had the sudden and ridiculous desire to sketch the contours of his broad chest that flexed effortlessly as he scrubbed a towel across his wet hair.

At the entrance to his tent, and clearly unaware he was being ogled, the whaler slung the towel around his neck. Grace's chest tightened as he turned his back, and she deduced that whaling must be infinitely more physical than exploring. His heavily corded muscles flexed beneath his bronzed skin and disappeared into his long johns. A small sound escaped Grace's throat as the tight fabric covering his firm behind contoured even more detail when he bent to enter his tent. A heady combination of grilled meat and smoked fish wafting over from the camp caused her stomach to rumble hungrily, and she guiltily blinked at her daughter.

"Here's as good a place as any for a picnic, isn't it, Miss Empem?" said Grace, swatting away a swarm of tiny insects buzzing about her head. The air was clear after the early morning shower. The grass was still a little damp, but the bright light of the spring sunshine tried hard to dry the earth. Jim stood guard, and soon the picnic table was set with a fresh white cloth and an assortment of delicious treats Toby had gathered from Cook Phillips's galley. The ever-resourceful ship's cook had managed to barter some excellent fare from the prison guards, and the table groaned with a smoked bacon hock, a fresh orange each, fresh bread, and most indulgently, a generous pat of butter. Grace threw a muslin cloth over the food to keep the flies at bay and ambled over to where Emily was scrambling to mount the eternally patient tortoise.

Unslinging his musket, Ben swivelled his gaze about the clearing on lookout. Grace lifted Emily up for a ride. After being thoroughly amused by the tortoise for an hour, Grace declared it to be lunchtime. Despite her groans of protest, Emily slid from the mottled carapace, scurrying eagerly to the table.

"Gentleman, care to join us?" invited Grace.

The three men eyed the table longingly. "Wouldn't be right, Mrs F.," said Toby shyly.

"Nonsense! You're always welcome to dine at my table." Grace stood with her hands on her hips, and Emily copied her.

Jim stepped forward. "Wouldn't be right for us to sit on duty. Captain'll string us from the yardarm if he catches us resting on our laurels."

"Fair point." She twisted her lips. "Tell you what, I'll prepare you a plate. You can take it in turns to eat while the others keep guard."

By the end of the meal, with only scraps left on the table, Emily excused herself and rolled onto the grass. "I's full!" She rubbed her bulging belly. "Ooo, look Mamam!" A chubby finger pointed to the sky. "A cloud rabbit." She tipped her head and pleaded. "Lie down. I want cloud stories."

Grace lay giggling at Emily's interpretation of the sky-rabbit's antics when she heard Ben growl. "Halt! Don't come any nearer!"

Grace sprung from the ground as though it were made of lava and straddled Emily.

"Mind, Mamam," Emily twittered from beneath her skirts. "Can't see."

"Hush, Emily. Don't move." Grace squeezed Emily between her boots, and the child stilled.

Grace recognised the approaching man as the man whose body she had recently scrutinised, and her scalp blazed beneath her straw hat. The man was balanced by a lidded basket in one hand and a small wooden bucket in the other. She glared at the intruder, her stomach giving a curious twist. He wore rough black trousers, and his shirtsleeves were rolled up. The buttons of his red shirt were undone at the neck. A peep of white under-shirt screened the well-defined chest she knew was under there. The reek of him confirmed he was indeed a whaler. Setting down the bucket a short distance away, the man whisked his torn leather hat off his head.

"Howdy do, ma'am," he said with an American drawl. "Didn't mean to scare you. Name's Albert Church, but folks call me Alby."

"State yer business," declared Jim, his musket pointed directly at Church's chest. Ben and Toby trained their muskets in sweeping arcs, scouring for further interlopers.

"I'm a whaler, with Captain Job Terry," Church announced with an expectant lift in his voice as though this would make sense to them.

"Who?" asked Jim.

"Ha! Thought every vessel in the Pacific knew Job Terry."

Jim shook his dark head. "Never heard of him."

Unfazed by Jim's curt reply, the whaler man continued conversationally, "He's ploughed the saltwater for forty years as a whaler. Reckons he's broken bread with governors and gamblers alike. Courted the likes of princesses as well as whor —" He broke off abruptly, eyeing Emily and smirking at Grace. "Ladies of the night."

"What's any of this to us?" Jim asked in clipped tones.

Church shrugged. "Nothing, 'cept you asked me to state my business." He levelled his kind gaze towards Emily. "I've gifts for the little lady."

He looked to be about thirty. The sinewy muscles of his forearm twitched minutely as he kept the basket balanced. His friendly, open face was at ease, despite having three muskets pointed at him.

"Look," he said, grinning. "Have your men inspect the basket and pail." He lowered the basket beside the bucket and backed away with his arms in the air, his tatty hat scrunched in one hand. His spiky brown hair had obviously not seen a comb after its earlier wash.

Beneath Grace's skirts, Emily shuffled about, watching the proceedings. Ben flicked the wicker lid open with the muzzle of his musket.

"What is it?" piped Emily.

"Hush, child." Grace drew Emily to her feet, keeping hold of her hand.

Ben turned back, his row of white teeth splitting his fiery whiskers in amusement. "'Tis a bucket of fresh milk and a little tortoise."

Emily gasped and pulled against Grace's grip. Grace yanked her back. Emily danced on her toes, desperately trying to peek over the edge of the basket.

Grace's gaze lingered on Church. He did not appear to be in any hurry to move on. "What can I do for you, Mr Church?"

The foolish grin slid off his square-jawed face, and he licked his lips. "Was hoping to have a confab with the captain, ma'am." Church held his worn hat against his chest, his muscular hands balancing it there delicately. "Reckon it's about time for a new job." He bowed his stubbled chin and sniffed at himself, wrinkling his nose. "The stench of whaling is enough to drive a donkey from his breakfast." He grinned as Ben sniggered. "Was hoping you had room aboard for one more?"

"Captain Fitzwilliam is away charting the islands," she said. "And I'm not sure that he's after any new hands."

Church dipped his head, his eyes flashing good-naturedly. "I'd appreciate a shot at persuading him myself."

Grace exhaled slowly, peering inside the open basket at the scrabbling miniature tortoise. The bushes behind her erupted into snuffling and grunting like two men scrapping, and she spun. She sucked her breath in horror. A large, black boar gouged the damp earth with its trotter as though digging in for a better grip on the ground. Its mouth gnashed nastily around its curved yellow tusks, and her fingers turned into a vice around Emily's arm. She eyed the musket laying in the grass. Blazing Hades, she would never reach it in time to load it if the wretched creature charged.

Church called softly and calmly from behind her. "Don't run, ma'am. That there's Satan's boar. He'll gut you as quick as you can blink. Back up now. Steady does it. Towards me."

Grace eased backwards, cursing the dry rasp of her skirts in the grass. The boar swivelled its beady, bloodshot eyes to her, and she froze. Emily whimpered, and Grace eased her grip on her daughter's small arm.

"Quietly does it," encouraged Church. "Keep coming."

Behind Grace, Jim's voice whispered, "I can take the shot."

"No," urged Church. "Miss and you'll infuriate it."

"I'll no' miss," replied Jim, his Scots accent thickening.

Grace winced at the hollow metallic click. A misfire—a sound that brought a cold dread to every marksman's gut. Oh, no! A gunshot would be a welcomed champion right now.

"Mother of saints! Misfire!" Jim growled.

"I *told* you not to fire." Church's voice was low and hard.

"Aye, and I told ye I wouldn't miss," Jim retaliated. "A misfire's no man's fault."

An explosion shattered the stillness and Grace jolted, instinctively yanking Emily into her. She buried her daughter's cries in her skirts. The black pig spun in frenzied circles, its shattered front leg hanging limply by shredded tissue.

"God's teeth!" The curse exploded from the American.

Squealing furiously, Satan's boar bolted from the greenery. Grace scooped Emily up and spun in one motion. Each thundering footstep jolted up her spine and into her brain. Bloody skirts! She gripped the back of Emily's head, pressing it tight to her shoulder to ready her for the impact.

Ahead of her, a curl of white smoke puffed from the barrel of Ben's musket. Jim was ramming a new charge down the barrel of his own, his face greyed with determination. Church, knife drawn, was sprinting towards her. She glared at Toby—her only hope. The muzzle of his musket swayed back and forth as he tried for a clear shot around her.

"Shoot it!" Grace shrieked. The pig's rage-filled squeals were right on her heels. Lord above, this was going to hurt!

Toby hesitated, his blond-bearded face scrunching in a tortured frown. Church speared his curved-tip flensing knife into the earth and snatched the musket from Toby. Shouldering it, he fired in one smooth motion as though it were an extension of himself.

The explosion reverberated in Grace's eardrums as the swine collided with her, the violence of the impact akin to being struck by a recoiling cannon broken loose of its breech rope. She cart-wheeled across the open grassland, the alternating spin of sky and grass dizzying her. When she halted, Emily was pinned beneath her. As though underwater, Emily's screams filtered through muffled.

Grace scrambled to her knees and bent over her daughter, who lay puce-faced and wide-eyed with terror. Grace's heart hammered behind her ringing eardrums, and her dress stuck to the perspiration on her back. She frantically searched the glade to gauge the boar's next charge. The limber American strode over, the musket slung over his shoulder. The man's face was pale and tight. His wide, hazel eyes scanned over her and Emily.

The knot in Grace's stomach twisted painfully. Where the blazes was the pig? She panted, fighting to control the rising panic in her chest as her head darted in every direction. "Where is it?"

"Stowed away, Mrs F.," said Ben, his own musket slung on his shoulder and his red hair flaring bronze in the sun.

The black beast lay dead in the grass, a dribble of blood

leaking from the hole where its left eye had been. *Oh, sweet merciful Lord, thank you.* Her comfort was short-lived as she spotted blood welling on Emily's face. The scratch ran high across her left cheek. It was long, but not deep. Grace patted Emily's hair and shoulders, desperately searching her little body for further signs of blood or disfigurement. She was unharmed. All was well.

She wrenched her daughter into her arms, rocking her as the scene replayed in her mind like jerking images flashing through a picket fence being walked past in haste. She pressed her lips into Emily's butter-blonde curls, her own sharp tang of fear mingling with Emily's sweet milkiness. "Shh, my darling. You're safe now."

Church knelt beside her and laid the weapon on the grass. There was nothing quick about his movements. Burnt gunpowder and the reek of dead whale wafted from him, but Grace's concern for her daughter overrode any offence the man's odour caused. Jim and Ben tore over, yelling excitedly, their words tripping over one another like runners in a steeplechase.

"Is our Em all right?" asked Toby softly. He swayed uneasily from one foot to the other and scratched his whiskers with a dry rasp.

"Crivens, 'twas close," said Jim, the warble in his laughter giving away the true measure of his nerves. He leaned the butt of his musket on the ground and bobbed down, his knees crackling. "Thought ye were done for, Mrs F. 'Specially after this bastard lump of iron misfired." Hysteria edged his voice. "D'ye see how fast the wretch ran on three pins? 'Twas out of its mind in pain with that hock barely hanging on." Jim wiped the palm of his hand along his trousers and swapped his musket over to wipe his other hand.

"Superb shot, man!" Ben thumped Church on the back. "Barely saw you snatch Hicks's musket before you'd shot the swine!" Ben ran his hands through his red hair, pacing in small circles. "Absolutely flaming remarkable."

By the degree of his concentration on her, Grace realised Church was ignoring the men's outbursts. His gaze was calm, and the skin at his throat pinched as he swallowed.

"Little lady don't appear injured, save for that small scratch. You hurt, ma'am?" Church edged over to Grace, his demeanour unruffled as he examined her.

Emily lay whimpering in her lap. Grace stared at Emily's curly head, her eyes wide with remembering. "It could have killed us."

A smile of reassurance curled his lips. "'Twas dead before it touched you—head and tusks already tucked under." He whistled through his teeth. "Boar that size could've done some mighty damage to such a lovely fine dame."

His warm grip on Grace's elbow reconnected her to the earth, back to her body, calming her humming nerves.

"Sure you ain't hurt, ma'am?"

Spotting the thumping pulse in his neck slow, she placed a hand of thanks on his crouched knee and laughed shakily. "My fingers and toes are all tingly."

"Happens when you've had a big fright."

"We're lucky you came along, Mr Church." Warmth returned to Grace's clammy fingertips, and she was glad her flip-flopping heart was not on public display.

"Alby. Please."

"Alby. I think you'll find Captain Fitzwilliam thoroughly persuaded to finding you a position aboard his ship."

Alby dipped his head. "Look forward to making his acquaintance." He rose, offering Grace his hand, the raised scars on his palm like a roughly textured relief map.

Toby scooped a blotch-faced Emily onto his shoulders and grabbed the tortoise basket. "Come on, our Em. Let's get you back to Petal. You can introduce her to ol' speedy here."

The little girl hiccoughed and clutched Toby's head, obscuring his eyes with her hands. With a light laugh, he pushed her hands onto his forehead and set off across the grassland with a bouncy gait that set her giggling.

Alby grasped Grace's fingers with a comforting strength, easily pulling her up. Her breath caught in her throat, their faces too near for the strangers that they were. She expected a flood of awkwardness, but none came. The whaler man stood still and boldly held her gaze. She smiled hesitantly, her gaze drawn to his lips as his tongue darted out to moisten them. She opened her mouth to speak, but no sound emerged. The corners of Alby's mouth twitched as he peered back at Ben, Jim, and Toby, who stood holding Emily, the muskets, and the remnants of the packed-up picnic.

"Gentlemen, lead the way." Alby's lazy drawl had a tone of satisfaction about it. Grace spotted the crew's nervous glances. She knew they would be worried about Seamus's wrath for failing their duty of protection. Never mind, it was a job best dealt with sooner rather than later. She hoped Seamus's gratitude towards Alby's heroic efforts, and his relief at having her and Emily returned relatively unscathed, would be enough to earn her three friends some leniency.

As they walked, Grace gave the stranger a quick glance and was thrown to find his unrelenting stare fixed boldly on her. A heated blush tingled across her chest. She took a short, sharp breath and turned on what she hoped was a polite smile. "Thank you for your kindness in dealing with my daughter. You have quite a knack with children."

"Only those who come attached to pretty mothers." His voice was low and thick. Overt interest replaced the smile in his eyes, and the liquid in her mouth evaporated with the ferocity of water splashed on a hot iron pot. She stared at the grass swishing past the hem of her skirts, desperate for somewhere else to fix her gaze other than his intense stare. She bit her lip.

"Keep chewing that lip, ma'am, and there won't be much left by morning."

"M-my lips are no concern of yours, Mr Church." The words tripped nervously from her. He laughed low in his throat, and her irritation piqued at the coveting flash in his eyes. "I'm a married woman."

"Was married once myself. Long time ago." Alby gazed unfocussed into the distance. No longer toying, a solemnity filled his tone. "Had a daughter too. Both were killed." He swallowed deeply again. "Fire."

Grace's cheeks blazed. "Oh, Alby. I'm so sorry. I had no idea."

"Feels like I've been running from their memories my whole life." His breaths were deep but his voice steady. "Thought I'd find solitude in the wilds on my own—trapping and hunting. But they're always there, their voices filling the silence. Filling my head." His footsteps were muted by the grass, but his stride remained steady. "When the anger came, I wanted to be alone." His hazel eyes were bright with pain, and he inhaled sharply. "So, I thought to flee as far away as possible from the Mississippi—from them. But they're still with me, on the other side of the goddamned world on a stinking whaleboat." His stride became heavier and longer, and Grace scurried to keep up.

She placed her hand on his bare forearm. "Sorry, Alby. I didn't mean to resurrect any painful memories." A knot of remorse twisted uncomfortably in the base of her skull. Yes, he was an outrageous seducer, but the man had just saved her life. Her sharp tongue was no way to show her gratitude. She would do her best to convince Seamus to take him aboard the *Clover*.

Chapter Twenty-Two

Seamus was impressed at how casually Church dismissed the heroic status bestowed upon him by everyone aboard the *Clover*. The whaler man found himself welcomed into the folds of camaraderie, enthralling everyone with his legendary story-telling abilities. In the snippets of conversation Seamus caught, the personable American had clearly led a colourful life on land and at sea, and the entertainment-starved sailors of the *Clover* lapped up his tales of adventure. He was certainly a boon to the men's spirits.

It was only due to Grace's plea for clemency that Buchanan, Hicks, and Blight escaped punishment for their misadventure. His lenience also stemmed from the fact that neither Grace nor Emily was injured. Seamus eyed Church in a crowd of off-duty sailors sitting in an enthralled huddle around their new shipmate under the shade of the cutter as he retold the sad tale of his wife and daughter for the dozenth time.

"Left the States with a sour taste in my mouth. Decided to travel to the furthest possible reaches to bolt from the memories. That's how I ended up in Nantucket as a whaler," said Church.

"Ah, and how you landed in the Galapagos!" chimed in O'Malley.

"Indeed," Church said, brightening his tone again. "Been a whaler for three years. I fled to sea to get away from the dying, but I found myself still in the midst of it."

"Eh? Wotcha mean?"

Church gave an uncomfortable shrug. "Nothing's quite as sad as watching a shattered whale rolling in exhaustion. Thick blood spurting out his spout hole, splattering your skin like hot rain. When he ogles you with such misery in his giant eye, you can't help feel he's staring into your soul. I felt such pity for the creatures."

"Crivens! Sounds barbaric!" exclaimed Buchanan.

Church punched Buchanan's shoulder, grinning amiably. "Which is why I've rung the changes and hopped aboard this leisure vessel with you idlers. Having the stink of a whaler man does little to attract the ladies—the pretty ones at least." The men's loud guffaws broke the sombre tension.

Seamus checked the compass and, as he shut the lid of the binnacle, he smiled at Emily with her brown-feathered friend roosting in her lap. Emily and Petal swung in the makeshift swing sweeping arcs across the quarterdeck from the long ropes rigged over the yardarm. The chicken's wings opened and closed like a concertina as it balanced to stay in her lap. Seamus shook his head good-humouredly.

The men below laughed again, and he studied them with piercing scrutiny. Some days Church's persuasion almost bordered on insubordination—including the liberties he took with addressing Grace—but Seamus reasoned it was the American in him. He had met enough of them to know not to measure Church against his own strict British naval ideology. Even though Church had no knowledge of surveying or mapping, and could neither read nor write, he confidently knew his way around a ship.

Eight bells announced the arrival of noon, and the men rose to prepare for the afternoon watch, their bright spirits following them in their duties. The day was fine, with clear skies, a brisk breeze, and a pleasant warmth to the high midday sun. Adding to Seamus's good mood was the sight of his wife leaning her elbows against the rail of the quarterdeck, inhaling deep breaths of the clear air.

He sidled up to her. "Glorious weather with my favourite kind of view." The endless swells of shimmering ocean passed alongside them.

Grace harrumphed. "It's the same boring ocean as yesterday, and the day before, and the day before that." She swallowed deeply.

He leaned against her hip. "I'm not speaking of the ocean but rather your pert derriere." Grace blushed and peered around to see who was in earshot, though Seamus had picked his moment perfectly.

She slid him a sly sideways glance and chuckled. "We've had fair winds so far."

"Indeed."

A clatter on the main deck drew Seamus's attention. Hicks righted a broom he had knocked over and dropped it in the barrel that housed the others. The blond-whiskered man flicked a glance to the quarterdeck but quickly looked away.

Buchanan bounded up the quarterdeck stairs and nodded at Seamus. "Sir. Mrs Fitzwilliam." His dark head bowed as he ducked into the charthouse.

Grace peered at Seamus, squinting against the sun. "You're not supervising Jim's cartography endeavours today?"

His gaze lingered on her striking profile with its pert nose, which suited her. Her brown brows were a shade darker than her billowing brown curls that refused to be tamed by bonnet or ribbon. By oath, she was lovely.

"Not today. I'm well pleased with Buchanan's ability to plot our points of discovery on the map. He no longer needs me hovering over his shoulder."

"Really?" Pride swelled her smile. "I hope you don't mind, but I shredded one of our bedsheets. Billy said the sickbay was running short of dressings."

Seamus cocked one eyebrow, and the corner of his mouth tugged higher. "A generous gesture. And no doubt a comfort to the men whose injuries now sport said dressings."

Below, Church appeared from the mid-hatch with Sail-maker Lester close behind. Between them, they carried a folded shroud of canvas and, judging by Church's inspection of the yardarms, Seamus figured they were heading upwards with it.

"It's heartening how Alby has transferred his skinning skills to sail making," said Grace.

He made a noise of agreement in his throat. "He seems well settled with the industrious role."

Grace's chuckle morphed into a low groan. She crossed her arms over the rail, resting her forehead on her forearms.

Seamus stiffened and laid a hand on her slim shoulder. "Are you ill?"

She exhaled slowly. "No. I'm bracing for another child of yours to mercilessly kick my ribs."

"Pardon... you mean you're—" His wave of elation was prickled by shards of panic and overwhelm. Blast! He truly wanted her to luxuriate in the fulfilment of maternity again, except he would have to find room for another body in their cabin. Where would they be when the child was born? Would they be on land like last time? He had just been thanking his lucky stars that Emily was no longer in clouts, but now boiling cloths—stinking of cauliflower past its prime—would become a staple in their home again. Still, it was the best news she could have delivered.

"Oh, Dulcinea! I could scoop you up and swing you about right now." He gave a breathy laugh.

The bow of the *Clover* tipped over another swell, and she raised one finger. "Hold that thought." The contents of her stomach followed the ship's motion. Grey, chunky remnants of porridge whipped away on the wind. Wiping her mouth with the back of her hand, she flopped her head back down with a groan. "Oh Lord, smite me now and be done with it."

"How long have you known?" He bowed down to where she lay on her cheek, studying him. Unlike his initial doubt when he had found out about Emily's impending arrival, he hoped his grin of expectation now would blow away any of his wife's concerns.

"A few weeks."

"Weeks! Why didn't you tell me?"

"I wanted to be sure. I wasn't sure myself, but my current state of queasiness confirms it. I'd rather swim back to England than endure the stench of Cook Phillips's boiled pork."

Seamus tucked a corkscrew of hair behind her ear. "Have I told you how happy you make me?" He scrunched his nose sympathetically as she screwed her eyes and blew out another steadying breath. "Should we tell our Em?"

"Not yet. She's too impatient. All those months of waiting would be agony for her."

One bell sounded the start of the afternoon watch. Seamus cocked his head to listen to the rise and fall of conversation of the men in the masts. Their indecipherable words whipped around in the wind, the ropes creaked with stretching, the water lullingly splashed against the hull. The cool slither across the back of his neck had nothing to do with the sea breeze. His jaw tightened as he scoured the ship, his hand capping the sunlight. The empty swing undulated in the briny breeze. "Emily?"

"I's here," her small voice piped from between them. Seamus stepped back, his neck craned down. Emily had Petal tucked on her hip under one arm. With her short arm unable to hold the whole chicken, one brown wing hung low. Despite the uncomfortable-looking position, the hen looked contented enough.

Seamus scooped up his daughter and her pet hen. Startled by the sudden movement, Petal's yellow-toed talons gouged his arm, and he hissed in pain. Wretched bird! Emily shrieked as the hen flapped and squawked. He lunged and nipped some wing feathers between his thumb and forefinger. For a moment the hen stilled, her bright, beady eyes fixing on Seamus from her topsy-turvy position, but then she gave another frightened flap and spiralled in a flutter of feathers over the edge of the gunwale. Seamus held up two feathers. *Shit!*

Emily squealed in alarm, as did Petal, whose squawk of terror trailed into silence. Seamus leaned over the railing, and Emily's little legs clamped tight around his middle. The hen landed with a small splash in the choppy water, her outspread wings like the support floats of an outrigger canoe. She screeched high-pitched trills of distress.

"Petal! Come back!" Emily's panicked blue eyes welled with tears and she leaned over.

Swinging Emily back over the rail, Seamus tipped her into Grace's arms, his lips set with resolve as he gripped the rail.

"Oh, Seamus!" Grace's face was devoid of colour. "What'll we do?"

He had never imagined adding drowning-chicken-saviour to his list of attributes. His mind raced. Even if he called for the ship to be slowed and turned, finding one speck of hen in a choppy ocean would be impossible. Blasted hell!

The squalling flock of seabirds that had been trailing the Clover for the last twenty minutes suddenly lost interest in the ship, instead circling and swirling over the floundering chicken. For pity's sake—though it was probably for the best; a quick ending was merciful. With a pretence solely for his daughter's sake, he roared, flapping his hands like a scarecrow whipped into a frenzy. The surface of the water erupted in a splashing, frothing mass, and when the birds swooped back up again, only a few floating brown feathers remained in the ship's wake. And with that, the world's most loyal chicken was dead. It was only a cursed fowl—so why did he feel so wretched?

Emily wailed loudly, and her tearful gaze drove a knife into his chest. "Petal!"

"Oh, our Em, I'm so sorry." He stroked her head, his fingers catching in her windswept curls. "I tried to chase them off." The anguish on his daughter's face did all sorts of preposterous things to his already churning insides. "Petal's in heaven now. Here." He offered her the two feathers.

She crushed the feathers in her chubby hand, sobbing. "Who be my friend now?"

Seamus rolled his injured wrist, savouring the release of the click, and looked desperately to Grace for help.

"Oh, my darling." Grace smoothed Emily's forehead and clicked her tongue empathetically. "Cappy and I have news."

Seamus arched one brow. Really? Now? He shrugged his shoulders. It certainly was a worthy distraction. Considering how infatuated Emily was with a chicken, he could only hope she might transfer that affection to a sibling.

"You're going to get a little brother or sister," said Grace.

Emily absently rubbed the edge of his collar between her thumb and forefinger as she always did for comfort. She wiped her nose with the back of her arm and gave a watery smile. "Now?"

"Soon, my darling. Very soon," said Grace, pressing a kiss to Emily's temple. She met Seamus's gaze over the blonde curls and widened her eyes.

Oh, well, cat's out of the bag now.

AS THE WEEKS PASSED, Seamus never tired of watching Grace's belly swelling outwards. He felt awfully sorry for her as she navigated the perpetually pitching deck with the same ungainliness that had plagued her the last time. He did not recall her being as big or as tired this early when expecting Emily. Poor thing. Between Hicks and Buchanan, Seamus ensured she had an extra pair of hands to care for Emily.

Hicks's reading and writing had advanced to the point where he could help Grace with the ship's books and read stories to Emily—a long way from his days in the forecastle of the *Discerning* when Grace had read to him. To ease Grace's burden, Hicks had also diligently taken over teaching Emily to read. Seamus was pleased that Emily recognised all her letters, could count to one hundred, and scratch out her name legibly enough. And thanks to Buchanan, Emily even knew how to load a pistol. He knew better than to argue with Grace on this point.

He also turned a blind eye to Blight or Church occasionally joining in with Emily's games on deck. His deepest restraint came knowing that his daughter's favourite chore was to help Hicks wash dishes. She had a basin of her own, filled with warm water to rinse the dishes, after Hicks had scrubbed them with a mixture of soap flakes and washing soda in a tub of piping hot water. Seamus always grimaced at how red and raw Emily's small hands were afterwards, but he held his tongue. A little hard work never killed anyone. And the distraction meant she stopped asking about her impending brother or sister for just a moment or two.

The first time Buchanan had played a game of pirates, with Emily and Hicks as his prisoners, he had them picking oakum. Seamus was on the verge of forbidding this activity when Grace caught his wrist.

"Where are you off to?" Her fingers intertwined with his.

"I'll not have my daughter undertaking a job reserved for a sailor's punishment."

"See how nimble her fingers are becoming," Grace said gently as Emily's pudgy little fingers unravelled the sticky old ropes into fibrous strands.

"The tar will never wash off," Seamus countered dryly.

"Come now, my love. You of all people know how essential such dexterity is aboard a ship."

He glanced at her sharply. "I've no intention of employing our daughter in any formal capacity. Certainly not on such menial tasks."

"She isn't coming to any harm learning the workings of a ship. There'll be a benefit to her knowing how those fibres she's spent hours plucking are used. I remember the first time Jim showed me how to hammer the fibres into the seams of the planks with a caulking iron. Though it was ages before he let me seal them with hot pitch to keep the *Discerning* watertight."

"You *know* I had no notion you were undertaking such tasks." He clasped his hands behind his back, stiff with the memories.

"I know." She ran her hand down his arm. "I'm only saying that it won't do her any harm to learn what I learned. And with the same men too. There's no one I trust more than Ben Blight to take our daughter up the rigging. When he thought me a lad, he'd take me above, where we spent many hours watching whales."

"I recall doing the same as a youngster." He curled a hand around the small of her back.

"Alby's taught her to whistle, you know?"

"Ah, so that's where she got it from." Seamus had tried to teach Emily how to purse her lips and position her tongue just right, but it had been in vain. Then one day, she had let out a high-pitched trill, and he had swung her around triumphantly. Having grasped a knack for it, Emily was soon whistling tunes, though none so pure as Church's.

Seamus taught his daughter a specific whistle that allowed her to call out to him like a bosun's call. It was useful for locating her on the ship and would work equally as well should she become lost in a crowd on land. Their next stop was the Antipodes. He hoped the governor there had better control of his prisoners than the last penal colony they had visited.

Chapter Twenty-Three

COLONY OF NEW SOUTH WALES, 4 JANUARY 1837

The *Clover*'s arrival at the settlement in Sydney Cove stunned Seamus. Instead of finding a grubby little settlement scratched into the earth, he discovered a thriving port town of windmills, white stone mansions, and grand government buildings shimmering in the summer heat. A clock tower stood above the roofs of the densely packed shoreline. The thick coastal forest had been slashed to make way for the settlement. While he would not consider Sydney Town a metropolis by any means, he felt a distinct undercurrent humming through the young settlement that gave it a promise of one day realising this potential. As though to reinforce its burgeoning status, a battery of long guns pointed intimidatingly out over the harbour entrance to the west of the inlet. The smoke of a distant bushfire to the east pricked inside his nostrils.

Despite the gleaming appearances from afar, Seamus was not surprised to find the docks at Queen's Warf were as insalubrious as all docks around the world tended to be—including the ubiquitous woody-tar reek of pier posts with their essence of seaweed. The injection of civilisation into this untamed land lay in the newly delivered supplies that lined the quay—boxes containing hundreds of thousands of nails, piles of axes bundled together, women's skirts and hoops and shoes, and even a printing press. The rowdy babble and caterwaul of compressed humanity closed the air around him tighter than in the stuffy sail storeroom on the *Clover*. Every second building was either a spirit shop, a musket seller, or a public house. Large wooden sheds lining the waterfront were filled with an assortment of goods being offloaded or re-loaded onto the waiting ships—the most recent delivery being a ship full of single women immigrants.

Seamus steered Grace by her elbow through the large crowd milling along the harbour shore. There were a few women and children but mostly men, some of them blind drunk. Emily clung tightly to his neck, and he sensed her fear of the swell of humanity—she was unused to the throng. On the whole, the tanned and weathered inhabitants were in fair condition, and not as ill-fed as some of the souls seen in London, even though their clothes were the same as those found in any English town. Still, the dock was no place for his wife and child. He tightened his grip on Grace's shoulder as some men, clearly only interested in the delivery of fresh female flesh, shouted ribald comments.

"You after a 'usband, love? Well, look no further—Ronan Thompson at your service."

"Wanna come home with me? I'll give ya a warm welcome to Sydney Town ya won't soon forget!"

"I've four bairns wi'out a maw. Ye wouldnae deprive the wee'uns of a mother now, would ye?"

"Pah! Look at 'em. Filthy whores, the lot of 'em. Bet there ain't a clean one in the whole bunch."

At this last comment, Seamus recoiled as one of the feistier women blew a white stream of spittle at the man. The crowd jeered and laughed, thoroughly entertained, and he winced at his wife. She was large with child and seemed more intent on finding a place to sit than paying attention to the rowdy goings-on. Seamus drew Emily's face into his neck as one woman lifted her skirts, provocatively flashing her legs as high as her thighs. Utter madness! The crowd roared in encouragement, and Emily's arms tightened.

He panned the crowd, dismayed at how many of the new females were not more than girls. They huddled together. Poor souls. Looked like they had experienced a devil of a voyage over from England. Most of them hugged their measly sacks of worldly possessions to their chests, though some were empty handed. Officials herded the women into a large, open shed. Seamus steered Grace in the opposite direction. Crowds of womenfolk milled about in the shed, waiting to have their papers checked. He saw Grace eye some ships' officers and other dignitary-looking gentlemen hovering outside the processing shed.

"Some lasses look to have already been claimed by the officers and gentlemen," Seamus offered tightly. "Probably be taking them as housekeepers and nurses for their children."

A pretty, young, mushroom-blonde girl, no more than fourteen, shuffled from the shadows of the processing shed. One of the uniformed officers grinned, beckoning to her. The two took off together, and Grace frowned at the departing couple. Seamus knew that, having lived with men, she was inclined to understand men's minds.

Her voice was clipped. "Fancy how it's always the pretty ones who are picked, rather than the robust, capable ones. How long do you think it'll be before she's with child and cast out on the street to fend for herself?"

Seamus shuffled Emily's weight to his other hip as Grace lifted the hem of her skirts above the mucous slick of mud and manure paving the wharf. He placed himself between Grace and a drunken woman lounging against the open door of an unsavoury establishment. She cackled bawdily, her rotting teeth spraying a reek of curdled milk and tumorous disease that smacked him back a step.

"Good heavens! No wonder those new women are in such high demand if this is the calibre of females on offer," he muttered through gritted teeth.

Just one street back from the docks, it was like another world, free of cloying odours and thronging noise. The winding streets—too narrow for carts—were full of unhurried people and slow-clopping horses. Remnants of cleared tree stumps interspersed the clay thatch-roofed houses wedged into niches in the hillside.

Seamus held up his hand to a uniformed officer of the mounted police riding by. The man cut a splendid figure above his white horse, with the gold tassels of his epaulettes swinging as he reined his mount to a halt. The policeman touched the peak of his navy shako, the feathered plume sprouting like a khaki fountain above his head.

"Excuse me, officer, would you please guide us to the nearest reputable accommodation?" Seamus peered up at the policeman, sitting ramrod stiff in his saddle.

Adjusting the scarlet-and-gold sabretache attached to his belt, the man spoke through thin lips that barely opened. "You're in the heart of a penal settlement, sir. 'Tis an unlikely place to haul your family. 'Tis even less likely you'll find reputable accommodation here in The Rocks."

Seamus stiffened. Beside him, Grace simpered and took a couple of sashaying steps towards the mounted man. What the devil was she up to? The narrow-eyed policeman glanced appreciatively at the sway of her skirts, his gaze snapping to her face as she spoke.

"Please, sir. We've travelled a great distance. We're after a clean bed and hot food." She blinked prettily and placed her hand delicately against her throat. "A gentleman such as you *must* know of a suitable establishment?"

Seamus nibbled the inside of his lips to hide his smirk. Coquettish little pixie!

The policeman coughed importantly, and his horse danced impatiently under him. "Just be sure to stay in town. A gang of miscreants robbed the bank last week. Last seen heading west. Blighted bushrangers are the scourge of this land." He glared behind at the swelling argument between two drunk men. Frowning, he turned his attention back to Grace. "Try the Sailor's Homecoming. Ask for William Wells, he's the owner. Tell him Major Winfield of the New South Wales Mounted Police sent you." He waved up the street and flicked his wrist to the right.

"Thank you for the warning and the directions, Major." Grace fluttered sweetly, resting her hand on his thigh. "Your assistance is much appreciated."

Sliding her hand from his trouser leg, she caressed the horse's neck. Seamus's throat worked hard as he choked back a laugh. Winfield's eyes widened, watching the same slim hand that had rested so intimately on his thigh stroke the horse's muscular neck. When Grace tilted her head at Winfield, the veins in his neck bulged.

"Have yourself a lovely day, sir." She smiled as she turned away, arching one brow smugly at Seamus.

Winfield let out a strangled burble, and the bridle jingled to life as he urged his horse on. With the policeman's back to them, Seamus could not control the twitch in the corner of his mouth.

"Absolutely shameless," he whispered, scooping his free arm around her waist. "Toying with a man's emotions like that. He's not likely laid eyes on anything as lovely or clean as you in months. See what a life among ruffians has taught you? Exploiting innocents with your beguiling ways."

"I'll reward you with more than just a swish of my hips, a pat of my hand, or a flutter of my eyelashes, if you're not careful."

Seamus laughed, taken by surprise at her boldness on the public, dusty street. He dipped his chin to stare at her and tightened his hand on her hip. "Promise?" He swallowed deeply, desire flooding warmly behind his breastbone. Emily twisted about on his arm, and he broke into a self-conscious grin. Grace nudged her hip into him and turned down the street Winfield had indicated.

With his wife securely on his arm, Seamus studied the ramshackle houses the locals had turned into bakeries, shops, and gin bars. Closer to the bay, the tantalising fragrances of sweet, fresh apples and earthy potatoes filled the markets, where an assortment of people were trying, outwardly at least, to earn an honest living. Infants wailed in the tumbledown homes with their cracked plaster and mud-splattered paint. Children shrieked as they chased each other, laughing as they tumbled to the ground wrestling. Women's voices cut across the narrow streets, shouting at children or chatting in loud conversations with neighbours. Pigs scurried underfoot, and dogs barked in every direction. Landlocked scents such as burnt, smoky air and horse sweat were always strongest in the first few days ashore.

Emily tensed, her neck craning in every direction to watch the children playing. "Wait, Cappy. I want to see." Seamus's shoes shuffled to a halt, raising a puff of dust that immediately blew away on the breeze.

A small gang of children were using two of the tree stumps as forts. Each tree stump had a leader who shouted out orders to his troops to launch glass bottles at their enemy. Seamus grimaced at the street littered with dozens of broken glass bottles. The road crunched underfoot as he set off again.

At the outer edge of The Rocks, the streets broadened. Seamus continued down a street along the foreshore. Emily's gaze was glued to the flocks of cockatoos and rainbow-coloured parrots squawking and bickering in the tall tops of the eucalypts. The aroma of fresh bread carried on the sea breeze—heavens, it had been months since he had savoured newly baked bread. His mouth watered. As they walked past the blacksmith, Seamus could taste the metal in the air. The burly smith finished off an apple and threw the core into the fire. With a sizzle and a pop, the sweet aroma of baking apples that reached Seamus was even more tempting than the bread, and his stomach growled.

He stopped before a three-storey sandstone building, sporting the hotel's name across its façade. Acquainting himself with the low light through the pipe fug, he examined the patrons crammed elbow to elbow at the long bar. Others perched on wooden benches at heavy tables, not unlike the tables in the mess on the *Clover*.

A trio of drinkers at the bar laughed uproariously, their hilarity clearly fuelled by the cheap gin that wafted off them in an almost visible vapour. Seamus pulled his lips tight as he took in the shabby surrounds of the pub, reeking of mutton fat and stale ale breath. *This* was the best establishment in town? He dubiously eyed the mix of seafarers, dusty sandstone quarrymen, and farm labourers. A couple of questionable women stood at the bar matching the men tankard for tankard, some perched unashamedly on the lap of whoever was paying them the most attention.

The publican behind the bar caught Seamus's eye and beckoned him over to the quiet corner. His full-whiskered face split into a welcoming grin. "Name's William Wells. Publican of this here alehouse. How might I be of service, sir?"

Seamus leaned in to make himself heard over the din of conversation and laughter. Emily leaned back in his arms, clearly uncomfortable with the proximity to the stranger. "A Major Winfield recommended your establishment as a place for my family to reside during our stay."

The publican's shaggy eyebrows shot up. He stopped twisting the drying cloth into the mouth of the glass and scoffed. "Pompous showboating fool. Aren't any places around here suitable for the likes of you." He held the clean glass in the dim light, examining it. Seeing Seamus's shoulders slump, he added, "Could offer you a room in my house across the way there." He waved the glass towards a large-paned window.

Through the grimy glass, Seamus spotted a brand-new two-storey sandstone colonial on the opposite street corner. "I'd like to rent your whole house, servants included, for the next month. I can make it worth your while," Seamus offered. A decent-sized emerald from Grace's pouch of jewels might do the trick. He dared not add any more promissory notes to his already unwholesome pile.

"Hmm," contemplated Wells, his pale brown eyes shifting between Grace and Seamus. "S'ppose I could stay in a room here at my hotel. I've only myself to consider."

This declaration of his bachelorhood did nothing to bolster Seamus's faith that the man's house would be anything more than sparsely furnished. Still, private accommodation was preferable to this establishment.

Wells slid the glass onto the wooden bar top with a thud. "Welcome to Sydney Town."

Across the street, the only hint the plain sandstone building gave of its interior was the white lace curtains. Seamus stepped up the small bank of steps leading to the dark-stained timber front door. He swung it open, blinking in surprise. Despite being a bachelor, Wells had impeccable taste and was obviously a man of comfortable means. In the entry hall, an elongated marble fireplace stood to the left of a surprisingly narrow staircase, leading through a panelled stairwell to the second floor. Emily tore upstairs with great abandon. Seamus followed.

His daughter darted into the first room at the top of the stairs, with its mint-green, vertically striped wallpaper. She sprang onto the bed, rumpling the cream bed cover.

"This one's mine!" She flopped onto the plump pillow in triumphant declaration.

Chapter Twenty-Four

COLONY OF NEW SOUTH WALES, 14 *JANUARY* 1837

"An invitation to the Governor's Ball?" Grace unfolded the thick parchment and scanned the meticulously written details. She arched her brows and laid down her toast. "To what do we owe the honour? We've barely been here a week. I can't imagine we've done anything to draw the governor's attention."

Seamus smeared quince jam onto his toast. "The invitation is from his daughter. Mrs Deas Thompson especially wants *you* there. No doubt your connection as Admiral Arthur Baxter's niece has great sway here."

Emily shuffled upright in her seat, sliding her teacup onto the saucer. "Me too?"

Grace twirled one of Emily's ringlet ponytails. "You're not old enough yet, Empem." Disappointment slid across Emily's face, and Grace cupped her round cheek, firm and warm like a peach hanging in sunlight. "I know how entrancing balls appear, but darling, they're such hot and noisy affairs."

"I want to dance with Cappy." Emily stood and, raising her arms, twirled around the dining room table.

Seamus coughed dryly, and Emily stopped instantly. With her cheeks flushing as red as fenberry juice, she plonked down heavily. He tapped one finger on her nose. "Young ladies first must learn not to dance around the breakfast table before they're allowed to go to balls."

Emily's pink lower lip pouted. "Sorry, Cappy."

Grace was relieved to see a reluctant smile replace his frown. He never could stay upset with their daughter for long. Leaning over, she wiped crumbs from Emily's mouth with her napkin. "You'll stay with Biddy for the evening."

Emily's eyes crinkled. "I like Biddy! She tells good stories."

Grace rubbed her protruding belly and blew out a long breath. "I'm not up to doing any jigs."

Seamus's eyes softened as her hands settled on her stomach. "I'm sure Mrs Deas Thompson is after your company, rather than to judge you on your dancing skills."

She sighed. "I must see which gown still fits." She patted her stomach again. "My sapphire gown should suffice."

ON THE AFTERNOON of the ball, Seamus gawked boyishly at his wife in the upstairs room of Wells' residence. "Grace! Where are your sleeves?" He pried his gaze from her bare arms and scowled.

She thrust out her chin. "I removed them." Seeing Seamus's furrowed brow deepen, she elaborated, "I'm not baking myself alive in this heat. Besides"—she readjusted the bow on the cream, pleated, silk fichu draped over her shoulders—"the tops of my arms are covered."

He gave a short, dry cough. "It's transparent! I can see every bit of your shoulders."

Amused by his indignation, she inclined her head. "There isn't going to be another man at that ball who gives me a second look in my condition." The sheen of blue satin was tight over her widened midriff.

Seamus's scowl slid into an appreciative hum. "I doubt I'll be dancing either. This heat is oppressive!"

In the ballroom of Government House, the toe-tapping notes of the Bonnie Highland Laddie swelled from the orchestra. Two lines of revellers facing each other danced in time with the music, as finely festooned onlookers clapped encouragingly. The bagpipes swelled, adding a passion to the song that the dancers on the floor responded to enthusiastically. Grace coughed and pressed her handkerchief to her nose. The cloying scents of powders and perfume mingled with the tang of sweat and damp horse-hair wigs was too much for her already delicate stomach.

Richard Bourke, the Governor of New South Wales, greeted them. Grace smiled politely at the balding man's face flushed with conversation. His droopy jowls, squashed against the high collar of his scarlet army uniform, made Grace realise that she was not the only one suffering the pomp and ceremony in this climate. Bourke greeted Seamus with bowed head, and Grace studied the military medal on his chest. Bourke noticed her interest.

"Civil Knight Grand Cross Star of the Order of the Bath." The words rolled off the governor's tongue in a lilting Irish accent.

"I beg your pardon?" said Grace.

Bourke touched the medallion on his chest. "My knighthood, madam," he said, bowing deeply. "Your humble servant, Mrs Fitzwilliam."

"The pleasure is all mine, Sir Richard." She curtsied.

"Governor Bourke, if you please," he clarified. "May I introduce my daughter, Mrs Anne Deas Thompson." A fresher, less flush-faced woman stepped into Grace's line of vision, and offered a kindly smile.

"Welcome, Mrs Fitzwilliam." She dipped her head politely, but her clear eyes were focussed and interested. "I hear you've had *quite* an exciting and daring journey. I'm simply dying to hear all about it."

"I'd be delighted," replied Grace, fanning herself with her handkerchief. "But first, I must beg a window or door. I'm unused to being dressed in all my finery in such heat."

Seamus loosened his grip on her arm as Mrs Deas Thompson waved to an annex along a bank of windows. "Of course. Let me escort you to a seat."

Sliding her hand free of her husband's arm, Grace allowed herself to be guided. An enormous gilt chandelier hung from an embossed feature in the middle of the high ceiling. Grace eyed the monstrosity—harbouring a childhood distrust that it might come crashing down—and was glad when Mrs Deas Thompson steered her around it. She could not deny that the crystal beads catching the flickering candlelight cast a mesmerising shimmer of light around the great hall.

She stopped before a line of chairs, sinking into the one remaining spot with a sigh. To her left, sitting alone and looking utterly terrified, was a young lady, barely more than a girl. Grace thought her high-necked, frilly gown was more suited for Paris than a penal colony. To her right, an older matronly type in black widow's weeds stiffened, her rheumy eyes sliding sideways at Grace.

Mrs Deas Thompson waved at the wide-eyed creature beside her. "Mrs Adelia Barclay, this is Mrs Grace Fitzwilliam, wife of the dashing Captain Fitzwilliam over there with my father." Mrs Barclay's gaze skittered around the room, and she nodded at Grace in minute acknowledgement. Poor thing looked painfully shy.

"And this," said Mrs Deas Thompson, waving to the older woman, "is Mrs Petunia Crunk."

"*Widow* Crunk," corrected the grey-haired woman primly.

Widow Crunk's brittle manner did not seem to perturb Mrs Deas Thompson, and Grace appreciated her gentle voice. "I'll come and find you later, so you can tell me of all your adventures. Alas, guests are still arriving and duty beckons." With a flurried swish of skirts, she swept away.

Waving an airy hand, Widow Crunk leaned forward, scrutinising Grace with the same critical eye that the officials had given the new arrivals at the dock. Grace raised her chin and straightened her back.

Widow Crunk sniffed and spoke nasally. "Haven't seen you before. Don't imagine you've been in town much longer than Mrs Barclay here. Though you do carry a little more weight as a captain's wife."

By weight, Grace hoped the sour-faced woman meant Seamus's social standing and not her burgeoning midline. Could a perfect stranger possibly be so rude? Next to Grace, Mrs Barclay smoothed out her skirts, and her eyelashes fluttered as though she were blinking back tears.

Grace swivelled her head back at the old woman's snippy voice. "*She's* the new wife of Elijah Barclay, owner of the largest sheep station out west. Comes from a long line of Lombard Street bankers. But she's embarking on a new life here in the colonies, aren't you, dear?"

Mrs Barclay nodded mutely.

Grace's gaze flicked back to Widow Crunk as she continued, "You're both no doubt *scandalised* to find yourselves in such company." Her wrinkled lips pursed, and Grace followed her rheumy glare. A respectably dressed woman stood easily on the arm of a distinguished gentleman in a black suit. Widow Crunk cleared her throat. "I don't know *what* the governor was thinking when he invited *them*. Just because he's a barrister and statesman doesn't elevate *her* into a superior position. Once a convict, always a convict, I say."

Grace stiffened at her tone, watching in empathy as Mrs Barclay fixed her gaze to her lap. It was clear the poor girl had been subject to Widow Crunk's sharp tongue already. The widow reached across Grace and tapped Mrs Barclay's knee with her folded fan. "Truth be told, dear, if it weren't for *your* connections back in London, Mr Barclay wouldn't have had a look in tonight, what with him being a self-made man *and* sheep farmer to boot. You've undoubtedly elevated *his* status a great deal."

Mrs Barclay balked, her pale cheeks colouring. She lowered her lashes, and Grace caught the tremble in her chin.

Grace gripped the old woman's sinewy wrist. "Widow Crunk!" At her sharp tone, the snooty widow jumped, glaring at her with yellowing eyes. Grace tempered her scowl into a meek smile. She arched back in the chair, accentuating the bulge of her belly. "It's rather hot in here, and I'm parched. Might I trouble you to fetch me a drink?"

Scoffing, the widow rose from her chair and peered down her long nose. "I'll find you a *servant*, Mrs Fitzwilliam." She sauntered off, her head cocked importantly.

Grace shuffled over beside Mrs Barclay. "Never mind that stuffy old potato."

Mrs Barclay's eyes widened at the insult, but a girlish giggle burst out. "I'd be too scared to ask any of the servants for a drink." She leaned in, whispering, "My husband tells me they're *all* ex-convicts!"

Grace pressed her lips together. "They're all *ex*-convicts because they've finished serving their time. They've as much right to be here as you and your husband." Mrs Barclay's gaze slipped to her lap again. Grace patted her knee reassuringly. "That Widow Crunk thinks she's the Queen of Sheba, when she's but a shrivelled bat seeing out her days in some backwater hole."

Mrs Barclay whipped her head up, her brow furrowed. Realising what she had just said, Grace gasped. "I'm sorry! I didn't mean to insinuate your new home is some backwater hole. I'm sure your husband runs a respectable sheep station."

The gold specks in Mrs Barclay's hazel eyes dimmed. "I haven't yet seen it, though I imagine it's a far cry from my parents' home in London. In the few days I've been here, I've seen precious few gentlewomen about. Did you know they have *no* theatres or bookshops or galleries—no exhibitions of intellectual life *whatsoever*."

"Well, I say pooh to London. The strict hierarchical structure of society there is utterly stifling." Grace waved a hand at the room. "I fancy this egalitarian way of life in the colonies. You can be your own person here, even if it *is* hotter than a blacksmith's forge." She fanned herself with her handkerchief again. "Besides, what's to stop *you* from opening your own theatre or bookshop, Mrs Barclay?"

Mrs Barclay scowled. "But wouldn't that put me at the same level as the working class?"

"Think of it as a charitable service—to import some culture to town." Grace waggled her brows. "Besides, did Widow Crunk herself not just describe your husband's sheep station as the *largest* in the colony?"

"Yes."

"Well then, your husband sounds like a respectable self-made man who puts in an honest day's work for his rewards. He may not be gentle born, but he's no convict either. You should be proud of him. To hell with what the Widow Crunks of the world think."

A resolution settled on the young woman's face as she spoke. "This place might be the back of beyond, but it's my home now." She smiled shyly. "You speak frankly, Mrs Fitzwilliam."

"Please, call me Grace. May I call you Adelia?"

Mrs Barclay's thin champagne-blonde eyebrows arched, and her small mouth curled up. "You may indeed, Grace." She swallowed deeply. "If it isn't too impertinent to ask, I'd very much like to be your friend."

Grace chuckled. "I'd like that too." She scrunched her nose.

Adelia shuffled upright. "Well, in that case, I'd like to invite you and your family to stay with us at Wooloongilly Downs— Gilly Downs for short. Wooloongilly is such a mouthful, don't you think?" Adelia paused as Grace bit her lips together.

Gilly. It had been a while since she had heard that name spoken out loud.

"My apologies, Grace. Have I said something to upset you?"

Grace laughed lightly. "I'm more nostalgic than upset. I had a friend named Gilly, but I lost him years ago." She swallowed the lump in her throat before beaming brightly. "I think Gilly Downs is a fine name."

"Truth is," said Adelia, gnawing her bottom lip, "I do hope it lives up to its name. Since Mr Barclay and I arrived a week ago, we've been staying in town while he sees to some business."

"By the sounds of things, it must be quite grand. Having the reputation of the largest sheep station can't come lightly," encouraged Grace.

"I must warn you, it's a four-hour ride on horseback from town." Adelia blushed again and became flustered. "You *do* ride?"

Grace straightened her spine, arching her nose in the air. "All respectable young ladies in London are taught to trip around Hyde Park."

Adelia chortled. "No tradesmen on shaggy ponies there."

"I'll speak with Captain Fitzwilliam. If he's agreeable, then yes, I'd love to visit your new home." Laughing freely with her new friend, Grace wondered how amenable Seamus would be to a visit to Gilly Downs.

"I'll be ever so glad to swell the numbers of our travelling party. Mr Barclay was just bemoaning how the criminal element of this town always seem to head west across Gilly Downs when they flee. That last lot who robbed the bank call themselves the Gentlemen Callers."

Grace laughed. "What? On account of them popping in to pay farmers a visit?"

"You laugh, but they've a fierce reputation for luring indentured servants away with promises of freedom and fortune. Mr Barclay says they're the blight of the earth."

The humour in her dried up as quickly as an ephemeral stream after a rainstorm. Her new friend's word of warning were unsettlingly similar to Major Winfield's. Even Billy had been imprisoned with a bushranger from this part of the world back in Newgate. Were they truly this plentiful in these parts?

Shaking off her gloomy thoughts, Grace patted Adelia's hand. "Well then, we'd best both don our dreariest day dresses for the occasion. Highwaymen are inquisitive creatures, drawn to shiny trinkets like magpies. We shan't give them anything to look at."

Chapter Twenty-Five

Seamus readily accepted the invitation to Wooloongilly Downs. Elijah Barclay's business nous preceded him. If Seamus was to establish any commercial connections in this remote part of the world, Barclay was his man.

Now, he tightened his grip on the leather reins as his horse wandered past the grand homes and cultivated gardens of the senior officers and government officials. Reaching the outskirts of town, he admired the neatly laid houses of soldiers and their families and, beyond that, the cultivated fields and scattered farms. The surroundings quickly turned to rough bushland. The odours of dog excrement and unwashed humanity were replaced by the fresh citrusy mint bouquet of the eucalypts. He could see Emily was in heaven on her own pony, even though it was secured to his saddle by the leather reins.

Seamus undulated in time with his horse's leisurely pace. Barclay wiped his forearm across his tanned brow to clear the perspiration. Tipping back a water skin, the grazier's Adam's apple bobbed with deep gulps. He handed the skin to Seamus.

"Drink plenty in this heat," cautioned Barclay. "Or you'll topple from your horse before long."

Swallowing several mouthfuls of the lukewarm water, Seamus winced at the brackish flavour. Still, it did the trick. He handed it to Emily. Peering across wide-open grasslands and through dry bush at the flaky trunks of the paperbark eucalypts, Seamus listened contentedly while Barclay pointed out kangaroos to Emily. Large black birds cried harshly from the treetops, competing with the humming summer song of insects.

"Look," hooted Emily, pointing excitedly.

Holding onto his hat, he squinted against the sun. "A crow?" A blasted big one, too. He turned to Barclay. "What on earth are English birds doing all the way out here?"

Barclay's ruddy face broke out in a grin. "It's a raven. These ones are native to New Holland. As you can see, they're bigger than the English ones."

"How can you tell the difference?" asked Emily, kicking her legs into her pony's sides and catching up to Seamus.

"Well, ravens go 'aaar, aaar, aarrrrrrrr' and crows go 'ark ark ark'. Or something to that effect." The red of the grazier's ruddy cheeks deepened. Emily burst into bubbles of laughter. For the next hour, Seamus endured Emily's repeated squawks at the black birds in the trees.

Barclay pointed at a flock of large white parrots with marvellous yellow crests, and shook his freckled fist. "Wretched flying rats! You leave my vegetable patch alone, d'you hear?"

Seamus laughed as the parrots' yellow crests flared into indignant fans at the insult. "At least your sheep are in no danger of being raided by the local birdlife."

"Indeed. The only danger in sheep farming is being unable to ship the wool to London in any decent amount of time." Barclay slapped his cheek, and the flattened carcass of a fly fell to the ground.

Seamus drew his shoulders back. His weary muscles, unused to riding, were forgotten at the prospect of a new business proposition. "What's the nature of merchant ships in this part of the world?"

Barclay tutted and shook his head. "Unreliable at worst. Sporadic at best. Even when a ship's found, it takes months to return to London."

Swiping the perspiration from his top lip with his thumb, Seamus sank into thought. Would he be able to persuade another investor into such a venture? Perhaps, if it were profitable enough. Until he could find out what in Neptune's name was going on with Hamilton, he needed to establish new business acquaintances. He resolved to ask Barclay to show him the figures later—arm himself with enough knowledge for a decent business proposal for a future investor.

By midday, the heat beat down on Seamus like a despotic tyrant with a fiery flail. Seamus removed his coat and rolled his sleeves, glad of his large straw boater. Beside him, Emily windmilled her arms at the swarm of flies buzzing around her face. He peered back at Grace and Mrs Barclay bringing up the rear of the riding party. His wife's heat-pinkened face blazed with affection. He was glad she had some female company for a change.

By the time they trotted past a large, blackened gumtree, he was shifting uncomfortably in his saddle. He did not think his backside could tolerate another minute in the hard leather seat.

"This old gum's the start of Gilly Downs," declared Barclay proudly. His sun-kissed face shone a cherry red that clashed with his coppery hair. The sheep station blossomed into view over the crest of a hill, spread out in the dip of a sunburnt valley with a brown stream cutting through it.

Hearing a short, sharp cry, Seamus twisted back in his saddle. Mrs Barclay's pink mouth moved wordlessly as she pivoted her head. Seamus turned to study the homestead he knew she was seeing for the first time. It was easy to understand where her horror came from. At first glance, even he could not tell much difference between the rudimentary main cottage and the slatted storage shed, both roofed with matching bark cladding. The two windows at the front of the cabin were dressed with wooden shutters fastened back by leather thongs. The horses ambled down the long, curved track, their hooves clopping over the low wooden bridge of the stream. Swirling dust devils greeted them in the dooryard.

"There's no glass in the windows." Mrs Barclay's voice trembled. Barclay dismounted and tied his horse to the sandy hitching post. Either he had not heard his wife's dismay or he was ignoring her. Dismounting himself, Seamus gripped Emily's waist as she slid out of the saddle. He supported Grace as she slid cumbersomely to the compact earth beside him.

Barclay helped his wife down, and Seamus offered her an encouraging smile. "At least those eucalypts offer the homestead a generous cover of shade in the afternoon. A godsend in this heat." He patted his trousers, and puffs of powder clouded around him.

Mrs Barclay whimpered, her reply drowned out by the desperate, high-pitched bawls of calves in the calf pen. Their mothers replied urgently with deep bellows. Seamus hoped the plumes of white smoke from the separate kitchen building, curling and dissipating into the clear blue sky, meant a hearty midday meal might be on offer. His stomach growled in agreement.

Chickens roamed freely around the dusty yard, clucking and pecking curiously at the dirt. Emily squatted, and a hen strutted over to her, its head bobbing on its scrawny neck. The hen made a watery clucking noise as it stepped within her reach. She tickled the back of its neck with her finger, and it gave a fluttery ruffle of pleasure, its feathers puffing and its eyes closing.

"Best not get too attached," cautioned Barclay. "'Tis likely to end up on your dinner plate." Standing beside Mrs Barclay, he shuffled from one foot to the other and pointed up the hillside to a high-roofed shed. "See that, lambkin? That's the shearing shed. I'll take you there this afternoon to watch the shearing."

Mrs Barclay made a small noise of agreement in her throat, and looked uneasily at Seamus and Grace. "But first, I must see our guests are made comfortable."

The hunched figures of the shearers bent over a row of upturned sheep. Beside the shearing shed, a flock of thickly fleeced animals bleated agitatedly in the fenced stockyard. Warm sweat trickled down the middle of Seamus's back. *Heavens, how do they manage such a laborious task in this heat?*

Mrs Barclay spat as a persistent fly crawled between her lips, desperately seeking moisture. "Come," she said, overly bright. "Let's go inside."

The front door swung open on its looped leather hinges. Mrs Barclay sucked in a sharp breath and stepped inside. From the doorway, Seamus could see the entirety of the hut's layout. At the heart of the home, a rough wooden trestle masqueraded as a dining table. In the bedroom to his left, the leather, plaited bed base—drooping between the wooden stumps of legs and the bed cover—appeared to be cowhide. Old wooden crates, slid into a homemade frame, made up a rudimentary, yet functional, chest of drawers. The room to his right could hardly be branded a parlour, but he supposed it must be with its one settee, a lace curtain the colour of tobacco spit, and a moth-eaten rug. Unaired in the unbearable heat, it stank of stale dust and old feathers. The place was perfectly practical, and Seamus could see how a man might proclaim this a home. But Mrs Barclay's tight-lipped smile and straining neck muscles told another story.

Barclay rubbed his hands together and they rasped dryly. "You can wash at the pump in the dooryard. Privy's behind the kitchen. Be sure to check for snakes."

Grace's warm, slick fingers slid into his. His courtship with Grace had been an unconventional one too, though he was glad they had not shared this awkward atmosphere at the start.

"Right," said Barclay briskly. "I'll just let Cook know we're ready to eat." He darted through the doorway, his boots crunching on the gravel.

Washed and refreshed, Seamus eyed the platters of sliced smoked ham, the generous wheel of cheese, and the freshly baked bread wobbling on the uneven table. Barclay ducked to wedge a woodchip beneath the leg, and the table stilled.

"Sorry there's no butter for the bread," he said. "Turns to oil in this heat. But there's cheese aplenty."

Seamus, diplomatically avoiding Mrs Barclay's red-rimmed eyes, carved a chunk of the hard cheese.

Mrs Barclay sniffled, her words thick. "It looks delicious. Thank you, husband."

Grace shifted slightly, and Seamus realised she had taken Mrs Barclay's hand under the table. He turned to the red-headed grazier, eager to inject some life into the stilted conversation. "What's the order around here, Barclay? You must keep a tight ship to manage a property this size?"

"Couldn't do it without my stockmen." Barclay nodded. "Tomorrow, if you're up to it, you can head out with me to deliver them supplies?"

"How many livestock are in their keep?"

"Five thousand head of sheep and seven hundred head of cattle."

"Heavens above! That many animals on an unfenced property? How will we find them?"

"By the dust clouds on the horizon. Requires hard riding to catch up with them."

"Cappy, I come too?" Emily asked.

Glancing at Emily's eager grin, Seamus turned and arched his brows at Barclay. The grazier shrugged and said, "We'll be in the bush for three or so days, but she can ride and sleep in the supply cart." He tapped Emily's shoulder with a freckled finger. "You can nurse the orphaned lambs we gather along the way."

Emily sucked her breath in through her grinning teeth, and Seamus glanced over to Grace to gauge her approval. She nodded and smiled, the pale dust on her skin accentuating her smile creases.

After the meal, Seamus followed Barclay to the shearing shed, with Emily bounding around him with the energy of a lamb in springtime. Grace remained with Mrs Barclay in the cottage to help her unpack her trunk. The new mistress of Gilly Downs needed a healthy serving of encouragement, and Seamus knew his wife was the one to deliver it.

AT DAWN NEXT MORNING, Grace dispatched Seamus and Emily off with Elijah. Before the bite of the sun took hold, she tended the vegetable patch with Adelia and took cheese-making lessons from Cook.

"Right," said Cook, wiping her hands on her grimy apron. "Now we must prepare the slush lamps for this evenin'."

Grace spotted Adelia nervously eyeing the empty treacle tins awaiting the rendered mutton fat. "Can't we just use candles?"

Cook's weatherworn face creased. "Why'd we waste candles like that? Slush lamps do the job well enough."

"Yes, but they—*stink*," Adelia squeaked. "I'm sure my husband can afford proper candles."

"Master don't like to waste." Cook tutted. She pointed to a wooden cabinet on the wall that housed hanging rows of tallow candles, the saltpetre-dipped wicks reeking with amniotic similarity to the outhouse. "Them's for special occasions only."

"But they're tallow. Where are the beeswax candles?"

Adelia's face was pale beneath the two heat patches on her cheeks.

"No need to waste coin like that." Cook bristled, sliding an empty treacle tin towards her.

With the vile job done, Grace steered her trembling friend into the homestead parlour. "Come now, Adelia, dear. Let's sit a moment. I'll help you sew those new shirts Elijah asked for."

Although the parlour barely earned itself that title, Grace pressed back into the lumpy horsehair settee as though it were a velvet divan. She desperately wanted to draw Adelia's attention away from the tattered lace curtain fluttering in the hot afternoon breeze, and the patchy carpets that were a necessity due to the splintery planks. Pretending the room was an arena of repose and beauty, Grace chatted easily. "Mr Barclay will look dashing in these new shirts."

Adelia's chin trembled. "He's not half as attentive to me as your husband is to you."

Rough furnishings aside, Grace was relieved to be out of the sun and away from the screeching cacophony of cicada beetles. She smiled kindly. "Give it time. You're newly married and still trying to figure each other out."

"I warrant you and Captain Fitzwilliam needed no time to figure one another out."

"On the contrary. He didn't give me a second look for the first few months that I was under his nose," said Grace.

Adelia scoffed and swiped back wisps of hair stuck to her glistening forehead. She nodded at Grace's bulging belly. "I'd say that's been well and truly remedied."

Ow! Stinking rats' tails! Grace flinched as she pricked her finger for the third time. "It's true!" Arching her brows, she explained her colourful start on the *Discerning*. "I'm sure it won't be long before you've your own bunch of red-headed babes to run after." She grinned.

The excitement in Adelia's eyes faded as she lowered her

eyelashes to her sewing, her cheeks the same deep red as the thread on her needle. "Not likely."

Grace lowered the half-tacked shirt into her lap. "Why not? You're a respectable married woman now."

Tears welled in her friend's light hazel eyes and she blinked hastily. "Mr Barclay and I have not yet... you know"—she fixed her gaze to the floor, her voice trailing off—"*consummated* our marriage."

Grace empathised with her friend's embarrassment. She often thought back to her own wedding night at Abertarff House. Seamus had shown her the true measure of his love that night, but she knew it was not so for all wives.

"Do you love your husband?"

Adelia's hands curled tight around the cotton fabric in her lap. "I barely know the man. He entered my father's library six months ago and asked for my hand without even meeting me. We were married two months later, and three months after that, I arrived here in New Holland."

"Oh, my. I'm sorry. I didn't realise the circumstances."

"I'm my father's fourth daughter. My other sisters are already in what *he* calls 'solid' marriages grounded on good business principles. Mr Barclay convinced my father that invest-ment in the colonies was the way to go. Being an astute busi-nessman, my father threw me into the equation to ensure he could keep an eye on his investments through the family connection."

Goodness! This was uncomfortably similar to her own circumstances with Silverton. Not a day went by that she was not glad to have dodged that life. She let out a soft sigh, her shoul-ders slumping. "Don't you have even the slightest attraction to the man? He appears kindly enough." *Unlike Silverton,* thought Grace, an invisible shudder rippling beneath her skin.

"He is kind, but kindness won't result in infants if he doesn't touch me." Adelia bit the thread on the shirt, her gaze wandering over to Grace. "How did you garner your husband's interest?"

Grace's discomfort slithered away as she understood that the new bride was sincerely interested in pursuing her new husband's attention. Not knowing what advice she might have offered if the opposite had been true, she settled herself on the settee, prepared to school the inexperienced woman as best she could. Thankful that she had learned these nuances under her husband's expert tuition, Grace took a deep breath. "Firstly, I assure you that as a red-blooded man, your husband will most *definitely* want relations with you. It appears you must both overcome your shyness of one another."

"And how do we do that?" Adelia sat forward in her chair, her interest fixed.

"Don't be afraid to fully disrobe before your husband."

"And let him see me—*without any clothes*!" The whites of Adelia's eyes bulged.

"Of course. Let him see what you have to offer. There's nothing quite as alluring to the male species as a woman's form. I assure you—that *will* pique his interest."

"And if it doesn't?" Adelia pressed her palm to her blazing cheek.

"If he still doesn't know what to do with you, then you must show him."

Adelia dropped her hand. "*Me*? Show *him*? I—I wouldn't know what to do."

Grace regarded her friend momentarily—she was leaning forward so intently, she was on the verge of dropping off the edge of her seat. "You do know the fundamentals, don't you? Which bits go where?"

"Well… yes—in a fashion. My older sister, Victoria, told me how her husband placed himself inside her." Adelia winced. "Though she didn't appear to gain any pleasure from it. She said these things were a duty to be endured."

"Poppycock! Don't be afraid to touch your husband."

"What? *Down there*? I couldn't possibly! He wouldn't let me... would he?" Adelia crossed and then uncrossed her ankles, squirming. Her chin jutted as she stared openly at Grace, waiting for an answer.

"Oh, he most definitely will—that I can promise you. But I don't only mean *down there*. Use your hands to study the shape of him, the curve of his jaw, the firmness of his chest, the contour of his buttocks. And don't be shy to look him in the eye when you do that."

"What then?" Adelia's voice hitched, the skin of her throat tightening as she swallowed.

"Then have him do the same to you. I particularly love it when Seamus traces his fingers over the soft part just above my knees."

"Your knees?" Adelia wrinkled her nose.

"You'll know your spot when he runs his hands over you. And don't be afraid to let him know either. Men aren't mind readers. They're simple creatures really. A little instruction goes a long way."

"How will I know where his spot is?"

"Of course you'll earn a reaction from him by reaching *down there*, but if you're truly intent on giving him pleasure, then watch for the signs. A quickening of breath, a dilation of pupils, gripping the sheets, ripples of gooseflesh—that sort of thing."

"Sounds like a rather time-consuming process. Victoria said Herbert is usually done in less than ten minutes." Adelia's lips twisted sideways.

"Oh, it *can* be," said Grace, smiling knowingly. "And sometimes that's not a bad thing. But in the beginning, take your time. Get to know your new husband."

"Will it hurt?" Adelia asked. Grace could hear the anxiety in her voice. "Victoria said it did and that for the most part, it's quite uncomfortable."

"It might, a little, the first time. It's a bit like learning to dance with a new partner. You may step on each other's toes a few times in the beginning, but with practice, your body will soon know what his wants."

Adelia pursed her lips and shuffled back in her chair, her sewing motionless in her lap. Grace smiled at the far-off look in her eye.

A dry scrape of shoes arrived at the parlour door. A young boy, with ragged black hair that looked as though it had been hacked with sheep shears, hovered in the doorway. The glass jar in his hands oozed golden strands that dripped onto the floor, and Grace guessed by the small insects buzzing furiously about the gummy mess that it was a pot of honey.

"May I help you?" Adelia asked primly.

The youngster flashed his neat row of milk teeth, and a flicker of familiarity twinged in the recesses of Grace's mind. Squinting, she took in the boy's round face and his wide ears, peeling from sunburn.

"Good day to ye, missus," greeted the grubby imp, his large eyes warm and alive like a recently stirred cup of cocoa. "My name's Nevin. My da thought ye might like a spot of honey? Newly fetched. Fresh as ye can get."

"Who's your father?" asked Adelia.

The youngster puffed up. "Rory Buchanan. Head shearer."

Good Lord! The needle jabbed into Grace's finger again, and she yelped. *Blast this wretched needlework!* Of course! Jim had said his father was head shearer at a station here in New Holland. Moaning softly, she sucked the stinging tip of her finger before releasing it with a light pop. "Buchanan? Is your uncle Jim Buchanan?"

Cocking his head, the boy scratched one of his protruding ears. "Aye. Do ye know him?"

Know him! Holy rats' tails! She had been living with the man for the past five years! And she had known him much longer than that. Grace steadied her thrashing heart with a couple of slow breaths. "Yes. I do."

Nevin's black brows tightened together in the exact same fashion as his uncle's. "Da said he was coming. Has he arrived?"

"Yes. He's my husband's survey assistant. Aboard the *Clover*. Do you live at Gilly Downs?"

"I do, missus. Was born here. Me grandmaw and grandda came out to Port Jackson when me da was but a boy."

Shuffling to the edge of the settee, Grace leaned her elbows on her knees, barely believing this good fortune. "Go on."

Nevin flushed under her scrutiny, but he grinned. "My grandda had his own flock back in Scotland before the filthy landlord kicked him off his land." Licking his glossy fingers, he wiped them down his shirtfront.

Grace sucked her bleeding finger again to stop herself laughing out loud at his outrage that had clearly been learned by repetition from an indignant Scot. She knew her fair share of them. "I'm familiar with the Highland clearings. Rotten business. Is your grandfather still here?"

"Nah. Old bugger died a few years back. Thrown from his horse during a muster." Nevin paused, a shadow of sadness darkening his eyes. "Me grandmaw weren't far behind him. Snake got her when she was hanging the washing." Nevin shrugged matter-of-factly, his black eyebrows pinching familiarly. "That's how me da came to be head of the shed. It'll be my job one day too when I'm grown up."

"And your mother?" queried Grace.

Nevin rubbed his eye with the back of his hand, leaving a brown smear across his cheek. "Never knew her. She died having me."

Adelia uttered a small sound of anguish and pressed her hand to her chest. Grace tilted her head, her voice gentle. "Sorry to hear that, Nevin. Do you have other family about?"

Catching another drip of honey with his finger, he shook his head. "Me Uncle Calum moved north to a cattle station, and me two aunties live in Sydney Town. They're both housemaids."

Grace rose and dropped the shirt into the sewing basket. She stepped nearer to Nevin, absorbing the family resemblance. "Goodness, you're just like your Uncle Jim."

"Ta for the grand news, missus!" He thrust the sticky vessel into Grace's hands. "I must go tell me da!" His leather-soled shoes patted across the floorboards, thumping on the gravel as he jumped over the front doorstep. He bolted towards the shearing shed as though a platoon of redcoats were chasing him.

A FEW DAYS LATER, Seamus, Emily, and Elijah returned to the homestead. Seamus was barely given time to rest before being put to work repairing the windpump. Grace stepped from the wooden kitchen hut and headed across the dooryard towards the metallic clangs, the tin mugs of tea sloshing on her tray. Seamus's white cotton shirt, transparent with sweat, contoured his back muscles as they bunched and jolted with each hammer blow. He stopped hammering and, passing the bent rod he had removed from the pump to Elijah, descended the wooden rungs on the leg of the windmill, his long, powerful legs making light work of it.

Grace studied his dusty boots and drew her eyes slowly up his body, enjoying the view. He fixed her with a look that told her he knew exactly what thoughts she was having, and she arched one eyebrow in response. A tiny trill of victory burbled in her chest as he blinked and broke away first.

"I'm heading back to the *Clover* tomorrow," he said, clasping a mug of tea and handing it to Elijah. "I'll deliver Jim his news about his kin. Give him a few days to visit. Mind you, he shan't be able to stay for long. I need him for the loading."

Lowering the tray to her side, Grace smiled. "I'd like to stay another couple of days. I'll head back with Jim when his visit's done."

Seamus nodded, but a shadow of disappointment darkened his eyes. Grace curled her arm around his back, tucking herself neatly along his damp flank. She inhaled his sharp male tang, appreciating the mix of clean sweat, dust, and pump grease—the scent of hard work.

"I'll accompany you, Fitzwilliam," said Elijah, slinging the bent rod over his shoulder and swigging his tea. "Must get this rod to the smithy. Have him straighten it out." He peered up at the large corrugated iron water tank. "We've enough water to last us a bit. But it won't do to prolong its fixing. Water is a scarce commodity out here."

Grace scrutinised the flakes of skin peeling off his lips from working under the intense sun, and she believed him.

The following morning, she stood in the open yard outside the back door, farewelling her husband. From inside Seamus's embrace, she had the perfect view as Elijah stepped awkwardly alongside his wife. The burly young grazier slid a broad hand over his wife's slim shoulder. Adelia stared up at him, blinking demurely.

"Adieu, lambkin," Elijah said softly.

Adelia's breath quickened as her husband kissed her gently on the cheek. They both blushed profusely, but Adelia caught Grace's eye, her innocent wonder slipping into a shy smile.

Grace chuckled to herself—clearly her friend had followed her advice. Surveying her handiwork, she watched as Adelia rested her hand on Elijah's chest, her chin tilted, her pert, pink lips stretched. Elijah pressed her hand to his shirtfront with a tender smile. Grace tightened her arms around Seamus, wanting to bury her face in his chest and shriek with joy. She peeked at the intimate scene from the corner of her eye.

"Mr Barclay," began Adelia shyly. "Might you enquire about

some glass for the windows while you're in town? My father's allowance should cover it."

Elijah's lips twitched as he cocked his head. "Mrs Barclay, I could buy glass for every house in the colony, should I wish."

"But how?" squeaked Adelia, waving a pale hand at the rustic cabin. "You've barely enough coin for proper candles!"

Elijah shook his head and waved away a fly. "Didn't have need of proper candles until you arrived, lambkin. If it's fancy candles you desire, all you need do is ask."

Adelia gave a watery laugh. "That—and a more comfortable mattress."

"I'll build you a castle if it ensures your happiness," said Elijah, pressing her knuckles to his lips. Adelia's cheeks coloured, and she nibbled her bottom lip.

Offering them some privacy in their intimate moment, Grace considered the rough, wooden walls of the cabin. So, this rudimentary but functional dust-trap was *not* how Elijah Barclay chose to make his mark on the world—even though he had the means. Studying her friend's flushing face, Grace appreciated that Adelia looked set to make her own mark. Ha! That would give old Widow Crunk something to sink her gossipy gums into!

Adelia whispered, "Be safe, husband. Return to me soon."

With a stiff, dry cough, Elijah turned swiftly, tugging at the leg of his trousers as he did a two-step dance to re-arrange himself before mounting his horse. Grace pressed her smile against Seamus's shirt front and breathed in the warm, earthy scent of him, thankful for this wholesome man who she loved with every breath in her body.

Chapter Twenty-Six

Through the kitchen window opening, Grace watched Nevin struggle up the hill with a heavy bucket, water sloshing muddy trails down his dusty legs. Rory Buchanan appeared from the shearing shed to help his son. Grace shook her head at their uncanny likeness to Jim. They both had the same dead-straight, jet-black hair, hacked in a similar unflattering style. The family resemblance ran strongly in their round faces and protruding ears. Her stomach fluttered in excitement—Jim was arriving at Gilly Downs this afternoon.

Standing on a low stool beside Grace at the kitchen workbench, Emily sunk her hands wrist-deep into the bread dough. "Can I play with Nevin?"

"Not yet, darling. He has morning chores to complete." She glanced out of the window again just as Adelia disappeared behind a freshly laundered bed sheet on the clothesline. Cook, who had been teaching her and Emily how to make bread, waddled across the dooryard to the storeroom to fetch some apples for that evening's apple and rhubarb pie.

Grace chuckled as Emily pulled her fingers from the dough, congealed white clumps sticking to her fingertips. The little girl rubbed her nose with the back of her hand, smiling ruefully at the sticky mess.

"You need more flour," said Grace, reaching for the flour tin and liberally dusting the sticky lump in Emily's hands. "I think we should leave the bread-making to Cook, don't you? Wash up now, Empem. Fetch your slate and chalk from the house. You must practise your letters."

Emily's right eye crinkled as she winced. "Must I?" She rubbed her hands together, rolling the sticky residue into little balls and showering the large lump of dough. "I don't like it."

Grace hid her smile by licking the salty sweat from the corner of her mouth. "All young ladies must learn the art of writing."

"Yes, Mamam." Emily washed and dried her hands then clomped through the back door, heading down the gravel path to the cottage.

Grace scrubbed her hands vigorously in the lukewarm water in the tin bowl, picking off the bits of gloopy flour along the edge of her nail beds. She dried her hands on the cloth tucked into her apron. Pulling open the cast-iron door of the brick oven, she squinted against the blazing inferno of the wood fire to check on the progress of Cook's current batch of mulberry and quince tarts. A hot, spiced wall of baked berry and buttery crust aromas pushed her back. Nearly done. They would make a delicious afternoon tea delight. Closing the oven door with a dull thud, Grace turned at the sound of feet shuffling.

A silhouette of a man filled the doorway, his broad shoulders blocking out most of the light. She did not recognise the nonde-script man with flaxen hair. A large white scar cut across under his nose against his tanned complexion. He bowed deeply.

"Harley Suffolk, at your service." He straightened up. "And you are?"

Grace hesitated at the familiar name. Where had she heard it before? "Mrs Fitzwilliam."

The stranger stepped into the kitchen. "Boil us up a cuppa won't you, love? I'm parched."

Grace startled at his informality and forwardness. "Um, if you're after Mr Barclay, he's not here presently." Her gaze roved over the man's ill-kept clothes and bare feet. "If it's a job you're after, you'll find Rory Buchanan in the shearing shed. He's the man to speak to."

The man smirked, but there was no warmth to it. "Now you see, I already have a job." His overtly interested gaze peered at her through sun-freckled eyelids. "'Tis my job to relieve you fine folk of your belongings. See, what's mine is mine, and what's yours is *also* mine." The scar under his nose creased into a humourless sneer.

Suffolk? The name swirled in Grace's mind like a lone butterfly amidst a kaleidoscope of hundreds of other names. Of course! The bushranger Billy had told her about. The one chained beside him in the dank London prison. At the flood of recognition, Grace almost choked on her words. "Oh, good grief! You're *the* Harley Suffolk! The thief from Newgate Prison?"

"Oh, ho! So, my reputation precedes me?" The bushranger cocked his head arrogantly. "Good to be remembered for something rather than disappear into obscurity, I always say."

Goodness gracious. Was Suffolk one of the bank robbers Winfield had warned her about? The Gentlemen Callers? Grace pressed back against the workbench, one hand searching for the knife she knew was among the baking jumble. "I'm acquainted with Billy Sykes. You were imprisoned together."

The bushranger shrugged. "Been cellmates with many a man. Can't say I recall the name. Now, I'm no thief, mind you. I'll give you something of yours—in a fair exchange, of course—for all your muskets. I'm also keen on getting myself a double-barrelled fowling-piece, so I hope you're not going to disappoint me?"

Grace's fingers curled around the wooden handle of the knife. Her heart thumped painfully in her chest as she measured the number of steps it would take to reach him. "What could you possibly have that would have me interested in bargaining with you?" she asked with forced nonchalance.

"Take a look for yourself." Suffolk stepped back from the doorway. "Haul 'em out, lads." His voice rang out clearly across the dooryard.

She peered through the glassless window. Bleeding rats' tails! Two armed men herded the dozen unarmed station workers from the shearing shed at gunpoint. Three station hands, who had been grubbing out tree roots in the paddock over the creek, and the household servants, were corralled on the dirt patch outside the kitchen. Another two men pushed Adelia from behind the hanging sheets, nudging her over to the group.

Suffolk signalled. "Sit 'em down, lads."

With butts of muskets jabbing into several of the station hands' thighs, they dropped to the dirt with grunts and growls. Adelia tumbled to the ground. Cook sat with her arms folded over her apron full of apples, glaring up at the gang of bushrangers. One of them snatched an apple.

Cook gripped the folds of her apron and wrestled his thieving arm. "Them's crab apples. No good for eatin'!"

Growling, he swung an angry kick. Cook ducked but lost the grip of her apron, the red, round orbs scattering in the dirt like well-struck marbles.

Seeing she was outnumbered, Grace slid the knife back onto the bench behind her. Any recklessness on her part would likely earn her a lead ball in her heart. She narrowed her eyes and firmed her chin. "You can have food and clothing, but you're *not* having our weapons. We need them for hunting and putting down sheep."

The Gentleman Caller's eyebrows shot up, but his laugh was without humour. "'Tisn't the adults I'm planning to bargain with, Mrs Fitzwilliam." Suffolk waved his hand above his head. She clenched a fistful of apron as a man dragged Nevin into view. The youngster's hands were trussed behind his back, his mouth gagged with a wad of cloth. Seeing the small boy struggling in the hands of a more powerful man flared her long-held abhorrence of injustice. Flaming Hades! This was just like Toby's flogging all over again. She snapped her head around as the bushranger continued. "And not forgetting the young lady who wandered into the main house."

Oh, no! He had seen Emily! Grace's blood ran cold. She ground her molars as Nevin kicked out viciously, but he was no match for the grown man who laughed teasingly, easily dodging his wildly aimed blows. Rory Buchanan snarled and launched from his sitting position like a panther springing powerfully towards its prey. The old, grizzled bushranger standing nearest to Rory swung his musket stock, driving it deep into the shearer's gut. Rory dropped like a felled tree. Curled in the dirt, his groans of agony sent up puffs of dirt around his head. Nevin's eyes bulged, his screams muffled by his gag. Grace grabbed the doorjamb.

Suffolk darted from the kitchen building. "My colonial oath!" he snarled, stomping over to the grizzled man. "Eejit! What d'you go and do that for?"

The old bushranger's boots shuffled. "He came at me."

Suffolk growled. "Wasn't asking *you*!" He pointed to Rory, curled and groaning on the ground. "Was asking *him*."

The greying bushranger nodded meekly and shuffled back a few steps. Suffolk sneered at Nevin and then focussed back on Rory. "Your boy, I take it?" He tutted, rolling his eyes. "Bloody fool! You want shooting for being so stupid. Want your son to watch you bleed out?"

Grace's insides clenched at the lack of remorse in the bushranger's voice. This was no man to mess about with. She turned sharply as Emily stepped into the kitchen through the back door, chalk slate in hand.

"Look, Mamam, 'E' for Emily."

Grace clamped her teeth onto her bottom lip. Snatching Emily's arm, she pressed her finger to her daughter's lips. "Shh," she cautioned. Emily's mouth twisted open in silent objection, her eyes flicking to Grace's firm grip on her arm. "There are bad men out there. Hide in the cellar."

Emily's pupils dilated and her bottom lip quivered. "But it's dark."

Steering her urgently across the room, Grace snatched a candlestick and matches from the sideboard. "You go in there all the time with Nevin." She fought to keep the panic out of her voice.

"But I'll be by my own."

She struck a match, but the head snapped off. Wretched thing! With trembling fingers, she struck another and it flared. "No, you won't. I'll be here in the kitchen the whole time." She thrust the lit candle at Emily and wrenched open the trap door. "Come on, Emily. Down you go."

"Yes, Mamam." Grace's heart lurched at the fear in her daughter's voice.

Compared to the uncouth state of the buildings above ground, the cellar Elijah had built was quite a luxury. Adelia had explained to Grace that he had followed the advice of a neighbouring grazier to build a proper underground storehouse. It kept perishable food from spoiling in less than a day in the sub-tropical sun. Grace sagged as she lowered the trapdoor into place.

Freed of her worry for Emily, Grace's thoughts shot to the flintlock pistol in the kitchen dresser—kept there for just such an event. She flicked a glance outside the window. With his back to her, Suffolk's muffled voice droned as he addressed his captives.

Stepping lightly over to the dresser, she pulled the two rings on the drawer front. The wooden drawer juddered with a dry scrape. She froze, listening for Suffolk's approach. Her trembling fingers seized the gunpowder horn and snatched the slim brass casing of the powder measure. Yanking the cork out with her teeth, she upended the horn. Pah! Gunpowder—tasted unsettlingly familiar as the sharp smell of cat piss. Beads of black powder jittered out over the edge of the brass measure, coating her fingers. Spitting out the cork and tossing the unstoppered flask aside, she wiped her blackened hand on her skirt and reached for the pistol. She had done this a thousand times in drill, and her hands worked instinctively. Holding the barrel up, the brass measure chattered against the metal rim of the muzzle as the black powder tipped out. Grace pushed the cotton wad into the upturned muzzle with a ball. *Come on. Come on. Hurry up!* She slid the ramrod from the underside of the pistol and forced the ball down the chamber, tamping it against the powder. Not wanting to waste time reseating the ramrod under the barrel, she laid it on the dresser beside the discarded powder horn.

A scream choked in her throat as a firm hand clamped her mouth from behind, the pistol twisted effortlessly from her grasp. She threw her head back, bracing for the impact of her skull on her attacker's nose, but he was quicker. Thrusting her against the rough planks of the wall, the man pressed his hard body against her, his belt buckle gouging into her upper buttocks. Grace bucked, kicking backwards, but he used the weight of his thigh to dampen her kicks. Anger swarmed like a buzzing cloud of hornets, her vision blurred by furious, hot tears.

"God's teeth, woman! 'Tis me. Stop fighting." Grace paused at the familiar cuss. Alby Church! His hand slid from her mouth, but he kept her pinned against the wall. She slumped her cheek against the jagged planks. Oh, good gracious!

Alby placed the pistol on the dresser and rested both hands on her waist. His accelerated breathing puffed against her neck, his heart pounding against her back.

"Alby, you're crushing me," whispered Grace.

"Oh, God! Sorry." He peeled away from her, twisting her gently to face him.

Bewilderment, relief, and undefinable happiness swept through Grace like an unrestrained wildfire. She threw her arms about his neck. He leaned in to touch his lips to hers. The softness of his kiss had a fierce passion behind it.

What in all the days on earth was he doing? She bucked like a wild horse again, shoving him away. His penetrating gaze blazed passionately, and he reached up to caress her face. She swatted his hand. "Stop it! What are you doing?"

"Wanted to do that since the day we met." Those soft lips she had just experienced curled in a self-satisfied smile. "You're a good kisser, ma'am. Could tell you wanted that as much as me."

She thrust hard against his chest. "No! Don't say such things, Alby."

He scanned her calmly. "Don't you care for me?"

"Of course, I care... but... not in *this* manner," she hissed, mindful of the courtyard full of armed men. "Just forget about it."

"How can I forget, when you kissed me back like that?"

"I didn't kiss you back. I'm *married*! And with child!" Grace squirmed under his intense gaze.

"I've learned to never leave things unsaid. None of us know what tomorrow holds."

"Stop it. You can't say that. I'm Seamus's *wife*. And happily so," she said, louder than intended. The air stilled as Alby sucked in his breath. She saw the burden of her rejection settling over him like a thick fur coat in the middle of summer. "What in blazes are you doing here?" The nail of confusion pounded into her headache.

"I accompanied Buchanan and Dr Sykes to fetch fresh supplies." Alby gripped her elbow.

She shrugged off his hand. "Where are they?"

"Outside. With Mr Barclay." He gripped her arm more firmly and reached for the pistol from the bureau. "Come. We can sneak behind the main house. Into the trees beyond."

She shrugged him off again. "I'm not leaving Emily."

He scoured the empty kitchen. "Where is she?"

"Down there." She pointed to the trap door, curling her hand into a fist to hide the shaking.

"I'll fetch her. Take this." He handed her the loaded weapon.

"No. Leave her be. She's safe in there."

Alby paused, his jaw muscles clenched. "You're not staying here. 'Tis too dangerous."

With her thoughts shifting to her daughter's safety, all the trembling left her body, and she turned from Alby with resolve. "I'm not leaving. You can't stop me." Newfound courage surged through her at the thought that Jim and Billy were outside.

"God's teeth, woman!" Alby snarled as he tried to grab her.

She neatly sidestepped him and, tucking the pistol into the back of her skirt, stepped in full view of the front doorway.

"Get back here. They'll shoot me if they see me." Alby lay flush against the wall, leaning well back from the doorframe, breathing heavily.

Suffolk, with his gun balanced across the back of his neck and his wrists hung limply over the length of it, levelled his eyes on Grace standing motionless in the open doorway. "Do join us, Mrs Fitzwilliam." The bushranger's invitation had an air of joviality to it.

Grace kept her voice light. "Unless you want lumps of coal in your haversacks, I suggest you let me wait for your mulberry and quince tarts to finish baking, Mr Suffolk." He smirked as she coolly placed her hands on her hips.

"Very well. You finish baking my tarts." He turned to address the seated men. "You're indentured servants, no better than slaves. Ride away with us. I see no walls, no bars keeping you here—only fear. Don't allow these imperialists to oppress the freedom of your new land with their tyranny. Come join the Gentlemen Callers." Suffolk waved his hand in the direction of the shearing shed. "Why eke out a meagre livelihood in this shithole, making graziers and government rich, when you can ride with me? Carve your own destiny. Be free men."

Grace spotted a few intrigued faces peering up at Suffolk from the sea of bowed heads.

He continued, "See the power you can have over those who lord their freedom over you. Power is for the taking, gentlemen. No one's going to give it to you." He swung his musket around, waving it inconsequentially over the crowd. Several men shrank back. "With a fine weapon like this, you can take all the power you want. So, who's with me?"

A deep voice rang out from the tree line. "I wouldn't do that if I were you." Eyes and musket muzzles swung in the same direction. Elijah stepped out from behind a tree, his hands raised. "The hellfire of Satan will rain down on you if you join this man and his gang. They're outlaws."

Chapter Twenty-Seven

Grace squinted into the shadows of the trees, looking for Jim's broad frame or for a flash of Billy's black hair. Where were they? She flicked her head around as Adelia wailed from the edge of the crowd.

Suffolk beamed genially at Elijah. "From your wife's reaction, you must be Barclay? How nice of you to join us."

Adelia whimpered again. Undeterred, Elijah strode on towards the bushranger. "Go around robbing banks and killing settlers, and the New South Wales police will put you down like a dog."

Suffolk laughed joylessly. "Those coppers couldn't run down a bloody poddy calf!"

Elijah stopped a short distance from Suffolk, and Grace admired his bravery. "I want no trouble. You clearly outnumber us, sir."

The bushranger glared suspiciously at the grazier's conciliatory tone. "Go on then, prove it. Have all your men step into the open." Suffolk's musket aimed steadily at Elijah.

Grace jolted as Elijah roared, "Show yourselves, men!" Jim stepped out from around the back of the shearing shed. Billy emerged from the same tree line as Elijah had.

Through clenched teeth, Grace growled at Alby, "Get outside with the others."

"No!" Frustration and dread soured his tone. "I'm *not* leaving you."

"Good gracious, Alby Church! You're not responsible for me!" Her barely audible words filtered through her gritted teeth and unmoving lips. "Get out of here before they find you and kill us both!"

Out in the dooryard, Suffolk frowned and turned. "Did you say something, Mrs Fitzwilliam?"

"Just cursing the wretched flies." Blood pooled from her face, and she waved one hand airily.

"Those tarts ready yet?" Suffolk asked.

"Almost. I must take them out to cool."

"Do that. Then join us." Suffolk turned, his gaze lingering over his shoulder. "Oh, and bring the girl, too. I know she wandered in there earlier."

Rats' tails! If he knew Emily was in here, was he aware of Alby too? Surely not. He would have sent armed men in to deal with him, would he not? Grace nodded and reached behind her back to undo her apron. In one smooth motion, she pulled the pistol from her waistband. Bundling the apron and pistol together, she placed them on the sideboard. Now was not the time for rashness. She wanted to fetch Emily and step outside where Billy was. She opened the trap door to retrieve her daughter. Blinking and wincing at the bright light, Emily's eyes widened with delight at seeing Alby crouched on the floor. With a waggle of his eyebrows, he pressed his fingers to his lips. Grace could see the worry in Emily's tight smile, but then he blew her a kiss, and her grin widened. Bloody Alby Church and his infernal charm!

"Alby," Grace whispered, "come out with us now." She eased her scowl as the whaler man nodded. "Don't do anything rash," she warned. Alby flashed his teeth at her. He looked smugly pleased with her concern for his welfare. She shook her head and hollered to Suffolk outside. "I'm coming out with my daughter now. And I've another man with me. He's unarmed."

Stepping neatly from the doorway with Emily, Grace cast a sideways glance at Alby. With his hands raised in the air, he stepped into the bright sunshine, half a dozen pistol and musket muzzles trained on him. Emily whined and hid her face in Grace's long skirts.

Billy lowered his head, tracking her and Emily's path from the kitchen. His lips pressed flat, and his face tightened as it did when he was deep in thought while diagnosing a patient. With a barely discernible flick of his head, he motioned for Grace to sit with the other women. Billy's eyes narrowed as Alby hovered nearby. He was a master of observation. Had he read her face? Seen her guilt?

As soon as Grace sat, Adelia launched into her arms with small bursts of panicky sobs. Grace squeezed her tightly. "Adelia, I know you're afraid, but you're scaring our Em."

Adelia exhaled through pursed lips, wiping the tears from her cheeks with the hem of her apron. She patted Emily's knee and pressed a brave smile to her lips.

Suffolk warily eyed Billy, his eyebrows shooting up. "By Lord, is that you, Pill Roller?" Suffolk strode towards the physician, stopping an arm's length away. "What're you doing here, my good man? Heard you were pardoned?"

Billy stepped forward and, from his tone, Grace knew he was not happy. "I was."

Grace winced at the gamut of emotions struggling for position on Billy's face. Beneath his scowling black brow, his eyes sparked with guilty delight at seeing the man who had saved his life by buying extra food and blankets all those years ago. She could not blame him.

Suffolk's bewilderment momentarily disarmed his tough persona, and the look of incredulity softened his features. He reached out his hand. "What in the blazes are you doing here, Pill Roller? Here by your own free will?"

"I am." Billy nodded shortly, shaking his old friend's hand with a firm grip. "I'm with Captain Fitzwilliam's ship. I'm a physician now."

"My oath, man! You've moved up in the world." Suffolk beamed.

Grace caught Billy's hesitation before he let Suffolk's hand go. Her heart ached with empathy as Billy's lips pressed white, his gaze sliding to Suffolk's musket.

"I see you're up to your old tricks again?" said Billy gruffly. "Thought you were banned from Sydney Town?"

"I was. I am." Suffolk rubbed the back of his head. "After getting out the nick the last time in London, I was nabbed for stealing the mare and carriage of the landlady of the White Horse Inn." Suffolk peered at Billy from under his eyebrows, his face a picture of contriteness. "To be fair, I was only borrowing it. I had a rather vexed husband on my heels." The bushranger laughed brashly. "He didn't take too kindly to my *acquaintance* with his wife. Needed a hasty escape from the hotel, and the lady's carriage was just the ticket. The judge weren't as sympathetic to my plight, though. Bastard sentenced me to transportation to Port Jackson—*again*. Though the minute my feet hit that stinking cesspit of a town, I did a runner. Been running ever since."

Billy shook his head with a grim smirk. "You're like a cat with nine lives."

"A bootless cat, no less." Suffolk shrugged.

Grace cast her gaze over to Elijah. He gave Emily a wink of reassurance, bringing half a smile to her daughter's face. The grazier stepped towards Suffolk. Grace heard Emily and Adelia suck in a breath as half a dozen muzzles swung in his direction.

"Look, Suffolk, I see the women and children are unharmed. I thank you for this." Elijah's Adam's apple bobbed deeply. "So, it's in this spirit that I give you fair warning. Major Winfield is heading this way."

Suffolk barked. "Ha! That bastard's too lazy to catch up with the likes of us."

Barclay's ruddy eyebrow rose and a hint of amusement played on his lips. "You're probably not wrong on that account, sir. The foppish popinjay is likely too busy looking in the reflection of his shiny buttons to bother coming after you. But speculation in town is that you'd likely cut through Wooloongilly Downs. 'Tis a big run."

Grace was relieved that Elijah's mockery towards Winfield neutralised the heavy undercurrent.

Billy added, "'Tis true."

Suffolk inclined his head. "And when exactly can we expect these reinforcements to arrive?"

Grace glued her gaze to Billy. Now was not the time to play games with Suffolk. Friend of Billy's or not, he was dangerous. Billy must have had the same thoughts because he answered mildly. "They're half a day away, perhaps a little less."

"I hear truth in your voice, my old friend." Suffolk's blistered nose scrunched. "Though, I'm not leaving until I've me fair share of clothing and provisions. And all of your weapons, powder, and ball." He raised one of his bare feet and waggled his toes. "Lost my boots yesterday after Banks over there got spooked—thought the coppers was on our tail. I was really enjoying my swim too. Left a real tart taste in my mouth to leave behind such a fine pair. Though those aren't half bad." He stuck his tongue out through his grinning lips as he ogled Elijah's footwear. "And I wouldn't half be obliged if your cook could whip us up something hot too. Been a while since we had a home-cooked meal."

Grace gripped Adelia's shoulder tighter at her low keening as the bushrangers ransacked the kitchen and cottage. The gang loaded several live chickens into baskets, and each man put on a new change of clothes from Elijah's trunks. Suffolk took Elijah's boots with a half-apologetic smirk. Cook placed the cauldron of mutton and vegetable stew that she had made for the shearers in the dooryard and served it with bread. The group of lawbreakers made quick work of the stew, tearing off chunks of bread and scooping the savoury meat straight from the cauldron, not seeming to care that it was tongue-blisteringly hot.

Grace flicked her head towards a movement in the tree line, her liver almost leaping up her throat at the wall of eight mounted police emerging like ghosts, with Winfield's green helmet plume jiggling at the fore. Oh Lord, nothing good would come of this. That pontificating showboat! Could he not have waited for the thieves to clear out before apprehending them?

"My, my, my. Isn't this the finest union of bushrangers and shearers in the colony?" drawled Winfield. He aimed his pistol at Suffolk. "Harley Suffolk, you are hereby under arrest."

Suffolk glared at Billy. "That's the fastest half-day's travel I've ever seen." He aimed his own weapon at Winfield's head, his bark of laughter filled with mockery. "Show me the warrant."

Winfield elongated his spine in the saddle. "By order of the Bushranging Act, a warrant is not required if criminal behaviour is suspected. And what I see before me looks suspiciously criminal. Am I right, Barclay? Is this lot causing you trouble?"

Elijah took a step towards Winfield and two of the officers trained their weapons on him. He stopped and raised both palms up. "Good God, Winfield, there are women and children about. Now is not the time to be a knight on a white charger."

Winfield's lips pursed, and he bristled. "It's my duty—"

"Duty, my arse!" scoffed Suffolk. "'Tis but your tangled

interpretation of the law. I'll be damned if I let you take me, Winfield." Suffolk snapped off a shot at Winfield, but it missed. The row of police riders swung their rifle muzzles up.

The seated shearers launched to their feet. Hunching over, they scattered like seeds of a dandelion in a stiff breeze to take cover behind the wooden buildings. Grace snatched Adelia and rolled atop her and Emily, hoping the volley of bullets would stay high. Sweet Lord, this was going to be a massacre. Keeping her chin tucked low, Grace searched for somewhere to hide. Right now even a blade of grass would do. Lord above, if only she could get to the kitchen—to the loaded pistol. No, she dared not risk dragging Emily to her feet—not with these fools' fuzzy aims. Emily quivered, both hands pressed to her ears.

Alby Church clambered past on his hands and knees. "Stay low!" he growled. The dark doorway of the kitchen swallowed him up. Grace spotted the barrel of the pistol poke through the window before bursting into obscurity behind a plume of blue-white smoke.

Rory Buchanan scrambled towards Nevin. Winfield, taking a moment longer to fire at Suffolk, steadied his pistol with his left hand before squeezing the trigger. Grace bit back a cry as Rory Buchanan doubled over as though punched in the gut. Jim's face contorted with fear and rage, his wide, brown stare fixed on the prostrate form of his brother. Good grief, no! The smarmy idiot had missed. Grace stared in horror at Rory's face—deathly pale, his dark-lashed eyelids scrunching with each gasp. Grace covered Emily's eyes with her hand.

"Da! Da!" Nevin's panic-pitched shrieks needled Grace's ears. With his captors preoccupied, Nevin threw himself across his father's body, burying his face in the crook of his neck. Wrapping his slim arms around the matching dark head, he shielded his father with the bravery of a gladiator facing a pride of lions in a Roman arena.

Grace swivelled her head at the thumping of Jim's thick-soled boots kicking up spurts of dust. *No, Jim! Stay down!* Grace gasped as her friend threw himself over Nevin and Rory. She would have taken the same risk if it were Emily.

The bursts of ignited black powder came from every direction, the white plumes adding to the chaos. Men's voices yelled in alarm and anger and agony. As quickly as the thunderous bedlam had started, it stopped. The ringing in Grace's ears negated the blissful silence that followed the brief and pitiless midday slaughter. Her chin scraped the dirt as she kept her head low, inspecting the carnage.

Six bloodied bodies littered the grassless dooryard. Two of the police horses were riderless but Winfield remained seated, viciously snatching the reins to steady his skittish horse. White eyed and frothy mouthed, the horse gnashed at its bit with yellowed teeth.

Elijah and Alby arrived simultaneously, both dropping to their knees beside Grace.

"God's teeth! Are you hurt, Mrs F.?" Alby's large hand gripped her arm. She shook her head.

"Lambkin?" Barclay dipped his head lower, peering under Grace's arm.

Adelia wriggled free, lunging into Elijah's arms, her jerky sobs renewed as he mumbled gentle sentiments about her courage and bravery. The stockmen and shearers poked their heads up from their hiding places behind the homestead buildings.

"For the love of all that's holy!" gasped Jim from beside his brother's quivering body. Rising to his knees, Jim gently peeled Nevin away, and rolled Rory onto his back. One half of the shearer's face was caked with dust, with tear-coagulated mud in the corner of his eye. Rory groaned, his calloused, grimy-nailed hand fumbling for Jim's.

Billy hurried to the injured man and tore open the bloodied

shirt front. He pressed the wad of his handkerchief over the dark blood oozing from the hole in Rory's stomach.

Grace pressed a kiss to Emily's forehead. "Stay with Alby. I'm going to help."

She slunk over to Rory, searching Billy's face for hope that all would be well. His eyes were fixed on his patient, though his jaw muscle jumped. *Please, Lord, no!* Jim had only just found his brother—he could not lose him like this. Incessant flies swooped towards the pooling blood like beasts around a watering hole. Breath quivering in revulsion, she waved them away, but they brazenly defied her efforts and swarmed down again. Flies and dust aside, the whole scene was starkly reminiscent of Gilly's death. She could not do this—not again. *Please, save him.*

"*Tha mi duilich.*" Rory's Gaelic plea was little more than a whisper, the effort to speak almost too much.

"Ye've nothing to be sorry for, brother." Jim's voice hitched. "Dr Sykes will see to ye." His thick, bushy brows joined into one as he glanced trustingly at Billy.

"Da," Nevin's high voice quavered as his fingers feathered his father's cheek.

Rory's brown eyes flicked towards his son, and his Adam's apple bobbed deeply. "My son. Be a good lad for your uncle." He shivered as though he were lying on a slab of ice rather than the sun-baked earth.

Jim's knuckles whitened around Rory's hand, anger tainting his words. "Don't speak of such things!"

Turning her head away, Grace's sobs came out in silent breaths. She did not want Nevin to see her anguish. Knuckling her tears, she swallowed, but the tightness in her throat made it impossible. Blinking, she turned her gaze back to the bloody scene.

With the same far-off look in his eye that Gilly had before he died, Grace knew Rory's time was near. She put one hand on his shoulder and her other on Nevin's knee, as though she could connect the two of them one last time.

Jim growled low in his throat as his brother's eyelid slowly drooped. "By all the holy saints. Stay, brother."

Billy cursed and wrenched off his shirt. The bloodied handkerchief plopped into the dirt, and the dust settled on it like sprinkled cinnamon. Billy went to press the wad of his shirt onto Rory's belly, but he hesitated. The trickle of blood had stopped.

The heartbeat in Grace's ears roared. *Oh, Lord, no!* The pain in her chest was unbearable. Devastation cut deeply into Nevin's and Jim's matching faces. A swelling ball of panic and grief threatened to burst her heart as Billy exchanged looks with them. His large, brown eyes were unable to shield his pain as he shook his head.

"I'm sorry. He's gone."

Nevin let out a pitiful yowl that burst Grace's ball of grief, and her vision blurred with tears again. The boy threw himself across his father's body. She glanced over her shoulder. Emily sat exactly where she had left her beside Alby, small and motionless. What a pitiful sight for these two children to witness—to be shown the cruelty of the world so young. Alby slid his hand across Emily's shoulders and the little girl curled her face into his side. Grace's earlier irritation at him evaporated.

Jim placed his hand on his nephew's small back, his fingers feathering up and down in comfort. "There, there, lad." Jim turned to Winfield, offering him a granite stare. "You killed my brother!"

Grace bunched her shoulders at the lack of regret in Winfield's cocked eyebrow. Heartless bastard!

Winfield pressed his lips together and waggled his head. "An unfortunate cost of war," he said, ramming his pistol into his belt.

"Jesus, Winfield!" exploded Barclay. "For lack of a little patience or a sensible strategy, you've killed an innocent man."

Grace noticed some of the indentured men's gazes glaring mutinously from the scattered dead bushrangers to the remaining police officers. This was how legends were made. Clearly, Elijah had spotted it too. His jaw muscles clenched and his gaze hardened as he panned across the crowd over Adelia's head. Elijah waved a hand at the shearing shed.

"There's a good life to be had here. An honest living for an honest day's work. Only a fool would consider joining the likes of Suffolk. No man lives long with a twenty-pound bounty on his head." Gasps and rumbles rippled through the men. Even the mutinous scowls of the indentured men melted into interest at the mention of the large reward. He narrowed his eyes at Winfield. "And I'm sure Major Winfield's report will tell of how Rory Buchanan assisted in taking down the Gentlemen Callers."

Winfield edged his horse towards Barclay, his face reddening. "He did no such—"

"Oh, but you'll report it as so, you bastard. Unless you want word spread that *you* murdered my head shearer with your lousy aim. That money will go to his son—now an orphan, thanks to you."

Winfield cast a shifty look over his shoulder at his men. Elongating his neck, he took a long breath through his nostrils and looked as though he were sucking lemons. "Very well, Barclay. I'll see what I can do." Winfield cocked his head at Jim. "The Colony of New South Wales thanks your brother for his assistance and offers its condolences."

With muffled obscenities, the shearers trailed back up the hill. Grace rose and, gathering Emily into her arms, turned away from the scene of devastation to let Jim and Nevin share in that intensely private moment when their beloved father and brother's heart stopped beating while theirs continued.

Chapter Twenty-Eight

S eamus glared at Grace in the bedroom at William Wells' house at The Rocks. The sounds of the town below the bedroom window were harsh and unnatural after the tweeting, chirping, and rustling of the bush.

"Church did *what?*" Teetering on the edge of a catastrophic eruption, he clenched his fists, the old injury in his wrist clicking. He shut the bedroom door quietly so as not to alarm Emily, who was downstairs chopping carrots for their dinner in the kitchen with Biddy.

"He kissed me," squeaked Grace, a flush creeping up her neck as she perched on the windowsill.

He eyed the open window. If the lulled conversations of the people below carried so clearly up to him, then his raised voice was likely spreading over the street below like a tub of dirty water. But he did not care.

"You don't seem too bothered by that." He snapped his hands behind his back and locked his knees against the agony of her betrayal. Her confession sat like a tombstone on their marriage.

Grace held her hands up and took a deep breath. He could tell how hard she fought to keep her voice measured and reasonable. "Seamus, I told you this because, on our wedding day, you said it felt good not to have secrets between us."

He scowled and tramped across the room. "And I never imagined on our wedding day that my *wife* would be standing before me, telling me she allowed herself to be kissed by *another man*." The tip of his nose almost touched hers, pinning her to the window frame. To hell with any eavesdroppers!

"I had Emily hidden in the cellar, for goodness' sake! You know how afraid of the dark she is—and I shoved her down that dark hole all by herself!" Grace yelled, shoving him backwards.

Grounding his feet, he cocked his head. She could push him all she liked, but he *was* going to have answers. "I don't see how our daughter's fear of the dark is a catalyst to you not stopping Church from locking lips with you."

"Don't make it sound so sordid. I was scared!" Grace shouted. "Scared for me. Scared for Emily. Scared for the child inside me. And when I saw Alby's face, I felt an unholy sense of gratitude. I hugged him with relief that he was there. And when he kissed me unexpectedly, I did push him away."

"Not until *after* he went in for a bit of heavenly bliss?" he seethed.

She jammed her hands on her hips. "It's no different to when you returned from the fort at Montevideo."

Seamus waggled his head in confusion at the tangent in the conversation. "Pardon?"

"You came back from the fort set to use me—what did you say"—she thrust her chin out—"in a foul and indecent manner."

"That's not the same and you know it."

"You were scared, Seamus! You wanted to take your relief of the aftermath—of the battle that never happened—out on my body. Your relief manifested itself in its basest form." Grace shoved hard against his chest, her fingernails raking viciously through the thin fabric of his shirt. When he did not flinch, she thumped his breastbone. He held his ground.

"At least I acted on it with my *wife* and not another woman," he thundered.

"What? You think because the man planted a quick kiss on me that I've sunk to spreading my legs for him too?"

The image struck Seamus with the force of a spiked club to the face. He needed to hit something—*hard*!

Hurt and disenchantment dulled her eyes, though she softened her tone. "Seamus, what I have with you, I will *never* have with another man. It's as simple as that."

He rolled his shirtsleeves and stepped around her. Christ! This was like Wadham all over again, except this time, the man in question was demanding his *wife's* attention. It was one thing to go toe-to-toe with a rival suitor during the parry of courtship, but he was not about to let that damned charismatic bastard steal one ounce of her affection. The Yankee already led his daughter like the pied piper, he would not have his wife too.

"Where are you going?" Grace asked, snatching at his arm.

He shrugged free. "No man escapes the consequence for kissing *my* wife." He pursed his lips wistfully at his weapons belt slung over the back of the chair. Leaning down, he snatched the small knife strapped to his calf from under his trousers and slammed it on the table. "Keep this."

"Seamus? *What* are you doing?"

"Defending your honour *and* teaching Church a lesson."

"There's nothing wrong with my bloody honour!" Grace snatched the back of his shirt as he gripped the bedroom door handle. "You can't do this. You're his captain."

"Not today, I'm not." His shirttails untucked as he effortlessly pulled away. He turned at the top of the stairs. "I'm an aggrieved man." Dropping down the stairwell, his voice bounced off the panelled walls. "Though Church might soon rather face me as his captain than as your husband."

"You're acting like a jealous schoolbo—"

The front door slammed out her words. Damn and blast! He had no evidence to suspect infidelity—in fact, he knew it was not so—but by Christ, he could not shake the dismay of imagining Church and Grace together. Suspecting that most of his men would be at The Sailor's Homecoming for their last night ashore, he strode across the street between the horses and carriages. His shadow stretched long in the late afternoon light, and his shoes made careful, strong contact with the earth.

The stone-framed entrance of the hotel welcomed him. Using the advantage of his height, he surveyed the fuggy alehouse. Church sat at a round table in the far corner with O'Malley and Blight. A wild-haired woman perched on Church's lap, and seeing his unbridled appreciation of her overflowing bosom, Seamus rolled his neck in irritation. Bastard had better not have looked at Grace that way! The four occupants looked up as Seamus snapped to a halt beside the table. O'Malley and Blight burst to attention, but the woman did not leave Church's lap.

"Good afternoon," said Seamus dryly. "Church. A word, if you please?"

Church slowly tipped the woman off his lap and rose, his eye-line meeting Seamus's. "Yes, sir."

Seamus ambled from the gloomy interior, and turned into the alleyway between the hotel and the haberdashery store. He weaved his way through the stacks of crates and barrels outside the delivery entrance of the alehouse, sidestepping a greasy-looking puddle that could easily be vomit. The blackened brick walls radiated a musty odour of urine-soaked grime and mildew. A cluster of discarded newspapers and dried leaves rustled along the edge of the wall. The window of the haberdashery store was secured by black iron bars—a measure against thieves exploiting the dingy, uninhabited alley. It was the perfect location for this task, thought Seamus, away from prying eyes. He did not need his humiliation turned into a public spectacle.

How long would this fistfight last? Seamus had seen plenty of scraps that ended brutally and rapidly, with one opponent usually being knocked flat on his back with one almighty punch to the nose. Others were scrappy and messy, lasting until one or both men dropped from exhaustion. He knew those were the ones that delighted the crowds, but there were no crowds here now. Would this fight be as violent and bloody? Would Church fight back?

Deep down the gullet of the alley, Seamus drew his rolled shirt sleeves above his elbows and flexed his arms, testing his range of motion. "Right, Church. You know why we're here."

Church stood, unwavering. "Your wife?"

"Blasted right, my wife! I'm here to defend her honour."

"What husband leaves a fine lady alone in the middle of nowhere?" There was no anger in Church's voice, but he slid off his jacket and lay it neatly over a discarded wooden gin crate.

Seamus might have laughed at this, but his pride stung like a thousand barbs of a poisonous sea anemone. "Grace Fitzwilliam is no lady. She even broke a man's nose once. Like this." His fist darted out, crushing the cartilage in Church's nose like a lump of limestone under a quarryman's hammer.

Church gasped as his head snapped back. Staggering, he swiped at the red torrent pouring from his nostrils. "I see you want no gentleman's fight, then?"

"What gentleman goes about kissing other men's wives?" Seamus took two steps forward, and Church took two back, his calves catching on a packing crate.

"The type that recognises when a husband is neglecting his duty. Didn't you swear to protect her in your marriage vows?"

Seamus was irritated by the purr of complacency in Church's

drawl. He had always disliked the glib way in which Church spoke to Grace. "My wife can take care of herself. This is between you and me now, Church."

"So, you'll not cry foul if I trounce you?" Church sidled around, giving himself the luxury of the open alley behind him.

The impudent lout! "I'd like to see you try!" Why could he not just trust her? This mistrust enraged him and left him vulnerable and exposed—like a child. No, he was a man, for pity's sake! Real and formidable—and incensed at his own jealousy. Though, as much as he hated Alby Church right now, he knew it was only an outcome of his own weakness, and this enraged him further. No man or woman had ever made him feel this insecure before.

Church launched with a gut punch, his head flicking aside and dodging Seamus's approaching fist. Seamus grunted, fighting the urge to double over. A burning pain wormed its way through his gut and felt like it might burst out of his back. By Neptune, he was quick! Not giving Church a second chance, Seamus feigned a right, then snuck his left fist under the American's chin. The impact jolted through Seamus's arm into his shoulder, and Church's teeth clacked together like the lid of a wooden chest slammed shut.

Shaking his head, Church's wavering gaze locked onto Seamus. He charged with his fists raised, his face open like an amateur.

Ha! Got him! Seamus shielded his face behind the wall of his fists, ready to strike like a cobra and put this bastard on his backside.

At the last second, Church dropped his berserker approach and ducked low as Seamus struck out. His shoulder ploughed into Seamus's solar plexus, the hard bone piling into his soft flesh. His breath exploded, and the already tender spot beneath his ribs exploded in agony, doubling him over. *The face! Protect the face!* Deadened by the waves of pain radiating from his core,

Seamus's arms stubbornly refused to obey. Scrunching his eyes, he turned his head, bracing. Church's uppercut struck his cheek, crashing into him like the lethal swinging pendulum of a wayward yardarm in a storm. Although he sensed the danger of its approach, Church's efficient delivery sent him sprawling in the greasy mud.

Blazing Hades—the man was the better fighter! He should have insisted on swords or pistols to settle this. Though, the physical release of his frustration was empowering, even if he was blasted well getting a hiding. Besides, it was not over yet.

Coughing and wheezing in the putrid alley air, Seamus rolled to his hands and knees before staggering upright.

"Had enough yet, Captain?" said Church, bouncing lightly on the balls of his feet.

How the devil could he look so calm? The anger heating Seamus's veins reached boiling point. Only one man would remain standing after this, and it was *not* going to be this bastard!

"You'll not have the pleasure of seeing that moment, wife stealer!" Seamus's lungs burned with each painful breath.

Church sniffed wetly and hawked out a spume of blood that splattered at Seamus's feet. His tongue flicked across his bloodied lips and he grinned. "There's no shame in throwing up the white flag, Fitzwilliam." He danced away at a respectful distance. "I'm happy to shake on a truce, if you are? There's no pleasure in showing you up like this."

Seamus scoffed. "What kind of naval commander would I be waving the white flag at a little bruised cheek?"

"The smart sort who accepts a sorry man's humble apology." Church's arms dropped to his side, and his feet stilled in the suspicious puddle.

"Raise your fists, you cursed bastard! Where's the sport—or honour—in surrendering?" Seamus squinted, one eye already puffing shut. His stomach felt as though it had been punched through the back of his spine. He swallowed a ball of bitter bile.

"Never meant any offence, sir." Church rolled his shoulders back, dropping them. "Can you forgive my impertinence, sir?"

"Why, in Christ's name, would I let you off so easily?" Seamus swung his fist. Church turned his cheek at the last second, but there was still a satisfying crunch.

Church staggered back, shaking his head. "Because I'll agree to leave your ship—to show I meant no harm. Weren't ever my intention to drive a wedge between you and Mrs F."

"Then why did you blasted well kiss her?"

"I'm but a red-blooded man. Never thought I'd feel again after my wife died, but Mrs F. showed me I could. She dismissed my reckless advance easily enou—"

Seamus's punch, straight down the middle, connected squarely, mangling Church's lips against his knuckles. "Shut your mouth! You'll not bring your sordid thoughts of my wife to light." Seamus rolled his wrist, but the sharp click sent a stab of pain through his forearm. Blasted hell! His wrist would not stand another blow to Church's face—not without inviting unwelcome injury. "Fight back, you bastard!"

Church stood swaying, arms limp at his side. "No, sir. I'll not raise my fists to you again."

To risk breaking his troublesome wrist on this waster's face was not worth it. In the cold, fading light of his anger, the prospect of crippling himself over a jealous spat seemed laughable. Admiral Courtney had once falsely accused him of acting impulsively over a jealous rivalry, and Seamus had worn the accusation with good grace. Christ! He had just fulfilled Courtney's allegation. Like the turn of the tide, the hot-headed husband in him eased back as the collected captain took control.

"Which ship will you join?" asked Seamus, lowering his shoulders.

"None."

Seamus frowned. "You're a fine sailor, Church. Even if you are a philandering dolt."

Wincing, Church shrugged back into his jacket. "Want to try my hand at farming. Plan to head north in the morning. Will you accept my departure as my apology?"

For pity's sake, it would be easier to hate the man if he were not so devilishly likeable. Seamus stared at the thick, calloused fingers on offer and took smug satisfaction that Church's red, swollen knuckles would be throbbing just as painfully as his. No real harm had been done to Grace. Seamus's blood settled. His mouth needed an ale more than it needed another punch right now.

He clasped Church's hand with a squeeze that delivered a finality to this whole wretched situation. "I accept."

Seamus stumbled from the shadows, rolling his jaw to ease the ache. Smatters of blood speckled the white shirt he tucked into the top of his trousers. His cotton shirt wicked the sweat from his back, cooling it against his skin. He swiped at the long, slimy streak staining the tan fabric from his hip to his knee. His hair had come undone, and large chunks clung to his sweaty cheeks. Yanking loose the leather strap and scraping his fingers through his hair, he tidied it back in place.

Beside him, the whaler's left eye was nearly swollen shut, and blood poured from the bridge of his nose as well as his nostrils. Most of the buttons on his red shirt were torn off, and he shuffled heavy-footed.

"Buy you a drink, Church?"

Church nodded, wincing as a lopsided grin stretched his puffy lips. Inclining his head, Seamus led the hobbling whaler man back into the alehouse.

Much later that evening, Seamus staggered through the bedroom door armed with a wavering oil lamp. The flames swam as he dropped the lamp on the bedside table with a clunk.

Grace shot up from the pillow, rubbing her eyes. "Where have you been?"

"Having a drink or two with Church," he slurred as he tried to remove his boot for the third time, losing his balance. Giving up, he swung around the bedpost and slumped onto the bed. Raising one leg in the air, he worried the boot with his stockinged foot.

"You beat the daylights out of the man—then went drinking with him?" She knelt beside him, making short work of yanking off his boot. She dropped it messily to the floor.

Despite his swirling drunkenness, he sensed the hurt of their earlier words lingering in the air like a subtle perfume. "Yes. To let him know there're no hard feelings." He unbuttoned his trousers and, lifting his hips off the bed, slid them down his thighs.

"I saw you both out of the window. By the state of his face, I find it difficult to believe he'd be in a forgiving mood."

Seamus struggled to wriggle out of his trousers, which had rumpled and become stuck above his knees. With a hard yank, Grace wrenched them off inside out.

He grunted. "He took his punishment like a man should. Said he was sorry. We shook hands. Then I bought him a round—or three or four." He sat up, fumbling with the top few buttons of his shirt and messily yanking it over his head. He tossed it towards the end of the bed.

"And that's it? Tomorrow we all go on as before?" Her voice rose sceptically.

Naked, he slumped back against the pillow and awkwardly peeled off his stockings in the same ungainly manner he had tried to remove his boots. "Matter's now closed. But there'll be no going on as before." Yanking off his final stocking, he plopped his legs onto the bed with a triumphant gasp. "Church is leaving the *Clover*." Sliding his hands behind his head, he angled his face towards her, hoping his enticing smile would lure her from her frosty mood. "You've invaded my thoughts all evening. D'you know what that's done to me?" He weighed her swollen breast in his hand, marvelling at the feel of it. "There's no finer sight in all the world than you filled with my child."

"Oh, so now you claim your right to me?" Her voice was tight.

Reaching for her hips, he drew her over him. Despite her tight-lipped annoyance, carnal desire darkened her eyes like the green of a lightning storm.

"Yes. You know full well how wedded we are." Seamus growled, "Come here—*wife*."

Grace's voice was breathy. "There you go again. Deferring to those dastardly base impulses of yours."

He flashed her a predacious grin. "Were my base impulses any trouble, you wouldn't moan so." He drew her down and kissed her deeply, drowning in her warm sleepiness that was quickly coming awake. Grace groaned—not helping her case. By Neptune! She tasted divine, like sweetened ginger tea. He ran his hand over the curve of her backside with an appreciative hum. "You've the hindquarters of a prize filly. I want you to ride me —*hard*."

He knew his usually rigid sense of propriety was uncensored by inebriation. Still, the image his words painted sent a thrill of desire coursing into his abdomen, and he squirmed in antic- ipation.

Her warm breath gasped in his ear, and he knew she felt it too.

He breathed a whisper against her smooth neck. "Right now, your pleasure lies solely in my hands, Dulcinea." His fingers pressed more firmly into her flesh, and she answered with a writhing groan. "And when you finally beg for me, I shan't stop until the patrons at The Sailor's Homecoming all know my name."

Seamus raked his fingers desirously down her spine, and her

thighs trembled against his sides. Voices of some stragglers from the alehouse below filtered into the room. To hell with the open window! He adjusted her hips over his. "Then and only then, wife, may you try to raise an objection to my dastardly impulses."

Chapter Twenty-Nine

The next morning, Grace awoke to the sounds of the flapping sails of the windmill at the end of the road, sounding much like the sails of the *Clover*. Beside her, her husband stirred and groaned hoarsely. She peeped over at him, one-eyed. He pressed the fleshy mounds of his palms into his eyes, moaning again.

"Good morning, Captain Fitzwilliam." She kissed him, withdrawing sharply, her nose wrinkling at the drunken vapours clinging thickly to his tussled hair and colourless skin.

"Nothing good about it," he murmured. He scraped his hands down his face, peering at her through slitted, bloodshot eyes. A dark bruise puffed under his left eye. Dried blood crusted the inside of his nostrils, and an unkempt fuzz of vintage-gold stubble lined his jaw.

"Regretting your impulse to teach Alby Church a lesson?" she said, smiling sweetly. He answered with a ragged moan, and she rolled out of bed to fetch him a glass of water from the dresser. Swaying, Seamus propped himself up on one elbow and swallowed deeply. Even after a second and third glass, she could see his insatiable thirst was hardly dented.

"By rights, he should be feeling far sorrier than I," he said, swinging off the bed to his feet. "I'm fair beggared to imagine he's feeling any rougher than I am right now. It's as though an anchor dropped on my head in the night." He grunted and clutched his middle.

"I daresay you're *both* regretting it."

He turned towards her, his red eyes flaring. "What would you have me do, Grace? Having you and Emily aboard the *Clover* has given me a joy I didn't know existed. But your presence also leaves me vulnerable. You know full well how others have strived to exploit my weaknesses. And whether you care to admit it or not—*you* are my weakness."

He snatched a clean pair of trousers from the drawer, but Grace noticed the bruises that were like purple islands on the chart of his pale skin. Clearly, he was in no better mood this morning than he had been last night. She rose and yanked her nightgown over her head. "Would you rather I'd not told you? Lied to you—like you lied to me about Babcock?"

"Yes. I would." His voice cracked as he spun away, head hanging. His deep breaths expanded his ribcage, but it must have hurt too much because his elbow clamped tightly as the anger ebbed from him. "No. I wouldn't," he said softly. "I kept Babcock's truth from you so you wouldn't see the depths I'd sunk to. Admiral Baxter called it a necessary business transaction, but let's be honest and call it what it is—blazing bribery and corruption!"

"Oh, Seamus." Sliding her arms around him, she pressed her forehead to his spine.

He twisted about, the bloodied corner of his mouth wincing. "Every time something happens to you, a piece of my soul dies. Especially when it's by my own actions."

She gentled her tone. "I've never considered the toll it takes on you anytime something bad happens to me."

His disappointment at her disregard swelled in his red-veined eyes. His back muscles tightened under her feathering fingers, twisting like strands of wire humming and quivering in the midday heat. She hated seeing him like this.

"I'm sorry, Seamus. For Alby. For my harsh words."

With her apology, it was as though the taut, unforgiving wires in him snapped, and he gripped her to him. "I'm sorry too, my heart. I said too much." He kissed the top of her head several times then eased her back, his hands planted on her shoulders.

"I didn't mean what I said either," said Grace, sliding her palms over his firm chest. Her scalp tightened. "You're the only man I've—"

"I know." He tried to inhale deeply but hissed in pain instead. "Though well within my rights to skewer Alby Church on the end of my sword for kissing you, I forgive him for taking advantage of you at a vulnerable moment. I owe the man a life for saving you from the boar. And from those wretched bush thieves."

A flood of relief filled her belly as his eyes twinkled mischievously. Attempting some levity of her own, she teased, "Don't you owe him *two*? One for me and one for Emily?"

"Hmph. I'm but a man. I've only so much forgiveness in me. Church best take care not to test the extent of my forgiveness a second time."

Grace stepped over to the windows and breezily whipped the curtains open. He squinted and groaned. She teased out a smile. "You're going to need your wits about you for our departure today."

"That's what first mates are for," he mumbled, reaching for a clean shirt.

"Will you leave the plotting of our route to Jim?" she chirped, enjoying herself at his expense.

"Buchanan's not coming with us." Seamus's scratchy voice quieted as he gingerly eased the shirt over his injured face.

Grace's good mood evaporated. "Why not?"

He peered at her from the safety of the shadows near the wardrobe. "Last night, at the alehouse, he asked to stay with Nevin at Gilly Downs. Reckons it's the only life the boy has known. After what happened to the boy's father, Buchanan doesn't have the heart to leave the lad."

"Can't Jim's sisters take Nevin?" A flutter of panic filled Grace at the thought of leaving Jim behind.

"Apparently not. As husbandless housemaids, they have limited ability to care for the boy. Buchanan has made him his responsibility."

"Can't Nevin come with us? Return to England?"

"I offered, but Buchanan maintains the boy's whole family is here. Doesn't want to uproot him. Barclay has offered him the job as station manager. Forty pounds a year with one per cent on the value of the wool clip in his first year, and an additional one per cent thereafter. Not a bad deal. Buchanan is set to call this place home."

"He has experience with sheep farming from when he was a lad in Scotland."

"Indeed. And he's a smart man. Won't take him long to learn the ropes around here. Also won't do us any harm to have one of our own in this new venture."

"But your charts?"

"I'll manage. Hicks has shown outstanding improvement in both penmanship and seamanship. And he has a fine head for figures. Besides being able to predict coordinates, I've also seen him give the sailmaker a damnably accurate estimate of the amount of canvas needed for each sail. When I questioned Hicks deeper on this, he said he knew the hoist of every mast and the spread of each sail in feet and inches. Again, he said he simply ran the calculations through his head. A smart lad like that'll have no issue assuming all surveying duties." Seamus reached for a clean cravat and sank onto the plush stool beside the dressing table. "Ugh! My innards feel like the greasy contents of a butter churn."

She could not imagine ship life without Jim. He had been alongside her on both voyages, and been her constant companion in London. Her pride at Toby's promotion contrasted with her deep sadness about Jim's departure. Stepping over to the dressing table, she helped her husband tie his cravat, taking care to not knock his bruised chin.

"That explains Toby's fascination with that book about steam engines," she said. "He told me it contains several complicated calculations. He wants someone to explain them to him." She laughed lightly. "I think he's well and truly reached the point of the student being able to teach the teacher now. Perhaps you could help him with the more technical components?" Her smile faded, heart aching as Jim's cheeky, round face with his spiky black hair came to mind. "I'm glad Jim is staying for Nevin. But our Em is going to miss him terribly."

"As am I. Buchanan is an excellent surveyor," agreed Seamus. He frowned at his nails, uncharacteristically caked with mud. Reaching for Grace's tweezers, he scraped out a field's worth of muck. "Oh, and Church is remaining too. Says he wants to try his hand at farming. Plans to head north this morning. Though I'm not sure if it was the whisky talking."

"He's leaving? Without saying goodbye?" She picked up her hairbrush and, scraping his hair into a tail, bound it neatly with a clean black leather tie.

"I said I'd pass on his farewell to you." His pale reflection in the mirror did not look angry, but his tone clearly finalised matters.

Grace knew Seamus was right, of course. Boundaries had been blurred, and her fiercely proud and protective husband had made sure they were clear and visible to all again. Her sea family was coming apart. She curled her arms around her husband's warm neck and shoulders, seeking comfort. He still reeked of sour whisky, but his fingers gently trailing along the skin of her arm were soothing and consoling.

Swivelling on the stool, he cradled the swell of her belly through her thin shift with the delicacy of an antique dealer holding a priceless Ming vase. "I hope to reach the Cape before the babe is born. I'd feel much better if you delivered in civilisation rather than out on the open ocean."

"I've a few months to go yet. And besides, I'll be fine wherever we are, as long as you're with me. And Billy too, of course."

He hummed in agreement. "We've a long way to go yet." Rising, he kissed the top of her unbrushed head. "We'll make a quick stop at the colony in Van Diemen's Land. I understand the settlers there maintain an agreeable high society."

"I find the patchwork of society here in Sydney Town rather refreshing. Beats the pretentiousness of those with long lineages in London."

Seamus chortled and shook his head. "If Van Diemen's Land isn't to your liking, you might find the more rustic outpost of the Swan River Colony preferable? We won't be staying in either place for long. The Swan River Colony is the last outreach of this vast continent where we can restock our supplies before we set off across the Indian Ocean."

"Speaking of food, I'm famished!" She reached for her dressing gown and stumbled over Seamus's discarded boots. "Would you care for some eggs?"

He grimaced, his face greying. "No offence, Dulcinea. You might have exquisite penmanship, but your culinary skills need some refinement." Gingerly rubbing his belly, he said, "Besides, I need the hair of the dog this morning."

She gave a huff of humorous indignation. "Have a chew of this." She scooped up one of his muddy boots, pegging it at his head with spot-on accuracy. He flung his arm up in time to deflect it, and his laughter followed her down the stairs.

JUST BEFORE MIDDAY, Grace and Emily stood alone on the dock with Jim. The accents of the voices were mainly British, but even then, the medley of accents from Cornwall to Manchester to Glasgow was dizzying to her ear.

Through wooden creaks and groans, the anchored ships in the harbour swapped stories of past adventures with one another. The strong offshore breeze that whipped Grace's skirts also pushed the stench of the immigration transport ships out into the open bay.

Jim's gaze slid from her face to his feet, and he thrust one hand in his pocket, the other pulling at his protruding ear.

"I guess this is goodbye then, Jim?" The words stabbed painfully at the back of Grace's throat.

Jim's soft, brown eyes glistened, and he flashed his teeth at her, his characteristic grin lighting his face. He drew his shoulders to his jutting ears in a slow shrug. "I don't know how to say goodbye to ye, lass." He licked his lips, and his hand fluttered to the back of his neck.

Emily clung to Jim's hand like a limpet on a rock, her eyes unusually blue above her quivering chin. "I'm going to miss you, Jim."

Grace's mouth dried as he laughed and ruffled her daughter's fair curls. "Aye, and I'll miss tripping over you and yer toys every day, our Em."

"But Jim," Emily beseeched, "Please come."

He dropped to his haunches. "Now then, our Em, ye know I must stay and look after wee Nevin." He tickled her under her chin and winked. "Though, I promise ye, yer the only lassie who'll ever have my heart." He gently circled his hand over his heart. "And I'll treasure ye in here all my days."

With a strangled cry, Emily's tears tipped, and she threw her chubby arms around his neck. One big hand shielded her whole back, the other cradled her head. Squeezing his eyes tight, he kissed the side of her head then stood abruptly.

Grace blinked hard, the back of her nostrils burning.

"Right then, our Em, run along now while I say goodbye to yer maw. There's a good lass."

Sniffling wetly, Emily scrubbed the tears from her face and balanced along the gangplank towards Seamus waiting on the docked brigantine.

"I'll miss you too," said Grace gently. She wanted to tell him she was going to pine for the easy way he spoke to her. Tell him that, although the rest of the crew were friendly enough to her, he was different. Tell him how much she appreciated that, even after he had discovered her to be a gentlewoman, he still treated her as he had when they were berth mates. Instead, she simply reached for his hand.

"Crivens, lass." His voice cracked. "Even though I knew this moment was coming, I wasn't prepared for how it would feel. You and yer wee lassie are fair cracking my heart in two." Sniffing, he pinched his eyes with his thumb and forefinger.

She swallowed the ball of tears forcing its way up her throat and tried on a laugh. "Isn't it amusing how each day nothing changes, but looking back, you realise how different it all is?"

"Aye." His black eyebrows wiggled. "I remember the day I first clapped eyes on ye, with yer sheep-shorn head." He studied her fondly, as though painting a picture of her in his mind.

"I do recall you saying something about the front of me being uglier than the back." Grace nudged his shoulder, and his eyes sparked with the memory. Pressing his fist against his lips, the corners of his eyes crinkled deeply as his shoulders jiggled.

Seamus's voice sliced through the bustling throng of the

harbour. "Mrs Fitzwilliam, the tide has turned. We must go." Grace glanced back at him on the quarterdeck with Emily in his arms and nodded briefly. She faced Jim, grasping his arm.

"Say you'll write to me? Tell me how you are." Urgency thinned her voice.

Her friend's gaze softened. "Of course, lass. Can't put all your hours of lessons to waste now, can I?"

Grace reached into the pocket of her skirt and pulled out a small, hard-covered copy of *Rob Roy*. She thrust it at him. "Here, I want you to have this." He took it wordlessly, biting his bottom lip and blinking rapidly.

The time for words was passed. She flung her arms around him as Emily had done. Jim buried his face in her neck, and she felt his body convulse, once, as though he fought the tide of sadness that swamped them both. His hair smelled of dust and hay and grass, not unlike the sheep at Gilly Downs. Grace let the tears pour freely down her cheeks, sobbing unashamedly as she purged the pain of their parting.

Chapter Thirty

CAPE TOWN, SOUTH AFRICA, 2 JUNE 1837

The *Clover* had docked in the bustling harbour below the majestic Table Mountain the day before last. Grace had watched Seamus disappear into the thick of the humming settlement, where he had gone to secure decent lodgings. Her pains had begun last night. Earlier this morning, she had bundled Emily out of the door with Toby, sending them off to the animal hold where one of the goats had recently dropped twin kids, and where a fluffy, newly hatched batch of chicks would keep Emily occupied for hours. As would Alby, the tortoise.

Now, pacing the length of the great cabin under Billy's watchful eye, Grace felt the familiar shift in her body and recognised the time was near. She roared and clung to Billy's arms as she collapsed to her knees, the grip of the contraction winding her.

"All right, flower. Time to hop up on the cot now."

"No, I can't. It's happening right now."

"There, there, lass. Let me help you up."

"No! I'm comfortable right here, on the floor," she hissed through clenched teeth.

"Can't let you do that. You're not an animal." He tried to pick her up, but she stubbornly went limp and shoved him away.

"Leave me be!" Another pain started, and she dipped her chin into her chest. "It's too late. It's coming now." She took a deep breath and emitted a low, guttural moan that lasted an eternity. Lowering her hands to the floor, Billy lifted her skirts from behind. The tiny, slippery body slithered down Grace's thigh into his cupped palms. With a victorious cry, she dropped her forehead onto her bunched fists in exhaustion.

"Oh, aye?" Billy laughed. "Not even born one minute and he's already christening me with a tinkle."

She flopped onto her side, spineless with fatigue. "Twelve hours," she gasped, glancing at the clock in the cabin and then through the scuttles at the soft afternoon sunshine. "Three hours shorter than our Em." She swelled with exhausted triumph.

Billy wiped the babe clean and tied off his umbilical cord. He swaddled the squalling infant and placed him in the crook of her arm. Reaching up to the birthing cot, he grabbed a pillow and slid it under her head. She sighed happily, studying her son's unhappy face and laughing at his pouting bottom lip quivering as he bawled. She kissed his little lips, and her son's cries decreased as he snuffled into her face.

"Born hungry, I see." She pulled open the front of her slip and pulled out an engorged breast, feeding her dark nipple into her son's open, furrowing mouth. "I can see I'm going to have a job keeping up with your appetite, little one." She gasped as his eager gums clamped down, suckling ferociously. "Take it easy, little Elias," she whispered, stroking the top of his wet head and running her fingers around the silky spiral on his crown. He smelled of warm sponge cake, and his little fists kneaded her like a kitten. She grimaced, clenching as a spasm rocked her body.

"'Tis but the afterbirth. It'll pass soon enough." He patted her knee reassuringly.

Within minutes, the babe dropped off to sleep, but the debilitating pains stole her breath again. "Something's wrong, Billy," she puffed. "Take him."

Billy bundled the sleeping infant into an open drawer. He knelt beside her. "I'll just help you along a bit here, lass," he said, his strong hands firmly massaging her belly. "We don't want this lasting much longer. I'm sure you could do with a rest and a hot cuppa about now. You've done a fine job." She drew her knees up as another wave gripped her. Billy's hands froze. "Move your legs out the way a minute, lass." His hands probed firmly. "Good God! There's another one in there!"

No. It was not possible! She was too tired! Billy's bushy eyebrows rose as he flicked aside his fringe. Grace lolled her head sideways. It felt too heavy to hold up. Everything was too heavy. "Oh Billy, I can't manage another one."

Billy took Grace's hand. "Yes, you can. Come on, flower."

"I'm scared. I need Seamus. Send for him." The fear that filled Grace was squeezed out by the grip of the next pain. When it passed, Grace's cheeks were damp with perspiration and warm tears.

"Captain's not here right this minute." Billy's voice was tinged with concern. "He's still ashore."

"I don't care where he blazing well is. Fetch him, now!" She glowered as she flopped back onto the pillow with a whimper.

He hesitated momentarily, his long face tight with indecision. "All right, all right. I'll see what I can do." Rising with a grunt, he staggered across the cabin before disappearing through the doorway.

When he returned, Grace could not read his face. Alarm and

misery jangled her nerve endings like the noontime bell. "Is he coming?"

"He will be soon enough." He sunk to his haunches. "Can we get you up now?"

"No. I'm perfectly comfortable as I am." She blew a steady breath out as she waited for the next tightening.

The doctor's brows dipped. "Your husband won't be happy to find out you birthed his children on the floor. Please, let me help you up."

Grace grated her teeth. "Try to move me one more time, and you can march right out of that door until you drop into the ocean."

Her friend blanched and took a deep breath. "Right you are then. I'll have a quick gander downstairs." He shuffled to her feet and lifted her blood-smeared skirts. "You're nearly there. Keep going, lass."

She sagged tiredly. "No more," she uttered. "I can't do it."

Instantly, the air around them reverberated, sucking the breath from her lungs. With a chest-crushing whomp, the atmosphere in the cabin shattered with a catastrophic *ba-boom*. Grace jolted violently, bolting half upright and grasping her raised knees in terror. She let out a primal roar.

Frowning, Billy peered over her knees and tutted. "Sweet Mary Mother, that didn't do the trick either." He shook his head. "Can't even scare the wee mite out." He scoured the back of his wrist across his forehead.

She flopped back heavily. "You tried to *frighten* my child out of me?"

"You've been labouring too long. I fear you haven't enough left in you to see this one safely born." He paused, holding her gaze with his look of gravity. "We've two options." He held up a curved surgical tool, its metallic jaws clanging together. "These won't favour the child, though."

Grace ground her teeth and shook her head. "No! The child

over me. You promised." She just wanted the muscle-tearing spasms to stop. If only Seamus were here. Then he could decide. She wailed. "End it, Billy. I beg you!"

The cabin closed in with the swell of bodies and voices. Toby's worried grey eyes swam briefly into focus. Billy's voice. "You four—lift her up here. Hold her down." The bitter-sweet, honey-brandied laudanum ignited her gullet. The brittle clink of metal instruments. The stale stench of unwashed men pressed in close. Billy's voice again. "Hold her still." Strong hands, grasping, squeezing. The blinding light of multiple lanterns. A fiery brand carved open her side—Billy's promise to save her child. Shrieking with raw agony, her hold on the world cracked and the last of her energy seeped from her body, sending her into the deepest, darkest fathoms of ocean.

GRACE AWOKE to the echoing cries of a babe. It was as though she were in a great hall, the cries bouncing back at her, filling her ears with multiple reverberations of the same wail. She opened her eyes to see Seamus picking up a tiny, squalling bundle from the chest of drawers. The grin he'd had on his face when Emily was born was missing.

Spotting her awake, he draped the newborn over his shoulder and slid his hand into hers. "My heart, you've come back to me."

"Hmm," she murmured, thankful she was propped up—it saved her from needing to move. Dear Lord Almighty! Did it hurt this much to be keelhauled?

She held her arms out as Seamus offered her the babe. She ground her teeth. It was as though someone had stuffed her belly with white-hot coals and then let a cart horse trample her. The squirming bundle's weight was almost unbearable.

Seamus placed the second yowling newborn in her lap. Their little lips smacked dryly, and Grace recognised the same jerky mewls Emily used to give when she was hungry, except now there were two! Both hungry at the same time! But unlike last time, everything hurt. Moving hurt. Breathing hurt. It would not surprise her if sleeping hurt too.

Balancing the bundled infants on her lap, she lowered the front of her shift, attaching one babe to each breast. She groaned as Seamus propped the babes into position with plumped pillows. She sucked in sharply at the searing sting as the two hungry mouths pulled greedily.

Her husband's bloodless cheeks spelled out his worry. "Oh, my heart. I thought I was going to lose you."

"I'm not going anywhere," she said with a half smile.

"Who would've thought? Twins." He placed a hand on her knee, his thumb rubbing in little circles.

Normally she relished the motion, but every hair on her body hurt. She lay her hand over his to stop his thumb. "Has our Em seen them?" The watery exhaustion in her own voice sounded peculiar in her ears.

"Briefly, before I put her to bed. I wanted you to rest. You've slept the sleep of the dead."

"When did you return?"

"Just before dark." He leaned in, studying their sons snuffling greedily.

She gently stroked the twin velvety cheeks. "How did you know to come?" She reached for the glass of water on the bedside table but winced as the movement cleaved her belly in two with a fiery pain. Seamus handed it to her, and she curled her fingers around the cool glass. The fresh water washed away the laudanum's bitter coating on her tongue. It tasted heavenly!

"Cannon fire has a tendency to rally all naval men to action," he said earnestly. His worry for her had clearly robbed him of any humour.

His blond brows dipped lower as she scrunched her eyes and gasped. The same squeezing pains that had accompanied Emily's early feeds returned. Grace had thought them painful enough before, but now it was as though someone were re-opening the wound from the inside with an incandescent sabre. She blew the pain out with a quivering breath, thankful for the tight bandages about her midriff holding her together.

"Sykes said you could have more laudanum for the pain, if you wish."

Chewing the inside of her cheek, she shook her head. "I'm all right."

He leaned in, speaking gently. "You scared me half to death." He wiped a warm thumb across her cheek.

One of the newborns slid sleepily off her breast. Seamus reached for the infant, the bundled babe almost fitting in the palm of his hand. His tall frame stood stable and upright.

"Now, who do we have here?" He peered into the round, sleeping face, the pink, pouting lips still instinctively suckling. He looked at her expectantly.

They had, of course, discussed names, but not two lots. Grace was not sure whether to laugh or cry. Neither—both would hurt too much! "That's Edwin." Her gaze caressed the babe.

"Edwin," he repeated.

"Do you like it?"

"I do. A lot," he said. "Though, how can you tell? They both look the same to me."

The look of wonder on his face diluted some of her exhaustion. She inclined her head. "Edwin has a more elongated face than Elias. Plus, his crown swirls to the right whereas Elias's swirls to the left."

Seamus stared wide-eyed. "You've figured out those differences already?"

The second infant dropped from her breast with a wet pop. Adjusting her shift, Grace squeezed the pillows tighter to her abdomen with her elbows, their softness lending her the comfort of protection that made it easier to think about getting up to use the chamber pot. "It's there for the seeing. I've just spent the last half an hour gazing into these darling faces and twirling their hair."

Seamus frowned at the sleeping infant in his arms. "I'll have to dot one on the forehead with tar."

She laughed breathily so as not to wrench her wound. "Not on my watch, Captain. Tie a ribbon on Elias's wrist, since he's firstborn."

"All right." His eyes scrunched in concentration. "A ribbon for Elias Alexander. No ribbon for Edwin Seamus." He kissed the tiny, downy forehead. "Forgive me in advance if I muddle you with your brother, my sweet boy."

Grace inspected the new, pink face lying on the pillow in her lap. What would Uncle Farfar make of this little chap and his brother? He already adored Emily, if the gushing sentiments in his letters were to be believed. With Seamus still to complete some surveying up the west coast of Africa, the twins would be more than eighteen months old by the time they arrived back in London, though that was probably a better age to introduce them to their grandfather. Grace had no doubt he would coax a smile from them in no time at all—he had doted endlessly on her when she was little.

But first, she needed to heal. Billy had kept his promise and saved her sons' lives, but he had gutted her like a fish in the process—or so it felt.

Knuckles knocked softly at the door, and Billy's dark head peered around. He expertly assessed her as he approached. "Ah, Mrs Fitzwilliam. You're awake."

Grace inhaled to speak but winced as the movement set her midriff alight. "Thank you, Billy. You saved our lives." She wanted to reach out her hand, but the effort scared her, so she offered him a tired smile instead.

"Simply discharging my duty," said Billy, offering her a ceramic bowl of caudal.

Grace breathed in the sweet, earthy aroma of the gruel. Forsaking the spoon, she tipped the edge of the bowl to her lips. The warm spiced wine danced across her parched tongue, sliding effortlessly down her gullet. She rolled the flavours around her mouth and discerned the familiar, bitter bite of laudanum. Billy clasped one fist with his hand, still and calm. She drew comfort from his presence, and from his draught that promised her some reprieve from this haze of pain.

"I'm sorry I shouted at you. And that I didn't do as you asked," she said, licking the sweet line of liquid from her top lip.

Billy shook his head. "No apology necessary, lass." He cupped his hand around the babe's head and smiled. A shadow of seriousness flitted across his warm gaze. "You've survived quite an ordeal—but 'tisn't over yet. If I'm to have any hand in your recovery, you've to do *exactly* as I say."

"I will, I promise. You kept yours to me." She cupped the empty bowl. "May I please have some more?"

Billy released a long breath that ended on a relieved chuckle. The corner of his mouth tugged up, and he nodded. "Aye, flower. When you awake again, you can have as much as you like. You'll need it to build your strength." Placing the bowl on the bedside table, he took the babe from her lap.

A woozy bliss descended, and she sunk her heavy head into the pillow. Even if the ship began sinking this very minute, it would be impossible to rise from this peaceful sensation of nothingness.

Chapter Thirty-One

After his initial excitement at spotting the first glimpse of England's shores off Lizard Point for the first time in seven years, uncanny nervousness fluttered in Seamus's chest as the great town of London emerged through the smog and smoke that cast a shadow over the earth. The Thames riverbank was congested with houses. Compared to the sparse smattering of civilisation in Sydney Town, London looked like an immense human hive—an icy, blustering hive.

Seamus caught Grace's reflection in the mirror as she brushed off imaginary bits of dust from his shoulder. He stood composed in his suit before turning to face her, his brow tight with concern. "Are you all right, Dulcinea?" The fluttering unease in his stomach returned as she took his hand.

"I know some of the men are keen to disembark, but..." Her throat moved as she swallowed. "This ship is my saviour. She's an extension of my body, and the men are my lifeblood. When everything around us disintegrated and our old life crumbled, this ship and her hands breathed new life into me. They gave me something to live for, to look forward to. Leaving the *Clover* feels as painful as hacking off my arm with one of Billy's bone saws—it feels impossible. And I'm afraid."

Seamus pulled her into a tight embrace, pressing his lips to the top of her head, her hair tickling his nose. He knew exactly how she felt. "I understand. I can't fault how loyally this old bathtub has served us. She handled everything Neptune threw at her, and still she delivered us home safely."

"But she *is* my home. Our home. I don't want to leave her." Grace's voice was thick, and she sniffed.

He drew back, smiling. "My home is where you are. Where the children are. It doesn't matter whether we've a canvas tent over our heads, or a bark-shingled roof, or even a gilded dome. As long as you're there with me, I'll *always* be home."

She lowered her lashes. "But London has too many memories."

He lifted her chin with his finger. "And we'll make new ones. Happier ones—with our children. With each other." He folded his arms around her.

"But what about Hamilton? And Silverton?" Her voice was muffled against his jacket.

He pressed another kiss to the top of her head. "Rest assured, my heart. I'll get to the bottom of their meddling."

Despite the reassuring beat of her heart against his chest, the clawed fingers of worry around his lungs tightened their clench. His first port of call was Admiral Baxter. He could appraise Seamus of all that had happened in their absence.

A WEEK LATER, Seamus unfurled a cluster of charts across the table in a private dining room at White's gentlemen's club. It was a frigid day, and both windows were sealed against the cold. Muted city noises from the street hummed unobtrusively. The corners of a pile of papers on the desk curled up, pinned under a silver salt cellar.

Baxter's chair creaked as he leaned forward, his fingers feathering across Seamus's meticulous topographical lines. "Ah, yes. Jolly good stuff." He drew on his cigar, his words curling around his head. "Seamus, my boy, you've outdone yourself."

"Thank you, sir." Seamus reached into the leather bag on the floor and drew out the ship's books. "The logs, sir. You'll find the voyage intimately detailed within." He flipped open the back of the book, the leather spine crackling. "And here is an account of the expenses I covered, including the repairs in Montevideo after the storm. I trust Colonel Hamilton will be here shortly?"

Seamus looked squarely at Baxter, whose grey gaze slid to the vexatious repair bill. Baxter tapped the end of his cigar on the ashtray, and Seamus braced himself for a frank discussion. Although he could account for every penny spent, he knew it was still a sizable amount, and he hoped that Hamilton would settle it fairly. Baxter would not meet his eye, and Seamus shuffled to the edge of his seat, stiff-backed. Heavens, the man's emotions were just as easy to read on his face as Grace's—a family trait.

"Is there a problem, sir?" Seamus enquired.

Baxter sucked his cigar deeply, his words eddying from between his lips. "There's no easy way to say this. Hamilton's not who I thought he was. Appears the man's a complete fraudster. He managed to dupe half of London, including the Lord Mayor, with his most brazen confidence trick."

"What's he done?"

"He fabricated an entire country in South America and sold land certificates to unsuspecting investors. Many who invested with him have lost everything."

"Where's the swindler now?"

"He purported to be taking his wife to Italy for her health but, by all accounts, he never showed up there."

The dread that had swirled in Seamus's gut as they had sailed up the Thames returned with a ferocity that forced him to shuffle forward in his seat to ease its gripping claws. "Sir? What does this mean? For the *Clover*? For me?"

"The ship will have to be sold to offset his debts and fulfil that trail of promissory notes you left in your wake." Baxter blew out a long breath.

Seamus exploded from his seat. Damn and blast that thieving charlatan! Snatching up his brandy bulb, he tramped over to the window, the frozen condensation framing the glass prettily. He sucked in deep breaths to quash his thrashing heart. Below, on St James's Street, the bustle of life continued, without any awareness of his misfortune. "Even if I sell my charts, I'll barely make the money back. It'll leave me back at square one. No ship. No commission. I'll have to consider joining up again."

Admiral Baxter cleared his throat and rubbed his thin, grey brow with his thumb. "Alas, there's no chance the Admiralty will have you back now. Not after your little lark in Montevideo."

Seamus stepped forward, his new leather shoes squeaking. "Do you mean the incident at the fort? In what way am I compromised?"

"You meddled in foreign affairs." Baxter, smelling of pungent cigar smoke, wrinkled his forehead in a grimace. "Sorry, my boy. You know if it were up to me, I wouldn't let a little mishap like this get in the way." He looked at Seamus through drooping eyelids that sagged with age, though the grey eyes beneath the salt-and-pepper brows were still sharp and glinted intelligently.

Seamus was glad Grace was not here to witness this humiliation. He blinked rapidly. "But Hood *asked* me to intervene." Lowering his glass to the table, he pressed the scar on his wrist, using the searing pain to distract him from his panic.

"I know, my boy," placated Baxter. "But you know how it is with governments choosing the least objectionable bed partners." He waved his hand and shrugged one shoulder. "You must understand that there is a wider political picture here. The British Government has already apologised to the Argentines for your intervention."

Seamus scooped up his brandy and took a deep swill. The smoky burn damped down the gorge rising up his throat. "I didn't take sides! Dias assured me he had political neutrality." Muffled footsteps grew louder on the carpeted hall outside the open panelled door, and a thick-set waist filled the doorway. What the devil?

Silverton stepped into the room and gripped the neck of the brandy decanter with his pink, pudgy hand. "May I join you?"

Seamus frowned. "No, you may not. This is a private meeting, Silverton," he said, sweat pricking in his armpits.

Unperturbed by the dismissal, Silverton's beady eyes widened with glee. "You've made quite a name for yourself, Fitzwilliam. Did you know certain citizens of Montevideo frowned upon your meddling as an act of British hostility?"

Seamus wanted to take the decanter stopper and plug Silverton's throat. Of course the swine knew of his business. He knew *everyone's* business. Seamus scowled and swung his head towards Baxter. "Is this true?"

Baxter nodded minutely.

Fire and damnation! "What of Hood? Has there been the same issue of complaint levelled at *his* interference?"

Baxter toyed with the curled edges of the chart, avoiding Seamus's gaze. "Hood is a visionary eyewitness—a rather old-school diplomatist, if you will. The Ministry rather like this in him. He's continuing in Lord Ponsonby's footsteps by cushioning the hot-headed ravings of the warring South Americans, while somehow managing to improve our trade agreements with both sides."

Silverton mixed a scoff and a laugh. He splashed the amber liquid into a glass. "Agreed. Hood's far too valuable an asset to use as a scapegoat."

"But I'm not, sir?" Seamus asked Baxter bluntly, his voice hard.

Baxter flicked him a regretful look.

"Christ, Admiral! I'm no fool," said Seamus. "I would never have willingly interfered in another country's political rumblings had I not had a politician tightening the thumb screws. I steered well clear of the Falklands the minute I learned of the anarchy that prevailed there."

"Come now, Fitzwilliam." Silverton took a deep drink and sucked air between his teeth. "It's not personal. It's political." He lowered his voice. "Though not even the admiral's influence can sway matters anymore since His Majesty's death. Political alliances have swung under our new Queen, leaving you and Baxter with few friends in the right places." His grey-stranded head motioned towards the portrait of the young Queen Victoria hanging on the wall. "Isn't that right, Admiral?"

Baxter tapped his cigar against the ashtray, the grey ash quivering as his hand shook. Seamus realised he was not about to dignify Silverton's question with an answer. Though he was not usually prone to queasiness, the room swirled around Seamus. His stomach rolled, and he fought hard not to vomit all over the clubhouse's maroon-and-navy carpet. Baxter silently blew out a long, slow plume of smoke.

Silverton finished the remaining brandy in his glass in one swig and tutted. "And between you both, you lost a pretty penny in that South American bond debacle too, didn't you?"

Curse the meddlesome bastard to the depths of hell! Seamus cracked his wrist and retorted, "Just as *you* lost a pretty penny in Hamilton's enterprise."

Silverton's tongue flicked at the sputum in the corner of his mouth like a toad catching flies—only he missed. "My recent loss is merely a coalman's wage compared to yours."

The heat rose in Seamus's cheeks. Heavens, he was in a shameful state, and the truth of Silverton's needling only made matters worse.

Silverton tugged down the front of his waistcoat. "Besides, do you think I'd lower myself to dabble in a commoner's pursuit like surveying? You'll find no evidence of my involvement with Hamilton. And a good thing too, considering the shame you've brought upon the British Empire, *Captain*."

Deep down, Seamus knew this was an exaggeration on Silverton's part. Two could play at that game. "I know you're involved, Silverton. I've a witness to prove it," he said. Except his witness—Babcock—was half a blazing world away. Plus, the priest's falsified letters had succeeded in convincing London he had died in Port Famine. By Neptune, how was he going to drag Babcock's wrinkled neck back here and make him speak?

Silverton chuckled, his jowls wobbling. "I didn't deny *any* involvement. I denied there being any *evidence* of it."

Drawing himself to his full height, Seamus strode over to Silverton and peered down his nose. "You've a hide to waltz in here uninvited. Leave. Now."

Silverton plucked at one of the folds of skin beneath his chin, his pressed lips forcing the foamy globules in the corner of his mouth to bulge. "An open door was just begging for a visitor. Perhaps you should have kept it closed? Then again, there's not much a closed door can do to hide your latest dishonour, Fitzwilliam."

Seamus took two slow breaths to steady the rising vehemence in him. His vision of Silverton narrowed to a shimmering, black-edged target, as though he were staring through a spyglass. "Well, it's about to be closed now. *Good day*, Silverton." Sweet Christ Almighty, if the man did not leave of his own volition,

Seamus would take great pleasure in shoving the pompous lump into the hall.

"Very well." Silverton's crystal glass dropped on the silver serving platter with a metallic clang. He swivelled his shifty eyes slowly towards Seamus. "Do pass on my regards to your wife. I believe she's spat out a few of your brats. Hope it hasn't ruined that delicate little waist of hers."

Seamus took a step towards Silverton, his right fist clenched. Baxter's clawed fingers bit into the back of Seamus's triceps, holding him back—though he felt the hum of Baxter's quivering rage melding harmoniously with his own.

"Get out," ordered Seamus. He slammed the door behind Silverton, and the portrait of Queen Victoria jolted and slipped off-centre.

"Good God, the man's a tyrant!" Baxter fell back heavily in the armed chair at the head of the table. He pressed his fisted knuckles to his forehead, his eyes screwed tight. "I'm sorry about the bond debacle, my boy. Seemed like a perfectly sound investment at the time." He lifted his head, and Seamus could still see the white press of anger in his lips. "Though it could be worse. Could've lost the lot."

Seamus chewed on his top lip. He *had* lost the lot. Especially with that loan against Abertarff House. Curse this wretched double humiliation! His cravat suddenly felt too hot and too tight. He tore it off. Men's voices shouting on the street drew him over to the window. Swaying like a prize-fighter winded by a brutal blow to the gut, he put out a hand to steady himself on the cold sill and bowed his head.

With Baxter's platitudes droning in his ears, he wrestled with his own thoughts. No chance of another commission now. Not even an anti-slaver. He was damned if he was going to beg the Admiralty for one! He was beggared. With no prospects of redeeming his career in the navy—waist-deep in debt, with no investor likely to back him for being foolish enough to be swindled by Hamilton—there was no light of redemption.

He just had to eke out the admiral's gems, to keep Grace in style, until he could remedy this mess. None would be any the wiser.

Chapter Thirty-Two

WALLACE HOUSE, MAYFAIR, LONDON, 20 SEPTEMBER 1839

Grace stepped into her old nursery at Wallace House. It was exactly as she remembered it, only smaller and mustier. Flicking her head in the direction of her rambunctious, maize-blond twins wrestling on the carpet, she smiled. How could they be two already? It felt like only yesterday they were born.

The wallpaper was decorated with roses. The pristine, cream, wing-backed chair sat in the corner as it had the day Miss Hargraves had banned her from sitting on it after Grace accidentally smeared strawberry jam on the arm. The tall sideboard still held her childhood possessions: the porcelain clown doll with a tear painted on its cheek, the miniature Royal Doulton china tea set, a painted wooden figurine of a mother deer with her fawn—all treasured but never used. Just like Grandmother Baxter's china—those blue-patterned plates had never left their cabinet either.

Sally McGilney had lit the fireplace, most likely to brighten the room, though the crackling heat did not spread far—it never had. Grace shivered at the cold, grey memories trapped in here with her.

After Seamus had pleaded with Grace to accept some help with the children, Uncle Farfar had offered for Sally to join their family at Abertarff House. Gilly's sister owned a double duty— one as housekeeper and the other as nanny.

Emily ran over to the sideboard and reached for the miniature tea set. Grace remembered Miss Hargraves' stern words whenever she had asked to play with it. Shaking her head to dismiss her old battle-axe of a governess from her mind, Grace beamed at Emily. "Having a tea party with Egbert?"

Emily propped a well-loved brown bear on its bottom and fiddled with one of its ears. "Yes, and then Nanny Sal said we can put him in the doll hospital to fix him. He's *so* old!"

Grace chuckled, smiling fondly at the stuffed animal that had been her childhood favourite. His ear was threadbare, and he was missing an eye. She winced as Emily pushed a bit of tattered rag back into the hole on Egbert's back.

"A good idea!" said Grace.

She was taken with the idea of having Gilly's sister around. Sally resembled him so strongly that her stomach fluttered with familiarity every time the woman stepped into the room. Even though Sally helped, Grace still bore the lion's share of the parenting. She thought back to the conversation between her and Seamus on the matter.

"I didn't give birth to three beautiful children only to have them raised by a servant," she had snapped when Seamus suggested getting a nanny. Her core chilled at the memories of the lifeless nursery. The rush of loneliness flooded back uninvited, and unexpected hot sobs had burst from her. Seamus had wrapped himself around her, holding her until her tears stopped.

He murmured into the top of her head, "I'm not advocating we lock them in a tower and throw away the key." Pulling back, his soft lips curved gently as he kissed away her tears. "Have I told you what a wonderful mother you are?"

Grace hiccoughed. "Then let me mother my children. Please."

"Of course. I was only suggesting an extra pair of hands now the twins are more mobile." Lifting her hands to his lips, he peered over her knuckles. "I'll never keep you from being with our children." He kissed her fingers. "I promise."

Their social counterparts were less understanding, though Grace did not give a fig about their opinions. She had shielded herself from their barbed comments behind her mothering instincts.

"I simply don't know how you manage the little monsters all day. I can manage an hour in the morning and an hour in the afternoon—and only if their father isn't around, of course. He prefers them neatly dressed and only to bid him goodnight each evening."

"You really should rest more, my dear. Those puffy bags under your eyes age you by ten years, if not more."

"What do you mean you've never used a wet nurse? How on earth did your children receive sustenance?"

"What? Both of them—at the same time? I can't imagine that being a discrete exercise. In fact, the thought of it is all rather primitive and vulgar. Turns me quite queasy."

"What do you mean you don't have a governess? Who on earth teaches your children? What? You?"

Back in the nursery, Grace's gaze wandered over to the mantel, her smile fading. An oval-framed portrait of Lord and Lady Flint stood on the corner of the stone mantel, with a portrait of herself as a five-year-old beside it. In the painting, she was immaculately dressed in a white frock with a pink sash. She sat rigidly on a wooden stool, chubby legs dangling, shiny black shoes hovering above the floor. Grace studied her plump, unsmiling lips, the memory prickling like a nettle—her mournful eyes filled with the agony of sitting so still for so long under Miss Hargraves' evil glare while the artist painted her likeness.

A familiar woody fragrance of tobacco snuck up behind her, and Uncle Farfar's hand rested on the small of her back. "A penny for your thoughts, poppet?"

"I remember sitting for this." Brushing her thumb over the curved, golden frame, she nudged the two edges until they touched—but that still did not bring the three people in the paintings any closer.

"This picture always broke my heart." Uncle Farfar's voice was deep and gentle in her ear. "The artist was good—he accurately captured the sadness in your eyes." Sliding his arm over her shoulder, he pulled her against his soft side. "Tell you what. I'll commission a portrait of your family. In fact, of all of us together. Yes?" He squeezed her elbow, his eyebrows rising above his kind eyes.

Glancing back at the tussling twins, she chuckled. "He'll need the patience of a saint to have those two sit still long enough to paint them."

A rumble of laughter rolled from Uncle Farfar. "Quite. Quite. Perhaps we'll wait until they're a little older, hmm?" He reached into his pocket and, with a familiar rustle, withdrew a wax-wrapped packet of pomfret cakes. She bit her bottom lip as she looked sideways at her children playing on the floor with Sally. She picked at the wax paper, admiring the twinkle in his eyes as he winked. "Just like old times, eh, poppet?"

The aniseed-fragranced sweet was her favourite flavour in the world, bringing aromatic childhood memories of Uncle Farfar's visits to mind.

"Mmm, delicious."

His grey brows shot up, delight pinkening his beloved face.

Edwin shrieked, and Grace slid from Uncle Farfar's warm embrace to grab each twin by the arm. "All right, you two. That's enough. We could all do with a walk."

"I want to feed the squirrels!" Emily pleaded, her blue eyes so much like Seamus's that Grace had to restrain herself from scooping her daughter up and nuzzling her neck.

"*I want* never gets," replied Grace calmly. Gritting her teeth, she pinned down Elias to tie his bootlaces. It was during moments like this that she truly appreciated Sally's help.

Sally backed a squirming Edwin into the corner and buttoned up his coat. "Stand still, Master Edwin. Gettin' you dressed is like tryin' to push a bleedin' octopus into a string bag." Sally jabbed him in the ribs with a triumphant grin as she successfully secured the last button. Edwin collapsed on the floor in a puddle of giggles.

Emily stood at the door in her summer coat, the high collar arching beneath her untamed mop of curls, the exact colour of Seamus's. Her likeness to her father had grown as she aged and, just like him, Grace knew that her daughter was sometimes driven to distraction by living with the twins' unruliness and untidiness. Grace still found Emily's transformation remarkable, especially considering that when they had disembarked the *Clover*, she was as untamed as a jungle monkey. Though she had soon gleaned a liking for pretty dresses and tea parties in the nursery, Grace knew that, when pressed, Emily could still take up a wooden sword against both brothers and trounce them easily.

"Squiwels! Squiwels!" yelled the twins in restless unison. Grace ran her fingers through their straight, golden hair. Most days she could tell who was who, especially when they were together. Elias's head was rounder, but even *she* got them mixed up when they were apart. The twins were used to being called each other's names and usually responded regardless. Though only yesterday, she had caught them trying to trick poor Bartel by giving him their wrong names.

"Come on then," she said, her voice warming as she offered her hands to the twins. "The squirrels will have gone to bed by the time you lot finish faffing around."

She hustled the twins down the street bustling with shoppers, appreciating how high and blue the sky was for a change. She tilted her head back momentarily, letting the sunlight spread across her cheeks. The warm air, permeated with the earthy tones of manure and the astringent odour of horse urine, did little to quell the children's excitement. Grace gave the boys' hands an extra squeeze as a reminder of their manners. She had learned from experience that it was easier to herd the two goats who had escaped in the *Clover*'s hold than it was to round up her sons once she let go of their hands. It was safer for everyone that they remained firmly in her grip. Their pudgy free arms clasped a glass jar of pearl barley to feed the swans at Hyde Park.

Crowds of shoppers and tradesmen jostled for position on the pavement, elbowing Grace precariously near to the curb. She drew the twins in, heartened by Sally's secure grip on Emily. A brown, wiry dog darted across the street, yapping and nipping at the horses' fetlocks. The horse pulling the carriage nearest the curb reared in alarm. Elias squeaked and jerked against her hand, his barley jar slipping from his grasp. Wailing in distress, he dove after it. His hand, slicked with sweat from the unseasonably warm day and the brisk walk, slipped from hers.

Elias! No! Grace sucked in a breath that jammed in her throat. He darted after the rolling jar. It trundled over the gutter, wedging to a stop against a fresh pile of manure. She lunged towards him but, weighed down by Edwin, she stumbled and fell, cracking her knee on the ground with a blow that sprayed sparks of pain through her femur. *Ow!* Grace dropped to her hands, glaring at the grime-blackened pavement. She grunted at each wave of pain pulsing up her thigh.

At first, she heard nothing, but then the screams and cries punctured the silence like panicked gulls swirling over a fisherman's catch. Beside her, Edwin's shriek ignited a fiery flash of panic through her core. Emily's pale face loomed, her blue eyes wide, her lashes clumped with tears. Grace tried to rise, but her limbs, heavy and uncooperative, magnetised her to the earth. Elias? Where was Elias?

"It's all right, Eddy. Mamam's all right." Grace heard the tight alarm in Emily's voice as she heaved on Grace's arm. "Get up, Mamam. Stop crying, Eddy."

Grace scooped Edwin into her lap, instinctively patting and shushing him. Oh, thank goodness! His blond head and puce, screaming face were unscathed. Tilting her head, she tried to make sense of the carnage. *Elias?* Several adults stood dazed and staring in horror; others bent over offering assistance, or words of comfort to crying women. *Oh, please, Lord! Where is he?* She stared past the clopping horses' hooves and whirring carriage wheels, her gaze alighting on a misshapen form laying in the street.

Oh, Lord above. No! Elias!

With the might of Hercules, she rose to her feet. Her world tilted and her vision swam. She thrust Edwin at Sally and, ignoring the flaming tendrils burning in her knee, limped over to Elias's inert form. She dropped weightily to her uninjured knee and rolled him over. Her chest slammed shut with terror. In the middle of his forehead, a V-shaped dent oozed a rivulet of blood that trickled down his face like macabre tears. Elias's long-lashed lids were closed.

Grace's mind slipped into an abyss like the tumbling turmoil of a muddy landslide. The world turned white and all noise ceased as she stared at his angelic face. She forgot how to breathe. It was not until her burning lungs forced her to gulp air that she became aware of the dancing black patent shoes in her periphery.

"Oh, God, I'm so sorry, milady. 'Twas an accident, I swear. Oh, God. I've killed 'im. He darted out so fast. 'Tweren't anything I could do, I swear. Almighty God, 'elp me!"

She tightened her grip on her son. An icy hand stroked the back of her neck, unfathomable pain constricting her heart to the point where she thought it would pop. She should never have returned to London. She should have trusted the ill-feeling in her gut at the docks. Looking down at Elias, her vision blurred with hot tears. Gripping her limp son to her chest, she struggled to her feet. Home. She had to get him home. And send for Billy. Glaring at the hackney driver, she gave him the address to Abertarff House.

"Oh, Jesus, missus. Of course. Anythin'. I'm sorry. I'm so sorry."

Grace clambered into the carriage, which whiffed of horse manure and leather wax. Sally bustled Emily and Edwin in behind. The carriage door slammed and Grace jolted, gulping in deep breaths of air that did not reach the bottom of her lungs. She lay Edwin across her lap. She wanted him to open his beautiful blue eyes. She *needed* him to open them. He was not breathing. He needed to breathe. She had given him life once—she would do it again.

She drew his chin down and blew hard into his mouth, still painted black from the pomfret cake he had been eating. *Breathe, my darling!* She blew again. And again. And again. It was no good. She could see the air was not getting in. Lifting his face to hers, she sealed her mouth around his and blew. *Oh, please, Elias. Just breathe.* Air blew from his nostrils and an aromatic liquorice fragrance puffed warm against her cheek. She jerked back. Was that a breath? She leaned in and blew again. Oh, good grief—it was her own breath. Why was it not blazing well working?

"Elias!" She shook his shoulders and his head snapped back and forth. "Wake up!" *Please, Lord.* She dropped her ear onto his chest, but all she heard was her own thundering heart in her ears. A heartbeat. He needed a heartbeat to live. She flipped him over her knees, as she had done when he was an infant, and jiggled him violently while banging his back. She knew she was being rough, but she was desperate.

On the opposite bench, Emily and Edwin cowered beneath Sally's armpits, their wide eyes fixed on their brother. All three sat in stunned silence. The hackney sped around a corner and Grace, feeling the back end of it slide out, gripped the leather hand strap. As it straightened out, the driver bellowed frantically. "Out the way! Move, ye bastard! Coming through!"

Grace flipped Elias again, catching his head as it lolled back. She pressed her ear to his chest. *Lord, help me!* Nothing.

Sally leaned forward, her dark eyes fearful like a fox cornered by hunting dogs, and laid the green woollen knee rug over Elias. "P'haps it'll help to keep him warm, marm?"

Grace tucked the scratchy fabric edges around her little boy. He looked like a swaddled infant, and she threw her head back, the agony of her cry bouncing off the canvas lining above. Gripping Elias to her chest, she tucked his face into her neck, willing her body heat to warm his cooling cheeks. She rocked him, just as she had when he was a babe. He always liked that. *Oh, my sweet darling boy. Stay. Stay with me. I need you.*

THE JANGLE of bridles and stony clopping of hooves halted outside Seamus's library window. He was poring over the bleak state of his finances in his ledger. His three-storey townhouse in St James's Square was blissfully quiet with Grace and the children not yet returned from their visit with Admiral Baxter. The clock on the mantel struck two. Outside, a horse snorted, and he stepped over to the window, curious who his visitor might be. Perhaps a letter from his publisher? He had written a narrative of their journey, and was waiting for word whether his book was suitable for print. Some days, it felt as though it took longer to write and publish a blazing book than it did to circumnavigate the world. Heaven knew how he needed the money!

At the sight of the hackney stopped at the foot of the town-house steps, a shiver of unease rippled across his back, the cold oddly out of place on this bright summer's day. The driver dismounted and opened the carriage door. McGilney materialised from the shadowed interior, handing the driver a large bundle wrapped in a knee rug. Back already? Where was Bartel with his carriage? Who needed a knee rug on such a fine day? Seamus shook his head. What on earth had Grace bought now? Something expensive if she was using a rug to protect it! He would have to have a word with her about her expenses.

Grace stumbled from the carriage, hanging heavily onto the open door as she did so. Her chin was dipped low, but Seamus's instincts flared as she placed her hand on the bundle in the driver's arms. It looked heavy. Surely he would not hand it to her? The folded edge of the rug slipped, and Seamus caught a glimpse of the blond hair of one of the twins, the small face pale and half concealed by the thick material. A sense of danger flashed in his gut like the flicker of an oil torch on a dark night.

He spun from the window and bolted into the hallway, his shoulder smashing into the door frame as his leather-soled shoes slipped on the polished floor. With an unnerving sense of disconnection, the passageway to the front door elongated before him. At the end of the distorted tunnel, the front door swung open. His footsteps thundered on the parquet floor, each step jarring his rigid spine. McGilney's usually bright face was grey and constricted in the rictus of distress.

He rushed towards his wife. "Grace, what is it?"

She stared vacantly, and the uneasy prickle on the back of his neck turned into a full-blown burn of terror across his entire body. He barely recognised her. Her face, so bloodless as to be translucent, twisted grotesquely. Before he even reached her, his breath shuddered. He knew that mask—he had seen it too many times before—*death*. Grace staggered as his feet skidded to a halt before her. He was panting sharply, swallowing deeply against the panic clawing its way up his throat.

Emily and Edwin wailed in distress and tore forward, clinging tightly to his legs, their buried faces muffling their sobs. McGilney stood stiffly, unblinking. Seamus peeled back the edge of the rug with tenderness and trepidation. He sucked in a sharp breath as the pale, bloodless face of his son stared back. A spiked orb of horror tore through his chest with the ferocity of a cannonball splintering a yardarm. *It cannot be! My boy!*

Seamus reached for his son. His wife crashed to her knees—and he sank into a sea of misery with her, as helpless and hopeless as a brigantine with both masts blown to smithereens.

Chapter Thirty-Three

The interior of Grace's London bedchamber was cold, bleak, and empty, like the grey November sky outside the open window. Even though it was winter, Billy insisted on airing her chamber. In the murky light, the colours of the room waned to silhouettes and ashen hues. The faint noises of the house—the shrieks of the children, the thudding of feet on the wooden stairs, the mutter of distant voices on the street outside—intermingled into a continuous garbled sound. None of this mattered, since she was a prisoner of her grief—held here for two long months already. The formless, shadowy terror had carried her to its lair. The harder she tried to scramble away, the more tightly it sunk its teeth into her. This was a thousand times worse than the darkness of Silverton's coal cellar.

She curled in the bed—sobbing—drowning. Even when her tears ran dry, she still heaved miserably in confusion and anger at the pointlessness of it all. Nothing could bring back Elias. Dear Lord Almighty, what was happening to her? She cuddled her pillow in consolation, the only recognisable point of reference in the black creature's lair. Even the *Clover* rolling over in the middle of the ferocious storm off Cape Horn had not felt this terrifying.

Seamus had taken care of the vicar, the undertaker, and the guests at the wake. He kept soldiering on, taking not only the weight and pain from her shoulders, but also the weight of being mother and father to their darling children, because her life had unravelled and there was nothing more anyone could do.

Every morning she awoke to realise it was still all too big and too real. Her head felt thick from crying too much, her eyelids swollen, her nose stuffy. Uninvited memories exploded into shards of glass, skewering the inside of her skull: fearful screams; the sweaty, little, warm hand slipping from hers; the dancing, polished shoes; the metallic tang oozing from the cherubic forehead.

At first, the pain of her grief was dulled by the liberal doses of laudanum Billy tipped into her. She should be thankful he had travelled from Oxford to tend her, but her gratitude soured when she had begged him for more drops and he refused. He said she did not need to add an opium dependence to her troubles. Curse him! Did he not understand? She *craved* the numbness the tincture provided. She needed more! She was desperate to fill the tearing hollow in her chest. But still he refused, and so she had told him to leave.

Now, the bedroom door opened, and Seamus entered with a tray. Her stomach lurched at the prospect of food and she rolled away, irritated he had disturbed the stillness. She heard the scrape of the silver tray as he slid it onto the dresser, and the aromatic fragrance of tea wafted over. The mattress dipped behind her as he sat.

"It's so dark," she whispered. Even if brilliant beams of sunlight were to filter across the pale blue bedcover, there were not enough suns in the universe to make it light again.

Seamus lay beside her, cradling her. She wanted to recoil

from his touch, but then she realised it was exactly what her soul craved, and she rolled over, laying her head on his warm chest. She needed his touch to bring peace to the raging, roaring darkness inside.

"Oh, Seamus, please stop the pain," she pleaded.

His arm tightened around her. "Perhaps you'll feel better if you get up? Put on a fresh dress. Take some tea in the parlour?"

A yellow bolt of anger ripped through her as she longed for something to wrinkle the smooth surface of his infuriatingly controlled demeanour. How did he not feel the agony? She tipped her face up, shocked by the red-raw rings circling his puffy eyes. "I can't," she whispered. "I just can't." He looked at her with such tenderness that her heart convulsed painfully. He caressed her cheek with his warm fingers, but she remained chilled. She wanted him entirely to herself, but how could he bear her when she could not bear herself?

"Do you know what I believe?" he murmured. "Elias lived a life knowing only love." His hand stilled and he peered deep into her soul, reaching a depth in her she did not think anyone could touch again. "Without you, I'm a fearful and discouraged man. I can't breathe without your love. Come back to me, Dulcinea. Please."

A soft shuffle of feet drew her attention to the doorway. Emily and Edwin hovered on the threshold, hand in hand. Edwin had taken to sleeping in Emily's double bed after Elias's death. Who was she to tell him he could not? The poor darling had never been alone a minute in his life, even from conception, and Grace struggled to imagine the loss of his twin. Realising that the horror of his young and innocent sorrow likely equalled her own hollow heartache, she beckoned.

"Come in, my darlings. Hop up." She patted the empty space beside her. Emily hoisted Edwin onto the high bed before scrambling up herself. Her son curled into Grace's free side, and Emily lay beside him, her blonde curls fanning on the pillow.

Grace kissed Edwin's head, his fine wheaten hair tickling her nose. His familiar, clean scent reminded her of Elias. They even smelled the same. Edwin's chubby arms gripped her neck tightly. The hug was firm—not enough to stop her breathing, but it did. With her breath choked in her throat, she squeezed her eyes shut.

"Mamam?" Edwin's voice was small in her ear. "Me see Elias again?"

She tried to swallow the lump, but it jammed fast.

When she did not reply, Emily sat up and faced Edwin. "Yes, Eddy, you will, one day. Elias is an angel in heaven now. He's looking down on us all. Right, Mamam?"

Grace sucked in a quivering breath, still unable to speak, but she nodded, teeth clamping her lips so as to not cry. She was desperate to reply, but she had no answer. She did not want him in heaven. She wanted him here, with her. She spotted Edwin's innocent acceptance ease his tightened brow. Oh, if only she were blessed with the same naivete, how much easier this torture would be.

Emily shuffled around, crossing her legs. She reached for Grace's hand. Grace curled her fingers around the small hand, still sticky with jam from breakfast. With her family surrounding her, she realised the sounds of bird song outside were no longer muted. It was as though someone had thrown open the theatre doors of an orchestra. Their trills and tweets blared through the ajar window—their joy felt wrong.

Edwin wriggled beside her as Emily asked, "Are you looking for something, Mamam?" Peeling her focus away from the window, Grace peered around, marvelling at Emily's innocence shining cleanly in her genuine smile.

How could she dismiss her daughter without being cruel? She did not have the energy to figure it out—it was easier to answer truthfully. "Yes, I'm looking for something."

Emily's freckled nose scrunched in concentration. "Is it your smile? Cappy said when Elias died, he lost his smile."

Grace visually caressed her husband. His eyes were as blue as the sky she had just been staring at. The corner of his mouth tweaked up cautiously. Turning back to her daughter, she licked her lips and swallowed. "Yes, I'm looking for—my smile." Her breath quivered as she inhaled. "I'm just not sure I'll ever find it again."

"Me help you find it, Mamam." Edwin's tiny fingers curled around Grace's wrist.

She knew she had to do something. Even if she could not shake this gloom, she did not wish to make Seamus and the children pay the price for its hold on her. "Perhaps I'll try to get up today," she said.

"Cappy will help you, won't you, Cappy?" said Emily. "You always treat Mamam like a queen."

Grace spotted Seamus's deep breath expand his chest, and his mouth curved into a full smile. "Since I treat Mamam like a queen, what does that make me?"

Without hesitation, Emily blurted, "A servant!" She clamped her dimple-knuckled hand to her mouth and giggled.

"Really?" said Seamus, one brow quirked.

An unexpected fizz of laughter rolled from Grace's mouth as his handsome face lit with humour. He froze. Clearly, her laugh had stunned him too.

"It's good to see you smile again, Dulcinea."

Her cheeks blazed at having been caught laughing, and she gritted her teeth to keep her smile transfixed. Seamus's cautious grin faltered, constricting her heart, but Emily's babbling drew his attention.

"Yes," nodded Emily, her blonde curls bobbing. "You're always saying 'Your servant, madam' or 'Your servant, sir' to people you meet."

Grace laughed tiredly. "Oh, Empem. You funny little thing." She patted her daughter's knee.

Seamus swung his legs off the bed and rose. He turned

smartly with shoulders drawn back and pale brows arching. "Right. My dignity and I will now pick ourselves off the floor. Time you powder monkeys go brush your teeth, before the tickly octopus comes out to play."

Accepting sticky-lipped kisses on her cheek, Grace watched Emily and Edwin scamper from the room squealing. Seamus held out his long-fingered hand. She slid her fingers into his dry palm, nodding to confirm the unspoken promise that she would rise and pretend everything was normal.

Chapter Thirty-Four

ABERTARFF HOUSE, ST JAMES'S SQUARE,
LONDON, 4 FEBRUARY 1840

Seamus sat with Grace and Admiral Baxter in his library before the fire, studying the bulbous glass of brandy on the table before him. Inverse images of the room shimmered and danced in the amber liquid. Grace was wrapped in her red tartan shawl, staring tranquilly into the flames. At least she was rising from her bed these days, even if she did not venture out.

Seamus took a deep, burning swill of brandy to swallow down the utterly irrational guilt that he had failed to protect his son. He looked away from Grace's forced calm, wanting desperately to forget that Elias's death had happened. The unreachable sorrow in her eyes tore at his guts. The space Elias had left in his soul now housed only memories and, some days, they were not enough. He missed his boy—missed the weight of his chunky little body in his arms; the squeal of his laughter when Seamus tickled his ribs; the soapy, clean smell of him tucked in bed at night.

With hands splayed on his thighs, Seamus rotated his right wrist, waiting for the click that would ease the stiffness. He wished he did not have to add such bad news to his wife's grief. Then again, he preferred being the messenger rather than having her find out elsewhere when she might be alone. It was a mistake he had made before and not one he wanted repeated. He cleared his throat.

"Grace, we have a grave matter to discuss with you." He flicked his gaze over to Baxter, whose normally soft features were tight. Seamus watched him take another sip of brandy, before his own gaze trailed back to her. "Admiral Baxter overheard that fermented bag of wind, Silverton, speaking ill of our sweet little Elias at the clubhouse." His voice cracked, and he coughed.

"Pah!" Baxter launched from his seat, slopping brandy over the rim of his glass. A log in the fire crackled, sending a shower of sparks into the silence.

"What did he say?" asked Grace woodenly.

Seamus's innards clenched, and he shook his head. He could not possibly repeat Silverton's filth. It would destroy her. "The details matter not."

Her eyes rose slowly to meet his, and her jaw firmed. "Tell me what he said."

"Come now, poppet," said Baxter. "Don't trouble yourself with that beast's vile spewing. I—"

"*Tell me*," she murmured.

Seamus frowned as the colour drained from her already pale face, her lips whitening into a tight line. *Oh, Dulcinea, why torture yourself so?* Looking over to Baxter, he nodded once. He reached for Grace's fingers, as thin and cold as the uppermost twigs of a beech tree in winter.

Baxter squeezed his eyelids shut and let out an unsteady breath through his nostrils. "He blames you for Elias's death."

Grace's fingers clenched around his. "How?"

He gently stroked her tense jaw with one finger. "There's no merit to what he said, but…" He swallowed the sulphurous poison that coated the words he was about to repeat. "He said that had you better control of Elias, the accident wouldn't have happened."

She inhaled sharply, her gaze of devastation shifting to Baxter.

Misery greyed the old man's round cheeks as he spoke. "He questioned why the children weren't at home, in the care of their nurse." Baxter put one hand on the mantle to steady himself. "He went on to tell all who were listening that the driver couldn't be blamed for… for…"

"For what?" she asked, her voice small.

"For your parenting ineptitude," whispered Baxter.

Grace stiffened. "And where is the coach driver now?"

For pity's sake! This was the worst bit. Seamus squeezed the bridge of his nose as he took a deep breath. "He took his own life. The weight of Elias's demise clearly corroded the man's conscience." With nothing further for the courts to determine, this unrelenting nightmare yielded no closure.

"I never blamed the driver." Grace withdrew her hand from his and tightened her shawl.

"I know you didn't, my heart." He did not blame the man either.

She tucked her hands into her armpits. "I should've held Elias's hand tighter."

"You're not to blame either, my heart. It was an unfortunate accident, with the most wretched of outcomes. For all parties."

"If Silverton believes it, so will others."

Seamus slid his palms down his thighs. "I wrote to him, demanding he cease discussing these matters since they're a private affair. I insisted he offer our family a formal apology for his slanderous insults." He shifted to the edge of the settee. "The bastard may not be responsible for the accident, but he *is* responsible for his loose tongue. And our family has been in the firing line of it for long enough." He circled his thumb around the scar on his wrist. "Silverton responded with a letter of his own, refusing to apologise. So"—he hesitated, bracing himself for her reaction—"I've challenged him to a duel."

"No, Seamus!" Her voice pitched and she slammed back against the settee. Her cheeks flared red in the rosy firelight.

He cupped her face. "Grace, it's time to end this. We'll never be rid of him if I don't see this through." Heaven knows she gave it her best shot when she stabbed him!

Baxter stepped away from the fireplace towards Grace. Indecision coated her face, even though Baxter assured her. "It'll be all right, my darling. Seamus has done me the honour of inviting me to be his second." He set his mouth grimly.

"No, Uncle Farfar! Not you too!" She bounced to the edge of the settee as though to rise, and Seamus gripped her hand. She beseeched, "I couldn't bear anything happening to either of you."

Seamus stretched his neck to alleviate the heavy weight on his shoulders. "Grace—it's time."

"I tell you"—Baxter's voice trembled with emotion—"if *you* don't kill the bastard, *I* will! Make your shot count, my boy."

He regarded Baxter calmly. "Have I not proven myself to have a steady nerve in a confrontation, sir?"

"Indeed, but the ammunition fired in the coming weeks will be far worse than any steel ball. Silverton's depravity has no end. He'll exploit your vulnerability to its fullest with his verbal tirade." Baxter flicked a wary look at Grace before firming his gaze on Seamus. "Are you prepared for that kind of injury?"

"If the end result is for me to put a ball through his heart, then yes, I'm prepared," said Seamus. Grace's chin rose. Encouraged, he continued, "Our family has endured this man's barbarity long enough."

Grace's voice was steady. "And if he refuses?"

"Ha!" snorted Baxter. "We'll put a notice in the paper denouncing him as a poltroon for refusing to give satisfaction to the dispute. The man's enormous ego won't allow him to be publicly slated as weak or a coward. This we already know from his fabrication of being attacked by a highwayman instead of by you." His wrinkled face was ashen with anger.

Seamus swallowed deeply, his own voice muted in his ears by the blood pounding inside his head. "I'm sorry I've let you down. I may be a ruined man, but I swear by every Commandment, I *will* avenge our son."

Baxter cocked one eyebrow. "Come now, Fitzwilliam! You're not ruined."

"I beg to differ, sir." Seamus frowned at his own empty brandy bulb, wondering if the fumes had gone to the admiral's head. He was most definitely ruined. He had not a penny to his name—not to mention that threat of foreclosure against Abertarff House currently stuffed in his writing bureau. Damn and blast! His hand was forced—even selling Abertarff House would not clear the debt. Idling away life in debtor's prison would be worse than pumping the wretched bilges of a ship—at least that task had purpose. He was sailing this tide of gloom alone, not wanting to add to Grace's distress nor face a shameful confession to Baxter.

"You might have encountered some misfortune, but your wife still has means," explained Baxter.

Seamus's confusion deepened. "But Lord and Lady Flint disowned her long before they died."

Grace's shoulders stiffened. He slid his hand into hers. What would she say when she learned the true measure of his miserable state of affairs? His gut clenched as though getting ready to expel a batch of bad oysters.

A shadow of regret danced across Baxter's face, but he nodded. "That they did. More's the pity."

"Are you referring to the gems you gave me?" Grace asked.

Baxter's grey brows arched. "Good God! You mean to tell me you still have those? I'd thought they'd be long gone by now."

They were! Seamus had used those gems to afford Grace the lifestyle she was accustomed to, but the funds of the last diamond were dwindling—fast. Christ, was Baxter about to ask for them back? Seamus rose and poured himself another brandy, hoping the alcohol would soften the ragged edges of this uncomfortable conversation that grated down his spine like a blunt wood saw.

Baxter drew deeply on his cigar and waved the ashen end at Seamus. "No, no, they're a mere drop in the ocean. Keep them for a rainy day."

That rainy day had long come and gone. "I'm not sure I follow you, sir," said Seamus.

Baxter slumped into the armchair beside him, a whoosh of air billowing from the leather-upholstered seat. "I feel perfectly wretched that you invested in those bonds on my recommendation. And I must be honest, I'm wracked with guilt about Grace losing her inheritance. My brother may have cut her off at the knees, but as you know, the inheritance passed to me. Which is jolly fortuitous, because now I can do with it what I like."

Seamus glanced at his wife's pale face. Her eyes narrowed in interest. Pressing his lips, his silence invited Baxter to continue.

"I'm gifting you and Grace half of the estate. No need for an old codger like me to sit on such a pile. Needs to go to you young ones who still have a long life ahead."

What the devil? Had Grace told Baxter of his financial predicament? But how could she know? He had taken such care not to burden her with it. How could a wave of fate sweep away one fortune and instantly wash in another? There had to be a catch. Seamus had never heard of another man struck with such luck.

He turned as Grace gasped. "Oh, Uncle. I... we... how..."

Baxter chuckled. "To save you the discomfort of asking how much, I'll just tell it straight. Eighty thousand pounds."

Seamus snapped upright. "Heavens above, sir! You could purchase a small country for that!" Not to mention clear all his debt in one fell swoop.

Baxter shrugged, the motion wrinkling the loose skin on his neck. "Not quite. But it's enough for you to build one of those new-fangled packets."

Seamus gave a joyous bark. "Ha! We could build a whole fleet for that!"

"The opium run's a profitable venture. You can't go wrong steering in that direction." Baxter ground out his cigar stub. "Though I'm not dictating how you spend it. It's yours and Grace's to decide."

"Actually, sir," said Seamus, "we had considered the wool run to the colony of Port Jackson. We've contacts there with the Barclay family. They're graziers with a substantial flock and a shortage of transport to see their wool to London."

"Well if I were you, my boy, I'd be making that Mr Barclay an offer *tout de suite*," said Baxter earnestly. "Half the battle with these ventures is finding the right person to do business with, and by the sounds of things, you already have your foot in the door."

"Yes, sir. Indeed, we do." Seamus smiled at Grace, the calculations running wild in his head. He would construct the best ship money could buy. Make her the fastest in the world. Fate had delivered him and Grace another opportunity to leave London. As a warm wave of hope rolled across his goose-bumped skin, the feeling of absolute certainty hit his core. One way or another, they were going to be all right—his family— they were going to be all right. Even if Seamus did not survive the duel with Silverton, Baxter would take care of Grace and the children.

Seamus offered his hand to the admiral. "Thank you, sir." What more did you say to a man who had just paved the path of your future? The quicker he got this ship built, the quicker he could whisk Grace from the horrors of London.

But first, he had a man to kill.

Chapter Thirty-Five

A week later, Seamus discovered that Baxter was correct —Silverton accepted the challenge. After a few more weeks of negotiation via letter between Baxter and a Mr Rigby, Silverton's second, it was determined the duel would be held on the grounds of Clovervale Manor, with a set of officer's duelling pistols owned by Silverton. Both parties were allowed to bring an additional witness.

The morning of the duel arrived with a haste that unsettled him. His carriage made good speed out of the hustle of the town, and he took in the painstakingly familiar route along the country lane. The cold hand that had caressed his neck the last time he travelled this road slid down his spine. He knew the Reaper was heading to the same killing field as them, but just who He was there to harvest was unknown.

Seamus perused the other occupants sitting in reflective silence as the carriage bore them towards the moment of judgement. Admiral Baxter puffed on a cigar, the tremor in his hands threatening to unbalance the ash. Grace stared out of the carriage window, and he slid his hand beneath her slick palm. Her clear gaze met his and she smiled reassuringly, though he did not know whether it was for his benefit or her own.

"Grace, I'm still not convinced you should bear witness to this. I don't want you there should events not work in our favour."

"I've the utmost confidence in your shooting abilities," she said.

"But Silverton is an unpredictable and dishonourable hound. I can't risk having you in his presence when my attention will be occupied elsewhere."

"Your husband is correct, Grace," said Baxter. "A duel is no place for a woman. I'm not even sure that Silverton or his second will permit the duel to proceed with you there."

"I doubt that. Silverton's overblown pride won't suffer a forfeit." Grace squeezed his hand. "Your worry is comforting, but I shan't have it any other way. I *will* watch Silverton die today."

He took a deep breath and looked up at the roof of the carriage. *Please, let justice prevail today.* The crack of Bartel's whip urged the horses on faster. They pulled through the gates of Clovervale Manor, and the horses slowed as they swept through the topiaries and up to the front entrance.

A short, salt-and-pepper-haired gentleman stepped into Seamus's periphery. Baxter thrust back in the seat in surprise, and Seamus twisted his head sharply towards the open carriage window. Christ Al-blasted-mighty! Hamilton! Forcing himself against the door, Seamus barrelled from the carriage, crashing into Hamilton. The rotund man staggered back.

"Jesus, man! Have a care. You almost knocked me down," complained Hamilton.

Seamus snatched the man's lapel and swung him around, slamming his back into the carriage. Hamilton yelped.

Seamus snarled. "I'll do more than knock you down, you

sticky-fingered quack! I'll knock out all your blazing teeth." He curled his fist in readiness. "I want my money!"

Baxter swung out of the open door and planted himself beside Seamus, hemming Hamilton in against the spoked wheel. "Good God, Hamilton. You've a hide showing your face after all the trouble you've caused. What in Hades are you doing here?"

"I'm Silverton's second," growled Hamilton, unsuccessfully striving to shrug from Seamus's grip.

"His second? But my correspondence was with Rigby." Baxter frowned.

"I wasn't about to use my real name and announce my whereabouts to all and sundry, now, was I?" Hamilton grumbled through gritted teeth.

Seamus laughed dryly. "Oh, I assure you, the *whole* of London Town will know you're back, if I have anything to do with it. I'll make sure you rot in Newgate for the rest of your days."

Grace's head appeared out of the carriage, and Seamus released his grip on Hamilton to help her alight.

Hamilton arched one brow at her. "What the devil is a woman doing here? She cannot be your witness. I won't allow it."

"My wife has every right to be here," said Seamus. "To see Silverton answer for his sins. He has aggrieved her as much as he has me."

Hamilton chuckled coldly. "Most audacious." Oblivious to Seamus's bristling hostility, he coolly continued, "Though it doesn't surprise me. Knowing your predilection for spicy adventure, Mrs Fitzwilliam, I'm sure today's events won't be half as arousing compared to some of your *other* escapades."

"God's truth, man!" exploded Baxter. "Is that *any* way to address a gentlewoman? In which den of iniquity did Silverton find *you*?"

Seamus felt Grace tremble as she pressed into him, but he

marvelled at her levelled response. She smiled prettily at Hamilton. "Pray, do keep speaking, Colonel. Perhaps you might entertain us with something delightfully intelligent." Despite the gravity of the situation, Seamus bit back a snort of mirth. She had not lost her witty tongue.

Hamilton cocked his head. "Eh?"

"Hamilton!" Baxter stepped forward, pushing Hamilton back against the carriage with a wave of invisible authority. "Show us to the meeting point. We'll await Silverton there."

Hamilton scraped the air before him, his voice dripping. "Of course. Lord Silverton has chosen the apple orchard." The hem of his grey coat flicked Seamus's legs as he spun towards a grove of trees. Seamus scoured their surroundings, doing a double take at the flutter of an upstairs curtain. He slipped his arm around Grace as they followed the portly figure ahead of them.

The trees in the apple orchard stood in orderly rows like files of Royal Marines at attention, the brown, crispy leaves their uniform. He noted the ground was damp but firm underfoot. His shoe slicked across a decayed apple, mashing its contents into the grass like a stepped-in cow pat.

With their boots crunching and cracking the fallen twigs on the ground, Baxter and Hamilton headed over to where Silverton's butler stood with a wooden box in his arms. Seamus recognised him from his last visit to Clovervale—Dickson! Brazen smuggler and henchman. Seamus deposited Grace at the edge of the clearing in the cold shade of a tree.

"Well, if it isn't the whole happy little family," droned a voice behind him.

Seamus skinned his knuckles on the rough bark of the tree as he whirled. Silverton ballooned before him, his putrefying scent —likely from the man's unwashed creases where a sponge could not reach—wafting by on the breeze.

"Silverton." Seamus's anger bristled around him like the static on a wool blanket in winter.

"Grace, my sweet. Delightful to see you, as always," said Silverton, peering around Seamus's shoulder. "Perhaps you might join me for some tea at the house once all this business is over?"

Seamus heard Grace gasp, and she grabbed the back of his coat—whether for support or to stop him launching at Silverton was not clear. "Hold your tongue, Silverton. My wife's name has no place in your polluted mouth."

Silverton's wide nose scrunched like a pig snout as he leered at Grace, chuckling. His eyes tripped down to her waist, and he scrunched one cheek in evident disappointment. "Alas, as I feared. Your spawn has ruined you. Pity."

Seamus's back muscles bunched in a slab of fury. *Control yourself, man—the hour of death is upon the bastard.* Grace was stonily quiet behind him, though her hand gripping his coat shook violently.

Silverton grinned as though enjoying the acute discomfort his presence caused. Flicking his tongue at the residing glob of sputum at the corner of his mouth, he feigned disappointment. "Never mind, I've always found her tongue to be too shrewish for my liking anyway."

Goad me all you like, you bastard. You shan't get a rise out of me! "Are we here to talk, or are we here to duel?" said Seamus flatly.

Silverton scratched an eyebrow with his thumb, his gaze wandering across to the group of men deep in discussion on the other side of the grove. He sighed as though bored. "Best get on with it then, heh?" His jowls wobbled as he trampled across the glade to the colonel.

Grace tugged Seamus's coat, and he turned. Seeing her ashen cheeks, he kissed her clammy forehead. "Are you all right?"

"Make sure you kill him!" she whispered tightly. He appreciated her conviction.

"I fully intend to." He kissed her again and whispered, "Stay strong, my heart. I'll return soon."

He paced across the open ground between the trees, assessing the lie of the land and the shadows. The air was filled with the cloying aroma of new flowers, almost as nauseating as the stench of the decaying fruit.

Silverton waved his hand at the open box inlaid with two immaculately polished duelling pistols. "Guests first. Pick wisely. Though you have me at an unfair advantage what with me providing you with a significantly wider target." He pouted his slimy lips. "Never mind. *I* have the unfair advantage of never missing my shot."

Ignoring the gibe, Seamus made his selection.

Baxter and Hamilton measured ten full paces and marked the spots with a sword stabbed into the rich earth. They cast lots for the choice of position and agreed that Hamilton would give the word. Seamus and Silverton loaded the pistols in each other's presence and faced one another as Hamilton ran through the rules.

"Gentlemen, when the parties are placed at their stations, I'll ask the principals whether they're ready. They shall answer in the affirmative. After this, the principals shall present and fire *when they please*. If one fires before the other, the opposite second shall say, 'One, two, three, fire,' and the principal shall then fire or lose his opportunity to do so." Hamilton's grey head pivoted between Seamus and Silverton. "Though I'm sure there'll be none of that nonsense. There's no room for cowards here today." He took a deep breath, his voice ringing out clearly, "To your stations, gentlemen."

Seamus reached his embedded sword and turned to face Silverton. The calm that settled over him reminded him of the surreal state of being aboard a ship while watching an ominous storm rolling in from a distance. Baxter stood behind him.

Hamilton asked, "Are both parties ready?"

"I am." Seamus's clear reply funnelled through the avenue of trees as he glared murderously at Silverton. *This had been a long time coming. Foul beast!*

"Indeed," drawled Silverton, carelessly waving his pistol. "Pity you didn't bring a physician along, Fitzwilliam. You'll be needing one."

Hamilton drew himself upwards with a deep breath and bellowed, "Present!"

Seamus took aim, and a cloud of gunpowder burst around his head as he shot first. The birds in the surrounding trees rose in a black swarm, darting away in synchronised panic. When the smoke cleared, his gut spasmed to see Silverton still standing, smirking smugly. Seamus glared at his smoking pistol. Goddammed smooth-bored piece of rot! He should have demanded to use his own better-quality weapons. They, and purer black powder, would not have resulted in this miserable miss.

"Ha! You missed!" Spittle sprayed from Silverton's thick lips. He raised his weapon at Seamus's chest. "Your naval medals aren't going to save you now, Fitzwilliam."

Seamus swung his head towards Grace for one frantic final look at her. "Grace!" She lunged towards him, the terror in her eyes tearing his heart from its roots.

Dulcinea! I'm sorry!

"Seamu—" His wife's scream was cut short in his ears as the second shot fired.

Seamus blinked rapidly in the momentary stillness, drowned out by the ringing in his ears. Silverton's eyes bulged, and his tongue wiggled like a fat worm in the hole of his open mouth. Seamus still held his empty pistol, raised in position, as tendrils of smoke swirled over his shoulder from behind. He stared at Silverton's face. Blood trickled down his fat forehead. The gargantuan frame toppled backwards, hitting the ground with a wet thud.

Grace collided with Seamus, throwing her arms around him and squeezing the air from him. "Oh, Seamus! Are you shot?"

Lowering his pistol, he gripped her to him with his free arm, mumbling into her lavender-fragranced curls, "I'm unhurt. I'm all right." Her quick, short breaths were warm on his neck.

"Murder!" Hamilton screeched, dancing agitatedly on the spot. His round face flushed cherry-red as he glared at Seamus. Grace swung her head in Hamilton's direction, but she did not relinquish her grip about him.

"He stepped away from his mark," said Baxter. Seamus glanced back over his shoulder as the admiral lowered his smoking pistol. "As Captain Fitzwilliam's second, I have the right to shoot Lord Silverton for stepping away from his mark."

Hamilton's fists bunched by his side, and he huffed like a struggling steam engine. "'Tis murder, I tell you. Saw it with my own eyes, as did my witness." He swung around to glare at Dickson, who stood by still holding the pistol box.

The dour-faced butler stared unblinking at Hamilton for a while before declaring, "Admiral Baxter is correct, sir. His lordship stepped away from his mark. As Captain Fitzwilliam's second, the admiral was well within the rules to shoot him."

"You disloyal dog!" Hamilton snarled. "After everything the man has done for you!"

Dickson snapped his head towards Hamilton. "Coward deserved what he had coming!"

"What are you on about?" growled Hamilton.

"I turned a blind eye to his philandering all these years —'tweren't my business—but I warned him to steer clear of my niece." Dickson thrust the pistol box under his elbow. "She needed that job to feed her family, but the fiend couldn't keep his wretched hands off her."

"Your niece?" echoed Grace.

"Nicolette Lloyd. Taken into his service as *your* lady's maid," sniped Dickson, thrusting his chin at Grace.

Hamilton blustered, "Good God, man. Are you fool enough to have brought your kin under Silverton's roof knowing his propensities?"

"Especially after what happened to her cousin, Jenny Parks," added Grace, her voice thin. "Silverton pinned Miss Parks's death on her fiancé—when Silverton was *clearly* the perpetrator."

"Hold your tongue, madam!" snapped Hamilton. "Unless you've proof of such outrageous accusations?"

Seamus's gaze darted to Dickson. The butler said, "My niece's bruised face was proof enough of what Silverton was capable of. He gave me his word he wouldn't lay a finger on her, but the bastard taught my Nicolette a lesson for conversing too freely with *her*." Dickson aimed a venomous scowl at Grace again. Seamus tightened his arm around her as she jerked against the accusation.

By Neptune's trident! The girl on the stairs! Seamus frowned at the recollection of the day he went to confront Silverton about Grace's whereabouts. The maid had been polishing the banister when he asked for the mistress of the house. He remembered the terror on her pale face, with one side purple and grotesquely swollen.

"Did Silverton kill her?" asked Grace, her voice trailing away.

Dickson shook his head. "No. Told his lordship I'd take care of her myself. I squirrelled her away to my sister in Aberdeen."

"Is he dead?" Grace's voice was followed by a void of silence, as all heads swung towards Silverton's immobile mass.

Seamus glared at the mound of flesh. "Well and truly," he said quietly, dipping his lips to her ears. "It's done. It's over." He felt her breath judder from her, and he stroked her back.

Hamilton wrung his hands together and strode over to the felled man. With a roar, he kicked Silverton swiftly in his bulging side. The kick ricocheted across the body, the excess flesh wobbling like a whale carcass on the shore being pounded by the surf. "You goddamned bloody fool!"

Seamus released Grace and sidled over to Hamilton with the pretence of inspecting Silverton's body. He grabbed Hamilton's arm, twisting it up his back. "Right, you thief. I want answers and I want them now." He tweaked Hamilton's arm higher, and the man shrieked. "Who are you, and what's your acquaintance with Silverton?" demanded Seamus, nudging Silverton with his shoe.

Hamilton pinched his lips, his breath coming hard and fast through flared nostrils. Seamus knew the look of a man prepared to keep his secrets. Oh, he would make him talk, all right. He caught a movement in the corner of his eye and twisted his neck.

The butler approached, the polished wooden box tucked under his arm. "He's *this* devil's spawn," offered Dickson, jabbing a finger at Silverton.

"Shut your mouth, fool!" Hamilton snarled, dancing on his toes as Seamus wrenched his arm higher. "You won't survive the night if you breathe another word."

"You don't scare me," scoffed Dickson, dropping the pistol box onto the damp earth with a dull thud. "I know all of Silverton's dirty little secrets, including *you*. With him dead and you disowned, there's nothing for me to fear."

Seamus's head volleyed throughout the confusing conversation. He shook it to clear his thoughts. "You mean to tell me that Hamilton is Silverton's son?" he said. He jerked his head around at the sound of Grace's voice beside him.

"I thought Silverton had no children?" she asked.

"He had no *heirs*," clarified Dickson. "But he had *this* bastard." He inclined his head at Hamilton. "He's the product of his lordship's dalliances with one of his many maids. Bishop Carmichael—"

"Carmichael?" burst Seamus. "Heavens above! Same Bishop

Carmichael who arranged Father Babcock's passage aboard the *Clover*?"

Dickson nodded. "Yes. The bishop arranged for the bastard infant to be raised by a childless duke and duchess. They passed him off as their own, with his lordship as his godfather. Lord Silverton paid for Hamilton's commission in the army, but the privileged fool couldn't even manage to keep that. Took to swindling like a duck to water."

Hamilton sneered, "You've room to talk, Dickson. You're an outright smuggler!"

Dickson's brow dipped. "Those wines and spirits are well insured. The wine merchants don't lose out. And the many hands that pass the goods along are well rewarded. I don't swindle anyone out of their hard-earned coin like you. I help men make a decent living."

"A dishonest living's more like it," spluttered Hamilton.

Dickson smashed his clenched fist into Hamilton's jaw with a meaty thud. Hamilton's head snapped back, the force jerking him from Seamus's grasp. The colonel tripped back over Silverton's mountainous form, landing heavily on his backside. The heels of his boots scoured troughs in the mud as he scrambled to his feet, his rotund cheeks quivering like they were fit to burst.

"You insolent serf! You dare lay hands on a gentleman!" said Hamilton. Seamus hooked his arms through Hamilton's elbows to prevent him launching at Dickson, and Baxter barricaded Dickson with an arm across his chest.

"Cease this instant! The both of you!" Seamus bellowed.

"You're no gentleman, Hamilton. You're a plotter of murder," said Dickson.

"What murder?" Baxter gripped Dickson's shoulder.

"Shut your mouth, brigand, before I shut it for you," groused Hamilton, fear flashing in his eyes like the grey glint of sun on a pistol muzzle.

Baxter turned to Dickson. "If you've evidence against this

scoundrel, you'd best speak it plainly now before witnesses." He swung his restless gaze towards Hamilton. "Before he has a chance to hide behind any influential connections."

Seamus noted the sag in Dickson's shoulders, and Baxter released his hold on him. This was an interesting turn of events and one that held Seamus's full attention. He concentrated his gaze on the butler's sweaty top lip.

"You transported a Father Babcock on your last voyage, did you not, sir?" Dickson tilted his head.

A jolt of surprise jerked Seamus as though Dickson had poked him with a hot handspike. "Yes. What of it?" Seamus asked warily.

"Did you encounter any... *unfortunate incidents* along the way?" asked Dickson.

Seamus rolled his shoulders back at the tight unease that stretched across his shoulder blades. "Yes." He shook Hamilton's arms, and the man's head jerked back and forth. "I know you planted Babcock as a saboteur, Hamilton. What I don't know is *why*."

Hamilton cast a fearful look over his shoulder, droplets of blood from his swollen lips spraying as he snapped, "It wasn't me!"

Wiping the warm droplets from his cheek, Seamus shook his head. "Was it the bishop who paid the generous stipend to rid himself of Babcock? I have no quarrels with any bishop. It makes no sense."

Hamilton shook his head. "It wasn't the bishop, though he was in on it. It was Silverton. *He* was the one who had me source a disgraced man to plant aboard your ship. One who was destined for the gallows—who would do the utmost to see your journey fail. But clearly, bumbling Babcock failed his task before he got himself speared to death."

Seamus gnawed the inside of his cheek. He could mention that Babcock was still alive, but since it would only prove another of his failings, he held his tongue. He did not want Hamilton diverted from his current thoughts.

"Why?" All heads swung in Grace's direction. Her pallid cheeks were drawn, but her eyes blazed like an emerald in a fire.

"My father was a vengeful man," said Hamilton, kicking Silverton's blubbery belly again. The corpse lurched as though alive. "The man held grudges for life. Just ask me." His chin quivered. "Nothing I did was good enough. When the *Clover* returned to London with you two still alive, he followed through with his threat to write me from his will." Hamilton's voice warbled, and Seamus eased the grip on his arms. "He held me responsible for the failure because I was the one who recruited Babcock."

"But *why*?" repeated Grace. "Why did he want us dead?"

"Because he couldn't have *you*," bit Hamilton. "Failure was not an option for my father. His failure to secure your hand in marriage was a thorn in his side. And you, Fitzwilliam, stuck it in deeper when you married her, essentially wresting all opportunity from him. If my father couldn't have her, he wanted *no one* to have her."

"I stuck more than a wretched thorn in him!" said Grace.

Seamus pressed his lips at the memory of the bone knife handle he had found beside Highgate Pond.

"All that did was poke the dragon," said Hamilton. "He had only planned to cripple Fitzwilliam financially, but after you stabbed him and ran back into Fitzwilliam's arms, he vowed you'd both pay with your lives."

"Good God, man!" exclaimed Baxter. "If he wanted them dead, why not just do away with them here in London? Why all the pretence and expense of a world voyage?"

"Because he enjoyed the game. The chase was always his favourite part of the hunt. Outwitting the other party."

Ha! That explained Silverton going to the trouble of hiring O'Reilly to kidnap Grace from the *Discerning* all those years back, thought Seamus. Realising that Silverton had wanted Grace back on *his* terms, Seamus drew his shoulders back. As much as he wished she had not been here today, he was glad she had heard these reports first-hand.

"Well, he failed miserably on *all* accounts as far as I'm concerned," said Grace, her chin jutting.

Indeed! Seamus thought triumphantly. Silverton had always sorely underestimated Grace's tenacity. "You'd have thought he'd reconsider his score after our son was killed. A more compassionate man would." He bit hard on his molars, the tension searing down his neck.

Hamilton ducked his chin, his stare fixed to the ground. "A regrettable incident. But one that only served his purpose to goad you into today's meeting." He raised his eyes to meet Seamus's. "I'd hoped you might rise above his provocation."

"Rise above!" Seamus gasped. "The man made a mockery of my dead son's name and accused my wife of being an unfit mother. No amount of rising could clear those insults. If it's all so woefully regrettable to you, Hamilton, why are *you* here today? Supporting *him*. How did he draw you out of hiding?"

Hamilton inhaled sharply. "He promised, if I stood as his second today and the outcome fell in his favour, that he'd write me back into his will." Hamilton's gaze darted venomously to the body. "But now he's dead. And it's too damned late!"

Baxter scoffed. "I'd say it is. You're going to prison for a jolly long time, Hamilton. You'll have plenty of time to mull over your regrets."

Chapter Thirty-Six

ABERTARFF HOUSE, ST JAMES'S SQUARE, LONDON, 15 JUNE 1840

Grace awoke to the tinkling of cutlery on crockery. The swelling hum of voices and sliding chairs signalled the meal was over. She had missed breakfast—again. She studied her chamber with its overtones of furniture polish and beeswax. The hearth lay grey and empty. Soft, hesitating chords of Emily starting her piano practice filtered into the quiet room. Normal sounds of life.

The door swung open slowly, and Seamus filled the door frame with a tray before him. She swung her legs over the edge of the mattress, her faint smile inviting him in. He nudged the door closed with his foot, sealing off the stilted music. Clearing his throat, he shuffled forward and slid the tray onto the dresser. He was thinner than usual, and his deep blue eyes were dark with wariness. He eased himself into the wing-back chair beside her. Entwining his fingers on his lap, he pressed his shoulders into the chairback. His features had sharpened over time and lost their youthful naivety. Usually this gave him an air of a man with everything well under control, but not today. Grace waited a beat for him to say something, but when he did not, she spoke.

"You're a little pale." She instinctively reached to feel his forehead. The weight of her arm reminded her of her fatigue— and she did not have the strength to bridge the gap between them. She lowered her arm, and he closed his eyes. He looked so disappointed that she could not bear to touch him. But that was not true! She wanted nothing more in this world than his touch. No, not wanted, *craved*.

He opened his eyes when she spoke again. "Are you unwell?"

"I'm not ailing from a fever, if that's what you mean," he said, gripping his scarred wrist and flexing his fingers. The clock on the mantel ticked, and his unshaven growth rasped loudly as he scratched his neck with his thumb.

"Did something happen?" she asked. She noticed the effort it took him to answer.

He pinched the bridge of his nose. "I'm sorry I've not been as good a husband as you deserve, Grace."

She shrank back, unsure whether she had the strength to walk through the door his statement had opened. He studied her a moment then tentatively reached for her fingers. His were dry and robust; hers were clammy and limp.

She stared dully at the floral-patterned carpet beneath her feet as she listened to his heavy voice. "I've never considered myself a coward, but I am, you know."

Grace snapped her head up sharply. "Pardon?"

He gave a mirthless laugh and collapsed back in the winged chair beside the bed, his fingers drawing away from hers. "I've always justified my decisions by convincing myself that I was protecting you—keeping Babcock's story from you, the state of my financial affairs." He scraped his fingernails over his scalp, disrupting the sleek set of his hair. "I should have been there for you. When O'Reilly took you. When Silverton attacked you. When the Gentlemen Callers forced their way onto Gilly Downs. I should have been there to protect you. It's what husbands are supposed to do—protect their wives—and I've failed you." His voice was hoarse and jagged with agony. "But my biggest shame is not sharing in your pain over Elias. Christ, I miss him," he whispered with such tenderness that Grace's breath snagged in her throat.

His first sob caught her by surprise. He clasped his hand to his mouth, trying to stifle it. His shoulders heaved violently as another sob burst out, followed immediately by another. He curled into a ball, his face buried deep in his hands, tears leaking through his fingers, trailing a path through the coarse hairs on his wrists.

Grace's fermenting anger and fear burst, the wooden splinters shredding her grief. She inhaled sharply at the pain, but compassion bubbled through her bloodstream and she shivered. She had felt nothing for so long that she had not believed she would ever feel anything again. Grace knew her anger towards her husband's lack of visible grief for their son was unjustified. Now, seeing the raw power of his loss, she realised that he was hurting just as much as she was. And she had not been there for him.

Grace handed him the handkerchief tucked in the shoulder of her nightgown. He balled the linen square in his fist, pressing it to his lips, muffling the even louder cries that juddered from him. She lowered herself onto the arm of the chair. She cooed and murmured softly as she did when the children were upset, her fingers gently caressing the back of his head. "Oh, Seamus. My love."

She waited patiently for him to expunge his grief. Afterwards, he lay back in the chair for so long with his eyes shut that she thought he had fallen asleep. She took his long, firm fingers

in hers, absorbing the essence of his touch—quenching her deep
need of it. Pressing his knuckles to her lips, she breathed him in,
warm and familiar, tainted by pungent traces of distress that had
moistened the armpits of his shirt. Their fingers fitted together
familiarly, perfectly. Grace ran her thumb over the ruck of scar
tissue on his wrist. He shivered and opened his eyes.

"You're staring," he whispered. Although red-rimmed, his
blue eyes were clear and calm. No lines pulled at the corners of
his mouth. He looked serene. Matured like a fine cognac, his
skin had the glow of weather-beaten copper, and the permanent
creases in the corners of his eyes showed the face of a man who
smiled often.

"I'm enjoying the view." She smiled shyly as she lowered
herself onto his lap. It had been so long since she had touched
him, she was afraid he might not want her now. She blew out a
breath as he pulled her tighter against his torso.

A sense of peace settled over her as she examined him, reac-
quainting herself with the person she once knew. His sleeked-
back hair was a blend of hues, like sun-kissed wheat stalks just
before harvest. His cheeks were lightly stubbled. His lips looked
dry, as though he needed a drink, and she ran her thumb over
them.

Grace realised that the fire of her rage had burned off the
dross, leaving behind pure gold memories of Elias. Dispersed in
the ashes was her hatred for Silverton. She no longer felt the
choking animosity—everything somehow felt lighter. Was this
what forgiveness felt like? A new rush of emotion flooded
through her. Guilt. She held Seamus's gaze, drawing strength
from the familiar curves of his eyebrows and square set of his
jaw. "I've been a terrible mother—and wife."

He stiffened, his puffy eyelids widening. "Don't say that."

"I've been absent from my duties. Disinterested and disen-
gaged. Oh, my poor Emily and Edwin. What must you all think
of me?" Grace cupped his cheek in her palm, the icy despair in

her fingers thawing against his warm skin. "Thank you, Seamus. For having the strength to carry on when I couldn't."

"You know, Dulcinea, we are both full of past suffering, but with you by my side, I'm no longer frightened by what has been —life's too short for that." He pressed her hand against his cheek.

"I understand. With Silverton gone—truly gone—I feel like I can breathe again."

He nodded, his relief softening and crinkling the moist corners of his eyes. "You've no idea how happy it makes me seeing you smile again."

She relaxed against him, enjoying being so near him again. Grace laid her hand on his chest, remembering the firm contours, familiarising herself with the warmth of him. "You asked me to come back to you," she whispered. "Well, here I am."

She laid her head on his shoulder and heard him let out a long, slow breath. With her forehead warming upon his neck, she realised his body temperature was also rising at their nearness. She closed her eyes as she breathed in the lemon muskiness of him—the scent of home.

Grace found herself transported through flashes of memories: the stony fissures of the church ruins; his icy, wet hair pressed against her cheek after the storm; his tender kiss under the stars; his hands fanning sensually over the swell of her maternity; the dip of his blond head as he bent to kiss a newborn Elias. Finding her mouth suddenly dry, she swallowed deeply and opened her eyes.

The crease to the side of his mouth deepened as a smile played on his lips. "I've missed you." His voice was thick. He kissed her eyelids, her cheeks, her forehead, her chin, and at last, her lips—the growth of his stubble scratchy, his soft lips sweet and tender.

Seamus curled both arms around her and pressed his cheek to her breast. She sighed, letting her own nervousness release. He no longer held her with calculated consideration. He simply held her as he always had. "What precisely have you missed?"

"I've missed you cursing like a navvy."

"I don't curse like a navvy—not anymore—well, not much. Do I?" She smiled, tipping her head like a cat listening to a far-off sound.

He shrugged one shoulder with a hum of consideration. "I've missed you speaking out more boldly than is wise."

"I'll give you bold, Seamus Fitzwilliam." She tweaked the hairs on his chest through his shirt. He yelped, chuckling and shaking his head. "Go on then, what other endearing virtues of mine have you missed?"

"Well, there are your feminine qualities." The corner of his wide mouth twitched as his long fingers gently cradled her breast.

"*Other* than that."

"You're the best-smelling sailor I've ever sailed with." He inhaled her hair, and she suddenly wished that it was freshly washed. Clearly he disagreed, and he murmured his approval in her ear. "I can't say I've missed your raisin hard-tack, though it was an improvement on the old—I'll give you that much."

"Really?" Grace wrestled with her smile. "Crusty old sea biscuits is the best you can do?" She squirmed on his thighs. She had always felt safe pressed beside his bulk, and it was no different now.

"All right, then. Your eyes. I've missed the brilliance of your eyes looking at me and seeing—*me*. I could sell them to a duchess for the price of diamonds. *That's* how brilliant and alluring they are."

"Hmm, diamonds? A much better offering than sea biscuits," she encouraged.

"And you're brave, and kind, and gentle."

"Don't forget patient."

"Patient?" he said. Grace arched one brow as he pretended to ponder for a moment, lips pursed, eyes rolled to the ceiling. He continued, "That isn't a virtue that comes to mind. I recall *you* pressing me rather impatiently for *my* attention on several occasions."

"I'm not sure I'm ready for *that*," said Grace, her voice trailing into a regretful whisper. "Not yet, anyway."

"That doesn't lessen my need of you," he breathed, leaning towards her.

His tender kiss reached into the dank, dark hold inside her and dragged her into the sunshine, shaking her out like a musty ship's blanket and laying her on the familiar warm rocks of their home shore.

He laid his head back against the chair, studying her.

"How much longer must we stay in London?" she asked, spotting the pulse on his neck pick up at her question.

"I received a letter from Barclay the other day. Gilly Downs is growing. They can sell their wool at half the price in Sydney, or wait for a better price from London—though at the moment that takes months. He's as keen for us to sail as we are."

Grace hummed. "Just think, I'll be able to see Jim again and meet the new Barclay children. Adelia's latest letter said they were already expecting number four." Seamus withdrew her hand from his shirt, and his lips caressed her fingertips. "I wonder if Jim has found himself a wife yet? Do you think William Wells will let us rent his house again? Will you have much of a chance of finding any of the old hands from the *Clover*?"

"Did I mention I've missed your insatiable questions?" His eyes sparkled, and Grace was delighted to see a glimpse of the old Seamus.

He curled his arm around her back and spread his hand over her hip, hitching her closer. "Would you like to come and inspect the ship with me this morning?" he asked.

As she trailed her lips over the rhythm in his neck, a warm

throb of hope pumped through her own veins. She nodded. "I would love nothing more."

GRACE WAS surprised by the advanced state of the ship, even without masts and raised on the open-air dry dock. She thought she was coming to inspect the giant ribcage of the new frame, but the vessel looked surprisingly whole. Men scurried up and down pulleys or scaffolding like worker ants in a nest, shirtless and glistening with sweat in the warmth of the summer sun.

Toby Hicks was waiting on the upper deck. His crisp, black frockcoat painted him more as a scholarly gentleman than as a deckhand these days. His sandy-whiskered face split into a wide beam as she approached. He nodded at Seamus in greeting. "Mrs Fitzwilliam. Lovely to see you again."

Grace reached out and squeezed his hand. "Oh, Toby. It's been too long. I'm so glad you agreed to come today."

"Wouldn't miss it for the world," said Toby, glancing round at the new ship and lowering the brim of his hat against the sun. "It's been an honour to be included in her design and build."

Old Stormy Willis, the shipbuilder, made a noise of agreement. "I've appreciated your input, Hicks." He turned to Seamus. "You were right, Fitzwilliam. Hicks's mastery of figures is unlike any man's I've met. I'll turn him into a master ship-wright soon enough. I'm confident we've created the sleekest, fastest vessel yet."

Grace smiled at Toby's beet-red cheeks, though he did not lower his eyes like he used to. He had a new air of confidence about him that she admired. He nodded. "Yes, sir. I look forward to trialling her at sea."

She had expected the ship-building yard to be more elaborate but, other than the impressive hulk of the ship and the small wooden office, little else occupied the dirt patch near the river's edge. She wrinkled her nose against the rotting stench of the Thames, but the new ship's smells—pitch and tar, varnish and paint—injected a vibrancy into the air that set her heart pounding. "I'm surprised with four months still to go on the build that we're able to walk around her."

"We've already got eight months' building under our belts," said Seamus.

Willis harrumphed. "'Tis not the frame that takes the time, despite it being the largest bit to construct," he explained. "'Tis the trim and fittings that take the longest. Devil's in the details, ye know?" he said, winking.

Grace found Jock Willis to be a likeable fellow. Although his snowy-white whiskers hung to his chest, his face was clear of any deep lines. His particularly pronounced cheekbones made it look as though he had two small apples on either side of his nose, but he had a debonair air about him that seemed out of place among the rough workmen in the shipyard.

Willis, Seamus, and Toby pored intimately over the ship's progress—the position of the knightheads at the bow, the integrity of the five-inch-thick teak planks of the wales. They discussed whether the stern design was too slim and whether this would cause the clipper to lose buoyancy or risk having her back end engulfed by the sea.

Grace was drowning in a tidal wave of design details. She waved an airy hand. "Gentlemen, I'll leave you to contemplate the specifics. May I have a look around?"

Willis shook his head curtly. "Not without a companion, Mrs Fitzwilliam. A ship's not the easiest to navigate on a fine day, let alone one that's only half built—and 'specially not in skirts." He cocked one brow and flicked his eyes at Grace's hem. "Once yer husband and I have finished mulling over the details, perhaps he can take ye about then?"

Grace held her tongue. He would have no notion of her shipboard abilities. Disappointment slithered down her spine. She had hoped to explore the ship more freely. She shrugged one shoulder at Toby.

"Pardon me, Mr Willis," said Toby. "Might I escort Mrs Fitzwilliam about?"

Willis's bushy brows shot up. "Eh? Och, aye. Ye know this ship as well as the two of us." He waved at Seamus. "I don't mind, if you don't, Fitzwilliam?"

Seamus smiled, and a warm quiver of excitement replaced Grace's discontent.

"I don't mind a bit," he said, running a warm hand over her wrist and squeezing her fingers. "I'll be along shortly to join you."

Peeling the red folds of her shawl off her shoulders and slinging it over one arm, Grace wandered towards the stern with Toby by her side. "Leave them to the technicalities," she said, hooking her hand in the crook of his elbow. "We'll take heed of the practicalities."

Toby chuckled and gently squeezed her closer. "I know you can make your way around unaided, Mrs F., but I'd best not be seen shirking my duties."

She leaned into him. "I've missed you, Toby. With everything that's happened, I haven't been the best company."

Toby patted her hand, his palms soft now that he was no longer hauling ropes for a living. He had the hands of an educated man, and Grace's heart swelled with pride. "Now, now, Mrs F. Let's not bring up the past. Let's look to the future, eh? Starting with the cabin that's to be your home."

The great cabin was more delightful than Grace had imagined. She stood on the upper deck, studying the carpenter's handiwork on the cabin's front wall. The top half was inlaid with leaded glass panes, the latticed lead creating small diamond-shaped windows. In the middle was the cabin door, with matching glass panes.

"Look." Toby pointed to a plaque above.

"Abertarff House," read Grace. "Home!"

"By the smell of that varnish on the panelling, I'd say it's still wet," cautioned Toby as they stepped into the interior.

"It's all so neat and orderly," said Grace. Typical Seamus! "You know, although the spaces are still a bare shell, as a whole, this great cabin is positively gargantuan compared to the one on the *Clover*."

Toby smoothed his whiskered cheeks with his knuckles. "Captain's not spared any expense to ensure your family's comfort. And it's a mighty sight better than the fo'c'sle of the *Discerning*."

Grace tilted her head, catching a fleeting squeal of a child's laughter—no, it was the rhythmic squeak of one of the many blocks and tackles positioned around the ship to pulley materials onto the deck. She glanced around at Toby. "Gilly said it would be many a year before I made my way up to the gunroom, but I got there in the end."

"You surpassed it, Mrs F. Made it all the way to the great cabin, and not just because you married the captain, either. You've earned it. You're as fine a sailor as ever I've seen."

"Come on," she said, tugging his arm. "Before you start singing shanties at me again."

Directly through the main cabin door was the entry into a central, walled-in dining room. They turned to the right.

"These are cabins for the officers, the children, and their servants," explained Toby, leading her down the larboard passage. "Each cabin will house a double bunk."

Grace nodded at the light, airy space of the cabins, each with a sizeable scuttle to allow fresh air. "I'm sure Miss Lissing will be happy to share this cabin with Sally."

"Who's that?" asked Toby.

"The children's new governess."

"I hope she's up for the adventure," chuckled Toby. "I can't imagine all lasses taking to the sea like you did."

Grace nodded. "She's not only agreed to accompany us to New Holland, but she's done so with unbridled enthusiasm. I have no doubt she's up to the challenge." Despite a nanny's status being lower than that of a governess, Grace knew the two women got along admirably, and neither had an objection to sharing a cabin.

"Ah, another spirited lass, then. Hmm?" murmured Toby, winking. "Known one or two of those in my life."

He followed her to the stern and waved at the last tiny cabin in the row. "The head. A little more respectable than the men's heads."

"And no tow rag," said Grace, laughing. She pictured the time Jim had first explained how the heads worked on the *Discerning* and her horror at the piece of rag dangling on a rope in the water below.

A large space opened up across the stern. "The saloon," announced Toby, running his hand along the mantle of an iron-enclosed hearth.

"This'll be the heart of our home," whispered Grace wistfully. "I can see it now. The children sitting over there, learning lessons. The family sitting before the hearth, taking books from that bookshelf." Her eyes roamed the empty shelves along the bulkhead.

"Sounds heavenly," he said.

She peered at the lead-lit skylight with matching diamond-shaped windows. It let in little rhombuses of sunlight that checked the sleeve of her dress. The same pattern was scattered across the bare wooden floorboards. Closing her eyes, she let the warmth of the sun caress her nape. With her ears pricking at the sound of pattering feet, Grace glanced around expectantly—almost instantly, she recognised the sound as the end of a rope slapping the wooden deck as it was coiled. Her heartbeat tapped loudly in her ears. She swore she could already hear the children's movements aboard the ship.

Along the starboard passage, Grace clapped her hands in glee at the small galley. "I know I'm no cook, but it'll be handy to have food for the children without having to fetch it from the main galley."

"That little stove will be handy for boiling cocoa on a frosty morning. If you can manage cocoa, that is?" He grinned.

She swatted his arm. "Yes, I can manage cocoa, you cheeky sod." She warily eyed the fire-heated laundry tub and mangle. "It won't smell half as nice as cocoa in here when I'm boiling the laundry."

"Bit of hard work never scared you, Mrs F. I'm sure you'll manage."

She stepped into the main chamber that would house their double-sized berth as well as a small lounge setting. Scanning the empty cabin, she noticed the narrow doorway along the back wall. "Now *that's* a luxurious head! And so private." The carpenter had courteously built a lid for the head in the corner. She studied the sizeable, enamel-coated bathtub nestled into a raised wooden platform. "And a private bath too! You and Seamus thought of everything."

"Well, we'd have asked for your input, but you were a little —" He hesitated, lowering his lashes.

"Preoccupied. I know," she said, patting his arm. "It's all right, Toby. I'm fine now." She indicated the last cabin on the starboard side of the passageway. "And what's this?"

"Captain's lounge," he said, his spine straightening as though he were showing a prize bull. "I'll likely assist the captain with his business from behind that desk. You'll be able to entertain your guests in here too."

"There are plenty of wonderful cupboards and drawers. Excellent for squirrelling away our personal possessions."

"And for packing away loose items during rough weather," added Toby, his lips twisting wryly.

Grace's heart lightened. "Even the prospect of bad weather

is not enough to dampen my spirits. It's perfect!" She stepped into the main passageway that ran in a square around the central dining room, into which she now popped her head. "Wonderful! Plenty big enough for a table of eight. I can see it now—rich wood panelling, ornate brass sconces. Fit to host the Queen!"

She stilled as a shadow flitted across the diamond-speckled bulkhead. Her stomach lurched and she swallowed dryly. Who was that? Just as quickly as it had appeared, the shadow disappeared. Grace whirled, gasping as the entry door swung open. Seamus beamed like a child with a new toy, but his brows dipped when he caught sight of her.

"Are you well, Grace? You look a little pale."

Her gaze flicked to the wall where she had seen the small shadow. Her husband's solid, broad-shouldered silhouette was the only shadow there now. She wrapped her shawl around her shoulders again as a cold shiver tinkled across her skin. "I'm fine," she said, smiling.

He looked at her for a beat longer, then spanned his gaze about. "Had a good look around?"

"Yes. Toby's been showing me everything. It's superb!" she said, the wonderment returning to her voice.

Toby dipped his head at Seamus. "Excuse me, sir. I must pop down to inspect the hold."

"Indeed, Hicks. We must make the most of every inch if we're to fit as many bales of wool in there as possible."

"Yes, sir. My thoughts exactly." Toby bowed to Grace. "Mrs Fitzwilliam, a pleasure, as always."

"Thank you, Toby."

The cabin door swung silently on its new, oiled hinges and clicked shut. Seamus padded over to Grace, curling his arm around her back. Unnerved by the peculiar sights and sounds, she was glad of his presence and his warmth—reassuring and familiar.

"I've been thinking…" His jaw clenched and his throat dipped deeply as he swallowed.

"About what?"

"About a name for her. For the ship." He had an unfamiliar look of indecision on his face. He braced his shoulders as he took in a breath, steeling himself. "What do you think of the *Elias*?"

Grace pressed a clenched fist to her mouth. That was it, she realised—the ship had been delivering allusions all afternoon. Either that or her boy was here with her now. Shaking off the superstitious chill, she smiled. With the ship named after him, Elias would be with her. Always.

"I love it," she said. "With all my heart."

"As I do you, Dulcinea."

She smiled at this passionate, wilful man, who sometimes drove her mad with his stubbornness, but who always drew her back from the edge of destruction with his love. Rising to her toes, she pressed her lips to his.

ALSO BY EMMA LOMBARD

For an extended bonus scene of when Grace visits Billy in Oxford,
read here:

https://www.emmalombardauthor.com/bonus-oxford-scene

Thanks for reading *Grace on the Horizon*. I hope you enjoyed it! If
you're interested in Seamus and Grace's next adventure, you can find
out more about it here:

https://www.emmalombardauthor.com/grace-arising

OTHER BOOKS FROM EMMA LOMBARD

Discerning Grace

The White Sails Series, Book One

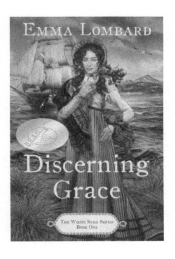

A rollicking romantic adventure
featuring an independent young
woman, Grace Baxter, whose
feminine lens blows the ordered
patriarchal decks of a 19th century
naval tall ship to smithereens.

Grace Arising

The White Sails Series, Book Three

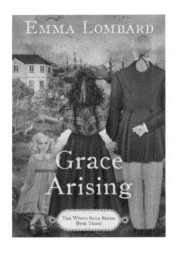

A new clipper ship means a new adventure. With Seamus gravely injured, and the First Mate an incompetent risk-taker, it's up to Grace to see the crew and her family to safety. Can she reach the New Holland wool market ahead of their competitors, and in time to save Seamus's life?

Lightning Source UK Ltd.
Milton Keynes UK
UKHW010708090223
416681UK00007B/1627